Sword-swinging stories
by authors who know Xena best . . .

In "Immortal Desire," by national bestselling author Jennifer Roberson, Ares invades the dreams and desires of Xena and Gabrielle.

New York Times bestselling author Josepha Sherman takes it straight from the horse's mouth in "Argonaut," a clever tale told from the point of view of Xena's noble steed, Argo.

Gabrielle is captured by a bloodthirsty lamia in "Bard and Breakfast" by *New York Times* bestselling author Greg Cox.

Ever wonder how the "man in the street" really feels about Xena? Keith R. A. DeCandido answers that question in "Recurring Character."

In "Leaving the Past Behind," series scriptwriter Melissa Good tells a touching story of Xena's birthday . . . when Gabrielle receives an unexpected gift.

. . . And ten more tales of adventure featuring
the Warrior Princess . . .

SEP 4   2001

THE FURTHER ADVENTURES OF

XENA

WARRIOR PRINCESS ™

Edited by
Martin Greenberg

Based on the Universal Television Series Created by
John Schulian and Rob Tapert

ACE BOOKS, NEW YORK

This is a work of fiction. Names, characters, places, and incidents either are the product of the author's imagination or are used fictitiously, and any resemblance to actual persons, living or dead, business establishments, events, or locales is entirely coincidental.

THE FURTHER ADVENTURES OF XENA: WARRIOR PRINCESS

An Ace Book / published by arrangement with
Universal Studios Publishing Rights, a division of Universal Studios Licensing, Inc.

PRINTING HISTORY
Ace mass-market edition / September 2001

Visit our website at
www.penguinputnam.com

Check out the ACE Science Fiction & Fantasy newsletter
and much more on the Internet at Club PPI!

ISBN: 0-441-00852-6

ACE®
Ace Books are published by The Berkley Publishing Group,
a division of Penguin Putnam Inc.,
375 Hudson Street, New York, New York 10014.
ACE and the "A" design
are trademarks belonging to Penguin Putnam Inc.

PRINTED IN THE UNITED STATES OF AMERICA

10   9   8   7   6   5   4   3   2   1

CONTENTS

INTRODUCTION

It is the end of an era.

With the unfortunate decision not to renew *Xena: Warrior Princess*, a golden age for both fantasy lovers and television itself has come to a close.

When it began as a spinoff show from *Hercules: The Legendary Journeys* in 1995, no one expected *Xena* to achieve such phenomenal success. But week after week, more and more viewers tuned in to watch Xena and Gabrielle taking on Ares, Callisto, Hera, Aphrodite, and many more, allying with such varied folk as Joxer, Salmoneus, and Autolycus. Together, the Warrior Princess and her stalwart companions traveled a fantastic ancient world that combined the wonder and glory of the civilizations of Greece and Rome with a modern, tongue-in-cheek sense of humor and adventure.

In their travels, much has happened to both Xena and Gabrielle, from profound joy to the deepest sorrow, from noble sacrifices to the simple, comforting bonds of comradeship. Throughout everything they have experienced, their friendship and devotion have remained unquestioned, and, indeed, have even grown stronger. Along the way, they've taught an entire audience important lessons about honor, trust, and belief in oneself.

As the final season drew to a close, we knew this could not possibly be all of the adventures of the Warrior Princess. With that in mind, we asked some of today's best fantasy writers to continue the adventures of Xena, Gabrielle, Joxer, Ares, and the rest of the characters living in a world that lies just beyond our imagination. So join us now, in these fifteen stories that bring all of the adventure, excitement, and intrigue that fans have come to love and expect from Xena. From Esther Friesner comes a humorous take on a chance encounter with

Aphrodite, who's up to her usual mischief. David Bischoff takes a look at Xena's involvement in the fastest-growing sport in Greece—professional wrestling, under the promotional auspices of Salmoneus. Even other characters get in on the act, with Joxer taking center stage in a tale of romance and peril by Diane Duane. Finally, we are pleased to be able to bring you a never-before-published story by Melissa Good, one of the writers for the show, who gives us a tale of Gabrielle, Xena, and Eve that could have been written directly for the screen.

So grab your chakram, saddle your horse, and prepare for wild adventure with the one and only—Xena, Warrior Princess!

IMMORTAL DESIRE

Jennifer Roberson

It was a dark and stormy night—

"No," she muttered, bent over the creased parchment scroll unrolled against a plank of wood cradled in her lap. "That's not it." And scored a thick black line of ink through the words. Her mind worked furiously to invent a new opening line.

"Gabrielle."

The day dawned like a lover's caress—

She got as far as *lover's,* with *caress* still in her mind, not on parchment, before once again obliterating the line of rapidly scribed text.

"That's not it *either.*"

"Gabrielle."

The afternoon was too beautiful for words—

Probably because she couldn't *find* any words. Not any that worked. Not any that didn't just lie there on the page, evoking neither image nor emotion. There wasn't any *resonance* in the words, no singing rhythms, no compulsion to keep reading to find out what happened next.

"Gabrielle."

Abrupt frustration sought release in a garbled, indistinct, yet eloquent exclamation—something between a howl and a roar as she clutched her head in despair.

"Gabrielle!"

Startled by Xena's battlefield bellow, Gabrielle glanced across the coals of their breakfast fire. "What?"

"You've been muttering over that scroll ever since breakfast," Xena declared. "It's a beautiful day, Gabrielle. We had a good dinner, a good night's sleep in a cozy little glade, an even better breakfast, and there's a lovely water hole just down the slope, ideal for bathing—which I know, because I've used it already."

Gabrielle blinked; she did have some dim recollection of Xena calling out to her that the water was perfect. "Are you implying I *need* a bath?"

"I might imply you should go soak your head," Xena enunciated, "but no. I'm merely suggesting you stop fretting over whatever it is you're doing. You're ruining my day."

"You're mending gear," Gabrielle noted, marking the pile of leather in Xena's lap as well as a length of sinew clenched in her teeth; no wonder her words had been slightly distorted. "How can I be ruining your day?"

"I happen to *like* mending gear," Xena explained, "when I have the time to do it in peace. When warlords aren't attacking, and villagers aren't dying, and gods aren't disrupting my life. None of which, for a change, is happening, and I'd like to enjoy it." She paused. "If you don't mind."

"Sorry." Gabrielle heaved a huge sigh. "I just can't get it to come out right."

Xena pulled the sinew from her mouth and threaded the awl. "Another poem?"

Gabrielle waved a declarative hand, absently noting ink flying from the reed pen in a gloppy dollop a goodly distance away. "No, I've given that up. I'm no good at poetry. *Joxer's* better at poetry than I am."

White teeth flashed briefly as Xena grinned. "Then try writing a song. If he can, you can."

"You don't understand," Gabrielle said plaintively, "I'm blocked. I can't find a good beginning."

Xena hitched one shoulder upward in a negligent shrug. "Why not start at the end?"

Gabrielle stared at her. "You can't start a story at the end!"

"Why not?"

"Because you have to learn what the story is *about* before you write the ending!"

Xena observed her with an infuriatingly bland expression. "You can't make up the end first?"

It was exceedingly aggravating discussing this with someone who couldn't understand the craft. "How am I supposed to know how it ends when I don't know how it *starts*?" Gabrielle demanded. "It's—it's rebelling. Refusing to let me find how it wants to be told."

"How it *wants* to be told?"

"All stories have opinions," Gabrielle explained. "You have to find one you can deal with, and then begin."

Xena's eyebrows arched. "You make it sound like it's an enemy."

"No, not an enemy." Gabrielle frowned down at the scroll with its crossed-out beginnings. "A friend, but sometimes a difficult one. A stubborn one."

Xena grinned. "No basis in real life, then."

Gabrielle grunted faint appreciation of the comment, distracted by the blacked-out lines on the scroll. What was the perfect opening?

Xena went back to mending gear. "So, you're saying you don't know how the story ends, begins, or what happens in it?"

Gabrielle nodded glumly.

"How do you expect to write a story if you don't know what happens?"

"I never know what's going to happen," Gabrielle explained with some asperity; someone who wasn't a writer couldn't possibly understand. "Part of the fun is discovering what comes next." She looked meaningfully at Xena's mending. "Stories aren't like gear. "It's never one stitch after another, each one identical—"

"My stitches are never identical," Xena put in dryly.

"—but a collection of unexpected happenings." Gabrielle

ignored the interruption. "You string them together, and eventually you see what the story's about."

"Well, if you don't know how the story starts or ends, or what's going to happen in between, why do you even bother?"

"Because it's a *challenge*," Gabrielle explained. "It's an *adventure*."

"Uh-huh." Xena chewed thoughtfully at the awl, eyeing the scroll. "You're always scribbling something . . . where do you get your ideas, Gabrielle?"

Joxer had asked that once before. She never knew how to answer it. How could anyone *not* know where ideas came from? They were always there in her mind, arguing over who deserved to see the light of day first.

Of late, no one in her mind was arguing anything.

"Inspiration," Gabrielle replied despondently. "But I seem to be lacking it lately."

"Well, what's inspired you before?"

"You," she said promptly. "Hercules. Autolycus. Some of the adventures we've had." She shrugged. "I don't know. Just—things."

Xena's smile was slow. "Love?"

Gabrielle, recalling the second attempt at an opening line with its reference to a lover's caress, felt the blush creep up from throat to forehead.

Xena's knowing smile grew into a grin. "Uh-huh."

"There's nothing wrong with writing about love," Gabrielle muttered.

"Especially when there's no . . . appropriate male in your current life. Your *real* life."

Gabrielle, mouth twisting, couldn't suppress a resigned sigh. "That's an understatement."

"Well, then—write about *that*," Xena suggested. "Write a story about your perfect man. Someone who could sweep you off your feet. The man of your dreams." Xena's expression was languorous, her tone slow and suggestive, freighted with feminine innuendo. "The ultimate fantasy."

The blush remained. "I don't have one," Gabrielle muttered.

Xena snorted. "You're the writer," she said. "Make one up!"

The water *was* perfect. So was the glade, the sun, the day. Gabrielle set aside her scribbling long enough to partake of the water hole, washing strawberry-blond hair, scrubbing at skin left untended too long. She was too fair to tan the way Xena did, but she had gained enough permanent color so that she didn't burn too badly anymore. And calluses to boot; her training with Xena and the Amazons had accounted for many of them. There was little about herself Gabrielle felt was truly *feminine*, the way men supposedly liked their women, but she had taken to the active life. She thrived on it now, even if it allowed no time or opportunity for a so-called normal life.

Gabrielle pushed off the shallow bottom of the water hole, floating on her back. She employed hands and arms as fins to keep her body moving slowly. She wore only a thin gauzy tunic, chopped off at shoulders and thighs, too self-conscious to swim or bathe in the nude while out of doors. Odd, she thought, that she had no compunction about baring her midriff in everyday clothes, but when it came to getting in a lake or river, she wanted the illusion of more propriety. You never knew when a stranger might show up.

Just now there were none. Only Xena a short walk away, camped behind a screen of reeds and fern, still assiduously mending gear. Certainly Xena would chase off any importunate strangers who hoped to catch a glimpse of a nearly naked Gabrielle.

"Not that it would precisely inflame their desires," she told the sky overhead, floating comfortably. "Maybe Xena's right . . . maybe I should make up the perfect man, and write about him."

Drifting there, she thought about it. *Was* there a perfect man? Could there ever be a perfect man? Handsome men, yes; she'd seen her share. Kind men, even. But the Perfect Man would have to combine all the elements Gabrielle found most attractive and compelling, binding them together in a stunningly masculine, strong, handsome body—because of course she did have her preferences in how a man looked, and moved, even though she'd never seen it put together just the way she'd like it.

Well, maybe. "Hercules comes pretty close," she murmured. "Tall, strong, broad in the shoulders, narrow in the hips, in perfect proportion, tanned . . . though actually I think I like dark hair better." Hercules was a mountain lion, all sun-kissed skin and hair. But Gabrielle had always found the black panther more compelling, more dangerous.

Dangerous? she thought. *Is that what I want?*

No. Of course not. She wanted someone who was kind and gentle and unafraid to be tender, a man unafraid to speak of his innermost emotions, a man unafraid to cry. A man willing to *communicate,* and to listen to *her* innermost thoughts and feelings.

Gabrielle's mind began to knit together the attributes and aspects she found most intriguing. Suddenly the picture presented itself, the image of the ideal man, *her* ideal man. She stood up abruptly, busily writing in her head, and splashed through the water to the bank. A cursory toweling with a rough length of old curtain dried her enough to stand the faint breeze against her skin, and then she knelt and gathered up the implements of her craft, left sitting beside her clothing: wood plank, parchment scroll, reed pen, and a small pot of crude ink.

The sunset behind him was glorious. But he was even more so.

Gabrielle sighed. Inspiration. At last.

Having scribbled away half the day, foregoing all but a swig or two of watered wine and an apple, Gabrielle stretched out languorously in soft green grass, drowsing on the bank beside the water. The nap was blissfully pleasant with the gentle sun warming her skin through the now-dried tunic, the faintest of breezes teasing her hair. She smelled coals, woodsmoke, herbs and flowers, the scent of crushed grass, the barest tang of drying ink. Best of all, she couldn't smell *herself* anymore; Xena had been right about the bath.

Gabrielle stretched in casual abandon, eyes closed. She smiled, pleased with the day's work. All it had needed was the right inspiration—

"What is this crap?"

Gabrielle sat up and spun around onto her knees with a stifled gasp of shock. A man. A *man's* voice. A man *right there,* standing over her.

Holding her scroll. *Reading* her scroll.

Suddenly she wasn't afraid anymore. Only angry. And somewhat embarrassed. Gabrielle sprang upright and attempted to snatch the scroll out of his hand. She failed.

He dangled it over her head. She was not tall; he was. Short of attempting to leap into the air after the parchment, which would be exceedingly undignified, there was nothing she could do. A smirk and edged smile she found most annoying curved his mouth, outlined by a thin black beard.

Gabrielle summoned the tone of command she had heard Xena use. "Give. That. Back."

The smile widened. "And permit you to write more of this—drivel? I think not."

"Ares," she growled. "What are you doing here?"

His feigned innocence had never fooled her. "Passing by."

"You're a god," she said pointedly. "You never 'pass by.' You only come when there's a reason. When *you* have a reason," she amended; the gods knew she and Xena never had a reason to want his company.

Ares arched eloquent brows. He was tall. Dark. Handsome, if in a cruel way. He was unquestionably strong. He wore black leather. He moved like a panther.

Gabrielle blushed.

He waved the scroll at her. "Is this what women want, Gabrielle? Is this what women really want in a man?" He paused suggestively. "Is this what *you* want?"

The blush deepened. But so did the anger.

"Ohhhhhh," he murmured in mock solicitude, "have I offended you? Or have I merely uncovered your fantasy?" He had an infuriating smile, and employed it to good effect. "Do you dream of me at night? Were you dreaming of me just now?"

Gabrielle crossed her arms tightly, wishing she had her staff. It wouldn't do any good against Ares, but she wanted it anyway. She glared at him.

And then realized she was wearing next to nothing.

With a garbled blurt of dismay, Gabrielle snatched up the damp curtain-towel spread on the nearest bush and swept it around her. It wasn't dry yet—clammy against her flesh—but it did cover much of her against his amused observation.

Ares grinned, displaying white teeth. "I can see through that, you know."

Gabrielle clutched the fabric more tightly, still glaring. "A *gentleman* would never say that," she declared between her teeth. "A gentleman would never look."

He waved the scroll again. "According to this, a gentleman is not what women want. According to *this*, women want what bears a striking resemblance to . . . me." He spread both hands, striking a pose that threw all of his more masculine attributes into relief.

She gritted her teeth. "You are *so* arrogant!"

"So is the man in here." He dangled the scroll before her face, then abruptly tossed it aside.

She followed its path with her eyes, wanting to snatch it up and guard it against him. But he had already read it. And now he'd make it a weapon against her—if she let him.

Gabrielle straightened her shoulders, lifted her head, met his eyes squarely, not flinching from the man who wasn't a man at all, but a god, and one who took so much pleasure in discomfiting people, as well as sending them off to kill one another.

"No," she said, "you are not what women want. The man in there may bear a slight resemblance to your physical appearance—strictly superficial, I do assure you—but he's nothing like you. There's kindness in him, and tenderness, and honesty, and loyalty, devotion—"

"You make him sound like a *dog,* Gabrielle. Do women want a dog?"

"—and gentleness, and a good sense of humor. He's willing to laugh at himself, to not take himself too seriously, to honor his mother—"

"Hera insists on that."

"—and to admit when he makes a fool of himself—"

"Sorry. No can do."

"—and he likes dogs and cats and children . . . and flowers in the meadow, clouds in the sky—"

"But can he juggle?"

She'd ignored his interruptions up till then. That stopped her. "Juggle?"

He waggled dark eyebrows. "I never take myself too seriously, Gabrielle. But then, I don't take anyone too seriously. Certainly not mortals. How could I? You exist for our amusement."

She realized then that she didn't need her staff. She didn't need a dagger, or a sword. She didn't need any kind of weapon when she had her tongue. And a certain knowledge.

Gabrielle smiled at the god of war, then presented her challenge and victory in one unerring blow. "*Xena* doesn't want you, Ares."

Oh, indeed. That worked. Well enough that he was momentarily struck speechless, something she'd never witnessed before, and attempted to cover it by disappearing in a shower of sparks.

Gabrielle grinned deliciously. "Gotcha." She bent to pick up the discarded scroll, brushing it free of debris. She unrolled it, reading swiftly. "Now, where was I?"

Xena awoke just after dawn. She lay there a moment beneath the blankets, savoring the warmth. Automatically her senses stretched out to make note of Gabrielle. Still sound asleep from the sound of it. Gabrielle had come back from the water hole grinning gleefully to herself, obviously pleased with what she'd accomplished. Xena had asked her how the writing went, but Gabrielle had waved her off, saying something about telling her a story later; but after eating a quick dinner she'd lost herself in the scroll again, muttering about 'getting it down' before the light died, and Xena never did find out what the story was.

She supposed it didn't matter. Something had sparked Gabrielle's imagination again, which was far preferable to listening to muffled exclamations of dismay and frustration.

She sat up, finger-combed her hair out of her face, then peeled back the blankets. Her bladder desired relief; then she'd start breakfast. They needed to get back on the road.

Xena rose, thinking about a bush, and paused. Disorientation swept in, seizing her without warning. For a moment she was in darkness—and then abruptly she was elsewhere. The small encampment was gone. Gabrielle was gone. The morning was gone.

She stood in a meadow at midday, blinking in sudden sunshine. "What—?" she began, and then fell silent. The meadow spread out before her, sweeping across rolling hills, displaying a vivid carpet of every wildflower known to man.

"Do you like it?" he asked. "I did it for you."

She swung around, hand grasping for a weapon. But none existed. That, too, had changed.

"Ares?"

"Do you like it, Xena?" He bent, plucked a crimson flower, held it out to her. "Isn't it lovely?"

She stared at him. The expression was not one she recognized. She wasn't sure his face did, either; it seemed uncomfortable with the new arrangement of his features.

"Or would you prefer a blue one?" The flower in his hand was no longer crimson.

He seemed nonplussed when she didn't answer. Abruptly the flower disappeared entirely. An instant later he was pressing something small, warm, and furry into her hands.

"Here. You like kittens, don't you?"

She cradled it absently, noting its purr as it nestled against her breasts. "Ares—"

"Or I can get you a puppy . . . would you rather have a puppy?"

"Ares—"

"Look at the clouds," he said, gesturing skyward. "Aren't they lovely?"

"Lovely" was not a word she'd ever expected to hear from his lips. Not in describing *clouds*. She gave them the most cursory of glances, then fixed her eyes on him again. "Are you ill?" she asked. "Or is this some kind of a joke?"

His brows drew together. "You wound me," he murmured, moving closer. "I created all this for you, and you insult me." He was very close now, and insufferably large. Xena stood her ground. "I think—I think you've hurt my feelings," he told her.

"You don't have any, Ares."

"See? You *have* hurt my feelings." Broad shoulders

drooped. Lips turned down. He was the picture of absolute dejection. "Can we talk about this, Xena?"

"What's *wrong* with you?" she blurted.

"Nothing that a smile from your lips could not cure," he told her earnestly.

Xena blinked. "I must still be asleep. This has to be a dream."

"No," he said, shifting closer yet. "This is real, Xena, every bit of it. The meadow, flowers, clouds . . . the kitten."

She could smell him. It was a clean, masculine scent, with the faintest undertang of something she couldn't name. He was a god, after all; could she expect him to smell like a man? And what was he doing standing so close, so intimately?

And then the kitten was gone, though she couldn't say when it had disappeared, and her hands were clasped in his. "Xena," he murmured, pulling her down to the grass. "Look at the flowers. The clouds—"

She jerked free and stood up. "I don't want to look at the flowers," she said. "I don't want to look at the clouds. I want to know what you're doing here, and what you want."

His face reflected hurt. "I'm here to spend some time with you, Xena. To see if we can't make a new beginning."

She stared down at him. Even seated on the ground, he was a large man. A large, leather-clad man. A large leather-clad man with black hair that somewhat disconcertingly curled against his neck. A thick and corded neck, perfectly balanced by extremely broad shoulders.

Xena promptly pinched herself on the arm, hard enough to elicit a brief hiss of pain. The meadow remained. So did the flowers and the clouds. The kitten was still absent.

Ares was abruptly standing next to her again, reaching for her arm. "Let me kiss away the pain."

Xena took one long step backward. "Are you *mad*?" she demanded. "Did some idiot steal your body when you weren't looking? This isn't you!"

His face was set in lines that, on another man, might be called kindness. "It's who I am now," he told her warmly. "For you."

"For me? For me?" She stared at him wildly. "This *is*

some kind of joke. Well, I won't fall for it, Ares! Underneath that pasted-on facade of tenderness is a monster who isn't happy unless men are dying for him, invoking his name in pointless battles. This—this charade you're undertaking now won't get you anything, Ares. I know you too well."

He merely continued to smile. "Am I tender, then?" he asked. "I was so hoping you'd notice."

"Flowers?" she said, imbuing the word with abject disbelief. "Clouds? A *kitten?* Is this a new kind of campaign, Ares?"

He reached out for her again, recapturing her hands. "Xena, let me be gentle. Let me be tender. Let me be kind. You know the other part of me, the tall, strong, handsome warrior-god of undeniable sex appeal, who can protect you against all harm . . . now let me *listen* to you, Xena. Let me know what's in your heart. Let me share what's in *my* heart."

" 'Undeniable sex appeal'?" she echoed.

"There's much more to me than that, Xena. I've just been unable to let you see it. I've been too—shy—to let you see it."

"Shy?"

"But now I see I should. Now I see I must." His head was bent over her, lips hovering. "Let me show you who I *really* am, Xena."

"Gabrielle!" she shouted.

Gabrielle started awake. That battlefield bellow again. She scowled sleepily up at Xena, who stood over her. "What?"

"Time to get up," Xena said, turning away to the fire. "You must have been sleeping like the dead; I called your name four times."

Gabrielle levered herself up on one elbow, peeling hair out of her face. "I was dreaming . . ."

"I know. You were talking in your sleep."

"It was the *strangest* dream, Xena . . ."

"I know that, too. You muttered something about clouds and flowers and kittens."

Gabrielle sat upright, now wide awake. "I did?"

"And something else about tall, strong, and handsome.

With undeniable sex appeal." Xena tossed her a grin across her shoulder. "Guess writing about your perfect man gave you something good to dream about."

"Perfect man," Gabrielle echoed. Then, "Oh, *ick*!"

" 'Ick'?" Xena tossed her the water skin. "That's all you have to say after dreaming about the man of your fantasies?"

Gabrielle let the water skin flop next to her as she dropped back down to her bedding, sealing her eyes shut with her hands. "He wasn't," she muttered. "Not the man of my fantasies—or yours either!"

"Well, shake it off," Xena advised. "I want to get going."

The dregs of the dream were starting to slip away, which was precisely what Gabrielle preferred. Nodding absently, she climbed out of her blankets and staggered off into the brush, looking for a suitable tree or bush. Afterward, she went down to the water's edge to wash her face, trying to clear her muzzy head of the incongruous images her too-fertile imagination had conjured up.

"Gabrielle."

She leaped to her feet and spun around, vowing to never again go anywhere without her staff.

Black leather and a blacker expression loomed over her, scowling fiercely. "You lied," he hissed. "*None* of it worked."

And then the grassy verge was gone from beneath her feet and she was in the water, rump planted in the sandy bottom, legs splayed out. After a shocked moment she spat water from her mouth and slicked hair back from a face that felt numb.

"Gabrielle?" It was Xena this time, observing her with raised brows. "I thought you took a bath yesterday."

Gabrielle blinked at her. "Is he gone?"

"Is who gone?"

Gabrielle opened her mouth to answer, then clamped it shut. She didn't dare speak his name, or Xena would know that somehow, unbelievably, *inconceivably,* she had managed to invoke Ares while writing about her Perfect Man.

That she had managed to dream he was *Xena's* Perfect Man, Xena's ultimate fantasy.

No. It would not do to tell her that.

Her face was burning. "Never mind," Gabrielle muttered, and climbed out of the water.

TWO AGAINST THEBES

Robin Wayne Bailey

Xena woke suddenly and flung aside her coverlet. On the ground beside her thin pallet she found her sword and unsheathed it as she sprang up. Fully alert, listening, she turned, searching the darkness.

Moments passed.

The stark silhouette of Mount Parnassus loomed in the south, a black pillar upon which revolved the pale stars of night. To the east, just beside Parnassus, the smaller Mount Elikón stood, its peak illumined with just a hint of the frosty moon that hid behind it.

The embers of a waning campfire cast a dull red shimmer on her naked blade as she lowered it. She moved a step closer to the dwindling warmth and exhaled a breath of feathery softness. An unseasonable chill had fallen over the Boeotian Plain while she had slept.

What sound had awakened her?

She frowned when she failed to spy any threat. The night breeze teased through wisps of her dark hair. With a quiet sigh, she brushed them back from her face and tried to relax.

Perhaps there had been no sound at all, only an outcry

from her dream; yet another dream of battle and slaughter. Her dreams were torment tonight, visions from her past, red as the embers whose edges she nudged with a booted toe.

But for the wind and the slow movement of the heavens, all was still. She stared across the darkened landscape— Boeotia. It seemed to whisper to her tonight, to speak in muted tones of its history and its tragedy. Beoetia—where more wars had been fought than anywhere else on Greek soil. Greek against Persian. Athenian against Spartan. Beoetia—where men by the thousands had died.

Was that truly the wind at her ear? Or did she hear the laughter of Ares and of Hades as they counted the men who had fallen here?

Or was it all just the imagination of an insomniac woman?

She had nearly convinced herself it was so. With another soft sigh, she sheathed her sword and prepared to lay back down. Then the sound she thought she had heard came again.

A moan!

On the other side of the campfire, as if in a dream of her own, Gabrielle shifted under the gray folds of her blanket. Xena watched her friend with an inexplicable unease. What nightmare, she wondered, could trouble that innocent heart?

For long, watchful moments Xena stood above her friend. Gabrielle lay still again with the blanket drawn almost over her head. Slender fingers that might have clutched a doll or a feather pillow, with a similar intimacy instead lightly clutched a stout staff. That brought a weak smile to Xena's lips, but she wondered again, as she had so many times, if she had made the right decision in letting the younger woman travel with her.

After a while, Xena turned away and crouched down to warm her hands above the coals. At least Gabrielle was getting some sleep, however troubled. Xena doubted she herself would close her eyes again. Something about the night, some dreadful quality, gnawed her nerves. Despite the embers' warmth, she bit her lip and shivered.

Another moan. Gabrielle turned over onto her back. With face still half-hidden beneath her cover, she screamed.

Xena shot upright.

Gabrielle continued to sleep.

An icy sensation tingled along Xena's spine. How could anyone sleep through such an outcry? She stared in anticipation of some waking sign. None came. Gabrielle lay still again, as if frozen, as if . . .

Xena's heart quickened. She moved around the campfire, bent, and shook her friend. There was an edge in her voice. "Gabrielle?"

The blanket slipped down from Gabrielle's face.

Xena gasped. The blond hair was the same, but the face was not her friend's. The lips were thin, not full, and red as berries even in the dark of night. The cheeks were gaunt, almost hollow, beneath a narrow brow. The skin held an unnatural sallow glow.

It was a face Xena knew. "Antigone!"

Eyes as bright and large as emeralds opened as if in answer to that hushed name. The woman on Gabrielle's pallet made no other move, but turned her head to fix Xena with her gaze. A nearly forgotten yet too-remembered voice issued from a lean mouth.

"That which was given is neither mine, nor yours;
What becomes a throat, a bloody hand defiled;
Beside the wine-dark sea, by sacred shores,
A crown that is no crown crowns king reviled."

Emerald eyes closed again. Xena flung herself forward and snatched the blanket aside to reveal, not Gabrielle's form, but that of a young woman richly draped in white funereal raiment. "Gabrielle!" she called in confusion. Then, "Antigone!"

The wind rushed across the embers; a sparkling swirl of smoke and ash rose up and spiraled around Xena's face, stinging and blinding her. She wiped furiously at her eyes.

"Xena? What's wrong? What is it?"

Worried hands clutched Xena's shoulders. Gabrielle's pale eyes, so blue in the sunlight, filled with alarm as she bolted up from her pallet. "Xena, were you having another nightmare?"

Then, she spied her blanket still clutched in Xena's hand.

Alarm gave way to a look of puzzlement, then smugness. She glanced at the fading embers and grabbed her blanket back. "Oh, I get it. Your blanket wasn't enough, so you tried to take mine." She flung the rough-spun cloth around her shoulders and clutched it tightly with both fists as she lay down again and indignantly turned her back to Xena and the campfire. "Well, I'm too alert for you. I don't sleep as heavily as I used to."

Xena's eyes narrowed. She stared sharply at Gabrielle, rubbed her eyes with her knuckles, then stared again. She hadn't dreamed the previous few moments, and she hadn't imagined them. She had seen Antigone. Or rather, she had seen Antigone's ghost, for Antigone was quite long dead. She rose to her feet.

"Get up," she ordered, reaching for her armor. "We're leaving."

Gabrielle rolled over and raised up on one elbow. "Leaving?" she protested. "Xena, it's the middle of the night. Where are we going?"

"Delphi," Xena answered as she fastened straps and buckled on her sword.

Gabrielle glared stubbornly at Xena for a moment. Finally, with a sigh of long-suffering exasperation, she shook her head and began rolling up her bedding. Xena did the same, and in the deep of night, they set off at an urgent pace for the black shadow of Parnassus.

For the first few miles, Xena ignored Gabrielle's persistent questions and kept her silence. It was easy to do; Gabrielle's was only one voice in her ears as she walked. The ghosts of old friends and acquaintances walked with her now. She heard them, saw them vaguely in the shadows of boulders or gleams of starlight. Her mind raced with questions of her own as she sifted through grim memories.

Finally, however, she relented.

"You knew Antigone?" Gabrielle said. Awe colored her young voice.

"After the death of her father, King Oedipus," Xena answered, "her two brothers warred against each other for the throne of the city of Thebes. Antigone's younger brother,

Eteocles, seized power, while Polynices, the older brother and legitimate heir, was away."

Xena paused in her story, wiping her hair back from her face with one hand, slowing her pace only slightly to allow Gabrielle to catch her breath. "It was a wild time," she continued. "Polynices put together an army of seven warlords to attack Thebes. Eteocles held a strong position behind the city's walls. Still, he feared his brother's might."

Gabrielle ventured a guess. "Eteocles asked you to help defend Thebes?"

Xena nodded. "Polynices had already asked me to join his army, and his was the more virtuous cause. Not that I had much truck with virtue in those days," she added in a self-deprecating manner. "But a few months earlier I had met Antigone and her sister, Ismene, in Colonus near Athens. Their dedication to their father greatly impressed me."

Gabrielle interrupted again. "Oedipus was with them?"

In the brightening moonlight, Xena's face turned grim and angry. "He had blinded himself for what he perceived as his sins—killing his father, marrying his mother—and fled Thebes with his daughters as his guides. But in truth, Gabrielle, the fault had never been his. Like all the children of Cadmus's line, Oedipus was a plaything for the gods."

"I've heard of a great play written by Sophocles," Gabrielle said. "I hope to see it someday when we visit Athens."

Xena grew quiet again. She looked from side to side as she walked, still hearing the timeless echoes of battle on the winds that blew over the Boeotian plain. But she resisted the urge to stop and turn her gaze toward the northeast.

There lay the haunted ruins of the city of Thebes.

Gabrielle adjusted the pack on her shoulder as she kept pace with Xena. "But you say you saw Antigone's ghost tonight, and that she brought you some kind of message?"

"A riddle," Xena answered. She hadn't told Gabrielle how Antigone had seemed to appropriate Gabrielle's form, nor how that had disturbed her. "The House of Cadmus always had a thing for riddles."

Gabrielle hummed thoughtfully. " 'That which was given is neither mine, nor yours,' " she repeated.

"No need to recite the entire verse," Xena told her. "The solution is easy."

Gabrielle looked dubiously at her companion.

"The answer is—the Necklace of Harmonia."

Gabrielle stopped in her tracks and leaned on her staff. "You've seen it?" she exclaimed. "Xena, the Necklace of Harmonia is almost legendary. Aphrodite gave it to Cadmus's wife, Harmonia, on the occassion of their wedding. It's fabulously beautiful—I've heard." She scrambled to catch up, for Xena hadn't stopped.

"It's more than just a pretty piece of jewelry," Xena said. "It's the true crown of Thebes. By tradition, only the man whose wife wears the necklace can call himself king of Thebes."

Gabrielle scratched her head. "Then how could Eteocles seize the throne from Polynices?"

A smirk turned up the corners of Xena's mouth. "Sometimes tradition yields to force of arms. If Polynices hadn't been caught off guard away from the city when his father died, he would have chosen a bride and given her the necklace his mother had once worn, and the throne would have been his."

"What if Eteocles had married and given his wife the necklace?" Gabrielle asked.

"Then, no matter his birth order, the citizens of Thebes would have recognized him as king," Xena said. "Unfortunately for Eteocles, he thought his brother was his only enemy. With his ambition and cruelty, he had incurred Antigone's wrath, and before he could lay his hands on the necklace, she stole it."

"That which was given is neither mine, nor yours," Gabrielle murmured. Her eyes suddenly brightened. "She gave it to you!" She hesitated, staring at Mount Parnassus, which loomed ever larger before them. "And you took it to Delphi!" She beamed proudly at having solved the riddle. Then a look of puzzlement overcame her pride. "But I still don't get the last line—'A crown that is no crown crowns king reviled.' "

Xena increased the pace without replying. She wasn't cer-

tain she understood it, either. But the possibilities filled her
with a rare dread.

Halfway up the slopes of Parnassus, Gabrielle gasped.

Xena allowed a small grin. She turned back toward her
friend. "Tired?" she asked. But it wasn't fatigue that caused
Gabrielle to stop.

Night had yielded to dawn, and the fire of a new day's
sun shimmered on the blue waters of the Gulf of Corinth,
which lay visible between a gap in the misty foothills. Gabrielle leaned on her staff as she stared with awe-widened
eyes. "Beside the wine-dark sea," she murmured, "by sacred
shores. Xena, it's beautiful!"

Xena nodded as she lay a hand on Gabrielle's tanned
shoulder. For a brief moment, her worries melted as she
regarded the splendid panorama, and she felt a rare stirring
of pride in her Greek homeland. But when she glanced at
Gabrielle, the sun dazzled her eye, and it was Antigone she
saw.

"Xena?"

Xena blinked.

"I said how much farther is it?"

Xena passed a hand over her face. Despite the rising sun,
her mood darkened again. "Not far," she answered.

The road to Delphi was well-traveled, for many pilgrims
and petitioners had made their way to Apollo's legendary
oracle. Xena and Gabrielle followed in their footsteps, up
and around the graceful slopes to a small plateau nestled
halfway up Parnassus.

White stone buildings rose on either side of the road.
Gabrielle walked side by side with Xena now, her gaze darting left and right, an expression of wonder on her face. They
passed a stadium, an amphitheater, a spring, a public bath.

Near the bath, a man gestured to them from a makeshift
booth as he arranged his wares on a table. Xena studied him
dubiously. "You're up early," he called, "but never too
early, I say. Get your souvenirs right here. Your official
Delphic souvenirs." He held up a garment; displayed upon
it were neat letters that read, MY PARENTS VISITED THE DEL-
PHIC ORACLE, AND ALL I GOT WAS THIS LOUSY CHITON!

Xena brushed the garment aside. "Where is everybody?" she said, indicating the empty streets.

Gabrielle fingered a string of beads, then a red-glazed kylix upon which was written, I LOVE APOLLO! She made a face as she set it back.

The merchant frowned, then shrugged. "It's the off-season," he said. "Besides, some idiot warlord attacked us about this time yesterday morning. Right at dawn, you know? The tourists ran like it was Marathon all over again, and most of the locals are still hiding in the hills." He picked up a doll that was dressed in a tiny gray robe with a lightning bolt clutched in its miniature fist. He thrust it hopefully at Gabrielle. "What, you don't love Apollo? Maybe you love Zeus. I got all the gods here." He waved a hand over his display. He turned his attention back to Xena. "But like whose got time to hide? I got a son at Plato's academy, and a daughter off at Sappho's finishing school, and I got a business to run."

Xena leaned across the table. "What warlord?" she asked.

The merchant looked irritated. "How should I know what warlord? They all look alike to me, all that armor and leather and crap." He ran his gaze up and down Xena. "No offense. I mean, who attacks Delphi? It's like just inviting some god's immortal boot up your backside!" He shot a look toward Gabrielle. "Hey, you gonna buy something?"

Xena touched Gabrielle's arm, and they moved on.

The street ended at the Temple of Apollo. It was the oldest of the thirty-eight buildings that made up Delphi. Its gleaming columns rose against the dramatic backdrop of Parnassus itself, and it faced the sea below like a watchful eye. With a certain reverence, Xena hesitated, then led the way up a cascade of marble stairs to a pair of great doors.

The interior was darker than Xena remembered. In the center of the ceiling, there hung a strange ball of faceted reflective glass. Xena had never seen its like before. It spun slowly, catching the firelight from the dozen braziers standing about the vast chamber and casting it back with swirling, dizzying effect. For the first time she noticed a music and drums that beat an intoxicating rhythm.

The air smelled with a potent and unfamiliar incense. Her

head felt as if it were swelling, and her face flushed with an inexplicable warmth. Her pupils seemed to dilate, making the weird lighting still more weird.

Gabrielle touched her hand. Without thinking, Xena drew her into a dancer's embrace, then propelled the smaller, un-resisting woman through a series of spins and turns that ended with Gabrielle bent backward in a sweeping dip.

From the far end of the chamber came enthusiastic applause.

Her lips dangerously close to Gabrielle's, Xena seemed to wake from a spell. The music ended; the rush of heat faded from her skin; she dropped a breathless Gabrielle like a stone and straightened. "I've come about the—"

"Necklace of Harmonia," said a voice out of the darkness.

Xena frowned and cocked her head. "I can't see you."

A patient chuckle. "My predecessor was killed yesterday," the voice said. "I'm her replacement. I've made a few changes. I know she was very open and public, but I think an oracle should surround herself with a little bit of mystery, don't you, Xena?"

Gabrielle picked up her staff and took her usual place at Xena's side. "She seems to know you," she whispered.

"Who are you?" Xena called.

A shaft of dim light penetrated the darkness. Within it, a black-haired woman Gabrielle's age sat revealed on a thronelike chair. Beneath the chair a narrow fissure breathed forth a thin whitish vapor.

The young woman rose to her sandaled feet. "I'm Disco," she answered, "the Delphic Oracle." She raised her hands, gesturing to either side. The light brightened, and the darkness drew back as if a curtain had parted. "And these are my psychic friends."

A quartet of middle-aged crones all dressed in black smiled vacuously and wiggled gnarly fingers at Xena and Gabrielle.

"I need to know about the warlord who attacked you yesterday," Xena interrupted. "Did he take Harmonia's necklace? Do you know what he plans to do with it?"

Disco put on a pouty face. "Well of course. What's the

point of being an oracle if I don't know all the answers? I have Apollo's ear, you know!"

"Maybe you'd better give it back before he misses it," Gabrielle muttered.

The oracle braced her hands stubbornly on her hips. "Mellow out, little sister. It's only out of the kindness of my heart that I'm refraining from revealing *your* future." She folded her arms over her breasts and gave an exaggerated shudder.

One of the crones leaned forward and cackled. "Want to know if your boyfriend's cheating on you?" she said to Xena.

Another leaned forward. "Want to know if you'll be rich?"

"Or get a better job?" inquired the third.

"Of course he took the necklace," said the fourth with a gesture of disdain. "What else do you think he came for? We don't do prostate exams."

Gabrielle shot a quizzical look at Xena.

Xena moved past Disco and stood before the fourth crone. "Old mother," she said respectfully, "I don't understand all these changes, but I can tell that you appreciate the traditional ways. Can you tell me what I need to know?"

"Hey, I'm the oracle here!" Disco snapped.

"And Xena is the future of Hellas!" the fourth crone shouted back, "while Disco's time is shorter than it takes to tell us! Your act's a load of crap! There's a sound at your door—wake up to the rap!"

Xena turned her back and headed for the door. "Excuse me for striking a sour note," she said. "I don't have time for your squabbling."

Disco made a rude hand gesture to the sour-faced old crone, then called, "Wait, Xena. Don't leave your cake out in the rain! I may dance to a different drum, but I know your song!"

Xena halted, then turned around with a set face, her expression humorless.

Disco struck an audacious pose, then seated herself ceremoniously upon her throne. She closed her eyes, lifted her head. After a few moments, a low melodic hum escaped her lips. Words formed a soft chant. "Oh," she moaned, "love to love ya, baby! Oh, love to love ya, baby!"

That same rhythmic pounding they had heard earlier rose again. A puff of white smoke hissed upward from the fissure under Disco's chair. A second followed it. Gabrielle began to sway again. A tendril of vapor passed under her nose. "What a rush!" she whispered, entranced.

Xena, too, felt the effect of the smoke, the flushing of her skin, the sudden warmth. She resisted a powerful urge to seize Gabrielle for another spin about the room. On the dais before her, the four black-robed crones—even the recalcitrant old mother—rose and moved together in a peculiar kind of line dance.

"Oh yeah!" Disco cried, her voice rising to a crescendo "I feel it! I feel the power!" The smoke flowed from the curious crack, swirled around her. Disco abandoned her chair and began to spin in a slow pirouette, round and round, her arms outflung, black hair making streamers about her face as she dipped and turned in dreamlike grace.

Like a puppet on Apollo's strings, Xena thought with sudden reverence, for though Disco's unsettling style, she abruptly spied a revelatory beauty.

Or maybe, though she fought it, the smoke was affecting her judgment.

"To the east your song must take you," Disco intoned, her words building a cadence with the unseen drums, "to Cadmus's city on the plain, where friendship will be tested and ghosts wait to be slain."

Xena struggled to keep her eyes open. She felt the insistent throb of the music, and though her feet remained rooted, she swayed to its time. Gabrielle danced around her with lithe movements that mirrored those of the oracle. Yet, with each whirling turn her face seemed to change, becoming Antigone, then Gabrielle . . . Antigone . . . Gabrielle . . . !

Disco sang on. "A warrior princess must fight for Greece when dragons' teeth are strewn, or Creon will be king when Parnassus spears the moon!"

The music's beat intensified; the fissure seemed to open wider in the floor spilling even more smoke into the air. The oracle faded in its pale embrace, then the crones. Soon the smoke became so thick they could not be seen at all. As mysteriously as it began, the music also faded.

Gabrielle collapsed to the floor. Barely able to stand, Xena flung herself down beside her friend. The smoke seemed to rise above their heads in slow, swirling eddies and waft away. When it cleared, Xena and Gabrielle found themselves alone.

Gabrielle looked up and blew a strand of hair from her face. "Sometimes, I wonder," she said, "if it's too late to go home, settle down with a couple of my father's cows, and spend the rest of my days quietly as an ordinary milkmaid."

Xena got up from the floor and brushed herself off. "You'd miss the action," came her dry comment.

Gabrielle sat up and hugged her knees. "Xena, how are we going to get to Thebes?"

"Think of it as part of your conditioning," Xena answered as she headed for the door. "We've still got most of the day."

"Conditioning?" Gabrielle shouted in exasperation. "Most of the day? We're going to run? All the way to Thebes?"

Xena paused at the top of the stairs. The streets of Delphi were finally beginning to fill with people. A carnival atmosphere was developing with more merchants and souvenir hawkers setting up tent-shops or wandering among the increasing throng. A stilt-walker moved toward her with a sign around his neck that read, EAT SOUVLAKI AT TASSO'S. A midget juggler weaved in and out of the stilt-walker's legs. A trio of belly dancers worked the crowd at one corner, collecting drachmae in their tambourines.

"Can't we at least grab one honeyed date or a baclava?" Gabrielle begged. "We've walked most of the night, we didn't have breakfast, and I'm starving!"

Xena shook her head. "Last one to Thebes grooms Argo for a month." She took off down the stairs of Apollo's temple and through the streets.

An annoyed Gabrielle called after Xena's back. "Yeah, like I'm going to win that one! If you'd brought Argo along, instead of turning him loose to go studding around the countryside, we could have ridden to Thebes!" Then, with a sigh of resignation, she chased after the warrior princess.

•   •   •

Late that night, far eastward and back on the Boeotian Plain, Xena stood quietly and watched the moon sliding down the side of the black splinter that marked distant Parnassus. Her thoughts wandered back again to that war between brothers and the fall of Thebes. She had sat on the sidelines then, refusing to choose sides. Had she done the right thing?

Antigone, her friend, tried to mediate a peace, but in the end, Polynices lay dead on the field outside the city, unmourned and unburied, by Eteocles's order. Enraged, Antigone defied that order and buried her older brother. In turn, an enraged Eteocles commanded that Antigone be entombed alive.

Then Xena might have taken action to save Antigone, but Antigone forbade it. To shame Eteocles and her uncle, Creon, who supported him, she staged her own funeral, dressed herself in the finest raiments, and had herself carried through the city's weeping throngs to the place of her interment. And to spit in Eteocles's eye, she stole the necklace that would have made him king and gave it to Xena to spirit away.

"What happened to Eteocles?" Gabrielle asked. She sat beside a campfire roasting the rabbit she had earlier clubbed with her staff and baking a fish Xena had caught from the lake beside which they were camped. With her hair tied back, the red sheen from the fire played eerily over her young face.

Xena turned and crouched down beside Gabrielle. "Three days after Antigone's burial, his guards found him torn to pieces in his bedchamber. Some said it was the work of the Furies, punishing him for mistreating his family. Others said Apollo himself had done the deed."

Gabrielle poked at the rabbit with a dagger Xena had loaned her, and juicy grease fell sizzling into the flames. "And Creon?" she asked.

Xena hesitated a long time before responding. "He vanished," she said lowly. "And that was the end of Thebes. Its citizens packed up and abandoned their homes. The city was haunted, some claimed. Invaders moved in, but none stayed.

Then an earthquake toppled the walls, the great buildings, even the temples."

Gabrielle took the fish from the hot stones upon which it cooked and blew on the smoking flesh to cool it. She filleted it, then, and divided the pieces onto clean stones she had washed in the lake. She handed one to Xena.

"Xena," she said, before taking the first bite of her own share, "why would Creon risk so much to steal Harmonia's necklace? If Thebes is in ruins, why would he want to be its king?"

Xena gazed off into the darkness. She had been pondering that same question all day. "Don't scorch the rabbit," she warned.

They ate the rest of their meal in silence. When only bones remained, and when fingers had been licked clean, Gabrielle unrolled her bedding, yawned, and prepared to sleep.

Xena watched her with a quiet pride. "You've done well today, Gabrielle. I set a grueling pace, and you stayed right by my side. And you conked that bunny as neatly as anyone could have."

Gabrielle didn't hear. She was already asleep.

With a sigh, Xena unrolled her own blanket. Before she lay down, however, some sense alerted her. Gooseflesh rose on her arms; a chill shivered down her spine. She shot to her feet, and her hand went to the chakram at her hip as she whirled about.

A pathetic figure, pale and thin as smoke, stood over Gabrielle. A dirty bandage covered eyes that leaked a horrid redness. Blood and filth matted his dark beard. Though mighty-thewed, he leaned upon a staff like a bent old man.

Xena could see right through him—to Parnassus and the rising moon.

She breathed his name. "Oedipus!"

Once the king of Thebes, and Antigone's father, he held out a hand in warning. In a voice that was stern, yet dry as death, he said, "Friend of my daughter—beware!"

Oedipus spoke no more, but faded away. Xena stared at the place where he had stood, half disbelieving the vision.

Then she felt a vibration in the earth through the soles of her boots, heard the sound of swiftly approaching horses.

"Gabrielle, get up!"

Xena drew her sword with one hand and with the other hand scooped a burning brand from the fire. A weary-eyed Gabrielle stirred, then noting Xena's attitude and hearing the hoofbeats, she seized her staff and sprang up.

Six riders charged them. Xena and Gabrielle struck together, and two armored warriors went down hard. With a high-pitched battle cry, the warrior princess leaped into the air, flipped, and landed on the back of a third rider. With her sword's pommel, she knocked him off and steered his horse into the path of another attacker, leaping free an instant before the two beasts collided.

Gabrielle's staff crashed onto the horse-haired helm of yet another attacker. Without hesitating, she spun low and expertly swept his feet from under him.

Then, an unexpected seventh rider rushed from the darkness. Xena cried a warning. Too late, Gabrielle turned and raised her staff. Her eyes widened at the size of the horse. She tried to dodge. A great black shoulder brushed her, knocking her nearly into the lake.

The seventh rider drew back sharply on the reins. The horse reared and let out a terrible whinny as its hooves thundered against the ground, and it stood still. Radiating cold hatred, the rider faced Xena. A leather-gloved hand rose and cast aside a concealing helmet. A cascade of blond curls spilled out.

Xena lifted the firebrand higher, the better to see the rider's face. "Ismene!" The name hissed through Xena's teeth.

The armored woman glared, showing no fear at all, though she bore no obvious weapon. "Leave this land, Xena! Your business here ended years ago when you let my sister die!"

Xena bristled. "Antigone chose her path," she answered. "The same as you chose yours when you ran away in the middle of the conflict."

Ismene spoke with icy intensity. "I'm older now. I no longer run from a fight."

Xena cocked her head. "Well, it looks like you've got one if you've sided with Creon. He killed an oracle of Apollo to seize Harmonia's necklace. I don't know what he's up to, but I intend to find out."

Ismene spat scornfully. "What did you ever care about Apollo or any of the gods? I warn you, Xena, leave—or die!"

Ismene jerked on the reins and rode off into the night. Her six men scrambled after her, some on horseback, the rest on foot. The sounds of their groaning and stumble-footed retreat could be heard for minutes.

A dazed Gabrielle sat up on the shore of the lake, one hand still in the water, her hair and face black with mud. "Don't tell me," she grumbled when Xena knelt down beside her. "Sisters? Antigone and Ismene?"

Xena's mouth drew into a grim line as she stared off the way Ismene had gone. "This is turning into a real family affair."

Gabrielle gave a caustic look as she squeezed mud from her hair. "Seems to me a family affair is what started all this." She followed the direction of Xena's gaze, then, in an accusing tone, added, "We're not going to sleep anymore tonight, are we?"

Xena allowed a weak grin and patted Gabrielle's knee. "Take a moment to wash," was all she said.

Noon found them jogging toward the barren outlands of what had once been the Theban city-state. Though the sun beat down with a harsh heat, Xena could still not shake off a chill. No matter how swiftly she ran, she couldn't leave behind the image of Oedipus's ghost.

They walked for a bit to catch their breaths. Gabrielle had grown quieter, too, for a change. Her blue-eyed gaze seemed constantly to be searching the land, and her face was set in a hard expression that seemed more Antigone's than her own.

After a while, though, she spoke up. "Xena, how did Ismene know we were coming? How did she find us in the dark?"

"Our campfire might have given us away."

Gabrielle was unconvinced. "That could explain how she found us, but not how she knew."

Xena sped up to a trot. Gabrielle's questions only filled her with a greater urgency. She didn't have answers, and she disliked not having them.

In late afternoon, they reached the end of their desperate journey. Though overgrown with grass and weeds, they could still see the ruts of the road that led across the plain to where the gates of Thebes had once stood. Stone pillars, once mighty but now broken, marked the main entrance.

There was no sign of Creon or Ismene, nor of any army. A soft wind rustling over the plain, whistling among the ruins, made the only sound. The only movement came from white clouds sailing a low course across the deepening sky.

In sullen reverence, Xena and Gabrielle entered the city. Walls that had withstood the long seige of Polynices and his allies lay crumbled. Flattened buildings looked as if an angry god had struck them. They moved without speaking among the rubble, climbed over shattered temple columns that blocked the streets, prowled through abandoned dwellings and homes. Gray dust from dangerous roofs showered down on them. A wall collapsed at a touch from Gabrielle's staff.

In the open streets, reflecting off white marble, the sun roasted them. In the shadows or in the gloomy interiors, they shivered.

Of the palace, nothing at all remained save a wide flight of granite steps cut into a hillside. The steps led up to the summit of a narrow plateau in the city's heart, where Cadmus had built an amazing edifice as a gift to his bride and as a tribute to the god Apollo.

At the top of the steps, upon the summit, Xena and Gabrielle turned as one and stared back. The palace offered one singular view—of Parnassus.

Though night had not yet fallen, a white and ghostly moon hung in the western sky. It sank slowly, inexorably, toward the very pinnacle of the sacred mountain, as if to impale itself.

" 'Creon will be king,' " Xena whispered, " 'when Parnassus spears the moon.' " She squeezed her eyes shut as she repeated the prophecy silently. Then she snapped them open again. "I'll never let that bastard be king. Not of Thebes, not even of its ruins!"

Gabrielle touched Xena's arm. "Xena?"

Xena turned to Gabrielle with an intense gaze. "This was Creon's fault, Gabrielle!" she explained. "Oedipus discovered that he'd killed his father and married his mother. But it was all a horrible mistake, a great tragedy! The Theban people understood that. They forgave him and wanted him to continue as their king. But Creon convinced Oedipus otherwise and urged him to leave the city. With Oedipus out of the way, it was Creon who urged Eteocles to seize the throne and make war on Polynices. Eteocles was young; Creon would have wielded the real power!"

The sky took on a blacker color. The last rays of sunlight withdrew behind the edge of the world; the moon brightened.

"Xena," Gabrielle said, pointing. "We've got company."

Armored soldiers filed through the street below and toward the granite steps. Leading them came an old man with gray hair arranged about his shoulders and a braided beard that hid his throat and brushed the top of his chest. At his side, sternly erect and cloaked in black, walked Ismene.

"Is that Creon?" Gabrielle asked. "He's older than I expected."

Xena nodded. "Ambition acknowledges no age." She drew her sword and struck a pose at the top of the steps. "Creon!" she called. "That's far enough!"

Squinting, the old man looked up and tilted his head questioningly. "Who are you?" he shouted weakly. A tremor marked his voice.

An angry Ismene caught Creon's arm. "Xena!" she challenged. "I warned you not to interfere!" She waved the soldiers forward. "Kill her!"

At Ismene's command, they streamed up the steps. Moonlight flashed on sword blades and spear points and helmets. Hoarse battle cries filled the night.

Xena met the first of them at the very edge of the steps. Her sword and booted foot drove a pair back. The others rushed on. A spear thrust at her gut. Gabrielle's staff deflected it.

"I owe you for that one!" Xena cried, skipping back.

Gabrielle swung her staff and danced back, too. "Then *you* groom Argo for a month!" she replied.

Outnumbered, they gave ground to the charging soldiers. Xena's battle cry soared. On the wider plateau, on the very foundation of the old palace, there was more room to fight. Xena's sword sang. Gabrielle fought with an uncharacteristic violence. Men fell to left and right of them, and the tide began to turn.

"Xena!" Gabrielle shouted suddenly as she knocked the helmet off one attacker and sent him reeling. "Look at them! They're *old*!"

They were, too, old men, and slow. Though their eyes burned with determination and purpose, age had stolen the strength from their arms, diminished their reflexes, dulled their skills. Only their numbers made them dangerous.

Ismene and Creon achieved the summit behind their warriors. Creon looked only confused, but Ismene's face was twisted with rage as she led her uncle around the edges of the fighting.

The wind caught the cloak she wore, and it fluttered open. Around her neck, gold flashed—the Necklace of Harmonia!

Xena gave a cry. Leaping into the air, she flipped over the heads of her attackers to land before Antigone's sister. The point of her sword flicked at Ismene's throat. "You're behind this!" Xena shouted. "Who are these old men?"

Ismene laughed. "All that's left of the Theban army!" came her haughty answer. "Men who still love Thebes and will risk their lives to see it rise again!"

"With Creon as its king?" Xena said scornfully.

Ismene lifted her head. "And me as its queen! Queen of Thebes—then all of Greece!"

"Sounds like another family problem to me," Xena replied coolly. With a subtle movement, her sword's edge severed the necklace. It slithered down Ismene's breast and fell to the ground.

"You leave my niece alone!" Creon, though little more than a dotard, flung himself at Xena, and they fell backward together with his arms locked around her.

Xena flung him off. From the corner of her eye, she

glanced toward Parnassus. The white discus of the moon balanced on the pinnacle!

Xena grinned as she often did at desperate moments. "You'll never win with this army, Ismene!"

Ismene emitted a serpentine hiss. "That's why I brought another!" She opened her fist, revealing a collection of ivory thorns. "With Apollo's help and the teeth of a dragon, Cadmus built this city. Now with my mistress Hecate's help and those same teeth, I intend to rebuild it. Thebes will be great once more!"

With an outward fling of her arm, she scattered the teeth. They caught the moonlight, and the air filled with a sparkling and glittering. They fell to the ground, an unholy seeding, on bare earth or stone foundation, it didn't matter. Wherever they touched, an armored soldier sprang up.

But no human soldiers! From the teeth of a dragon they rose, and children of a dragon they were! Their hands were green-scaled skin and clawed. Reptilian faces peered out from under their helmets. Red eyes burned with fierce blood lust.

With shields and swords, they turned, not just on Xena and Gabrielle, but also on the old Theban soldiers. Ismene laughed with insane glee as she scooped up the Necklace of Harmonia and helped her uncle to his feet.

Xena's eyes widened in horror and disgust. She met the nearest reptilian attacker. With her first blow, she knocked away its shield. With her second, she struck the monster in the neck. The impact of the stroke shivered up her arm. It was like striking stone! She struck again, and still her blade drew no cut!

Gabrielle made a similar discovery. "Xena! You can't hurt them!"

But Xena had seen the creature stagger when she knocked away its shield. Maybe cutting it wasn't the only way to beat it! She pivoted and kicked her dragon soldier in the chest with all her strength. He stumbled back a step, and before he could recover, she kicked him again, then again. Over the side of the plateau he tumbled to the ground far below. She watched him strike and lay motionless.

Then he got up.

All around her the old Theban soldiers screamed. Though they fought furiously, they fought against magic, the powerful magic of Ismene and the witch goddess, Hecate! Though the Thebans had tried to kill her, she felt for them now and pitied their helplessness. If they were to have any chance at all, she had to disarm the dragon spawn! *A warrior princess must fight for Greece when dragon's teeth are strewn!*

She drew her chakram and flung it. Against a sword blade it flashed, then ricocheted, striking a shield and another sword blade, a broken stone column, then yet another sword blade.

Xena's heart sank. The unnatural swords were stronger than her chakram. None of them had shattered!

Then, a thinly muscled arm shot out, and a delicate hand snatched the chakram from the air.

In amazement, Xena called, "Gabrielle?"

Gabrielle turned.

It wasn't Gabrielle!

Antigone raised the chakram and launched it again. With an uncanny precision that matched Xena's own, it flew from one sword to the next, smashing them each just above their hilts. *A warrior princess must fight—*

Antigone was a princess—a princess of Thebes!

Again, she caught the flying chakram. A dragon soldier leaped into her path. She struck out with the chakram's edge. Greenish blood spurted from a severed throat. Pushing him away, she leaped onto a bit of fallen cornice and flung the chakram high into the air. Up and up it sped, spinning, catching the moonlight.

It hung in the air like a second orb, gleaming, brightening.

Down below, in the streets of Thebes, hundreds of figures began to move toward the plateau, ghostly figures, wan, almost transparent. Yet they glowed with the moonlight and the light of the chakram.

Antigone sang, and they came! The ghosts of Theban soldiers, of Theban citizens, the ghosts of men, women, and children, the generations of a city. Up the granite steps they came, and up the sides of the plateau, climbing like insects. They seized the dragon soldiers, fell upon them, ripped them apart like bloody paper and cast the pieces over the plateau's edges.

Ismene screamed as she saw her mad dream destroyed. "No!" she cried. "Thebes must rise again! Through me, the House of Cadmus must rise and rule again!"

Creon caught her hand. "Daughter! Daughter!" he said in a feeble voice. "The gods are against us, as they have always been! Lead me home, child! Guide a blind old man . . . !"

Ismene lashed out. "I'm not your daughter! I'm not . . . !"

Under the force of her blow, Creon stumbled back. His heel caught on a bit of rubble.

Even the ghosts that crowded the summit seemed to stop their carnage, catch unnatural breaths, turn as one, and watch as Creon fell with dreamlike grace. A long sigh seemed to escape his lips as he sank backward.

A broken stone makes a harsh pillow.

One by one, two by two, the Theban ghosts faded away.

Ismene screamed again, a sound as unnatural as anything that had transpired this night. Picking up a Theban sword, she ran at Xena. "By all the gods, you have no right to live when Thebes is dead! You stood by, a mere witness to it all, when you might have acted to save us!"

Xena countered Ismene's guileless attack. Frustrated, Ismene lunged again. Xena sidestepped. Off-balance and carried forward by her own momentum, Ismene gasped, then tumbled head over heels down the long steps. Halfway to the bottom, broken and upside down, she stopped.

"You were right about one thing," Xena murmured. "You don't run from a fight anymore."

She glanced toward Parnassus, which was now a black splinter deep in the moon's heart.

Antigone, in Gabrielle's body, came to Xena's side. In one hand she held the chakram, in the other the Necklace of Harmonia. "You will always be my friend, Xena."

Xena laid her hand affectionately on the face before her and answered softly, "You will always be mine. I'm sorry, Antigone, if I let you down."

Antigone smiled. "You did exactly what I asked of you, no more and no less. Sometimes, that's the hardest thing of all." She turned away for a moment, toward Parnassus, then gazed upward toward the heavens. "I could keep this body, Xena. We are well-matched, this Gabrielle and I. I could live again."

Xena hesitated, then swallowed with difficulty. "Not at the price of Gabrielle's soul."

With that same eerie sense she had experienced before, Xena suddenly knew they were not alone. She turned.

Oedipus stood behind her at the top of the steps. He held out a hand, but not in warning this time. "Come daughter," he said gently to Antigone. "Guide me as you have always done. Guide us home."

It was Antigone's turn to hesitate. With a sigh, she reached up and kissed Xena's cheek. "Good-bye," she whispered, "my friend." She walked to Oedipus and took his hand.

At the edge of the steps, she turned back to Xena.

It was Gabrielle.

"Who is that?" Gabrielle asked as Xena came to her side and they looked together down into the ruins of Thebes.

A pair of figures walked slowly toward the gates, a father and a daughter.

Xena said nothing.

... WHEN THEY
BEAR GIFTS

Diane Duane

It was three hours after sunrise, somewhere in the western
lands of Dacia, and the sun spilled down from behind the
three of them into the valley toward which today's road led,
laying their shadows out long against the white dust, and
(when the road curved) against the green-gold of the fields
of ripening wheat to either side. Ahead of Gabrielle strolled
a figure few people ever got to see: a warrior princess actually at ease for once, lazy, almost unfocused, even chewing idly on a blade of grass, her dark hair swinging a little
with her stride and shining in the sun. Behind Xena, on the
long rein, the golden mare Argo ambled along, trying to
snatch bites of greenery from the roadside as they went, and
occasionally succeeding.

Gabrielle breathed out in pleasure at the absolute peace
of it all as she walked. High up, larks were singing against
a sky of cool deep blue, one which would later be a hot
deep blue if she was any judge of the weather. As they
walked, Gabrielle was already eyeing the landscape for possible shade, and finding it here and there, even this high up,
where outcroppings of old trees reared up, scattered among

the corn lands on either side. Down ahead of them, as the
road descended into the vale, the greenery grew thicker, less
scattered, combining into a genuine forest. And in the midst
of the forest, maybe eight or ten miles distant, she thought
she caught the occasional glimpse of one or two tall stone
buildings. What they might be, she wasn't sure, but Xena
didn't look even slightly concerned, which was always a
good sign.

The rolling countryside around them was delightful, and
much more so since Gabrielle knew that it was now a lot
safer than it had been when she and Xena had first arrived
in these parts. No one wants to have to live in the neighborhood of a chimera, but when the things suddenly change
their hunting grounds in the spring, anyone might suddenly
find a creature with a lion's front, goat's middle, and a
snake's tail holed up in one of the local caves, setting things
on fire with its inflammable halitosis and eating the live-
stock. So it had been with Meleia, the little village she and
Xena had left yesterday. Xena had predictably enough been
begged to help do away with the creature, which had already
killed the two village hunters who had tried to take it on.
The ensuing hunt had taken the better part of a day and
night, but the outcome had never been in doubt: chimerae
were not all that intelligent, and when the beaters, Gabrielle
leading them, drove the chimera into the narrow gully where
Xena was waiting for it, everything was over in a few
minutes and the flash of a chakram. Now at least there were
no more of the creatures within a fifty-mile radius, and
everyone could relax.

Xena, ahead of Gabrielle, glanced toward a coppice of
trees that stood close to the road, about fifty paces ahead of
them. "Thinking of stopping?" Gabrielle said.

She watched Xena glance down toward the forested vale
as they walked. It was rare to see her companion this relaxed, but even a woman so driven had to let up on herself
sometimes or go mad; and this was apparently one of those
times. Argo wandered past Xena, her ears pricked up, her
attention apparently on one down-hanging branch. "Maybe,"
Xena said, her voice sounding lazy. "It's not as if we're
expected anywhere."

Under the tree, something rustled. Xena stopped still, her hand on her chakram, and Argo kept on heading for the tree, making a soft whickering noise in her throat. Gabrielle gripped her staff, brought it up to the ready.

Something scrambled up out of the underbrush. Or rather, some*one* . . . and Gabrielle groaned softly at the sight of him.

He looked, as usual, like a collision between a delivery cart from Joe's Discount Armorers of Corinth and an unmade couch. The earnest face, the slightly gawky form, the battered, mismatched gear and weaponry, the general air of being unready for anything: they were all too familiar. "Fear nothing," he said as he scrambled to his feet, brushing off various leaves, twigs and opportunistic bugs: "Joxer the Mighty is here!"

Xena relaxed again, and rolled her eyes expressively. "I suppose we all have to be somewhere."

Gabrielle raised her eyebrows, but lowered her staff to lean on it, and paused there next to Xena in the road. "Just how did you know we would be coming this way?" she said.

"Easy. I simply followed the sound of triumph. Shouting crowds, maidens throwing flowers, the usual . . ."

Xena threw Gabrielle a dry glance. "I've got to try to get them to make less noise throwing those flowers."

"Then I took a shortcut across the fields last night, and had a nap here." He scratched himself reflectively. "So where are you two headed now?"

"Off for a few days' peace and quiet," Gabrielle said, "in private." Though now there seemed precious little chance of that. *Did I really think it was going to stay quiet for a little while?* Gabrielle thought. *So much for that.* Joxer's presence never made for a quiet life, especially for her.

"Well, never fear. I shall come with you," Joxer announced in a heroically magnanimous tone of voice, "and protect you."

The look Xena threw him was choice. Even Joxer's ego had to take note of it, and he said, "Well, at night, anyway. I can share the watches with you."

Xena chuckled.

"*Oh* no," Gabrielle said.

"Gabrielle," Xena said, "if he's offering, why not? You were the one who was complaining last week about four-hour watches that never let either of us get enough sleep."

"But—"

There was something slightly wicked in Xena's expression, an almost provocative laziness. "Let him share our road for a couple of days," she said. "It's safe enough around here. What's the harm in that?" And suddenly Gabrielle understood the expression. *And if he gets too intolerable, then one night when he's asleep somewhere safe, we'll slip away "on business." We've done it before. . . .*

Gabrielle raised her eyebrows. *Xena must really be in a good mood, otherwise she wouldn't be suggesting this. And who am I to ruin her mood when it's good for a change . . . ?*

She breathed out. "All right," Gabrielle said. "But one thing, Joxer."

"Anything."

"No singing!"

He pouted.

Gabrielle scowled at him.

"All right," Joxer said at last, disappointed. "But there are nineteen more verses of 'The Ballad of Joxer the Mighty' since I saw you last. You're missing out on some great material."

"I'm sure we are, and doubtless posterity will judge us harshly," Xena said. "Meanwhile, let's get going."

Argo reached up to tear off a mouthful of leaves from the nearest tree, and then stepped out behind Xena. Joxer and Gabrielle followed.

They walked on down the dusty, white road, looking out across the countryside, an astonishingly fertile and gentle-looking land, set among the little low hills. Joxer looked out over the rolling waves of gold-green and said, "This looks like a pretty well-kept place . . ."

"It's one of the little kingdoms between the empire and the city-states," Xena said. "Eluria, its name is, if I remember correctly."

"I didn't know there were kings around here," said Joxer.

"Well, there's one here, all right," Xena said. "King

Enomaeus. And he doesn't have the most wonderful reputation."

Gabrielle raised her eyebrows, noting that Xena didn't
look terribly concerned, even as she made this pronounce-
ment. "Really? The name's slightly familiar, but I don't remember hearing anything all that bad about him."

"Oh, apparently he was all right," Xena said, "until some
years back. He married one of the local princesses, and they
were happy together; but then there was a child, and the
queen died . . . and after that, there were rumors of trouble. . . ."

"What kind of trouble?"

Xena shook her head. "Gods, I don't know. But you hear
all kinds of stories, and how likely they are to be genuine,
or just rumors started by annoyed neighbors, is always the
question. . . ." She raised her eyebrows. "He had a good
name as a warrior, Enomaeus did, when he had cause to go
abroad. But apparently at home he started to acquire a reputation for enforcing the country's laws more rigorously
than he needed to. A real stickler for the rules. Not a position
calculated to make your subjects particularly enjoy your
rule."

"Huh," Gabrielle said.

"Is he oppressing his people?" Joxer said eagerly. "Should
he be deposed?"

Xena rolled her eyes. "Don't start," she said.

"Certainly not without evidence," Gabrielle said. *Hey,
that's it*, she thought, *maybe we can get him to go ahead
and "gather evidence" . . . and then slip off some other way
while he's doing it.* But *that* was no good. Joxer was certain
to get himself in some kind of trouble, and it would be Xena
and Gabrielle who were responsible for it. Then they would
have to get him out of it again. *Simpler to just let matters
take their course . . .*

"Well," Joxer said, "maybe we should look the situation
over. As responsible heroes, I mean."

"Maybe," Xena said, "we should mind our own business
until we have reason to do otherwise. Hmm?"

She walked on ahead. Gabrielle threw Joxer a you-stay-
here look and hurried a little to catch up with Xena.

When she did, Xena was smiling. "What are you thinking of?" Gabrielle said under her breath.

"Nothing in particular," Xena said, "except what I was thinking about before we were so rudely interrupted . . . stopping for a midmorning snack. For Argo, if not for us." She gazed ahead of them. "That glade up there—it looks like a good spot. There's water there, if I'm reading the terrain right. One of the little streams that leads down into the valley."

"I meant," Gabrielle said, "what are you thinking of as regards *him*." She gestured with her head at the young man following them.

That smile got lazier. "Gabrielle, you of all people should know how he is. Run away, he just chases you faster. Slow down, pay no attention to Joxer, and he gets bored and goes elsewhere."

"Not after creating a lot of trouble first!"

"Less than if you run. And I don't feel like running anywhere today. Nothing urgent is happening. Let's take it easy for a change. We'll be rid of him soon enough."

"Easy for you to say . . ." Gabrielle muttered. But Xena was already ahead of her again, making for the glade, and Gabrielle followed, while behind her, examining every shadow, came Joxer.

Gabrielle sighed and tried to start enjoying the morning again. It was futile, for behind her, someone was starting to hum.

"Joxer!"

The humming stopped.

Gabrielle sighed and kept walking.

The glade did indeed have a brooklet running through it, one of several that wound their way down from the hills on this side of the valley. A little mossy pool lay among the roots of the big smooth-trunked beech trees there, where the trunks of older, fallen trees lay as well, and Argo waded down to stand fetlock-deep in the clear rippling water, sucking it up for minute after minute without stopping. After a good while she moved to settle down to some serious grazing by the banks of the stream above the pool, and Xena went to her to undo the cinch and lift her saddle off.

Joxer was poking around among the huge boles of the trees, looking impatient, and the sight made Gabrielle immediately feel like sitting down and relaxing, if only to irk him. As she did so, and started going through her pouch to see if there was one more piece of nutbread left from the last baking, Joxer came out from around another tree and looked over at Xena. "How long are you planning to stay here?"

Xena strolled over to where Gabrielle sat and took the piece of nutbread she held up for her. "Argo needs to eat. Even I need to eat. What's your hurry?"

"There are deeds to be doing," he muttered.

"They'll get done, believe me," Xena said. "Half an hour's rest now won't make that much of a difference . . . and you may be glad of it later."

Joxer made an impatient face and vanished behind one of the largest trees, downslope.

Gabrielle and Xena watched him go. Gabrielle raised her eyebrows, saying, "How far do you think he really followed us?"

"There's no telling with that one," Xena said, and sighed. "Maybe it was really only since Meleia." Behind them, Argo whinnied softly; Xena looked around to make sure her reins hadn't slipped down so that she could step on them, a favorite habit of hers. "Maybe he—"

She stopped. Gabrielle, chewing on a mouthful of bread, glanced at Xena, saw her shocked look; followed her glance.

And stopped chewing.

On a log near the pond, dangling her perfect toes in the water, sat an extremely beautiful woman with long wavy cascades of golden hair. All she wore, besides that splendid mane of hair, was a very scanty band of some glittering material around her chest, and another one around and below her hips. The air around her was sparkling slightly, the sparks falling gently to the surface of the water, where they skated around briefly before vanishing.

"Aphrodite," Xena said softly. "Very . . . eye-catching."

The Goddess of Love and Beauty smiled charmingly. "Just my divinity showing," she said.

Gabrielle privately considered that there was a whole lot more showing than just divinity.

"Oh?" Xena said. "Funny . . . Ares never seems to feel it necessary to indulge in that kind of display."

Aphrodite rolled her eyes, annoyed. "I do *not* wish to discuss my ex."

Gabrielle's eyebrows went up. "You mean it's *true*, that story that—"

"He never did have any discretion," Aphrodite said, sounding exasperated. "He would come around the house while he thought Hephaestus was at the shop. Well, somebody tattled. Actually, Apollo. You just can*not* keep that one from looking in people's windows." She let out an annoyed breath. "And then we got caught together, and there was a big scene . . ."

"And why shouldn't there have been? You and Hephaestus were *married*. There's a word for that kind of thing," Gabrielle said severely.

"Yeah. Youthful indiscretion," said the Goddess of Love, and gave her a deadly look.

Gabrielle had been thinking of another word, like adultery, but for the moment she decided to let it pass, especially considering the expression on Aphrodite's face.

"Anyway, since then I've been trying to get out of the house more," the goddess said. "Do a little community service work on the side."

"Ah," said Gabrielle, somehow unconvinced that this was necessarily a good thing.

"But enough about you," Xena said. "Exactly what have we done to deserve this little visit?"

The goddess looked at Xena with amusement. "You always think everything that happens is aimed at *you*, don't you? Believe it or not, there are more things of interest in this neighborhood at the moment than just your august presence."

Gabrielle and Xena glanced at each other. "Such as?" said Xena.

"Oh . . ." Aphrodite smiled. "A small matter which requires the attention of a hero. Nothing serious."

" 'Nothing serious'? We're supposed to believe that?" Gabrielle said.

"Since when do gods lower themselves to fib to mortals?" Aphrodite said, and pouted prettily. "I would have thought you'd appreciate it when I came to do you a favor."

"Yes, well, I fear the gods even when they bear gifts," Gabrielle said, a lot more dryly than was probably necessary.

"Boy, and to think they say that the aphorism is a dead art form," Aphrodite said. "Thanks for sharing, Miss Buxom Bard of 380 B.C."

Gabrielle looked bemused. "What's a 'B.C.'?"

"Don't go there," Aphrodite muttered in a warning tone of voice. "I wish I didn't have to."

"Excuse me, but exactly what kind of 'favor' do you have in mind, goddess?" Xena said. "As Gabrielle says, the gods' favors rarely come without strings attached."

"Well . . ." Aphrodite glanced around her. "Joxer—"

"You're interested in *Joxer*?" Gabrielle said. "Things must be pretty slow up on Olympus this week."

The goddess's look was wry. It was not the response that Gabrielle had expected. "He might need some help shortly, that's all," she said. "Keep your eyes open."

"What kind of help?" said Xena.

"You're heroes," Aphrodite said, fretfully. "That's your specialty, isn't it, problem solving? Just deal with it." She started to go transparent.

"With *what*?" Gabrielle said.

"The princess."

"*What* princess?"

But it was too late. In a fizz of hot pink light, the goddess was gone.

Gabrielle and Xena looked at each other. From off among the trees, they could hear someone humming.

"*Joxer?*" Gabrielle whispered.

"A *princess*?" Xena whispered back.

"Dum, dum, tiddle dum dum, '*Joxer* the *Mighty* went *down* to the—' "

"*Joxer!*" Xena and Gabrielle said in unison.

A sudden silence fell, broken by some desultory splashing

in the stream that ran downslope from the pool.

"I remember you mentioning," Gabrielle said, "that Enomaeus had a child . . ."

"A daughter."

Xena went over to Argo, who had gone back to grazing,
and lifted her saddle from the log over which she had draped
it. Argo gave her a reproachful look.

"I'm not sure Aphrodite's doing us any favors," Xena
said, as she saddled the mare again. "Sounds more like she
wants us to do her one. But either way, when *she* turns up,
I start to get cautious."

She swung up onto Argo's back. "Let's get moving. But
let's stop in the next village before Enomaeus's main town,
and find out what's going on before we just walk into something we could otherwise avoid."

She rode gently out of the glade, and Gabrielle went after
her, while behind her Joxer said, "Hey, where's everybody
going? Are we leaving? Hey, wait for me . . ."

It took only an hour and a half or so for them to reach the
village at the edge of the forest, beside the road where it
dove into the woods, about six miles before Enomaeus's
castle. The village, called Tyche, was a comfortable enough
place, made up of fifteen or sixteen wattle-and-daub houses
tightly and neatly roofed with wheat-straw thatch. The people there were well dressed, for country folk, and well fed—
not one, but two huge communal bake ovens stood outside
the village, on the woodland side, with big stores of firewood stored nearby, held neatly stacked in thatched open-
sided sheds. The people there had heard of Xena, and made
her and Gabrielle very welcome; but Gabrielle saw them
spare some odd looks for Joxer—expressions of alarm or
concern.

"Stay for dinner," said the village headwoman, a handsome, tall brunette named Demis. A fire was kindled in the
middle of the village circle, and Gabrielle and Xena and the
villagers sat around it until fairly late in the evening, telling
and hearing news of the countries round about, while dining
on fresh bread and roast venison and drinking the good,
rough, country wine. But the only news they seemed reluc-

tant to discuss was that of Enomaeus's little kingdom, which was odd, since they were a part of it.

As people began to drift away from the fire and back to their houses, later in the evening, Xena took the opportunity to press the subject a little more with Demis. "We are going to be going to the castle in the morning," she said, "if only to look around . . ."

Demis threw an uneasy glance at Joxer, who was busying himself with the remains of a chunk of venison. "The king," Demis said, "is a good man . . . if a little abrasive . . . but he is, shall we say, a little vigorous about law enforcement."

"That hardly seems like a bad thing," Gabrielle said. "The land is peaceful, you're a fairly prosperous folk . . ."

"Yes, that's true. But there's no light lacks its shadow." Her eyes were resting on Joxer, rather sadly now. "The castle is probably safe enough for the two of you. But . . ."

Gabrielle followed the glance. "He's not likely to leave us at this point," she said. "What's the matter?"

Demis looked back at her. The expression was nervous. "I've said too much already," she said. "If the king should hear . . ." She sighed. "If you must stay . . . don't stay too long. It could be unfortunate for your young friend."

"Why?"

Demis shook her head. "It's forbidden to speak of it," she said. "But keep him out of there."

She got up and made her way to her own house rather hurriedly.

"We could avoid it," Gabrielle said.

Xena thought about that . . . then shook her head. "First of all," she said, "my curiosity's been aroused. But secondly . . . I have a feeling that with or without us, Joxer's likely to wind up there. And if he does, and gets in trouble . . ."

"As Aphrodite suggested he might . . ."

Xena nodded. "We'll go there, briefly, and keep an eye on him," she said. "It's all we can do."

Late that night, Joxer was still unable to get to sleep. He went out to the low-burning fire and sat there for a long time by himself under the stars of the early summer night, singing very softly in what he had been told often enough, and now knew, was no known mortal key. It was one of the many minor pains of his life. Inside his head, he always knew what his voice sounded like: pure, strong, clear, absolutely indicative of his mood—sad or glad, tender or reflective; and effortlessly so, a voice that would win all hearers to its agenda. Unfortunately, this perception was nothing like the reality the Fates were winding off the distaff for him, and day after day the thread of his life unreeled only a singing voice that made human beings run away. Even sheep and goats on lonely hillsides left for other hillsides lonelier still when they heard him sing. Joxer's heart had perfect pitch, but his throat had only the crow's voice, as rusty as the morning after the fox made it drop the cheese. People asked him to sing only when it was a slow midweek night at the tavern and they badly needed a laugh.

He bore this without too much complaint, as he bore most of the other disappointments in his life, which were ongoing and without foreseeable resolution, until Atropos should come along with the big sharp shears and put an end to it all. He glanced over at the little thatched house in which he knew Gabrielle lay asleep, and heaved a big sigh, secure in the knowledge that no one would hear it, and no one would care.

Not even her . . .

From the other side of the fire, a voice said softly, "Tell me about it."

"She is," he said, very low, "kind of spectacular."

" 'Kind of'?"

"Oh, more than that. She's the top. She's the Sphinx's pajamas! She's the top. She's—"

"Cut it out already," Aphrodite said, but she said it affectionately. "You think I haven't heard it a hundred times?"

Joxer stared at her. He could hardly avoid it. The goddess suddenly sitting there across the fire from him was wearing a kind of clothing he had never seen—nothing like a peplum or a chiton, but something that shone almost metallically in the firelight, fitted her all over from neck to ankles, extremely closely, and seemed to hug all her . . . charms . . . in an unusually candid manner. The garment was also excessively pink, not a normal color for clothes in these parts.

"Where did *you* come from?" Joxer said.

"Take a wild guess. Mountain? Starts with the letter omicron?—Oh, do you like the spandex?"

Joxer blinked and broke the stare by an act of will. "I haven't seen any of them hereabouts," he said, "but maybe the chimera scared them away."

Aphrodite looked at him kindly. "You really *were* left holding the empty amphora the morning they gave out the cognitive faculties, weren't you. Never mind."

"Mighty goddess—"

"Now there's a boy who knows how to ask politely. Who says flirting is a dead art . . . ?"

"I was just wondering if—" He looked over at the house in which Gabrielle lay. "If you couldn't . . . you know . . ."

"Not today. I've got another job on my mind, and if there's one thing you learn fast in this business, it's never to multitask," Aphrodite said. "Big career mistake for a god. You do that, pretty soon mortals start getting the idea that you're omnipotent, and then where are you? Answering prayers all hours of the day and night, not a moment for yourself to have a bath or read a good scroll on the—" She made a face. "Never mind. There is, however, one thing you can do for me, and I would be *really* grateful." Aphrodite wiggled her eyebrows at him several times in a most suggestive manner.

"What?"

"How would you like to win a princess's heart?"

Joxer burst out laughing. "That'll never happen."

"How do you know?" Aphrodite said. "The world is full of unexpected occurrences."

"*Me?* And a princess?" Joxer laughed harder, and had to undo his blanket so that he could wipe his eyes. "Look at me! I'm a penniless itinerant warrior of no particular lineage. Princesses like stability. Nobility. Cash," he added with the wistful tone of someone who had not seen a lot of that commodity recently. "There's absolutely nothing about me to attract a princess."

"You might be surprised."

"Cruel," Joxer said, looking up at the stars. "Cruel goddess, to so raise a poor mortal's hopes. Here I sit, alone, ever rejected and spurned, and you descend from cloudy Olympus to torment me."

"You could really get on my nerves," Aphrodite said, "if I wasn't so good-natured. Now stop whining and giving me weather reports, and pay attention. When it happens . . . I want you to do one thing."

"When what happens?"

"I knock on the amphora and it is empty, *empty,*" the goddess said to herself. "I don't know why I bother. Well, yes I do. But oh, what I go through to get anything done. Listen, you, I did *not* rise from the foam to play twenty questions with mortals! So just take my advice. When she asks you your name . . . don't tell her. Stall."

"Stall?"

"Stall. *Make her guess.* Got that? Do I have to carve you a bas-relief? No? Good. You do that, and after that just follow your hunches, and everything will turn out all right."

She disappeared.

"It doesn't sound right somehow," Joxer said, uncertain. "I thought the gods helped those who helped themselves."

"Believe me, this is the same thing," said her voice out of the air, and nothing more.

In the morning, no more than two hours' leisurely walk brought them from Tyche to the walls of King Enomaeus's forest castle. It was not a huge edifice, but handsome enough, a four-square walled building with towers at the corner, and a single, central keep. There was a cluster of thatched wooden houses in the shadow of the walls, and a small marketplace in the center of them. Stalls were set up there, and people moved casually among them, doing their shopping.

Xena tied Argo up at a handy water trough fed by one of the forest streams, and looked the place over. "Defensible," she said, looking at the "dry" moat, which had been dug around the castle and was filled with sharpened stakes. "A nice location."

"A noble edifice," Joxer said.

Gabrielle nodded absently, for there was something in the air that bothered her—a scent that had nothing to do with the usual marketplace smells, a faint, old fetor. "I think they need to do something about their drains, though . . ." But then the wind changed and carried the scent away, and she thought nothing more of it.

The three of them walked into the marketplace under the walls. Gabrielle glanced up, catching sight of some small, round, brown objects nailed up high on the stone of the walls. It was hard to see what they were. The sun was running high, and got in her eyes.

Xena, meanwhile, was also sniffing the air. "Someone's roasting venison again . . ."

"I thought you said you had enough of that last night."

"That was then. Besides, we missed breakfast. Here's our chance to catch up . . ."

The cook-butcher's stall was right under the walls. They paused there, and Gabrielle looked up again, now that they were in shadow.

"Oh," she said, and gulped.

Xena looked up too.

The brown dried-up looking things were the nailed-up heads of men. Above them, a few ravens sat on the battlements, looking bored, possibly because just about everything that could have been picked out of or off of those heads had been, and the remaining flesh and sinew was now much too dry to be appetizing.

Xena raised her eyebrows and turned her attention back to the venison roasting on the butcher's spits. "When Demis said they were keen on law enforcement around here," Xena muttered, "she wasn't joking."

"Well," Gabrielle said, "we can at least do some shopping."

"Yes," Xena said. "But I don't see any reason for us to linger. Once we've stocked up on supplies, we can head right out again."

Gabrielle nodded and turned her attention to shopping. The eternal nutbread had been getting boring lately, and here the variety of breads was surprisingly good, probably because of the plentiful firewood that the forest afforded. She went over to the bread stall and picked up a number of flat olive-oil loaves and some salted biscuit, and then moved on again to dicker with a neighboring stall holder for some dried meat. Suddenly Xena appeared at her elbow again, finishing a last piece of spitted venison.

"Gabrielle," she said under her breath, "have you seen Joxer?"

At that, Gabrielle's eyes widened. She had been so enjoying the peace and quiet, which meant he wasn't bothering her, that she had forgotten what his not bothering her meant. "Oh no," she said.

"Oh yes," said Xena. "I swear, you take your eyes off him for a second . . . Finish up there. Then let's find him and get out of here."

Joxer had swiftly become bored with the marketplace. When you got down to it, one village market was a lot like every other—meat, bread, beans, oil, wine, cloth, pots and pans . . . He had enough food for his own purposes at the moment, and besides, the structure and architecture of the castle was much more interesting to him. He walked under the walls for a little while, admiring the stone—it had apparently been brought some distance as there was no stone like this in the neighborhood—and the way it had been mortared together.

In front of the castle gates he stood for some minutes, admiring the gateway itself, a pair of high granite pillars bound in gilded iron, with a massive capstone around which the upper level of the wall had been built. The heads hanging to either side of it had apparently been there for some time. *Well, whatever they did, they probably deserved it. . . .*

A young woman came striding out of the gates with a basket over her arm. She was well dressed, tall and slender, with long chestnut hair hanging down her back over various layers of bright, gauzy muslin tunics, skirts, and vests in varying shades of russet, orange and red. Her face was beautiful, in a severe, classical sort of way—high-cheekboned, with slanting gray eyes—yet also weary, almost sorrowful.

Joxer stood there transfixed. *Will you look at her,* he thought. *What a beauty. A high-class servant of some kind. But why is she so sad?* He broke off the stare as she caught sight of him, looked him over, and then walked over to him.

"You're not from around here," she said.

"Uh, no."

"Who are you?"

The tone of voice was not that of a servant, however high-class. "Uh—" *Stall!* said something in the back of his mind, a voice suddenly very imperative. "I am, uh, the Unknown Hero," Joxer said. He paused, and then added, "Also called the Magnificent."

The princess looked him over skeptically. "And of what precisely does your magnificence consist?"

"Uh, it's supposed to be self-evident." He suppressed a sigh, for it seemed it rarely was.

He could hear footsteps coming up behind him, and glanced over his shoulder. Yes, as he had thought, it was Gabrielle, and Xena, at exactly the wrong moment. The princess raised her perfect eyebrows. "Many heroes," she said, "have passed through our golden gates before now, but few have made such a poor show as this." She looked over his shoulder at Xena and Gabrielle. "These are your attendants?"

"Not . . . really," Xena said, very slowly, in a way that made Joxer twitch.

"This is Xena," Joxer said hurriedly, "and the valiant Gabrielle."

The princess's eyes widened, though only marginally. "All know of the noble warrior princess," she said, bowing slightly to Xena, "and you and Gabrielle shall be made very welcome. And you then," she said to Joxer, "you are come to sue for our hand?"

"Our?" Joxer looked around him. "Is there more than one of you?"

The princess gave him a dirty look. "We are the only daughter of King Enomaeus," she said. "Hippodamia."

"Are we," Joxer said. "Ah." He was trying to figure out what had gone wrong with the pronouns around here.

"So are you here to ask my father for my hand, or what?" said the princess.

"Uh," Joxer said. "Well, now that you mention it, I wasn't sure that I—"

"—was adequate for my radiant glory, yes, that's what

they all say, let's just get it over with," the princess said
arrogantly enough, but to Joxer's ears there still seemed to
be a touch of weariness underlying the arrogance.

She led them through the castle gates and into the palace.
Xena, having seen palaces enough in her day, was plainly
not overly impressed. Gabrielle was glancing around her
with a dubious expression. Joxer could understand why, for
as he looked at the columns and tapestries they passed, he
got the feeling that this place might have seen better days—
it had a slightly seedy look about it, and the servitors' robes
had a much-mended look about them that was not well con-
cealed. One of them, passing by, caught Joxer's attention.
This was a young man, fair-haired, well-built, in rather
threadbare robes, and he did not so much walk by as skulk
by. But as he did, he glanced up at Joxer and favored him
with an expression of purest rage. Just a flicker of it, and
then the man was moving away, head down, hurrying.

Joxer blinked as he walked along behind the princess.
Why should he hate me? I haven't done anything to him—

The central hall of the palace was not very big, but it was
a little better kept than the antechamber through which they
had passed. At the near end of it was a faint quacking noise,
which proved to come from several nervous-looking musicians, playing shawms and other odd-looking wind instruments. Down at the other end stood a small cluster of men
surrounding a tall chair and partially hiding it. "Father—"
the princess said.

The five or six men standing there parted left and right,
bowing, to reveal the short, broad-shouldered man who sat
in the chair. He was not crowned, and he was wearing
clothes that were like enough to those of his subjects out in
the marketplace: a belted gray tunic, gray cross-gaitered
breeches, and sturdy sandals. But the face held royalty
enough, of a rather harsh kind, with an edge of cruelty to
it—eyes at a slight slant like his daughter's, but steely, and
a mouth that showed no signs of having smiled in a long
time.

Joxer bowed. "Here's a man who has come to ask for my
hand," Princess Hippodamia said.

Joxer straightened up. "Uh, it's a very nice idea, b—"

"What is his name?" said the King, in a deep, mellow voice.

This time Joxer was ready. "I am the Unknown Hero," he said. "And this is the warrior princess Xena . . . and her companion Gabrielle. In the meantime, I just—"

"You honor us with your presence, noble Xena," said the king, standing up. "And you, Gabrielle. Meanwhile, young man, I am sure that, having come here and asking what you ask, you know our law. Once you have set foot in my halls, I have the right to ask you to solve a riddle. Once you solve it, my daughter is yours. Should you fail to solve it, however, your head is forfeit, and will be nailed up on the walls as a warning to others."

Joxer went hot and cold with panic. *'They probably deserved what happened to them,'* he'd thought. *Oh, wonderful!* He swallowed, and started to say, "Excuse me, I don't want her, and I was just leaving." But instead, the words came out as, "King, is it not also the law that a man so challenged may in turn ask you or your daughter a riddle, which you must first answer before asking your own? And if you cannot answer, that man may go free, and demand one boon of you?"

Xena and Gabrielle stared at each other. Joxer would have stared at himself if he could have.

King Enomaeus blanched. "Someone told you that," he hissed. *"Who told you about that?"*

The musicians playing the wind instruments down at the other end of the hall squeaked and bleated to an abrupt halt, and a terrible silence fell. Joxer swallowed again, unwilling to answer the question directly. Fortunately he didn't have to, for the king's attention was immediately distracted by the courtiers and counsellors standing all around him, who were looking in every possible direction except at him. "Which of you traitors told him?" cried the king.

The most senior of the counselors, a distinguished-looking man with a long gray beard, turned to face the king then. "Sire," he said, "this man has only just now arrived, as you know. None of us have had a chance to speak so much as a word to him. And your people, knowing the law, would not dare. They know very well the price they would pay, and how it would be enforced."

The king subsided somewhat. "Very well," he muttered, glancing at his daughter. "It is the law. Ask your riddle."

"You must guess my name," Joxer said—or, rather, the voice inside him said, using his throat. "By tomorrow morning."

The king glanced at Xena and Gabrielle. Joxer watched the look Xena gave King Enomaeus: level, thoughtful, with just a hint of threat. Joxer was glad to see that, for it was occurring to him that what he had just said would be all too likely to put Xena in danger . . . and Gabrielle.

He was opening his mouth to tell the two of them to get out of there, that this was his mission and he would see them in the morning . . . but before he could, the king said, "Very well. Chamberlain—" He turned to one of the men standing nearby, who bowed very low. "See these guests to rooms befitting their station. In the morning," he said to Joxer, "my daughter will give you the answer to your riddle. Then you must answer hers, or die, by the time the sun reaches noon."

"Fine," Joxer somehow managed to say. The voice that had spoken through him had left him on his own as suddenly as it had come. "Oh, and would it be possible to get some lunch?"

"See to it," said the king, and waved them away.

As they went, Joxer shouldered close to Xena and whispered, "You should get out of here."

"Just when things are getting interesting?" Xena said, apparently not caring who heard. "Not a chance. We're with you, Hero."

Joxer gulped, and followed their escort.

For Gabrielle, it was a very peculiar afternoon. . . . partly because, when lunchtime came, she had to keep reminding herself not to call Joxer by his name as the three of them feasted at the king's table. The king was not there, having said that he had business to attend to. "Finding out the hero's name, probably," she muttered to Xena, while they watched Joxer put away the better part of a leg of mutton with a cheerful concentration all too reminiscent of that of a condemned man.

"All they have to do is go to Tyche for that," Xena said under her breath. "Except—"

"Except what?"

"Remember the lady we met earlier?" Xena said, more quietly still. "I don't think it's going to be that easy for them."

Gabrielle thought about that for a moment. "I hope you're right," she said. Trouble was, it was no use depending on the gods for anything. Their caprice could betray your expectations at a moment's notice.

They ate their lunch, and took advantage of the castle's facilities for a bath. Neither of them saw much of Joxer that day; he was walking around the place, looking it over with the air of someone spying out the strengths and weaknesses of a fortress to which he was about to lay siege. His seeming insouciance began to prey on Gabrielle's mind as afternoon slid into evening, and evening into night. There was another festal table set out for them all at dinner—a cold buffet— and various of King Enomaeus's courtiers met them there, all courtesy and insinuating questions about their travels, which Gabrielle parried as gracefully as she could. Xena had her reputation and her temper to shield her. No one bothered her more than once after she had turned that flashing, feral smile on them and told them to mind their own business, before she made them *hers*. Joxer, meanwhile, answered every question anyone asked him, except those pertaining to his own recent whereabouts. For those, somehow, he always had his mouth hilariously full, and the answers came out garbled past recognition. Finally the courtiers, making fastidious faces, gave up on him and left the three of them alone, and servants came in and began quenching all but a few torches.

Xena herself seemed to have become rather fed up with the proceedings, and she stood up and stretched. "It's been a rather odd day," she said. "I think I'll turn in . . ."

"Wait for me!" Gabrielle said. "Good night, . . . Hero."

" 'Night," Joxer said, not budging, but rather addressing himself straightaway to another piece of cold mutton.

The two of them headed up the stairs in one corner of the keep's tower toward the room they had been given. "Befitting their station" in this part of the world apparently meant fairly palatial. The couches were cushioned in silk and the room was scattered with beast-skin rugs—but, again, everything had that slightly tatty look. Xena sat down on one of the couches and started taking her greaves off. Gabrielle put her satchel aside and then glanced around.

"What?" Xena said.

"I left my staff downstairs."

"Oh, leave it . . . no one's going to steal it."

"No, I guess not." Gabrielle sat down on her own couch . . . then stood up again.

"What?"

"I just like to know where it is . . ."

Xena shrugged.

Gabrielle slipped out, eased the door shut, and stood still long enough to let her eyes get used to the reduced light. There were only one or two torches burning down in the keep's main hall, now, and none in the corridor. When her eyes adjusted, she made her way cautiously down the steps . . . then, just inside the doorway to the keep, stopped. Voices. . . .

She peered around the doorjamb. Joxer was still sitting at the table, and standing across it from him, looking down at him, was Princess Hippodamia. ". . . I don't know what it is about you," the princess was saying, "but you're not much like my other suitors, somehow."

Gabrielle, overhearing this, had trouble controlling her laughter, but she managed it.

"No," Joxer said, with the calm of complete self-assurance, on this count anyway. "I'm unique."

The princess shifted, an uneasy movement. "Look," she said. "I wish you'd give this up and leave. The result is so . . . predictable."

"I wouldn't say that," Joxer said. "I'm willing to take my chances. Especially since you have a result to produce, too."

There was a brief silence. *At his boldness*, Gabrielle wondered, *or because she really isn't sure she's going to be able to find out who he is . . . ?* "And when I do?" the princess said.

"Then if I can't answer your question," Joxer said, "you get to nail my head up."

"It's not me!" the princess said, sounding upset for the first time. "Everybody thinks that!"

"You sure haven't done much to try to change their minds," Joxer said.

"You don't know my father," the princess muttered. "He says he loves me, he says he only wants the best for me . . ."

"This is 'best for you'?" Joxer said. "Chopping off all the neighboring princes' heads and nailing them up to the walls? Kind of an unusual concept of good parenting, isn't it?"

Gabrielle's eyebrows went up at the sharpness of his tone. The princess said, "There's more to it than that. When my mother died . . ." She trailed off, her voice suddenly full of old pain.

There was a pause. Finally Joxer said, "He really loved her, didn't he."

"He did."

". . . And I don't suppose he was entirely happy to be left alone with a baby daughter . . ."

"Who he felt had killed his wife," said the princess. "No. You could say he would have been pretty ambivalent about that."

There was a much longer silence. "But you were all he had of her," Joxer said. "And when you grew up, and getting you married started to be an issue . . ."

"It's still a tradition here that a father gets to set the conditions under which his daughter marries," the princess said. "My father simply seems to have set the conditions . . . rather high." She shook her head. "For all his talk about how much he loves me, though, he never once asked me what I wanted to do . . . but then he never asks me what I want about *anything*."

They both sat in silence for a moment. Finally Joxer said, "What happens when I win?"

"You won't," the princess said.

Joxer laughed. "Then I'd better pick my best side," he said, "so your father can nail me up with that one facing out. And what happens afterward? When that blond guy I saw skulking around here finally gets up his courage to—"

"No!" the princess cried, and leapt to her feet. She stared at him like someone who had just taken an arrow through the heart. "No, you *can't* know, you—"

She fled.

Joxer stared after her. From her place of concealment, so did Gabrielle.

Joxer stood up, then, wearing a most thoughtful expression, and made for the stairway on the other side of the hall, the one leading to his own room. Gabrielle watched him go.

After a short wait to make sure the coast was clear, she made her way back to the room she and Xena had been given, and found Xena sitting in front of the fire, sharpening her chakram thoughtfully on a whetstone. Xena glanced up. "Gabrielle . . . your staff was right there in the corner, where you left it."

"Oh," Gabrielle said. "Yes."

"Where've you been?"

Gabrielle told her. When she was finished, Xena raised her eyebrows and went back to grooming the chakram's edge. "You'll have noticed that this place is beginning to fall on hard times," Xena said softly.

"Yes."

"Word has certainly gotten out about how the king treats his daughter's suitors. The royal line will die out, and the kingdom will be annexed by one of the other neighboring kingdoms . . ."

"Doesn't he realize what he's doing?" Gabrielle said. "He's destroying the place himself, as surely as if he'd set fire to it!"

"He may realize," Xena said. "He may not. Sometimes it's hard, when you're in the middle of your pain, to understand all the ramifications of what you're doing . . ." She fell silent.

"And J—the hero."

"Yes," Xena said, sounding thoughtful.

Gabrielle sat down. "What can we do to help him?"

"Right now?" The whetstone went *tshk, tshk, tshk* against the chakram. "Probably . . . nothing but wait."

• • •

In an upper room of the palace, Hippodamia and her father, the king, were waiting for the messenger. Hippodamia was pacing; her father was calm.

"It's nothing to worry about," King Enomaeus said. "Calm yourself, daughter. Everything will be fine."

"I had hoped it was all over," the princess said softly, pausing to look out the window. "It had been so long since anyone came . . . I thought it had finally stopped."

"It seems not. Well, never mind, we'll soon be rid of this one, too . . ."

She turned so that her father should not see her face. At the same moment someone knocked on her father's chamber door. "Enter—" said the king.

The door opened up just enough for the messenger to come in, and then shut behind him with a thump. The little man stood there, in his dark night-traveling clothes, looking distinctly nervous.

"Well?" the king said.

"I rode to Tyche village, just as you said, sire, and—"

"What's his name, then?"

The man fell to his knees. The princess stared. "Please, sire, the villagers, they—"

"They must have heard his name when the three of them were there: what's his name?"

"Sire," the shaking messenger said, "they've forgotten."

The king stood up slowly and began advancing on the man. "*What* did you say?"

"Truly, sire! They were so impressed with Xena and Gabrielle, they're so famous, that they paid hardly any attention to this nobody. None of them had ever heard of this fellow, after all, and he mentioned his name once or twice but none of them can remember it now, he seemed like such an *ordinary* type—"

The princess stood there, blinking with surprise, as her father grabbed the messenger and shook him as a dog shakes a rat. "You're lying! They're lying! I'll have all their heads—"

"No, sire, truly, they wouldn't lie, they know your law too well for that, and anyway, I know them all, they

wouldn't lie to me, and truly, on my oath, they don't remember his name—!"

The king threw the messenger to one side and stalked
back to his chair, hurled himself into it, and sat there with
his head in his hands. "No time to send any messenger any
further, the night is running—there must be something we
can do, otherwise this nobody, this 'unknown hero' is going
to be able to do anything he wants with you—"

"Father," Hippodamia said, moving to him. She bent over
him, put her hands on his shoulders. "Father. Leave the
problem with me. Aren't you always telling me how wise I
am? Let me handle it."

He sat there with his head in his hands awhile more, and
then turned his face up to her: a hard face, trusting, and
afraid. "All right," he said.

She went to get the pitcher that held his wine, and lingered a little longer than strictly necessary at the sideboard,
over the business of pouring out a cup of it for him. She
had half suspected something like this might happen, and
once the hero had refused to leave, she had come prepared.
"Here, Father," Hippodamia said, coming back to him with
the cup. "Drink this . . . then get some rest. Everything will
be all right in the morning."

He drank the cup off at one draught, and she would have
sighed with relief if she'd dared; she lived in fear that one
day he would detect the taste of what she'd slipped into the
wine from the hollow inside her pendant. "Go on, now," she
said, and motioned with her head to the messenger to get
out of there as she helped her father up out of the chair and
pushed him gently in the direction of his couch. "Go on . . .
sleep. And leave everything to me."

He lay down on the couch. Quite shortly he was snoring.
A few moments later, Hippodamia slipped out of his chamber and shut the door behind her.

The first quarter moon was riding high in an utterly clear
sky, one bereft of the usual summer haze, and more indigo
than black. Stars seemed to swarm in it like bees, more of
them visible every time one looked at a specific part of the
heavens; and the whole landscape spread out under Joxer's

window, the forest and the hills beyond, was unnaturally luminous with starlight and moonlight.

Joxer couldn't sleep. It was too warm, and there were things on his mind. Finally he got up, made his way out of the castle keep, nodding at the door guards, and began to walk around the keep in the warm summer night.

He started to hum . . . then stopped himself. *There are other things to think about. Like what I'm going to ask for . . . what I'm going to ask her . . . tomorrow morning.*

Assuming that things go my way.

He had no idea whether they would or not. It was useful to know that you had a goddess on your side . . . but goddesses were inscrutable, and sometimes changed their minds for fun. And what would he do then? *Suppose they do find out my name . . .*

Joxer gulped, but then he tried to hold himself straight and brave, as if it didn't matter. This lasted about five seconds. *I'm too young to die!*

Then again, since when is there a minimum age for dying? Here, or anywhere else. His mouth set grimly. *I may be committing suicide here.*

He paused, looking up at the castle keep. The window opening above him was the one opposite his in the tower: Gabrielle's bedroom window. There was a light there. She was awake, too.

Worrying about me, said one part of his mind, hopeful.

Not a chance, said another. *Or more accurately: not in the way you wish she was worrying. You know better than that. Her heart . . . is elsewhere.*

Joxer breathed in, breathed out: hope departing, light as a butterfly, on the breath, and leaving him sad . . . and suddenly resolute. *If I'm going to be dead of this adventure in the morning,* he thought . . . *why not? What have I got to lose? . . .*

And if I don't tell her now, I'll never have another chance . . .

He started to sing.

On her couch, in the near-darkness, Gabrielle heard the voice from outside the tower, and rolled over and buried her face in her arms. "Oh, no," she muttered. Joxer had plainly forgotten about his promise.

"No one's sleeping," she heard Joxer sing,

> *"none are sleeping . . .*
> *"Not even you, my princess,*
> *up there in your chilly bedroom,*
> *Look out to see how*
> *the blessed stars are trembling*
> *with love and longing!"*

Gabrielle had expected to be holding her ears by now. But to her utter surprise, in the middle of practically the first stanza, something unheard-of started to happen to his voice. It acquired a shape, and the notes Joxer hit, true ones for once, acquired depth, and power. The voice *grew*. Across the room, Xena glanced up from her seat by the slowly dying fire, a brooding look in her eyes. Gabrielle caught the musing glance, flinched from it, looked out the window again, unable to make out the figure that sang.

> *"But ah, my mystery's locked inside,*
> *My secret no one else will learn but you;*
> *and to your lips alone*
> *will I reveal it*
> *when dawn's rose splendor*
> *lights the sky!"*

All around them, in the castle, Gabrielle suspected that people were sitting up in their beds, wondering what had awakened them, and wondering who in the world had a voice like that. *In the world indeed*, Gabrielle thought, feeling, even for a man's voice like that, a most unaccustomed twinge of envy.

The voice paused, then went soft again, musing, and it was as if the whole night leaned in close to listen.

> *"Yes, it's my kiss*
> *will finally break the silence*
> *and make your heart mine!"*

From somewhere nearby Gabrielle thought she heard a somehow-familiar woman's voice, in sweet and rather stagy desperation, singing in response:

> *"The hero's secret no one knows,*
> *Yet oh, the hero's death is surely near. . . ."*

But the voice that was suddenly Joxer's, if it heard this, was not concerned. It pealed out in growing triumph and anticipation:

> *"Oh, hasten hence, now,*
> *holy night,*
> *and set, stars!*
> *Swiftly set,*
> *for my love*
> *will conquer come the dawn,*
> *come the dawn,*
> *come the dawn!"*

Summer thunder flickered along the horizon, like muted drums, and faded.

In another room in the palace, a young woman stood by the window, listening, listening with all of her being.

I never knew, Hippodamia thought. *I never knew* this *is what they felt like.*

She thought about the walls. She had stopped counting the heads a long time ago: had learned not to pay any attention to the suitors, their longing looks, their rich presents—because she knew what was going to happen to them. There was no moving her father, no hope of changing his mind. She knew what was still foremost in it, even after all these years: the memory of her mother, the queen, dying in the agonies of childbirth. A long time ago now, but that memory was still fresh for him. *And every time he looks at me, he sees me married . . . and then, after nine months or so, dying the same way.* The screams, echoing down these empty halls . . . sometimes she suspected he still heard them, through all the chatter of his courtiers, the squawk of the musicians he hired and fired and hired and fired again, because none of them could drown that sound out.

He loves me so much that he would do anything to protect me from that. Even kill them all, one after another . . .

She had been telling herself for a long time that there was nothing she could do to stop it. Yet now, terribly, she wondered. Hippodamia began to tremble at the thought of Evenus, who had been here for nearly two years now, hiding, pretending to be a servant and doing the most menial tasks to be near her, things that should have been utterly alien to his princely blood. She had not betrayed him: that would have been her death. But neither had she allowed Evenus to do what he so much wanted to do: come forward, take the challenge, meet the dare. For that would have lost him his life as well. Nor had she ever dared to tell him the part of the law that this unknown hero had somehow discovered. The chance of something going wrong, of losing him, was too terrible to contemplate. At least at the moment the two of them could catch the occasional furtive glimpse of each other during the humdrum palace day. But Evenus could never have the freedom to sing to her the way this hero did, though the same thoughts, almost the same words, must surely beat every night in his breast . . .

Loving me is a death sentence. And we are in prison. In prison together.

But never until tonight has there been a way out of jail . . .

Evenus had at last heard the loophole in the law, now: not from her, for her father had made her swear by the Gods never to tell, but from her father's own lips. Now he could challenge her father, and maybe even win. Then they could be together openly at last, and the killing would finally be over. *Finally! Oh, Gods, over at last!*

But there was still this nameless hero. And what if he should win her? She would have to leave her hidden prince and go to some strange country, and would never see him again.

No, Hippodamia thought, suddenly fiercely resolute. *Once and for all, it ends here. And I will not let this hero out of nowhere ruin everything when a way out for Evenus and me has finally become plain.*

She sat very still, clenching her mind around a growing plan as she might clench a fist around a knife.

Then Hippodamia got up and went to the door, opened it, looked down the hallway, and called the guards.

It was almost dark in the room—only the fire left, burned down to embers, and one little oil lamp on the nearby table. Sleepless on her couch, Gabrielle stared at it.

That voice . . . and the words it had sung.

That voice. It had been the kind of voice that sounded like it had been in training for a lifetime, and it wrapped itself around your heart and squeezed until you were breathless with longing . . . She had always known perfectly well what a hopeless case Joxer was, but this voice had nothing to do with that hopelessness.

And her memory said, *I fear the Gods even when they bear gifts . . .*

Orpheus must have sounded like that, Gabrielle thought, *down there in the Underworld, singing before the throne of Hades for the return of Eurydice. No one could possibly refuse him anything. It's not fair! You train for half a life, working hard to have some kind of voice, and then someone comes along with a god as backup and sounds like* that *after a single night!* She had to resist the urge to get up, go hunt down Aphrodite, wherever she was, and administer a good swift kick to her divine butt.

Yet at the same time, Joxer seemed to be manifesting signs of being seriously interested in someone else. This by itself was a good thing, and to be encouraged. *I should be relieved,* Gabrielle thought.

All the same . . . it was weird. Very strange to have that endless, annoying regard suddenly diverted from her. It was enough to make Gabrielle twitch a little bit: enough to make her . . .

Jealous? Oh gods, no!

But all the same, as Gabrielle twisted and turned on her couch, she had to wonder what was the matter with her. There was no question that this princess was absolutely no good for him, that Joxer deserved much better. *Especially*

*as she's likely to have his head nailed up on the walls by
tomorrow afternoon.*

*But was that just a rationalization? Am I thinking that
because . . . even though he and I can never be lovers . . . I
still want to keep him to myself? Because it would be too
much a wound to my pride if all of a sudden he ran off after
some princess?*

She made a face. *And why shouldn't he? What do I have
to offer him, compared to a princess?*

Not cutting his head off, for one thing, said another part
of her mind, unusually sarcastically.

Across the room, there was a soft sigh as Xena shifted in
her sleep. She had dozed off in the chair, and Gabrielle had
seen no need to try to move her. Indeed, she had been too
distracted, as the moon slid down the sky, and the echoes
of that voice rang in her mind and refused to fade.

And then she heard a sound that was not one of those
echoes, nor was it anything to do with Xena. A soft scrape,
outside the door. Faintly, through a crack between the
boards of the door, she saw a glimmer of light.

"Xena," she whispered: and got up, feeling around her.

A moment later the door swung open. It had been locked
from the inside. Gabrielle looked hastily away from the lamp
being carried in by one of the palace guards; caught sight
of the gleam of eyes behind the door; and stood up straight,
holding her staff.

Behind the guard, followed by another one, Princess Hippodamia came in. The guards were carrying drawn swords.
The princess paused, looked around her. "Where is she?"

"What are you doing here?" Gabrielle said.

"I've come to ask you a question."

"You might have come a little earlier," Gabrielle said.

"Not for this," said the princess. "Tell me now, and no
harm will come to you. What is his name?"

Gabrielle grinned, shook her head. "You're asking the
wrong person."

"I think not. Take her," the princess said to her guards.
They stepped forward.

The door swung back. Xena was there, wide awake,
reaching behind her. "Think again," Xena said.

The princess turned, as if not surprised, as if still resolute. The guards looked from Gabrielle to Xena.

"*You* think," said the princess, "and save us all trouble. You two have been traveling with him. You must know his name. We are not a poor land: not just yet. We have gold enough to give you to make the one word worth your while."

"And you seriously believe," Xena said, "that having been approached like this, by you, that we would tell you?" She laughed, and in her hand the the chakram flashed in the lamplight. "Or that we would betray our friend? Gold you may have in plenty here, but brains are clearly in short supply."

The princess's face went dark with anger, and she looked at the guards. The guards looked like they would much rather be somewhere else. "Now!" the princess said.

The guards turned away from Xena, leaped toward Gabrielle. But Gabrielle's staff was already in her hands, and the guards' attack was half-hearted, fragmented: they got in one another's way. A moment later one of them was on the floor, curled up like a poked bug, retching and holding his crotch. Gabrielle feinted, thrust with the staff at the second guard's head, then took the staff two-handed and drove it straight down onto the second guard's instep. He howled, and fell over sideways.

Gabrielle stood up straight again and watched the two men fight for floor space in which to writhe in agony. She shook her head. "You were right," she said. "They almost never armor the feet properly, do they . . ."

"When they do, they have to walk like ducks," Xena said mildly, putting the chakram away, "and men hate walking like ducks."

She looked up at Hippodamia. "Princess," she said, "go away. Don't bother us again. We'll send these poor creatures back downstairs when they've recovered. Meanwhile . . . if I were you, I'd start deciding what you're going to do when you can't answer the hero's riddle in the morning."

Hippodamia, now pale with rage and possibly with fear, vanished. "Come on, you," Gabrielle said, bending over the guard whose foot she had crushed, "come on, get up, I've got something you can put on that. . . ."

Xena was meanwhile hoisting the other poor guard up onto her couch, on his back. "You always amaze me," she said.

"How?"

"When you insist on patching these creatures up afterward . . ."

"It's not their fault," Gabrielle said. "They're only doing their jobs. Get me my satchel?"

Xena made an exasperated face. She got up, but first she went to the window and listened. But that remarkable voice had long since fallen silent. "Now I wonder," she said, turning back to get Gabrielle's satchel, "just where he is . . ."

Worried, Gabrielle looked up from getting the man's sandal off to look out the window. *Yes*, she thought sadly. *I wonder too . . .*

In the darkness of the main hall, Joxer sat by what was left of the fire in the big hearth. He was a shadow among shadows, but all the same, when one more shadow moved, he noticed it.

"Hold it right there," he said. "I have a sword, and I'm not afraid to use it."

"I dare say you're not," said the darkness, in a voice sharp as bright bronze, but very quiet. A man's voice.

Joxer nodded. His hand was on the sword's hilt, but not in any position that would make for an effective draw. He knew this, and he was sure the one who was watching it would know it, too. "Come closer," he said.

The shadow moved, became a shadow in long threadbare robes, with a hood. Joxer had been sitting in this near-darkness long enough to see the glint of blond hair under the hood, and the gleam of eyes. "What do you want?" Joxer asked.

"I'll help you escape."

"Why?"

"I heard you sing . . ." The bright voice was slightly dulled.

"And you think that someone with a voice like that shouldn't die so young," Joxer said.

The other hesitated, hearing the ironic tone in Joxer's voice, probably unwilling to agree to the lie.

Joxer smiled a small, grim smile, and shook his head. "I'm not going anywhere," he said. "There's something to do here first."

"You love her."

Joxer swallowed. By rights he should have been afraid, alone with this man who was desperate, who might do anything: but to his surprise, fear was far from his heart. It was too full of other things. "It's not what you think."

"You're crazy! Do you expect me to believe you? I heard you, I heard how you sang—"

Joxer shook his head. "You heard what I was singing, all right, but not who I was singing to."

"If you hurry," the man said, "I can still get you out of here."

Joxer laughed softly. "I'm not *that* many oars short of a trireme, buddy. There are no guards on the palace doors, and none on the gates outside. I could leave any time. Come to think of it, so could you."

"I can't," the man said. His voice was suddenly terrible, desperate.

"It's *her* you can't leave," Joxer said. "You think I don't know the signs? Do you think I don't know how it is—to want someone, and know you'll never be able to have them? Unless a miracle happens—" He swallowed. He was finding this hard, but it had to be done.

"It is about to happen," the man said, "but not to me. In the morning, they still will not know your name. And she will be yours."

"What if she were to be left free to ask someone else her riddle?" Joxer said.

A pause at that . . . the sound of breath sharply intaken. Then the man said, "It wouldn't matter. No one has ever answered it correctly."

"Oh? What is it?"

"The riddle is, 'What is the one thing that all women want?' "

Joxer frowned. "Yes," he said after a moment, "I could see where that one would be a real poser." It was hard enough figuring out what just *one* woman wanted.

"So you see, it does not matter . . . and it does not alter what will happen. She will be yours in the morning. Better I should be dead before then. Or better that you should—" There was the soft sound of a sword being drawn.

Joxer should have at least started to become nervous, but somehow it didn't happen. "I swear by the gods," Joxer said, with abrupt clarity, so that the room rang with it, "by mighty Aphrodite herself, that I do not love your princess."

Silence.

"But in the morning," the man said softly, "she will still be yours."

Joxer shook his head, gazing for a moment into the fire. "Don't bet on it," he said softly. "Besides . . . Just look at the word. *Yours.* As if people can own each other, like slaves. It's not owning that special other that you want, if you're really in love. You want them to have what *they* really want . . . and to get to be with them at the same time. But the two don't always coincide . . ." He sighed. "All you can hope for is that, at the right time, you think of the right thing to say . . ."

He looked back at the gleam of eyes under the hood. "Wait till morning," Joxer said. "See what happens." He paused. "And you might pray. A little prayer never hurts."

A pause, and then the sound of a sword going back into its sheath, uncertain, almost reluctant. "The gods," the man said, bleak-voiced, "are capricious and cruel."

"Not all of them," Joxer said. "Not all the time. And even when they are . . . what use are human beings, if we can't give them a good example, and try to teach them manners?"

Silent, the man's gaze lingered on Joxer a little longer. Then he turned, faded into the shadows, was gone.

Joxer sat and stared into the fire again, wishing he felt as certain as his words had sounded: for outside, pallid and uncertain, the night was shading into the morning twilight that would lead to dawn.

•   •   •

He did not move. People began gathering in the hall as soon as it started to get really light, about an hour before dawn. Someone from the kitchen stopped by his seat by the fire and pressed a cup of hot wine into Joxer's hand; he drank it gratefully, for the place had become very chilly overnight. Slowly, more and more people gathered there as the light grew, and finally he saw Xena and Gabrielle move through the crowd, and take a stand near him. Gabrielle seemed to be having trouble looking at him.

It was reciprocal: Joxer got very interested in the last of his wine. Xena, though, slipped over to stand by his chair, and said quietly, "How's your throat?"

"Sore. I think I'm catching cold."

She gave him an ironic smile, which suggested immediately to Joxer that if that was all that happened to him this morning, he would be lucky. "We had some visitors last night," Xena said. "Your princess, and a couple of guards."

"My" princess. Joxer smiled, but not with humor. "What happened?"

"Gabrielle dealt with them."

Joxer's eyes widened.

"She wasn't in the best of moods, last night," Xena said.

"Something she ate?" Joxer said, innocent.

Xena smiled and stepped back to stand with Gabrielle.

Away toward the rear of the hall, trumpets bleated a slightly off-key fanfare. Joxer got up from his chair. "Well," he said, "let's go . . ."

He and Xena and Gabrielle and all the various courtiers and counsellors, and a whole crowd of townspeople, who seemed to have appeared from somewhere, made their way down to the king's throne at the end of the hall. King Enomaeus was sitting there, looking slightly hungover and very depressed, and by his throne stood his daughter, in magnificent robes of silver and white, and the flame-colored veil of a bride-to-be. Her face was as still as a statue's, and expressionless. Only her eyes dwelt on Joxer—with dull fear.

Joxer took up what he hoped was a stately pose before the throne. There were some snickers from the crowd behind him: he ignored them. "King," he said, "yesterday, in accordance with your law, I asked you a riddle. Now you must answer it. What is my name?"

The king looked at his daughter. Princess Hippodamia looked down at him with a flicker of grief in her eyes, and shook her head. Then she looked up. "We do not know," she said.

Joxer stood up tall. "I," he said, "am Joxer the Magnificent!"

The king looked at his daughter, and Hippodamia looked at him, and then along with everybody else in the crowd, they shook their heads. "Never heard of him," said the king.

Joxer sighed.

"But that's of no account," the king said, his voice heavy with defeat. "By our law, I must now grant you whatever boon you ask. So ask your boon."

Joxer saw the princess go even paler than she had been. And as had not happened until now, for just a moment, the possibility hung burning before him, clear and real, within his grasp. Marry the princess, settle down, eventually become a king . . .

Then Joxer breathed out. This was not a fairy tale: this was real life, and his heart was bestowed elsewhere. Meanwhile, he hated to hurt Hippodamia, even fleetingly, but he saw all too distinctly what had to be done here.

He took a deep breath. "I want *this* man to answer the princess's riddle," Joxer said. And he pointed at what seemed to be a servant standing off to one side in shabby brown robes, a fair-haired, well-built man, who stood straight and tall, wearing the fiercely hopeless face of a man who is about to die, and knows he can do nothing about it.

The man came forward.

"Who are you?" the king said, while Princess Hippodamia stood there trembling and pale.

"I am Evenus, Prince of Arkheria," he said, "and I come to sue for the hand of the Princess Hippodamia!"

"*No!*" Hippodamia burst out. "I told you not to, we agreed that you would never—"

"There's no such thing as never," Joxer said. "Sooner or later, everything ends." Were they his words, or Aphrodite's? He couldn't tell. His heart was aching, as it had been for most of the day and night: but then it usually ached, one of the conditions he had become used to in life. Possibly this was why he was perfect for this job—he was already inured to the pain.

"I won't ask him!" Hippodamia cried.

"The law is the law, daughter," said the king, iron in his voice, but also fear. "You must ask him."

"Father—"

"Ask him!"

Hippodamia gulped.

And then she whispered, "What is the one thing that all women want?"

The courtiers stood, hushed, glancing at one another, shaking their heads.

Prince Evenus stood straight and proud, but his face was uncertain. He swallowed convulsively . . . and then his eyes went wide. *"Their way,"* he said.

Sudden, astonished, a great smile of joy broke over Hippodamia's face. The king looked completely stunned.

"Is that the right answer?" Joxer said.

"It is," the king whispered.

A huge cheer went up from the surrounding courtiers and townspeople. *It's not like that's not the one thing all* men *want, too*, whispered a voice in Joxer's mind, the same one that had plainly whispered to Evenus just now. *But phrase the question this way, and men always get bogged down in the gender details, and lose sight of the bigger issue . . .*

The prince cast off his worn robes and stood forth in the hitherto-concealed rich garments of a noble man. He and Hippodamia flung themselves into one another's arms, and the king stood up from his throne, suddenly looking very lost and alone.

"You have beaten me," he said to Joxer, as Xena and Gabrielle came up behind him.

"Not me," Joxer said. "The gods, maybe . . . with a little help from me. And you know, you might have a word with Aphrodite yourself. You can never tell what might happen."

The king looked at him sadly, then stepped away and vanished up the stairs.

"Now that you mention it," Xena said, "have you seen Aphrodite recently?"

Joxer shook his head. "Heard from her," he said. He turned to look at Hippodamia and Evenus, just now breaking out of their clinch, and said, "I think she's been busy."

The prince and princess, hand in hand, came over to them.

"How can we ever thank you?" the prince said.

Joxer immediately became flustered. "Oh, think nothing of it . . . though now that you mention it, travel expenses, some supplies . . ."

"I will never forget you," Princess Hippodamia said. "You won my heart . . . and then won it again, for another." She took Joxer's hand. "You are truly a hero . . . though how you should be an unknown one, I will never understand."

"Oh well, you know how it is," Joxer said, still more flustered. "News doesn't always travel everywhere at the same speed. There is, however, a ballad—"

"So I heard," Hippodamia said. "It changed my life . . . and I will remember it always."

She kissed the open-mouthed Joxer on the cheek, very softly, and then, hand in hand with Evenus, she went away.

The wedding happened the same day.

The next morning, having caught up on their sleep, Xena and Gabrielle and Joxer left King Enomaeus's castle, loaded down by Hippodamia and Evenus with as much as they could carry in the way of supplies and gifts, and a small but solid sum in gold. For the rest of the day they journeyed up out of the forest vale, and that night sheltered on a south-facing hillside, under the trees, looking out over the sunset grainfields and toward the southern plains.

Gabrielle sat up by the fire for a while with Joxer after Xena had rolled herself up in her bedroll and turned in. "How was it," she said, "having a voice like that?"

"I don't know that I had it," Joxer said, rather somberly, "as much as *it* had *me*. But it sounded the way I always sound, in here . . ." He tapped his head.

Gabrielle sighed. But when she looked up at him again, her expression was thoughtful. "Maybe," she said, "when we run into each other, occasionally, that's something we could work on. Getting the outside voice to sound more like the inside."

He looked at her, and realized that this was the best offer that she could make him: not at all the one he desperately wanted . . . but the best. "That would be nice," he said. "Thanks."

Gabrielle sat silent for a while more. Then, she said, "You know . . . I can't."

He sat silent too. "Yes," he said. "I know."

"For your sake," Gabrielle said, "I could wish that things could be different. But . . ."

He nodded, finding it difficult to speak. "That still means a lot," he said. "Just that."

Gabrielle nodded, then got up and went to her own bedroll, not so far from Xena's.

Joxer sat there by the fire for a long time, watching it burn. When he suddenly heard a soft *pop* like an ember popping, followed by a brief sizzle of pink sparkles in the air, he did not look up immediately.

"You used me," he said softly, so as not to wake the others up. "I was a *tool!*"

"Most mortals are," Aphrodite said softly. "And you know what? So are the gods, sometimes. There is a power even above Zeus, a power that sits above Olympus in the clouds and darkness, moving even gods to and fro. Destiny. . . ." She shook her head. "It's annoying, having to put up with that kind of thing, but you know what? You'll get over it. We all do. Meanwhile, what was I supposed to do? I'm the goddess of *Love,* for cripessake. Things were not going well here, and my rep was at stake. If the right tool comes along for the right job . . . should I just sit around and refuse to use it?"

She paused, looking at him. "Besides, you didn't really want to stay there. You want . . ."

"*You* know what I want." Joxer said, more softly still. "But it won't happen, not without divine intervention. I mean, Gabrielle . . . and Xena, they—" He fell silent. "They're so . . . close. There's no room for three. But all I want in the world is—"

Aphrodite sighed. "You're going to have to work that out

for yourself," she said. "If I just gave you what you want
without you working for it, what would it be worth, anymore? And anyway, do you think that force up there in the
darkness isn't moving *her* around, too? In ways even *I* can't
tamper with? I wish you luck." Her voice was compassionate. "Meanwhile . . . maybe *tool* is the wrong word to use.
Maybe you were more like a gift. If not to the one you
wanted to be made a gift of . . . well. But think how much
good you did."

Joxer thought about it. "Yeah," he said. "I guess." And
he started to acquire a small smile. "And after all," Joxer
said, "it's part of a hero's role, to make heroic sacrifices . . .
isn't it?"

"*There* you are," Aphrodite said. "What a clever mortal.
Hold that thought. And meanwhile . . ."

She bent toward him. "Nice work," said the Goddess of
Love. "Just remember . . . never give up hope." She kissed
Joxer lightly on the lips, and vanished. With little sparkling
lights, and in fragrance: and where she had been sitting,
small white flowers lay on the ground.

Joxer touched his mouth, wondering . . . then sat up and
looked into the fire, and threw another branch on it.

"No one's sleeping," he sang softly. "No one's sleeping . . ."

"Not with a voice like that singing, they won't," someone
muttered on the other side of the fire. "Joxer, *shut up!*"

Joxer shut up . . . and smiled.

CAME THE DAWN

Esther Friesner

The temple stood at the bottom of a small green dell, far removed from the major trade roads and a goodly distance off the rough goat track Xena and Gabrielle had chosen in an evil hour. They almost passed it by, for it was nestled away snugly in the heart of a grove of aged willows. In winter it might have been more conspicuous, when the whip-slim branches were bare, but this was spring, and the little building's smooth walls and slender columns were painted the same tender green as the newly uncurled willow leaves.

It was only pure accident that they caught sight of it. Xena was in a hurry and the goat track was thwarting her at every turn. Although the local terrain only consisted of moderate-sized hills and valleys, the path behaved as though it were leading them through the harsh heart of the Spartan mountains. Sometimes it curved back on itself like a fishhook, sometimes it took a sharp turn and headed straight up the side of a hill only to change its mind, make an about-face, and take them right back down again. Sometimes it seemed to vomit chunks of stone directly under their feet, then reverted to sand so soft that they sank in it up to their ankles. Xena took it all in stride, literally, but for Gabrielle, this supposed shortcut to Thebes of the Seven Gates was turning into the road to Marathon. When she twisted her foot on a particularly rocky stretch and snapped the strap of her left sandal, it was the last straw.

It was while she knelt to fix the broken leather that she spied the temple.

"So what?" said Xena when Gabrielle pointed it out.

"But Xena, isn't it *beautiful*?" Gabrielle exclaimed. "It's exquisite, a—a perfect *gem* of a building! And look at how well it harmonizes with its setting."

"Harmonizes or hides?" Xena snorted. "When a place or a person tries so hard to fade into the background, there's usually a good reason. I can name you at least fifteen venomous desert reptiles that do nothing all day but blend into the sand and bite the fools who just *have* to get a closer look at them. What they get is a closer look at the inside of Charon's boat when he ferries them to Hades."

"Oh, for goodness' sake, Xena, poisonous snakes aren't the only creatures that keep themselves hidden."

"True. So do mice, but only so the snakes can't catch them. Let it go, Gabrielle; we've got places to be. Nosing around a strange temple will only take up valuable time."

"You're not the *least* bit curious?" Gabrielle asked.

"I'm not." Xena's teeth flashed momentarily in a provoking grin. "But I can tell that *you* are."

"So we'll explore it?" Gabrielle hastily finished repairing her sandal strap and bounced eagerly to her feet. "Just long enough to find out *whose* temple it is. It won't take long."

"Not a chance. We're due in Thebes in three days."

"Thebes is only a two-day march from here!" Gabrielle protested.

"Two days to get there, one day to find out which of those damned Seven Gates they've got open. That paranoid idiot King Creon keeps changing it. He's almost as obsessed with security as he is with punctuality. Now come *on*." Xena turned her back on Gabrielle and started up the goat track again.

Seeing that the direct approach wasn't going to work,

Gabrielle switched tactics. "If we're so pressed for time, we could use directions to a better road."

"I don't ask for directions," Xena growled.

"No, you just take shortcuts like this one."

"There is no better road to Thebes short of the main highway, and that would take *four* days' travel."

"How much do you want to bet that the locals know a route to Thebes from here that's better *and* shorter?"

"What locals?"

"Where there's a temple, there are priests." Gabrielle folded her arms. "Q.E.D."

"What does *that* mean?"

"I don't know." Gabrielle shrugged. "Something Julius Caesar once said. He never asked directions either. You're a lot like him."

"Don't . . . *ever* . . . say that about me." Xena gritted.

"Well, what else can I say? *He* won't ask directions, *you* won't ask directions—"

"I'll asked your damned directions! Watch me!" Without another word Xena marched down the hillside double-time, bound for the willow-veiled temple, while Gabrielle trotted after, struggling to keep up and to cover her grin of triumph.

The temple grove was a sweet refuge of shade and fresh water after the heat and dust of the goat track. A modest stream laced its way around the roots of the willows and a gentle wind played through their branches. Gabrielle didn't know whether she was more enchanted with the temple itself or the grounds surrounding it. She looked everywhere, exclaiming over fresh attractions, while Xena headed straight into the temple in search of help.

"Always in a hurry," Gabrielle muttered, watching Xena vault up the well-swept marble steps and vanish into the temple. "She never takes time to stop and smell the roses."

"What roses?" said a high, whiny voice behind her.

Gabrielle whirled around, her staff ready for battle, and found herself looking right over the head of a curly-haired little boy who was diligently searching one nostril with a busy finger. The child didn't seem to be more than five or six, yet he had a truculent look that was somehow too old for him.

"I *asked* 'What roses?' " he repeated. "There aren't any roses here. All *she* lets them grow anywhere near her temple are morning glories. It's worse than tedious; it's egotistical. But what can you expect of a minor goddess like Eos? All that light and none of it ever reaches her brain." He removed his finger from one nostril and switched it to the other.

"Eos?" Gabrielle asked. "So this is the temple of the dawn goddess?"

"Bra-*vo*." The boy stopped picking his nose long enough to give her some very measured, very sarcastic applause. "And for your second question, can you tell me where they fought the Battle of Salamis? I'll give you a hint: It wasn't in a butcher shop."

Gabrielle frowned. "You're a very rude child."

"Rude? *Me?*" The boy opened his eyes as wide as he could and struck an offended pose worthy of an Athenian actor. "I am shocked—*shocked*, do you hear?—to learn that a woman of your obvious mental gifts finds me less than a perfect gentleman." He concluded this speech by making a vulgar sound with his tongue and skipping away.

"Wait a minute! Come back here!" Gabrielle called after the odd little boy in vain. He had vanished into a thick stand of bushes. She followed, breaking through the scratchy shoots and branches into a sundrenched clearing. In the middle of the grassy expanse a shallow fountain leaped and bubbled, watched over by the statue of a nymph. Her arms were full of small, chubby-limbed children and a host of others clung to her skirts, their plump little hands reaching up to her in supplication.

Gabrielle was captivated and came closer to get a better look. It was only when she leaned right against the lip of the fountain that she saw the expression on the nymph's carved face. The artist who'd created this work had known how to make solid stone show desperation, anxiety, and panic. On further inspection, the little ones ringing the nymph didn't appear to be holding up their hands in some childish appeal for attention. Rather, they looked like a pack of miniature wolves bent on tearing her to pieces. Gabrielle shuddered so hard she almost lost her balance on the fountain's rim.

"Careful you don't fall in, darling." Another juvenile voice, different from the first, sounded at her elbow. She glanced down at a second boy, a blond cherub with a winning smile. He couldn't have been older than four. "I wouldn't want anything to happen to such a beautiful lady."

Gabrielle was instantly charmed. She squatted beside the fountain and stroked his cheek. "Thank you, dear," she said. "Aren't you thoughtful. Do you live here?"

"Now I do." He put one arm around her neck and began to play with her hair. "Oooh, you're pretty. Can I sit in your lap?"

Gabrielle saw no harm in it. She sat on the grass and the little boy cuddled up, hugging her tightly around the waist. "My, you're an affectionate one," she said, a doubtful note creeping into her voice. She couldn't put her finger on it, but something about the child's behavior was starting to make her feel uneasy. "What's your name?"

"Orlo." He gave her a surprisingly powerful squeeze. "Will you be my friend?"

"Why, of course I will. Tell me, Orlo, do your parents serve in the temple? Could you help me find them? You see, I'm traveling with a friend of mine and we need to reach Thebes as soon as possible and—"

Orlo looked up at her, his soft little face the mask of Tragedy. "You *can't* go away!" he whimpered. "*Everyone* goes away! Everyone leaves me behind. Alone. In the dark. And I'm so small and helpless. Honestly, I am. You said you were my friend!"

"Yes, dear, but I really have to—"

"I don't have anybody but you!" he sobbed, covering his face. He made enough noise to be weeping his heart out, but Gabrielle had the sneaking suspicion that his eyes were dust-dry. "I'm just a little boy and I'm scared of all the monsters under my bed and they give me terrible bad dreams and I need someone just like you to keep me company and you *can't* leave me now! Can't you stay here just *one* night? With me? I'll let you have the best pillow."

"What you'll let her have is the *truth,* Orlo!" The air above the fountain shimmered and a female voice flooded the clearing. Clad in filmy robes of purple, pink, and saffron, crowned with radiant golden hair, glorious with youth and beauty, the dawn goddess Eos appeared before them.

Orlo let out a little yelp and scampered off. The goddess laughed and extended one rosy-fingered hand. "You'll have to forgive my sweet little Orlo," she said as she helped Gabrielle to her feet. "He's terribly naughty, but he can't do you any harm."

"I didn't think he could," Gabreille replied. "I hope you won't find me presumptuous, O Eos, but I believe you're going to have a problem with that boy. He strikes me as just a little too . . . mature for his age."

Eos laughed until the dew ran down her cheeks. "Orlo? *Mature?*" she finally managed. "There are times when he acts like a sixteen-year-old, and him a man of twenty-five!"

"Sixteen?" Gabrielle repeated, nonplussed. "Twenty-five? A . . . *man*? But he doesn't look—"

"And he's not my son. He's my seventh husband."

Inside the temple of Eos, Xena was fast coming to the end of her patience. First she explored the outer chamber, where the worshippers would congregate, then the smaller, inner chamber that housed the image and altar of the goddess. Both were deserted.

"Where there's a temple, there are priests," she muttered. "Q.E.D. my—"

She was about to leave in frustration when she noticed three doors in the rearmost wall. She was ready to swear on her chakram that they hadn't been there before. The first opened to reveal a storeroom full of charcoal, incense, and other supplies for the tending of the goddess' altar. Behind the second was a room crowded with half a dozen small cots and one full-sized bed. Children's clothes lay everywhere. She picked up one badly soiled chiton before dropping it in disgust and stalking out.

Then she opened the third door.

The room beyond seemed to stretch away into infinity, and infinity was plated with solid gold. Blinding light reflected from the glittering walls. Xena threw one arm across her eyes until she got used to the dazzle. Even then, blink as she might, she could see no end to the room and nothing inside but a wide-mouthed golden brazier, raging with flames. The fiery tongues leaped far too high for them to spring from any earthly fuel. Here was a mystery.

Xena didn't have time for mysteries. Unlike Gabrielle, unless the mystery in question was coming straight at her with intent to kill, she was perfectly content to leave it lying undisturbed where she found it. She was backing out of the golden chamber and had the door half shut when she heard a voice within whispering.

Xena's hand dropped to her sword. "Who's there?" she called. "Show yourself!"

ohIwouldifIcould, thatIwouldlovelylady

It was a rustly, crinkly, dead-leaves-in-a-pile whisper. Xena stepped back into the golden chamber, squinting against the glare, and let her ears guide her to its source.

overherewhereIhang, overhere

A tiny chrysalis dangled by a silken thread from the ceiling just above the raging brazier, sparkling with the same precious coating as the walls. The flames might be supernatural, but their heat was real enough. Xena flung her chakram, severing the thread and bringing the chrysalis to her hand on the return arc. She carried it back into a less garish part of the temple, all the while the chrysalis buzzed and trembled.

thankyou, Othankyou, lovelylady

"What are you?" she asked, setting it down on the pedestal holding the goddess' image.

afriendafriendafriendafr—

Xena gave the chrysalis a brisk shake. "Slow down. I can barely understand you."

Ow, said the chrysalis. It no longer buzzed like a hornets' nest; in fact, it sounded cranky. *You've got your nerve, girlie, shaking me like that. I'm an old man, not a baby's rattle. You ought to treat me with a little more respect.*

Xena shook the chrysalis again, harder. "Don't call me 'girlie' and we've got a bargain. My name is Xena. An old man, huh? A very *small* old man, from the look of things."

A torrent of unbelievably complex and old-fashioned profanity gushed from the chrysalis, curses so venomous and ferocious that the warrior princess was shocked to realize that she was blushing like a milkmaid. "Stop! Enough! Rein it in!" she shouted. "That'll be enough of *that* out of you, unless you want to find out whether I can hurl you clear to Corinth."

The chrysalis subsided. *Well, you didn't need to go casting aspersions on my manhood,* it grumbled.

"That's not what I meant when I called you small and you know it," Xena replied. "Now stop fooling around and tell me: What happened to you? Why are you trapped in this thing, kept in this temple? What's your name?"

The golden husk in her hand trembled with a sigh. *My name is Tithonus. Once I was a mortal man, strong and handsome and young, the son of King Laomedon of Troy. One day when I was out tending my father's flocks—we all tended our father's flocks in those days, even princes like me. None of this slacking off you get from young people nowadays, nothing but whining and excuses and sassing their elders and—*

"Get back to the sheep," Xena cut in.

Ahem. Yes. Well, there I was, tending my father's sheep just as the day was breaking when all of a sudden I beheld the most beautiful girl I'd ever seen. It was love at first sight, and not just what you whippersnappers call love. Ha! Like a tangle of ferrets in heat, you are. *Not like love was in my day, when it was pure and noble and clean and—*

"I'll bet if I throw you into the air and hit you just right with the flat of my sword, I can send you sailing all the way to Thrace," Xena remarked, tossing the chrysalis up and down casually.

Er, as I was saying, I saw this charming girl and fell in love with her on the spot. That was no wonder; what was incredible was that the first words out of her sweet, sweet mouth were a declaration of love for me! *And who do you think she was, eh? A goddess, no less. Eos herself, the rosy-fingered lady of the dawn. She whisked me away to be her love and begged the gift of immortality for me from Zeus himself. We lived happily, had three fine sons, and I even helped her raise four of her own lads from a, er, previous alliance: Boreas, Zephyrus, Eurus, and Notus, gods of the four great winds. I taught them everything they know.* The chrysalis stood up on end as if strutting with pride.

"It shows," Xena said, deadpan. "Especially when they blow hard."

Yes, especially when they— What *did you say?*

"I said you did pretty well for a shepherd prince. So when did *happily ever after* change into *stuck inside a cocoon*?"

The chrysalis didn't respond at once. Xena got the distinct impression that it was embarrassed. Finally it said, *Remember the part where I told you about how Eos got Zeus to grant me immortality? Eos is a lovely girl, a very lovely girl indeed. A man couldn't ask for a sweeter mate, or a more passionate lover, but the dear lass has one teensy, weensy flaw: She's a tad... impetuous. Doesn't think things through. Leaps before she looks. Forgets to tend to the details, and sometimes it's all in the details, such as—*

"—such as remembering to ask Zeus to grant you eternal life and eternal *youth*," Xena concluded. She stared at the chrysalis. "You poor chump."

Again the chrysalis sighed. *It didn't take long for Eos to notice that I was no longer the man she'd married. First there were the wrinkles, then the aches and pains, the gray hairs, followed by certain other, um, changes that are none of your business. I have to say she was very supportive, in spite of the—in spite of my—even when I couldn't—Well, that's none of your business, either. As soon as she realized her mistake, she went back to ask Zeus to restore my youth, but he said she should've thought of that in the first place. Wouldn't give her the time of day.*

"That's awful."

You don't know the half of it. At first Eos said that it wouldn't make any difference to her, that she'd always stand by me, that love would find a way. But as the years rolled on and I continued to age, she was forced to face the hopelessness of our situation. I didn't die—I couldn't die—but I did begin to wither away. I shrivelled up a little more each day, my body growing more feeble, my bones more brittle, my skin as crinkly as a shed snakeskin, my voice the weak, piping thing you now hear—or barely do. And Eos was still as young and attractive as the day we first met. Very, very attractive.

Xena didn't need the Delphic Oracle to interpret what Tithonus was getting at: "She left you for another man."

Left me? If only she had! It would've been kinder, in the long run. Instead, she placed me in this gilded husk you hold and hung me where you found me, for safekeeping.

Xena's heart was moved to pity. "I wish there were something I could do to help you, Tithonus," she said.

Nice of you to offer. Matter of fact, there is: Kill me, there's a good girl.

"But you're immortal."

I knew you were going to say that. But you could try. It would only be polite to make the effort.

"I don't think so," Xena said. "But I will take you with me." She tried to fit the chrysalis into her belt pouch, but it was full, so she tucked it into the front of her armor instead. "It's no good your just hanging around here. The known world's a big place: For all we know, the answer to your problem's somewhere out there. I'll help you find it."

Take your time, Tithonus murmured happily from his new resting place. *I think this may be the beginning of a beautiful—*

"Xena! *Help!*" Gabrielle's voice rang out through the temple.

Just when I was getting comfortable . . .

"Who are you calling a nymph?" Xena spat, facing down the goddess.

"It's only a temporary title," Eos said patiently. "Nymphs always take care of children. Zeus himself was raised by Cretan nymphs."

"Speaking of Cretans—"

"I don't think childcare's going to be an issue here," Gabrielle said. The three of them stood ringing the fountain while six pairs of eyes watched closely from the surrounding shrubbery.

"I'll say it's not," Xena affirmed, giving the dawn goddess a look fit to put her lights out for good. "I don't know who these children are that you've been jabbering about, but Gabrielle and I are *not* nymphs and we are *not* babysitters.

What we *are* is *leaving*. Come on, Gabrielle; we've got to get the Thebes."

Xena started off, but she hadn't gone more than thirty paces when something struck her a mighty blow squarely in the breastplate, sending her toppling head over heels, all the way back to the base of the fountain. She was on her feet in an instant, teeth clenched, sword drawn, searching for the assailant that wasn't there. Eos giggled.

"What's so funny?"

"*That* was one of my children," Eos replied. "Boreas, god of the north wind. As you can see, he doesn't need anyone to babysit *him*. He's all grown up, the same as his three brothers, and every one of them is more than willing to help me ... *reason* with hotheads like you. You assume you know what's going on, but you haven't any *accurate* idea of the situation at all." Her beautiful face was insufferably smug.

"You're the dawn: Enlighten me," Xena said drily.

"She doesn't need baby-sitters because her 'children' aren't children," Gabrielle broke in. "They're men."

"Little men?" Xena was taken aback. "Now there's a novel idea, even for a goddess."

"Don't be silly." Eos tossed her golden curls. "Boys! Boys, come here! There's someone I want you to meet."

The foliage rustled. Twigs snapped underfoot. One by one, six small boys ranging in age from two to seven emerged from the bushes. There was something distinctly unchildlike about them. It wasn't just their eyes, which held neither shyness nor fear when meeting strangers; it went further than that. Xena watched, amazed, as the two-year-old came boldly up to face her. She'd never before seen someone manage to toddle and swagger at the same time. When he took his thumb out of his mouth, laid hold of her hand, and kissed it with a gallant flourish, it was as if someone had opened an amphora full of understanding and up-ended it over her head.

"*You're* the ones!" she cried. "You're Eos's new lovers!"

"Not exactly," said Gabrielle's old acquaintance, Orlo.

"Not at the moment, anyhow," said the oldest looking of the bunch, a gangly towhead.

"She *calls* us her husbands," another added. "Which is neither here nor there, seeing as how in our present condition the role or husband *or* lover is unthinkable."

"I should hope so!" Gabrielle was appalled.

"You can do more than *hope* so." Eos gave her a cutting look. "You can rely on it. How *dare* you think such dreadful things of me? I'm a *respectable* goddess!"

"Who just happens to need a husbandsitter," Xena concluded. "*Very* respectable."

She was joking, but Eos reacted as though she'd spoken pure logic. "Then you *do* understand! Oh, I'm so glad. But of course you would: I saw you come dashing out of my temple. You must've spoken with Tithonus. Well, I can tell you right now, I'm not about to make *that* mistake again."

"No, you're going to make a whole bunch of *new* mistakes," Gabrielle muttered.

There was nothing at all wrong with Eos's ears. "What did you say?"

"Let her alone; she's right and you know it," one of the boys spoke up. He was a red-haired tyke, all blue eyes and baby fat. Solemnly he approached Xena and Gabrielle, bowing low. "Myron of Thebes, at your service. I used to be King Creon's favorite harper until I had the misfortune to take a holiday from my work and travel down to *this* scrofulous neck of the woods. There I was, minding my own business, drinking from that little stream over there, when suddenly *this* brazen creature appears before me and declares, 'Oooooh, you're *cute*. Want to be my husband?' "

Xena raised one eyebrow at the goddess. "Not too subtle, are you?"

"I believe in the direct approach," Eos responded haughtily. "And why shouldn't I? I am one of the Olympians. All wise mortals know what a great honor it is to be chosen to consort with us."

"And what a lethal mistake it is to decline that 'honor,' " Myron said. "As a harper, I've heard all the songs about the fates of mortals who try giving gods the brush-off. So of course I consented. At the time, I didn't see the harm in it. I assumed that she was after a quick liaison, no more than a night's entertainment. I *knew* I wouldn't find her beside me at dawn. Ah, but little *did* I know, for no sooner had she given me a most rigorous audition, so to speak, but she announced, 'That was *great*. You'll do.' And with that, she turned me into *this*." He touched his chest.

"She did?" Xena was puzzled. "How?"

Before the former harper could answer, Eos stepped in. "That will be enough out of *you*, Myron. Goodness, you'd think you weren't happy with the prospect of eternal life."

"In *this* shape?" The harper opened his arms wide, appealing for judgement to Xena and Gabrielle. "It interferes with my work in ways you can't imagine. I am a harper—a poet and a musician combined. My profession makes certain creative demands, especially when I need to compose a new song. Inspiration doesn't come easy."

"We're colleagues!" Gabrielle cried eagerly. "Where do *you* get your ideas?"

"I *used* to get them every week in a six-pack of *amphorae* from Arcadia, but now—? Do you realize just how little wine *this* body can hold?"

"Stop bellyaching," Eos said. "It's just temporary. The next time I ask Zeus to grant eternal life and youth to a mortal, I must be sure I've picked the right man. Eternity's a long time to spend with a loser. As soon as I make up my mind, I'll have Zeus return the rest of you to your proper ages."

"And when will that be?" Myron wanted to know.

"I'm not making any more snap decisions," Eos maintained. "What do you have to complain about? Don't I see to your every need?"

"You don't," Myron replied. "Gelassia does. Or did."

"I take it that Gelassia was your *previous* husbandsitter?" Xena asked the goddess.

The dawn goddess sighed and a refreshing breeze stirred the clearing. "Poor dear, she was such a good influence on the boys, so kind, so patient, practically perfect in every way."

"Until she cracked," said Myron.

Eos spread her hands. "I blame myself. Nymphs are such fragile creatures. I should have given her a vacation, only—"

"—only you were afraid she wouldn't come back," Xena concluded, and received a divine scowl for her observation. "What happened to her? Did Boreas and his brothers let her escape?"

"No, she's still here. Or maybe I should say still *there*." Eos pointed at the fountain.

"She was turned to stone?" Gabrielle stared at the statue, horrified. "And all of those poor children with her?"

"Nonsense," Eos said. "Do you think I collect husband candidates by the boatload? And she wasn't turned to stone. We haven't had a gorgon wander through these parts for ages."

"*I* made the statue," one of the little boys piped up. His wavy brown hair failed to cover the distinctive, star-shaped birthmark on his right temple. "Not some dumb gorgon. And if you think that's easy to do when you're this size, think again."

Xena looked at him narrowly. "That birthmark . . . I know you," she said at last. "The only person I ever saw with such a mark was Endemon of Naxos, the famous sculptor."

"The *famous* sculptor?" the boy echoed. "Since when am I famous?"

"Since you vanished mysteriously, fifteen years ago," Xena said. "Everyone thought you drowned. The whole island went into mourning."

"Really?" Endemon's eyes lit up. "Did my death help sales?"

"They can't find enough of your works to satisfy the demand," Xena told him. "An original Endemon is worth a fortune. This piece here would fetch a cartload of drachmas." She nodded at Gelassia's statue.

"Ooh." Endemon beamed.

Eos did not like being ignored and cleared her throat loudly to recapture their attention. "*As* I was saying, Gelassia was the daughter of a local river god. One day the boys were acting up more than usual. She couldn't take it—child care's not for the fainthearted—so in her distress she called upon her father and he rescued her the only way he knew how, by turning her into a spring. She's got a slightly metallic aftertaste, but she goes well with olives and goat cheese."

"Then that fountain's not—?"

"—the Fountain of Youth?" Eos laughed. "That's only a myth."

"So how did you make these men young?" Gabreille asked.

"And if you have that power, why didn't you use it on your first husband?" Xena added.

Yeah! Tithonus buzzed from inside her breastplate.

Eos cocked her head, puzzled. "That sounds like Tithonus. But how could he get out of my temple?"

Before the chrysalis could utter another sound and give itself away, Xena clapped one hand to her bosom as if shocked by what she'd heard and insisted, "Well, why *didn't* you?"

The goddess gave a small I-must-be-hearing-things frown, then replied: "It wouldn't work on him."

The lying little snip! the chrysalis hummed angrily. Xena's hand, still in place, muffled Tithonus' paltry voice so that even she could barely hear it. *She never even* tried *it on me!*

"What do you have to do when it *does* work?" Xena asked the goddess.

"It's really very simple, sort of a one-shot deal," Eos said. "I just need to tell a nice young man 'You'll do,' give him a little kiss, and *bang*!—he's a child again, never any older than two when the smoke clears. And he ages much more slowly than normal children, so even though I can't use the power twice on the same person, I've still got *oodles* of time to make my choice. The power's a gift from Zeus, something he gave me to make me stop nagging him about poor old Tithonus."

"I'm surprised he was so generous," Xena commented. "When Zeus wants someone to shut up, he usually sends them a thunderbolt, not a gift of power."

"Let's just say that there are some days that the Father of Gods and Men doesn't want morning to come any faster than it needs to." Eos smirked.

"Cute," Xena said, flatly. "All right, Eos, can we *try* being reasonable about this? I don't have a whole lot of mornings to spare between now and when we're due in Thebes. I'm not going to be your new husbandsitter, but I'm still willing to help. Since you can't make a decision about which one of these men's the right choice, let me do it for you."

"Pardon me, but I don't believe your title is Xena: Warrior Marriage Expert," Eos said coldly.

"Fine." Xena shrugged off the insult. "Then let Gabrielle do it. Let *anyone* do it, only let it be *done*. You're a goddess, but you're acting like a headless chicken. Stop dithering, choose, and let all of us get on with our lives!"

The light surrounding Eos darkened and crackled until she looked like the dawn of doomsday. "I don't take orders from mortals," she snarled. "I *give* them. I order you to stay here and take care of my potential future husbands or else I'll—!"

"—kill me?" Xena finished for her. "Others have tried. Even gods."

"*Kill* you?" The goddess was startled at the thought. "You can't take care of my darlings if you're dead. But you *will* do it, because—"

She vanished.

"—you'll have someone of your *own* to take care of, too!" The goddess's words filled the sky. Eos dawned suddenly, right behind Gabrielle. Seizing Xena's companion firmly by the shoulders she lowered her head until her lips were inches from Gabrielle's cheek and purred, "*You'll* do, too."

As the goddess' lips puckered to deliver the kiss that would seal Gabrielle's fate, the tranquil dell shattered with the wild, ululating sound of Xena's warcry. Thrusting one hand down the front of her breastplate, she scooped out Tithonus's chrysalis, tossed it into the air, and with the flat of her sword sent it zooming across the clearing in a blazing line drive that smacked Eos right in the mouth. The goddess hurtled backward, landing sandals-up in the fountain just as the air shuddered with the report of a tiny, golden husk bursting asunder. Streaks of fire and vast clouds of smoke erupted from the shell, engulfing the temple grounds.

When the smoke cleared, a tall, handsome man of about thirty-five stood beside the fountain, offering Eos a hand out of her soggy predicament. The goddess staggered to her feet, wiping water out of her eyes. "Ti-ti?" she quavered, blinking. "Sweetie, is it really you?"

Gabrielle sidled up to Xena and murmured, " 'Ti-ti'?" Xena just shrugged.

"I'll say it's me, little missy," the transformed Tithonus declared sternly. "A fine howdy-do it is when a man can't get his own wife to make him feel young again. Huh! But since I got another woman to do it for me, I suppose next you'll be mad about it."

"Oh, darling, how could I ever be mad at you?" Eos threw her arms around Tithonus's neck, half laughing, half weeping for joy. "I'm so happy! I never would've had the nerve to try the power on you. I was afraid of what might happen if I tried, you being so old and all. I thought that if I did attempt it, the shock of snapping all the way back to being a baby would've *killed* you!"

"Killed me?" Tithonus repeated. "But you had Zeus make me immortal, remember?"

Eos clapped a hand to her brow. *"Duh!"*

That was not enough to soothe Tithonus. "Maybe it wouldn't've slipped your mind if you hadn't been so busy running after every beefy young piece of *baklava* between here and Sparta!" he shouted. "Maybe if you really *wanted* me back, you could've figured out how Zeus's gift actually worked! Maybe you'd've noticed how whenever you snapped a man back to boyhood he only lost a certain *portion* of his years, a fixed *percentage* of his real age, which is why when the power worked on me, I *didn't* come back as a baby! Drat it, woman, why didn't you just *do the math*?"

Eos stuck out her lower lip. "But Ti-ti, sweetie, math makes my head hurt." Snuggling up so that her wet clothing plastered her body to his, she added, "Izzums Ti-ti mad at his little Eeezie-weezie?"

Tithonus tried to stay angry, but Eos kissed him—on purpose, this time—and he came up smiling. Sweeping her up in his arms, he said, "Sweetheart, we've lost too many years already. Let's not waste any more." He started for the temple, holding her close.

"Uh, yoo-hoo?" Gabrielle called after them. "Aren't you forgetting something?"

Tithonus turned. The six little boys stood drawn up in a row between Xena and Gabrielle. Eos giggled. "Goodness, what did I ever see in any of *them*?" she said. Lifting her eyes to the heavens, she called out, "O Zeus, Father of Gods and Men, harken unto me! Everything's settled, I made up my mind, thanks for all your help, put them back the way they were when I found them and . . . um . . . see you to-morrow!"

Xena quickly covered her nose and mouth, anticipating six puffs of smoke, but this time it pleased Zeus to restore Eos's rejected matrimonial candidates without benefit of flashy effects. One moment they were boys, the next, men.

Orlo looked down. "I'm not naked," he observed.

"You were expecting to be?" Xena asked.

"I didn't think this chiton would stretch *that* much. I just assumed that when I grew up, my kiddie clothes would rip apart, revealing me in all my astonishing beauty." He turned to Gabrielle. "I can imagine how disappointed you must be."

"Orlo," Gabrielle said, patting him on the shoulder. "Zeus may have made you grow taller, but I don't think you're ever going to grow *up*."

"*Now* where do we go?" one of the men asked.

"Anyone know the way to Thebes?" Xena suggested.

"I should hope to tell you I do," Myron of Thebes spoke up. Surveying the others he announced, "You're all wel-come to come along, unless you've got other places to be."

Endemon the sculptor nodded his head in Xena's direc-tion. "According to her, I've got a great career waiting for me. I guess Thebes is as good a place for a dead artist to live as any."

"Then it's settled," Gabrielle said cheerfully. "To Thebes!"

"To Thebes!" they all echoed, and fell into line behind Myron and Xena.

As they marched up the hillside, Xena turned to King Creon's harper and asked, "Are you *sure* you know the shortest way to get there?"

"Of course I do," Myron replied positively. "Although it

has been years since I left . . . roads change . . . paths get washed out . . ." Bit by bit, his confidence dribbled away. "I think we're supposed to go north . . . or was it west? My memory's not so great when it comes to this sort of thing. . . . Oh well, never mind." All at once his optimism was back. "Even if we *do* get lost, you can always ask for directions."

Xena's scream stripped every leaf from every willow in the grove of Eos, goddess of the dawn.

ARGONAUT

Josepha Sherman

Argo shifted her weight uncertainly from foot to foot, cocking first one hind leg and then the other. She straightened, ears up, snorting nervously.

Nothing. Still nothing. All around her, the forest glade looked and sounded like—a normal forest glade in a normal night. The moon was rising, sending glints of light flicking through the leaves. Argo, like every horse, didn't need the moon to know there was a fox hiding behind that bush, and a squirrel in that tree: Nothing alarming.

But the sense of wrongness was still there, subtle as a fly tickling her neck. Argo snorted again, then took in a deep, questing breath. The forest smelled of normal night, too, and under it, Argo caught the comforting, familiar scents of *her* human and *her* human's yellow-maned human friend.

She had tried to warn them earlier, sidling and whickering. But the humans hadn't understood, and she hadn't known what more to do. *Her* human had scouted the area, sword in hand, but had soon returned, shaking her head.

"Nothing out there, Gabrielle. No humans. No monsters. Not even signs of any animal predators."

"What's making her so nervous, then?"

"I don't know. The full moon, maybe. It gets to animals the way it gets to people sometimes." *Her* human had scratched Argo under the jaw, and the mare had sighed and relaxed. "Nothing bothering her now. Everything's all right, eh, Argo?"

And just then, everything had been all right.

Now . . .

Something . . .

Something wrong . . .

Where? What?

Argo brought her head up suddenly, ears shooting up in new alarm, then moved silently away from the humans, to the other edge of the glade—

The Other stood there, blazing white and beautiful in the darkness, neck arched and wings folding softly.

"Pegasus," Argo acknowledged in the Silent Speech of Horses.

"Argo."

They touched noses in greeting, breathing in horse fashion into each other's nostrils. Pegasus smelled strange and familiar in one: bird and horse. But the scent also bore a hint of worry, and Argo drew back, snorting.

"What?" she asked. "What is happening?"

The great white wings opened in a soft rush of feathers, then folded. Pegasus shivered, settling the feathers back into place. "There is great need. Come."

But Argo balked, glancing uneasily back at *her* human. "She sleeps . . ."

Pegasus' ears flattened in impatience. "There is no danger to her! No danger to either human!" The white tail snapped with an audible *crack*. "Come! I call you in the Names of the Stallion and the Mare."

Argo sighed. "In the Names of the Stallion and the Mare, I must obey."

She followed Pegasus down through the forest, together silent as two deer, to where it thinned away to the ocean's shore. Standing on the verge of the sand, watching the silver of the moonlight rippling on the waves, Argo flared her nostrils, taking in testing breaths of salty air, salty water, decaying and living green things . . . normal air, normal sea . . .

No. There was also . . . strangeness.

"What now?" she asked Pegasus warily.

"Now we hide," Pegasus said with an uneasy snort. "And wait."

They stood together behind a great, jagged rock, and Argo froze, tail clamped down with nerves, trying not to even stamp a foot or shiver her golden hide. Something was in the water . . .

Something was coming to shore . . .

Something that smelled of Horse and Death at the same terrible time. Every nerve screamed to Argo, *Run!* But at the same time, she knew with a sureness deeper than any instinct that to run was to attract that Death's attention and bring it down on her.

The being rose from the water, a great black shape in the night, dripping silver in the moonlight. It stepped out onto the shore, shaking the water from it in quick, bright drops. But no moonlight could lighten its utter blackness . . .

"The Black Horse," Argo breathed.

"The Black Horse," Pegasus agreed.

The monster was twice the size of a mortal horse, with not even a glint of light from its eyes. Something huddled at the feet of the Black Horse, a small, terrified creature, bleating like a frightened foal . . .

No. Argo tensed. "That is nothing born from a mare."

"Not horse," Pegasus told her, "but horse-kin. That is a Ki-rin foal."

Ki-rin! Yes . . . Argo realized, the furry coat was multi-colored, and that was the first tender nub of a horn on the small forehead. "This is wrong! That does not belong here!"

Pegasus twitched an ear. "No, it does not. It is the wrong-ness. And it must be allowed to go back to its rightful place in Cathay."

They fell silent as the Black Horse prowled around and around its small, terrified captive. Why had the Black Horse taken it? Argo could not puzzle that out. Perhaps a human might understand such things as . . . as . . . the need to take something free and keep it as a prisoner.

"What has this to do with me?" she asked Pegasus.

"You must free it."

"Me!" Fortunately, the roar from the sea hid that astonished sound. "Why? I am no one!"

"You are a hero."

"*My* human is a hero!"

"True."

Pegasus was too calm. Argo insisted, "*My* human is a great fighter, a true warrior. A true hero! I—I am a mortal horse, born of mare and stallion. Why me?"

"No human can harm the Black Horse."

"Then what of you—you have wings!"

"I am of Air, the Black Horse is of Water. We cannot fight."

Argo shook her mane. "Not me. I cannot do this."

"You are mortal."

"Yes! I wish to stay alive."

"By the Rules, you are the one."

Argo pinned her ears back, flat to her head, baring her teeth at Pegasus. "Why should I do this? Why should I not just gallop back to *my* human?"

Pegasus never moved. "Because you, of all horses in the realm, you of all your mortal kind, felt the wrongness. Because you know also that there is always a balance: Day, night, predator, prey—always. There must be this, or there is only Chaos. If the Ki-rin is not freed, there will be no balance."

Argo kept her ears pinned flat back, but she let her lips relax to cover her teeth. She knew what Pegasus was saying was truth, since no horse, not even one of Air, lied. She knew what must be done, and by whom—and she did not wish to do it.

But . . . this hesitation was how a human might think. A horse was too wise to quarrel with what must be done.

"Yes," Argo said simply.

And with no more than that, she gathered her feet under her and charged the Black Horse at a full gallop.

The Black Horse was so astonished by this sudden attack that it went back on its powerful haunches. Argo raced past, and dared a sideways bite. Pfah! Only a snatch of hide and hair, tasting foul as spoiled meat. The Black Horse roared, whirling and snatching at her mane. Argo squealed as she lost strands of hair, and twisted free, her hoovs scrabbling in the sand.

The Black Horse snaked its head forward, jaws gaping, teeth glinting, and Argo shied sideways. She lost her footing, rolled, terrified that she wouldn't find it again, and scrambled up, hearing the Black Horse's jaws snap shut behind her. Its breath smelled of blood.

Pushing off with her hind legs, Argo lunged forward, right under the Black Horse's neck. She tried another bite, aiming at the jugular, missed completely, and kept going. The Black Horse was fast, but it surely was too big to be as nimble as she—

Yes! Argo pivoted on her haunches and lunged forward again, this time at the Black Horse's unguarded flank. She whirled, and whipped out both hind legs in a savage kick. The Black Horse grunted from the impact. Staggering, it roared in rage, then snaked its head out again, teeth raking Argo's side. She leaped sideways, sides heaving. This could not continue! She was swifter, but the Black Horse had more strength!

Yes, but . . . she had seen *her* human fight against bigger foes, stronger foes, and win. Swift . . . and clever.

Argo stopped short, spinning around to face the Black Horse. Ears flat back, she neighed challenge to it, and rushed straight at it. The Black Horse reared, looming over her. All her instincts cried to her to shy aside—but Argo raced blindly forward. Before the Black Horse could crush her beneath its hooves, she was at its hind legs. Before it could shift its weight to kick, Argo bit down with all her might on a fetlock, just above a hoof, bit down through the hair and hide to the flesh.

The Black Horse screamed. It kicked, and Argo was tossed off her feet, still clinging to the Black Horse's fetlock. It kicked again, and Argo went flying, the night whirling about her, and landed with a great splash in the waves. She surfaced, snorting out water from her nostrils. This was the Black Horse's realm!

Breathless, the mare began swimming back. The Black Horse—

But the Black Horse was hobbling, three-legged. Argo wriggled back her upper lip in triumph. Her fierce bite had crippled a tendon! And now there was a chance.

Fighting against the water's pull, Argo swam on the crest of the last wave, letting it carry her in to shore, then leaped out of the water onto the sand, barely bothering to shake the drops from herself. The Black Horse hobbled about to face her, teeth bared. And the tiny Ki-rin was right in its path!

Argo leaped sideways left, right, like a playing foal, left, right, forcing the Black Horse to shift balance again and again. Panting, sides heaving, Argo darted forward, leaped back, taunting the Black Horse, drawing it away from the Ki-rin. But she was beginning to slow. Argo felt teeth like fire rake her side, and shrilled her pain—

But as it lunged at her, the Black Horse overbalanced. It came down hard on its injured foot. Its leg gave way, and the Black Horse fell with a thunderous crash.

"I cannot," Argo said. "I cannot."

But she forced her exhausted body into one last run, straight at the fallen Black Horse. This time her teeth closed on its throat. And Argo hung on. No matter how the Black Horse pitched and struggled, she hung grimly to its throat. There was nothing else, nothing but cling, and cling, and cling . . .

Suddenly, there was no Black Horse. With a thud, Argo landed on her side on the sand, then struggled up. She sniffed at a stream of blackish water pouring back into the sea, then wrinkled up her nose in disgust.

A thunderous clapping made her look up. Pegasus hovered for a moment on wide white wings, then came lightly down to a landing beside her.

"What happened?" Argo asked wearily. "I did not kill it."

"It does not die. But it cannot reform to solid shape for many an age."

"And the Ki-rin?" the mare panted.

But a small, multi-colored form was at her side. Eyes wide and wise beyond mortality looked up at her. The budding horn touched her injuries, the scrapes and bruises, and they were gone. The small nose touched hers, and breath sweet as new hay took the weariness from her.

Then the Ki-rin was gone.

"What . . . ?" Argo asked.

"The Ki-rin has returned to its home," Pegasus explained. "The balance is safe." The winged horse glanced sideways at Argo. "And you, as I said, are a hero. What now?"

"Now," Argo said with a great gusty sigh of relief, "I go back to *my* human. Hero or not a hero, I am still a *horse*!"

Gabrielle yawned, stretched, and sat up, brushing leaves out of her hair. Rubbing a hand over her eyes, she asked, "Xena?"

"Over here. With Argo."

Getting to her feet, Gabrielle stretched again, arms over her head. Scratching an arm, she went to join Xena. "Anything wrong?"

"Not a thing. But, well, look at her. Argo looks downright . . . smug, doesn't she?"

Gabrielle frowned, then shrugged. "I guess."

"Yes. Almost as though she knows something we don't."

"What secrets could a horse possibly have?"

"Ah well." Xena ran an affectionate hand along the line of Argo's jaw, scratching her under the chin. "Too bad that horses can't talk. Guess we'll never know what you've been up to, eh, girl?"

Argo, relaxed and almost asleep under the caressing hand, only snorted.

BARD AND BREAKFAST

Greg Cox

Apollo's blazing chariot—known to less poetic souls as the sun—had barely risen in the east when a familiar foot nudged Gabrielle awake. "It's your turn to start the fire," the warrior princess reminded her.

Never a morning person, the young bard groaned plaintively before crawling out from beneath her sleeping fur. Goose bumps sprang up over her exposed arms and legs; the forest clearing where she and Xena had camped for the night seemed much chillier than she remembered. Shivering, Gabrielle hastily donned a leather bodice and skirt, pulled on her boots, and looked around the empty glade. All seemed quiet enough, with Argo remaining safely tethered to a nearby laurel tree, and Xena having gone back to snooze upon her own sleeping mat, lying next to Gabrielle's. All that could be glimpsed of the legendary warrior princess was a crown of raven-black hair poking out from beneath her heavy fur blanket. Last night's campfire, alas, was now nothing more than a heap of cold ashes, and the prospect of lighting a new blaze struck Gabby as altogether too daunting this early in the morning.

"Tell you what," she called to her dozing companion, "I remember spotting a well about a quarter of a league back, by that abandoned temple. I'll go refill the water skins if you'll make the fire."

A grunt emerged from beneath Xena's furs. Gabrielle took that as a yes, and gathered up a pair of empty water skins, tucking them under her arm as she set off down the lonely country trail they had traveled the night before. Wild gooseberries grew alongside the path and she picked a hand-ful of the freshest berries, tucking them into the cleft of her bodice.

The task turned her sleepy thoughts toward breakfast, and Gabrielle began to think about what she wanted to make once Xena got the fire going. That it would be she who prepared their morning repast was not a question; despite her grogginess, Gabby wasn't addled enough to let Xena cook. *Just some simple gruel,* she speculated, *or maybe a few of those fruit-filled dumplings Xena likes so much?*

Rounding a corner, she spied the location she'd recalled. The ruins of a fallen temple presided over an overgrown, weed-clotted field that also contained a solitary brick well, several paces in front of the temple. Gabrielle paid little attention to the crumbling marble edifice in the background; her short hike had left her thirsty, and she prayed to Hermes, god of travelers, that the ancient-looking cistern had not run dry years before. From the looks of the sky, they could not expect rain anytime soon. *Just as well,* she thought. *Who, except maybe a hippopotamus, wants to hike through mud?*

Before she could draw nearer to the well, however, a lone figure detached itself from the shadows beneath the cracked and splintered pediment of the ruined temple and hurried toward Gabrielle, arms outstretched. Instinctively, the bard reached for her weapons, then realized that she had left both of her sai back at the camp.

Thankfully, the approaching figure didn't appear too threatening, for the bright light of dawn revealed an elderly woman clad in a shapeless black robe that fell past her feet and trailed through the low scrub carpeting the open field. "Help!" the old woman cried out in obvious distress. "For the love of the gods, help me!"

All apprehension fell away, replaced by an urgent desire to come to the stranger's aid. "What is it?" Gabrielle called. Dropping the empty skins onto the ground, she ran across the field until she came close enough to touch the old woman, who grabbed onto the bard's shoulders with surprising strength. The woman's hands were cold and dry, but Gabrielle was more concerned by the fear and desperation in the crone's voice. "What's the matter?" she asked intently. "How can I help?"

"My granddaughter!" the agitated woman said. The hood of her cloak obscured her features, but Gabrielle got a vague impression of an angular face with thin, anguished lips. "I just turned my back for an instant—only a heartbeat, I swear!—and she fell into the well!" The panicked grandmother tugged on Gabrielle's arm, pulling her toward the waiting well. "You have to help her . . . she's only three!"

"By the gods!" Gabby exclaimed. Her heart went out to the unfortunate woman. She had heard of similar tragedies occurring before. Hadn't Hercules saved a child from a well only a year ago? Gabrielle briefly considered running to fetch Xena, but decided to check the situation out herself first. *There might not be any time to spare,* she realized, letting the old woman lead her to where the little girl had disappeared. *I can always get Xena later if necessary.*

Built of chipped, weathered bricks, the circular housing of the isolated well rose as high as the youthful bard's waist. A battered tin bucket lay neglected in the dirt at the base of the well. "That's where she fell, poor little Semele!" The stricken grandmother pointed frantically at the open shaft within the brick housing. Anxious words tumbled from her aged lips, mixed with soul-rending sobs. "I thought I could hear her crying before, but now I'm not so sure. My ears, they're not what they used to be. . . ."

Hoping with all her heart that they were not already too late to rescue the lost child, Gabrielle leaned over the edge of the timeworn brick barrel. "Semele?" she shouted down the yawning abyss, trying to keep her voice as gentle and reassuring as possible, despite its volume. Peering into the tenebrous shadows, she glimpsed a faint glint of sunlight reflected on the surface of the murky waters far below. A long fall, she swiftly judged, but not necessarily a killing one; it was possible the child could have survived. "Semele? Can you hear me?"

Her cries echoed within the empty depths of the well, and Gabrielle strained to hear the reply she prayed would come, but instead two strong hands suddenly shoved Gabrielle from behind and she found herself tumbling over the edge of the well into the beckoning pit. A cold wind whipped past her startled face and golden tresses as she plunged head-first toward the subterranean pool below. *Oh no!* she thought, a second before hit the water. *Not again!*

"Gabrielle?"

Xena stirred beneath her furs, then sat up suddenly and looked around. Her beloved bard was nowhere to be seen. "Gabby?" Tossing the warm and cozy furs aside, Xena stood quickly, stretching her muscular limbs and taking stock of the campsite. Battle-scarred bones cracked loudly into place as the warrior princess readied herself, mentally and physically, for whatever the day had in store for her.

She said something about going for water, Xena recalled, *but what's keeping her so long?* Gabrielle should have been back by now, she realized, unless something had happened to her. Xena scowled and reached for her armor, lying on the ground not far from her and Gabrielle's sleeping mats. Over the years, she had learned to trust her warrior's intuition, and right now those instincts were telling her that Gabrielle was in trouble. *The Fates know it be wouldn't be the first time,* Xena mused wryly, *even though she's definitely gotten better at taking care of herself.*

Despite Gabrielle's improved survival skills, Xena's worries only worsened when she spotted her comrade's lethal sai lying forgotten by the bard's discarded bedroll. The matching blades silently testified that, whatever had befallen Gabrielle, she had clearly been unarmed. *Remind me to scold her for leaving them behind,* Xena told herself crankily, *once I get her back safe and sound.*

Moving with a speed and efficiency born of long experience, Xena donned her armor, the hand-crafted leather and brasswork fitting snugly over her tall, athletic frame. The morning sun was taking its own sweet time warming the clearing, and Xena would have killed for a convenient hot spring, but there was no time to light a comforting fire. Securing her sword and scabbard upon her back, and clipping her chakram to the catch at her hip, she strode over to where Argo was tethered.

"You stay here, girl," she whispered to her golden mare, untying Argo's reins so the horse would be free to run if danger visited, "unless you hear me whistle for you. Hopefully, I won't be gone long."

Although I wouldn't count on that, she reflected grimly. As an afterthought, she tucked Gabrielle's pair of sai into her own boots before setting out in search of her missing sidekick. Xena hastened down the trail, marching briskly at first, then breaking into a run as she caught sight of Gabrielle's bootprints in the dust and dirt ahead. Although tempted to call out to her friend, she kept her tongue silent lest she alert any potential foes to her rapid approach. The advantage of surprise was not one she intended to sacrifice needlessly, especially if Gabby really had run afoul of some nasty customers.

As she dashed toward the well Gabrielle had mentioned, concern for her companion's safety adding speed to her already powerful legs, Xena could not help wondering who might have ambushed the bard. Ares? Discord? Alti? Frowning, the warrior princess conceded that there were too many possibilities to count; between the two of them, she and Gabrielle had accumulated a veritable horde of vengeful enemies, any one of whom might have chosen today to settle some old scores. *Then again,* she thought, *maybe we're only talking a couple dozen armed mercenaries or slavers. That wouldn't be too tough. Practically a day off, really. . . .*

The broken-down temple, and nearby well, were just where she remembered, but any hopes Xena had entertained of finding Gabrielle peacefully drawing up some fresh drinking water were immediately extinguished by the fact that not a trace of the absent bard could be seen anywhere in the vicinity of the well. *All right,* Xena concluded, her dire suspicions confirmed. *This is no false alarm.* Fortunately Gabrielle's abductors couldn't have gone far; Xena guessed

that the bad guys had, at most, an hour's lead on her. *Unless
there's some sort of god involved,* she admitted. *In that case,
Gabrielle could be halfway to Chin by now.*

Hoping fervently that today's adversaries were merely
mortal, Xena took a moment to inspect the decrepit remains
of the old temple. Perhaps the ruins held some clue to the
bard's whereabouts . . . ?

The collapsed shrine had clearly seen better days. Toppled
Ionic columns lay atop one another like fallen tree trunks,
while cobwebs stretched across the looming stone portico.
Judging from the peacock motif on some of the surviving
portions of the frieze, Xena deduced that the temple had
once been dedicated to the worship of Hera, before falling
into its present state of disrepair and neglect. *Couldn't happen to a nicer goddess,* the warrior princess thought with
chilly satisfaction; she still hadn't forgiven Hercules's nasty
stepmom for that business with Prometheus a few years
back. Xena wondered momentarily if Herc himself had
wrecked this particular temple. *It looks like his work,* she
thought approvingly.

Still, she couldn't imagine why the Queen of the Gods
would have any sort of grudge against Gabrielle, who had
played a very small role in Prometheus's liberation, and
done nothing to cross Hera since. Besides, Xena wasn't feeling that peculiar tingling sensation she usually felt when
there were gods or goddesses about, so maybe those pesky
Olympians had nothing to do with Gabrielle's disappear-
ance. *We can only hope,* Xena thought emphatically. As far
as she was concerned, most gods were nothing but trouble.

Forgetting the temple for the moment, she turned her attention to the actual well and the area around it. Piercing
blue eyes scanned the ground at the base of the well, searching for the telltale signs of a struggle. To her vast relief, not
a drop of blood was in evidence, only two sets of tracks that
led from a point near the trail up to the very edge of the
brick well. The first batch of tracks clearly belonged to Gabrielle; Xena would recognize those petite bootprints anywhere.

The other tracks were a good deal more peculiar. There
were no actual footprints as such, just a wide trail of flat-

tened earth and underbrush, about half an arm's-length across and tapered at one end. An expert tracker, whose skills rivaled Artemis herself, Xena required only a few moments to identify the source of that serpentine track. Her fears for Gabrielle's safety heightened to an almost unbearable level as she realized what exactly the unarmed bard had come across, and she spit out the word with a mixture of dread and disgust: "Lamia!"

Stunned by her impact with the underground pool, Gabrielle barely heard something else land with a splash a few heartbeats later, then slither through the brackish water toward her. She was still sputtering and coughing up water when that same something grabbed her by the back of her bodice and began tugging her through the darkness at the bottom of the well. Within moments, Gabrielle felt herself dragged onto the mossy shore of some subterranean lake. The damp, slippery stone beneath her felt strangely smooth, as though polished by the frequent passage of unknown parties. *Where am I?* Gabrielle wondered as she lay sprawled upon the burnished rock. Water streamed from her blond tresses into her eyes. *What is this place?*

Cruel fingers seized a handful of Gabrielle's soaking hair and yanked her upright. "On your feet!" someone barked impatiently; Gabrielle scarcely recognized the voice of the old woman who had beseeched her aid only minutes before. No trace of grief or frailty remained in the crone's harsh tones. "This way," the woman said, poking Gabrielle in the back with the point of a knife.

The drenched bard spit out one last mouthful of foul-tasting water. "Let me guess," she said bitterly. "There was no missing granddaughter."

"Bright girl," the deceitful hag cackled, "but not bright enough, it seems." She gave Gabrielle a rough shove between the shoulder blades, causing the bard to stumble forward. "Get going," the old woman said. "I haven't got all day."

Prodded by another painful jab from her captor's knife, Gabrielle hesitantly made her way into what felt like some sort of cavern or corridor. Behind her a small shaft of sun-

light filtered down from the well overhead, but the farther
she walked from the underground reservoir, the blacker the
darkness became, so that Gabrielle had to wonder how the
crone could see at all, when the squinting bard could barely
discern her own hands before her.

The old woman clearly knew where she was going,
though, as she steered Gabrielle through a maze of cool,
clammy tunnels that led to only the gods knew where. Feeling her way with her hands, Gabby's palms brushed across
what felt like tuff, a soft volcanic rock that hardened when
exposed to air. Empty horizontal niches, large enough to
hold an ordinary-sized body, lined both sides of the tunnels.
Catacombs, Gabby guessed, *probably carved out by whom-
ever built the temple above.* Certain cults, she knew, preferred to bury their dead underground rather than simply
cremate them. But why did all the burial niches appear to
be empty? No matter how long the catacombs may have
been abandoned, shouldn't there still be some rotting skel-
etons tucked away in the stone shelves?

Despite the disadvantage posed by the Stygian blackness
surrounding her, Gabrielle considered trying to disarm the
knife-wielding woman behind her; there were a few Amazon
fighting tricks she knew that might catch the crone by surprise. But even if she successfully turned the tables on her
captor, the bard reasoned, where would she be then?
Trapped in the pitch-black catacombs with no idea how to
get out. Better to wait, perhaps, until a more promising moment arose.

Beyond her doubts about the cramped confines of the catacombs, however, Gabrielle also had reservations about the
true nature of her foe. She had not forgotten the unexpected
strength of the seemingly infirm old woman's hands, which
led the alert bard to suspect that the creature behind her
might be far more than she appeared. *All the more reason,*
she decided, *not to start a fight before I have a better notion
of what I'm up against. That's what Xena would do . . . I
think.*

And why was it, Gabrielle wondered, that she could hear
no footsteps behind her, only the unnerving rustle of something heavy sliding across the stone floor? Gabby shivered,

and not just from the chilly temperature of the tunnels. Her trembling fingers silently slipped between her breasts as she did what she could to help Xena find her. . . .

Finally, after many twists and turns, Gabrielle spotted a flicker of light ahead, coming from just around the next corner. The lambent glow of a torch or lamp painted dancing shadows on the roughhewn catacomb walls. "Ah," the gleeful crone cackled. "Home at last." She poked Gabrielle impatiently. "Hurry, girl!"

Grateful to see any light at all, the bard needed little urging to hurry around the curve before her. Relief quickly turned to horror, though, once she caught sight of what lay beyond. "By the gods!" she whispered, aghast.

The narrow tunnel opened up onto an enormous cavern decorated in a singularly ghoulish fashion. Human bones, most of them brown with age, covered the walls and ceiling of the vast underground chamber, arranged in intricate patterns and designs. Slender humeri and fibulae, laid knob to knob, framed macabre rosettes composed of artfully arranged ribs and vertebrae. Broad scapulae flared like calcified wings alongside mounted human skulls, while yet more skulls, too numerous to count, were piled neatly to form sturdy altars and pedestals. Even the elaborate chandeliers hanging from the ceiling were constructed of narrow collarbones radiating outward from the inverted pates of desecrated skulls. Burning candles blazed atop the dry bones, illuminating the charnel contents of the spacious cavern. Hades himself, Gabrielle marveled, could not have conceived such a morbid celebration of death and decay.

Nor could the appalled bard help noticing yet another unnerving detail: here and there, among the hundreds upon hundreds of moldering bones festooning this awe-inspiring ossuary, a few fresh white bones gleamed like polished ivory. Gabrielle didn't want to think about how those newer relics had come to join their ancient cousins.

"Well?" the old woman demanded, her cold breath upon the back of Gabrielle's neck. "What do you think of my masterpiece?"

"That you have way too much time on your hands?" The bard couldn't turn her gaze away from the ghastly spectacle.

Countless pairs of empty sockets stared back at the bard from beyond the grave. If nothing else, the mystery of the empty biers had now been solved; the supposed grandmother of little Semele had surely looted the catacombs to create her grotesque art.

"Fool!" the irate crone barked. "Unappreciative mortal!" She sank her sharp nails into Gabrielle's shoulder and spun the startled bard around, so that Gabby faced her mysterious captor at last. A gasp escaped the young woman's lips.

The supposed crone had discarded her concealing cloak, revealing her true, inhuman nature. The bizarre creature before Gabrielle resembled an old woman only from the waist up. Below her sagging, withered dugs, only partially hidden by her long grey hair, the monster's body transformed into that of an enormous snake. Adorned with silvery, iridescent scales, her serpentine tale stretched out behind her nearly as long as Gabby was tall.

A lamia! the bard recognized at once. She had heard of such fearsome creatures, although she had never laid eyes on one before. According to the ancient tales, the lamiae were the unholy spawn of one of Zeus's human mistresses, transformed by Hera's jealous wrath. A chill passed through Gabrielle as she recalled that the lamiae were said to feast upon the blood of mortal men and women. *I might as well be back among the Bacchae,* she realized with a sinking heart. The danger was just as great.

"What, no scream?" the lamia mocked her. Her yellow eyes were more like a snake's than a woman. A forked tongue flicked past her lips as she leered at Gabrielle. "You're braver than most, little girl."

"Well, I've had a lot of practice at this sort of thing," Gabrielle said glibly, while her eyes searched the cavern for a possible escape route. A gigantic open arch, outlined by a trellis of piled skulls, attracted her attention to the far end of the chamber, and she thought she could even smell a hint of salt water, leading her to suppose that another, larger tunnel led to an open cave somewhere along the nearby coast. *How fast can the lamia move?* Gabrielle wondered, thinking about making a run for it. Unfortunately, serpents weren't exactly known for their slowness. *Curse the Fates,* the frustrated bard thought. *Why couldn't she be half-tortoise instead?*

She was still weighing the possibilities of a dash for safety when the sound of heavy footsteps rocked the cavern, coming from the very tunnel through which she had hoped to flee. The massive tread of whatever was coming rattled the bones upon the walls and ceiling and shook the floor beneath Gabby's boots. *Now what?* she pondered in alarm, feeling as though she were suddenly caught between Scylla and Charybdis. *A bloodthirsty lamia wasn't bad enough?*

Apparently not, as, a moment later, a gargantuan (and horribly familiar) figure stomped into the cavern. The cyclops was so tall that he had to duck his head slightly to pass through the enormous archway, and the club in his hand was as thick as an oak. An old and ugly scar stretched across the ample brow where his single eye should have been, and he sniffed the dank air of the gloomy, unhallowed crypt with a pair of grotesquely big nostrils. "What's that?" he rumbled, licking his lips with a tongue the size of a ten-pound slab of steak. "Do I smell mortal meat?"

"Um, hello again," Gabrielle said, waving her hand weakly.

"YOU!" the blind cyclops roared. "I know that voice. You're the chatty little morsel that tricked me years ago." Anger contorted his already homely features. "You said you were going to kill Xena for me!"

"Er, would you believe I just haven't gotten around to it yet?" Gabrielle stepped backward involuntarily, almost treading on the lamia's tail. In fact, she *had* talked her way out of this very same cyclops's clutches a few years back, right after she met Xena for the first time. "Long time, no see."

The cyclops growled irritably, clearly not one to let bygones be bygones.

"Well, isn't this a pleasant reunion," the lamia remarked with fiendish amusement. She took Gabrielle by the arm and none too gently led her over to a pedestal made of piled skulls, where she forced the outnumbered bard to sit down upon the stack of grinning death's-heads. The lamia tied Gabrielle's wrists together with a strip of coarse leather whose origins did not bear thinking about. "My colossal friend and I have worked out a neat little arrangement over the last few years," the creature explained. "He gets the meat"—the lamia patted Gabby's well-muscled abs—"and I get the blood and the bones."

With her armored back pressed hard against the inner wall of the well, and the soles of her boots pushing against the bricks on the opposite side, Xena carefully inched down the vertiginous shaft. She had no doubt that she was heading in the right direction to find Gabrielle; since neither Gabby's nor the lamia's tracks had led away from the well, it was obvious which way they had gone. Xena only hoped that her purloined friend could hang on to all of her blood until the warrior princess could catch up with her.

Xena's back was already aching from her awkward descent, but she wasn't about to dive headfirst into an underground pool without checking it out first. Especially with lamiae about. *Gabrielle's going to owe me a good massage when this is all over,* she thought. *What is it with her and bottomless pits anyway?* Gabrielle seemed to have a remarkable propensity for falling down gaping holes, chasms, volcanic craters, whirlpools, and such. *I swear, she could find a way to fall from Tartarus itself.*

Such irritated musings merely masked a deeper anxiety. *Please let her be alright,* she hoped passionately. Gabrielle was her closest and dearest friend, and the most precious thing in her life. *The pain of losing her again would be more than I could bear.*

Despite the painful protests of her abused spine and leg muscles, Xena hurried faster down the well.

The lamia was feeling Gabrielle's bones through her clothes and skin, figuring out how best to fit them into her grand design. "What a lovely clavicle," she cooed, pinching the bard's collarbone with her cold, dry fingers. "Such a graceful, elegant curve."

"Thank you, I think," Gabby muttered, permitting the indelicate inspection for as long as it kept the two monsters from having her for breakfast. *I have to keep them occupied until Xena gets here,* she resolved, confident that her remarkable partner would stop at nothing to rescue her. "You know," she began, trying to start a conversation with the preoccupied lamia, "I'm an artist, too. A bard."

The serpent woman looked up from Gabrielle's collar, a flicker of interest in her reptilian eyes. "A bard, you say?" She stroked her pointy chin with bony fingers. "I have to admit that I haven't heard a good bard in years." She drew back from her defenseless captive, the lamia's human half resting atop a stack of scaly coils. "Very well then, girl. Tell us a tale."

"Hey!" the cyclops objected. He rose to his feet from an oversized throne of skulls, looming over them like a living mountain, albeit one clad in crude woolen garments. "What about breakfast?" An immense hand rubbed his mammoth belly. "Please, Ophidia. I'm famished."

"Patience!" the lamia hissed at him. "I caught this dainty delicacy, Conjunctivus. We'll feast on her when I choose." The cyclops opened his mouth to argue further, but Ophidia silenced him with a withering glance. "This won't take long," she promised.

That's what you think, Gabrielle thought. Taking a deep breath, she gathered her wits and went into full bard mode, projecting her voice so that it seemed to fill the vastness of cavern:

"In a time of ancient gods, warlords, and kings, a land in turmoil cried out for a hero . . ."

Her chakram clutched between her strong white teeth, Xena swam across the murky, stagnant reservoir at the bottom of the well. So far the subterranean pool did not appear to hold any lurking lamiae, nor any other nasty surprise, but the warrior princess wasn't taking any chances. As soon as her keen eyes adjusted to the gloom, she struck out for what appeared to be a shallow beach leading to an unlit opening in an otherwise unbroken wall of stone. *That looks like the only way out,* she concluded.

Powerful strokes swiftly brought her to the shore, where she returned her chakram to its place at her side, then retrieved a small pouch from a separate hook on her armor.

The bag of greased, watertight leather held flints and a candle, which Xena promptly used to create a flame to see by. Damp bootprints—obviously Gabrielle's—pointed her straight toward the cave entrance she had noted earlier. Xena nodded silently, her deductions vindicated once more. Candle in hand, she stepped warily into the apparently empty tunnel.

All her senses were at a heightened state of awareness, primed to detect the slightest hint of any waiting deathtrap or ambush. The desolate catacombs reminded her of many others she had explored in her travels, although she noted the curious absence of any human remains in the burial niches. Her habitual scowl deepened when the tunnel she was following first offered her a choice of branching corridors, leading no doubt to yet more detours and decisions. Xena paused to consider the problem: if these catacombs were at all like their counterparts in Rome and elsewhere, the network of tunnels could well extend for leagues. A careless person could easily get lost forever down here, but Xena had never been described as careless. Crouching down between two clammy tuff walls, she meticulously searched the floor for clues.

Gabrielle's wet bootprints had long since dried out, and the smooth stone floor did not readily retain ordinary tracks. Xena's eyes widened, however, when she spotted an odd yellowish stain smeared into the ground in front of the left-hand corridor. The stain was still wet and sticky to the touch, and she tasted it experimentally.

Gooseberry. Xena's razor-sharp memory instantly summoned up an image of the fruit-bearing bushes growing alongside the trail to the well. *Good girl, Gabrielle!* she thought, pride and renewed hope surging within her heart. *I should have known she'd find a way to guide me to her.*

The warrior princess sprang from the floor and hurried down the tunnel marked by the squashed gooseberry. She found still more berries along the way, invariably left behind wherever the trail veered off in a new direction. Xena could practically feel Gabrielle's presence in the lonely, sepulchral corridors.

Hang on, she pleaded with her stolen friend. *I'm coming!*

• • •

"Callisto again? I thought she was dead."

The bewildered cyclops scratched his coarse black hair in confusion. Dandruff the size of snowflakes littered the cavern floor.

"Pay attention, dolt!" Ophidia snapped at her elephantine accomplice. "Hera brought her out of Tartarus."

Conjunctivus just looked more adrift. "Hera? What about Ares?"

"Ares brought her back to life the first time. Hera brought her back the second time." The lamia snorted in disgust. "Can't that humongous brain of yours follow a simple story?"

Exhausted from declaiming nonstop, Gabrielle welcomed the momentary interruption in her narrative. Her mouth was as dry as the legendary deserts of Arabia, her throat equally parched, yet she feared to risk asking her monstrous captors for a drink of water. Frankly, she didn't want to do anything that might bring up the subject of refreshments. *I have to keep them thinking about the story and not about their stomachs. . . .*

Ophidia quickly noted that her captive bard had fallen silent. "What's the matter with you?" she demanded, giving Gabrielle a sharp poke with her finger. Piled coils rustled impatiently. "Keep going, girl. I want to know what happens next."

Feeling distinctly like a human pincushion, Gabrielle swallowed hard and launched once again into her tale. *I've faced tough audiences before,* she thought wryly, *but this is the first time I've ever had to orate for my life!*

Xena's candle sputtered, inciting the umbrageous shadows to close in on her. The warrior princess tipped the lighted taper, pouring off the pool of molten wax that had threatened to drown the lighted wick. Droplets of liquified tallow splattered the floor of the catacombs, as well as the toes of Xena's leather boots. She blew gently on the tiny flame, restoring it, and the encroaching darkness receded once more.

But a problem far more serious than a faltering candle

now faced her: an intersection with no helpful gooseberry to point her in the right direction. *Gabrielle must have run out of berries,* Xena guessed, *or else the lamia got wise and confiscated the rest of her supply.* In either event, the warrior princess was on her own now.

No point searching for footprints. The cavern floors were far too hard, and lamiae didn't even have feet. Instead Xena closed her eyes and sniffed the air. At first, all she smelled was dust and mildew, the odor of antiquity, but, wait, was that the faint aroma of salt water tingeing the musty atmosphere of the tunnels? Wetting a finger, she held it up experimentally before each of the branching corridors. Yes, there was definitely a slight, but detectable, breeze coming from the passageway on the left.

Possibly there was another way out of the maze? Despite the many twists and turns she had already taken, Xena felt certain that the feeble breeze was not emanating from the pool beneath the well; she had an almost uncanny sense of direction and would have known if she had circled back toward where she'd begun. The draft, with its hint of the open sea, had to lead to somewhere else, maybe to Gabrielle and the lamia.

Leaving a trail of cooling wax behind her, Xena rushed down the lefthand path. She prayed, to whom she wasn't sure, that she was heading the right way, and that the loathsome lamia had not already used Gabrielle to quench her vile thirst for human blood. *If that creature has so much as scratched Gabby,* the warrior princess thought ferociously, *I'll separate her snake half from her human parts!*

How long can I keep this story going? Gabrielle worried desperately. She had already exhausted all the adventures she and Xena had experienced during their first three years together, and there was still no sign of any imminent rescue. *What if I run out of stories before Xena gets here?* The weary bard realized she had to keep her narrative going for as long as possible. *I can't leave anything out, no matter how painful.*

"And lo', after many arduous journeys and adventures, the warrior princess and the bard were reunited in the leafy forests of Poteideia. Tears as salty as the briny deep stained their cheeks, and their wounded hearts pounded loudly in their chests, like the beating of mighty drums, and then—"

"Wait a sec," Conjunctivus interrupted. A titanic scowl twisted his ugly face. "You fell into a pit of fire, you and your demonspawn offspring. You should have been burned to ashes." A giant foot tapped impatiently against the bone-littered floor of the crypt. "How in Zeus's name did you end up in the woods?"

That's a very good question, Gabrielle conceded, wishing she had a more convincing answer. "Er, I got better?"

"Bah!" Ophidia spat, her forked tongue flicking angrily. "That's no good. You cheated!" She looked away disdainfully and nodded at the seated cyclops. "Go ahead. Eat her."

"Yes!" the one-eyed giant said, far too enthusiastically for Gabrielle's peace of mind. He lurched to his feet and groped for the bound bard. A trickle of drool the size of a small waterfall spilled from the corner of his blubbery mouth. "Breakfast time!"

"Wait!" Gabrielle called out. Instinctively, she raised her hands in front of her, even though they were still tied together at her wrists. "I haven't got to the best part yet!"

"I don't care," Conjunctivus snarled, baring yellow teeth that looked as big as tombstones. "I'm hungry enough to eat four of you."

"Just don't shatter the bones this time," Ophidia chided him, shaking a warning finger at her colossal accomplice. "They're no good to me broken, let alone all gnawed upon."

Desperately, Gabrielle tried to recapture the attention of her monstrous audience. "Wait! You haven't heard about the time we were trapped on Shark Island . . . or when Xena defeated Pompey's army!"

Alas, the salivating cyclops didn't appear interested in either women's prisons or Roman politics. He loomed over Gabrielle like a carnivorous mountain. Huge, hairy, brutish palms reached out for her.

"Keep your hands to yourself, Eyeless!" a defiant voice shouted fearlessly. All heads turned toward the back of the crypt, where Xena stood framed, chakram in hand, beneath an arch of skulls. She smirked at the cyclops she had blinded years before. "Seen any good sunrises lately?"

"XENA!" the giant roared, his nagging appetite displaced by a homicidal rage. He charged at the sound of the warrior princess's voice. "I'll tear you apart with my bare hands."

"You and what guide dog?" Xena mocked him. Blowing out her candle, she leaped into the air, effortlessly clearing the head of the cyclops lumbering toward her. Executing a perfect midair flip, she landed feetfirst behind the vengeful cyclops, less than a hundred paces away from Gabrielle and the lamia. "Gabrielle!" she yelled. "Get ready!"

Alerted to Xena's new location by her urgent cry to her friend, Conjunctivus spun around awkwardly and started stamping wildly at the floor before him. Brittle bones rattled alarmingly upon the walls and ceiling, but Xena deftly evaded the giant's murderous feet. Her blue eyes shone with feral glee and a wolfish grin stretched across her face; the warrior princess never looked half so happy as when she was fighting a battle to the death.

"Here goes!" she warned, flinging her chakram at the cyclops's enormous head. The gleaming steel ring flew from her hand, spinning through the air like a discus hurled by an Olympic champion.

"Conjunctivus, watch out!" Ophidia warned her sightless partner, and the cyclops ducked instantly, so that the chakram appeared to miss him, whizzing past his scalp to strike the ceiling instead, where it shattered a skeletal rosette, then came ricocheting back at Gabrielle. "Hah!" the lamia cackled triumphantly. "So much for the warrior princess's legendary aim!"

Most people would be afraid to have a disk of razor-sharp metal zooming at them, but not Gabrielle. She knew Xena *never* missed.

As the chakram came whistling through the air, the bard raised her bound hands above her head, pulling her wrists apart as much as the leather strap would allow. Sure enough, just as she had expected, Xena's most versatile weapon sliced cleanly through Gabrielle's bonds before striking the wall behind her and bouncing back to its armor-clad mistress's grip.

"Thanks!" Gabrielle shouted, yanking her wrists apart and

springing to her feet. She scrambled away from the bony pedestal, trying to put some distance between herself and Ophidia, who was now hissing in rage. Thankfully, the bloodthirsty snake woman was more intent on her partner's battle with Xena than with her escaping prisoner.

"No problem," Xena said casually. The cyclops tried to smash the warrior princess with an enormous fist, but she somersaulted between the giant's legs, then turned toward her newly liberated sidekick. Their gazes met across the roomy crypt and Xena reached into her boots with both hands. "Catch!" she yelled to Gabrielle.

The bard spied two shiny, metallic objects hurling toward her and reacted with reflexes honed by hours of diligent practice, grabbing both sai by their handles and snatching them out of the air. Gabrielle's chosen weapons felt strong and snug within her grip, the deadly blades flashing beneath the flickering light of the bone chandeliers. *Alright now!* she enthused, no longer merely a helpless hostage. *Time to kick some lamia butt!*

The depraved serpent woman was still trying to help her cyclopean cohort get his hands on Gabrielle's elusive rescuer. "Where is she?" the frustrated giant roared. His groping paws had found his stupendous club, which resembled a battering ram more than a simple cudgel, but the warrior princess remained one step ahead of him. "Tell me where she is!"

"To your left! No, higher!" Ophidia hollered, tracking Xena's every move with her cold reptilian eyes. The massive club obeyed the lamia's instructions without hesitation, lashing out again and again at the agile warrior princess, who leaped and rolled and cartwheeled away from every blow. "Now a bit more to your right—yes, that's it! You almost got her that time. Try again, a little lower!"

Just one blow from that ridiculously large club, Gabrielle realized, would be enough to flatten even Xena. *I need to cut off Conjunctivus's "eyes" at their source.*

Jumping atop a typically hideous altar, she kicked a dusty, brown skull at Ophidia's head. The dislodged death's-head hit the distracted serpent woman squarely on the chin, its yellowed teeth chattering as it bounced off the lamia's jaw and onto the stone floor of the crypt. "Hey, Grandma Scaly," Gabrielle taunted, slashing the empty space between them with her twin sai, "don't forget about me!"

Xena wished the lamia would just shut up. Keeping out of the way of Conjunctivus and his big, big stick was challenging enough without that withered old snake coaching him from the sidelines. *C'mon, Gabrielle,* Xena thought. *You know what to do.*

For a few more moments, the lamia kept on shouting instructions, like an Athenian guardsman directing traffic past the Parthenon. Xena listened as intently as Conjunctivus, making sure she never stayed put long enough to let the revenge-crazed cyclops zero in on her. Adrenaline poured through her veins, along with the intoxicating joy of combat, but Xena knew she couldn't keep this up forever. Her eyes scanned the spacious crypt, taking in every detail of the cavern-turned-battleground. Already a strategy was forming in her mind. *Yes,* she thought coolly, eyeing the grisly chandeliers overhead. *That could work.* Her mind quickly calculated the angles and directions involved. *Now if Gabby will just take care of that lamia....*

Right on schedule, the interfering snake woman fell silent. Xena didn't need to look back over her shoulder to confirm that the lamia now had a fighting-mad bard on her hands; she had faith in Gabrielle's ability to cover her back. After all, Gabby was a former Amazon queen.

Conjunctivus was acutely aware of his partner's sudden hush as well. "Ophidia!" he demanded. The cyclops held his club high above his head, so that its squat tip scraped the ceiling. "What's the matter with you? You have to tell me where Xena is!"

"Sorry, big boy," the warrior princess informed him, poised to spring away from the upraised club the instant it began its descent. The giant's enormous shadow seemed to cover the entire floor, but Xena only grinned all the harder. "You're on your own now."

One blind cyclops against the Destroyer of Nations? She almost felt sorry for the poor brute. Almost. A wicked kick caught Conjunctivus right below the kneecap, causing the giant to howl in pain and fury. He stumbled forward, nearly dropping his club on his own mammoth skull. "Kill you! Crush you! Grind you up!" the cyclops bellowed, lumbering after Xena like a minotaur in a china shop. Bones rained from the roof of the cavern as the heedless giant rampaged through the lamia's ornate ossuary. Conjunctivus shrugged off the falling debris, unable to think of anything except obliterating his relentless nemesis. "Smash you like a bug!"

"Come and get me!" Xena dared him, delivering another vicious kick before darting out of reach again. Facing the cyclops from only fifty paces away, she flung her chakram at a pillar of skulls that rose behind Conjunctivus's right shoulder. The god-forged ring shattered the towering column, the cacophonous clatter causing the giant to spin around and turn his back on Xena, who, getting a good running start, raced *straight up the cyclops's broad back.*

Caught off guard, Conjunctivus frantically fumbled behind himself with his free hand, but Xena was too fast for him. "Don't you hate it when you can't scratch those hard-to-reach places?" she taunted the cyclops as she used his yard-sized shoulder as a springboard to flip onto the giant's head. Xena's boots touched down on Conjunctivus's balding pate just in time to catch her chakram on the rebound and return the weapon to its rightful place on her hip.

"Yi-yi-yi-yi-yi-yi!" The warrior princess's ululating war-cry echoed through the crypt as, after giving Conjunctivus a headache-inducing stomp for his troubles, Xena launched herself off the cyclops's head and into the air. Her outstretched hands caught on to the bony arms of one of Ophidia's ghastly chandeliers. Xena turned the hanging lamp into a trapeze, swinging away from Conjunctivus until the soles of her boots brushed the ceiling, then came arcing back toward the unsuspecting cyclops.

She waited until the last minute before letting go of the chandelier and tossing her chakram at the same time. The whirring missile sliced through the chain that bound the swinging lamp to the roof. Xena's boots slammed into Conjunctivus's chest only seconds before the untethered chandelier collided with the giant's head, its overturned lantern setting the cyclops's receding hairline ablaze.

Conjunctivus landed flat on his back, crushing a stack of neatly organized ribs and mandibles to powder. Bright orange flames devoured his short black hair, before spreading rapidly to his filthy, grease-stained garments. Xena leaped off the fallen giant's midsection, fire literally licking at her heels.

"RRARGH!" Maddened by the searing flames, Conjunctivus scrambled to his feet and fled the crypt in a panic, desperate to quench the blaze in the sea beyond the cavern. He smashed through the decorative trellis around the exit, scattering skulls everywhere, before disappearing from sight. Xena was tempted to take off in hot pursuit, perhaps dispose of the man-eating monster once and for all, but what about Gabrielle? Slaying the cyclops came in a distant second compared to making sure Gabby was okay.

Letting the barbecued giant go, the warrior princess turned her eyes toward her bard.

Gabrielle had succeed in getting the lamia's attention. "Impudent brat!" Ophidia gnashed her fangs and uncoiled her long, serpentine tail. Her bony fingers were crooked in front of her, as though eager to gouge out the bard's sea-green eyes. "I should have drained your blood when I had the chance!"

"Better luck next time," Gabrielle replied, assuming a defensive stance. Despite her bravado, the eerie appearance of the lamia still sent chills down the sidekick's limber spine; she knew, though, that she had to keep the snake woman too busy to assist the cyclops. "No offense, but I have better things to do with my blood than feed an over-the-hill, old snake."

Ophidia hissed angrily, rising up on her tail until she towered over the diminutive bard, who gulped and tried to maintain a warlike expression. *Could be worse,* Gabby thought. *I could be fighting a younger and spryer lamia.*

But the elderly serpent woman was faster than her human half might lead one to believe; her powerful tail whipped out unexpectedly, knocking Gabrielle's legs out from under her. Xena's sidekick fell backward, landing supine upon the rocky floor. The impact of the fall knocked the wind out of Gabby, and her precious sai slipped from her fingers.

"Yessss!" the lamia said sibilantly. Like a striking cobra, the she-creature lunged for Gabrielle's exposed throat, only to be abruptly distracted by the clatter of falling bones. A look of utter horror transfigured Ophidia's gaunt features as she watched the crypt's morbid ornamentation be reduced to charnel chaos by a sightless cyclops gone berserk. "No!" she shrieked in despair. "My masterpiece!"

Gabrielle could sympathize with a fellow artist's anguish, but not too much. A skull thudded to earth not far from the bard's head, and she hooked her fingers into its empty sockets, then swung the skull at Ophidia with all her strength. The grinning *memento mori* slammed into the lamia's own noxious noggin so hard that the desiccated skull broke apart into dozens of tiny fragments of bone. Ophidia's eyes rolled backward, exposing blood-streaked whites, and the stunned lamia collapsed onto the bone-strewn floor.

An instant later, a silver chakram separated the monster's head from her body.

"Hope you don't mind me finishing her off," Xena said, catching her weapon as it ricocheted back to her. "You looked like you were holding your own just fine, but I figured I'd spare you the messy part."

"Sure," Gabrielle said. "Anytime." she clambered nimbly to her feet, then searched the crypt with inquisitive eyes. "What happened to the big guy?"

"He's not going to be bothering anybody real soon," the warrior princess assured her, crossing the crypt to join the bard. "Especially now that he's lost his 'eye' a second time." A growl, almost as fierce as any mythological monster's, escaped Xena's stomach. "Nothing like a little morning mayhem to work up an appetite," she commented, dropping a strong but gentle hand onto Gabby's shoulder. "So, what's for breakfast?"

"Hah!" Gabrielle laughed. "Let me tell you a story about that. . . ."

RECURRING CHARACTER

Keith R. A. DeCandido

It had been a normal day at Miltiades' tavern, which was just the way he liked it.

Within an hour of his opening, most of the regulars had come in. The ale flowed freely from the smooth wooden goblets into the patrons' gullets. The sturdy bar continued to withstand the onslaught of spilled drinks and clumsy drinkers. The two barmaids served the tables quickly and efficiently. The regulars knew not to mess with the pretty young women, and if anyone did, they were shown the door. A giant stag's head hung from the far wall, a gift from a local nobleman who appreciated the service Miltiades provided to the community.

Taborn, one of the regulars, spilled his ale laughing at one of his own jokes. As Miltiades wiped down that part of the bar, he smiled, extremely happy with life.

Yes, it was a perfectly normal day, the latest in a series of them.

Until the stranger walked in.

"Drinks for everyone, on me!" said the stranger, a young

man in leather armor, carrying a broadsword on a hip scabbard.

A ragged cheer came up from the assembled customers.

Miltiades did not share in that cheer. An ex-soldier himself, Miltiades knew that it was never a positive sign for a tavern owner to have a soldier in an expansive mood around. Such people tended to break furniture and annoy barmaids. Miltiades hadn't had a brawl since the winter solstice, and he hoped to keep that streak going.

Miltiades refilled everyone's drink before pouring an ale for the soldier. "What's the occasion, kid?"

"Quite simple," the kid said with a grin. "My name is Roxus, but everyone calls me Rocky. Remember that name, barkeep, because soon it will be known throughout Greece as the name of the man who killed Xena!"

Taborn, who was seated next to the soldier, turned, his eyes wide. "The Warrior Princess?"

Rocky snorted. "No, Xena the Goat-Herder. Of *course* the Warrior Princess!"

Miltiades sighed. Generally, the customer was always right, but he couldn't let this young idiot go off and make an ass of himself.

"Take my advice, kid—go home and forget about Xena."

"Are you kidding? I spent years honing my skills! This is my chance to prove myself against the greatest warrior of our age!"

"All you'll prove is that she *is* the greatest warrior of our age, and you're just some dumb kid who ain't got the brains to realize she earned that reputation for a reason."

Rocky barked a derisive laugh. "What do *you* know? You're just a barkeep."

"You know how many times I've heard that Xena was dead? Killed by Callisto in battle, killed by barbarians who hit her with a log, killed by Ares, crucified by the Romans. And you know what? It's bunk—*all* of it. Because Xena's unstoppable. I oughtta know."

"And how's that?" Rocky asked with a sneer.

Miltiades sighed. " 'Cause *I* tried. I used to live in a nice, quiet little village on the Parthian peninsula. Then one day this Darphus fella shows up and starts attacking folks in their homes. His boss was Xena. A bunch of us survived, barely, and decided to fight back. We didn't do too badly against Darphus, but then Xena stepped in. Mowed us down before we could blink. She gave me this." Miltiades lifted his shirt to expose the scar on the right side of his belly.

"When it was all over, the village was a pile'a charred wood, and only six of us were still alive. I didn't have any family, thank the gods, but I had nowhere to live. I'd done fairly well as a soldier against Xena—leastaways I survived, which put me one up on most of the others.

"So I looked for work. Finally hooked up with an arms dealer, name of Mezentius. That was a pretty good gig— mostly protecting shipments and the like. Went fine until Xena showed up. I'd heard rumors that she'd become some kind of hero, and they turned out to be true. She busted up a scam Mezentius had going. I tried fighting her at one point, and got knocked silly for my trouble. By the time I woke up, Mezentius was dead, Xena was long gone—and I was stuck.

"Working for Mezentius gave me some good contacts, though. Managed to score some work for King Xerxes fighting some filthy rebels. It went pretty decently till Xena showed up. She helped the rebels out and deposed Xerxes. She gave me this when I tried to stop her." Miltiades pointed to the scar on his cheek.

"With Xerxes gone, I was out of work *again*. And working for a king who was overthrown by a bunch'a rebels didn't exactly beef up my resumé. I finally got work with a warlord named Nestor. That was real sweet, until the big moron went after the Golden Hind."

"I thought they were extinct." Rocky sounded like he didn't believe Miltiades.

"There was one left. Unfortunately, she was being protected by—"

"Xena, right?" Rocky said snidely.

"No, Hercules, actually, and that friend of his, Iolaus. But after Nestor went and got himself killed, who should show up to help Hercules out but Xena? I was starting to think she had it in for me personally. Fine, I figured, I'd return the favor. I ran up to her, determined to take her out.

"It took her all of five seconds to take *me* out. She didn't even recognize me.

"That did it. I was fed up. It was time to get serious."

By now, the entire tavern had gone quiet. Miltiades's customers were used to the barkeep listening to *their* stories. A long-winded tale like this was cause for notice.

Besides, people *always* liked to hear stories about Xena.

Pouring fresh drinks for everyone sitting at the bar, Miltiades went on: "I spent the next month or so in intensive training. I went over Xena's fighting style in my head. I was pretty sure I knew her weak spot, and that the next time I saw her would be the last.

"A fella named Draco was building up an army. He and Xena used to run together, and they'd clashed up in Amphipolis after she went good. I figured, sooner or later, Xena would come after him, so I joined his troupe.

"And it paid off. Xena tried to stop a slave-trading scheme of his. I was thrilled. Finally, I thought, I get some of my own back. A bunch of us confronted her and that Amazon sidekick of hers outside a temple.

"This was it. My big moment. After she'd hounded me for years, I was going to kill her."

Everyone in the tavern held their breath—even Rocky.

"She took me out without breaking a sweat. And you know what the worst thing was? She *still* didn't recognize me. We'd clashed four times, and she had no idea who I was. She just kicked at my leg and sprained it, and I went down in a heap. By the time my leg healed, Xena was long gone. At that point, I made a solemn vow."

Rocky leaned forward. "That you wouldn't rest until you hunted Xena down and destroyed her once and for all?"

Miltiades rolled his eyes. "Do I look stupid? No, I swore I'd put as much distance 'tween me and Xena as humanly possible."

Blinking in shock, Rocky said, "But—but didn't you want revenge for all the indignities she'd lain at your feet?"

"No, I mostly wanted to keep my feet from gettin' any more indignities laid at 'em. So I went to Rome. The Roman Army's always lookin' for folks. An' I was right. Got a job as a mercenary, put down some Germans and Gauls. Good, honest, steady work, and nobody'd even heard of Xena. It was great till I got promoted."

"What's wrong with being promoted?" Rocky asked.

"Nothing, I thought. But they put me on prison guard detail—in Rome itself."

"Prison guard?" Rocky said with a curl of his lip. "How's *that* a promotion?"

"It was *in* Rome. Any job in Rome is a big step up from anything outside it. One day, I come on duty, and they've got some Gaul fella in the prison—and Xena! I couldn't believe it. Not only had Xena come to Rome, but Caesar himself captured her. They were planning to put her in the arena against the gladiators. I figured, great, all my problems solved.

"Then the Gaul tells me there's something I should know about this woman, meaning Xena, of course. I had no idea what he could tell me that I didn't already know—'cept it turned out she had a key.

"Next thing I knew, I woke up in one of the cells with a broken nose, and Xena was long gone. That was the straw that broke my back. I couldn't get away from her. No matter what I did, no matter where I went, I got beat up by Xena. It had to stop.

"I quit the guard and came back home to Greece. I'd saved enough to buy this place. And you know what? I'm better off. If I'd done this three years ago, I wouldn't have all these scars and my nose wouldn't look like this.

"So trust me, kid—no matter what you do, Xena will stop you. Caesar, Callisto, Draco—none of them could. And neither could I. Worst of all, she didn't even remember who I was each time she took me down. She won't remember you, either."

There was silence in Miltiades' tavern. Everyone looked at Rocky.

Before anyone could say anything, a woman ran into the tavern.

"Run for your lives! Bandits!"

Then she ran out again.

Miltiades heard horses at full gallop and voices crying out—probably the bandits in question.

Then he heard something else, something he'd hoped never to hear again:

"Ai-yi-yi-yi-yi-yi-yi-yi!"

Four-and-a-half seconds later, a man in once-brightly colored clothes went flying through the front wall of the tavern.

He was quickly followed by another through the side wall.

The patrons and the barmaids started making for the exit. Miltiades, though, couldn't move. He was in shock.

"C'mon," one of the bandits said, "let's get her."

Within a few seconds, both bandits, plus three of their buddies, came crashing through the walls.

Then *she* came in.

Xena.

She had that same smile on her face as when she beat him up in the past.

The smile stayed on her face as she walloped the bandits into insensibility.

And right into one of the supports for the tavern structure.

As his tavern collapsed on his head, Miltiades cried out, "By the gods, *not again!*"

When he came to, Miltiades saw Taborn standing over him, along with another regular, Grecox. "Are you all right?" Grecox asked.

"What happened?"

"Xena drove off the bandits," Taborn said.

"You should've seen it!" Grecox cried. "Her moves were *incredible!*"

Miltiades looked around. He lay on the ground about twenty paces from his tavern.

Or what was left of his tavern. What was once a fine structure was now a pile of kindling. Shattered goblets, broken bits of bar, and the caved-in head of the stag lay strewn about the ground.

Grecox carried on: "She actually let the bandits get away because she saw you were trapped. She pulled you out of there, made sure you were all right, and only *then* did she go back after them! It was *amazing!*"

"She saved *me*?" Miltiades asked, stunned. He felt something on his forehead—reaching up, he felt a bandage.

"Well, of course," Taborn said. "I mean, she's a hero, right?"

With that, the pair went off, probably to find another tavern to get drunk in. No doubt the other regulars were doing likewise.

As Miltiades struggled to his feet, he was surprised to see Rocky approaching him. Miltiades assumed the kid would be off chasing Xena by now.

"Barkeep," he said, "I just wanted to thank you. I have to admit, I didn't really believe most of what you said—I mean, c'mon, there's no way Xena could've gotten out of being captured by the *Romans*, that's just *crazy*—but when I saw her tear up your place, I realized that you were right. There's no way I'd even hurt her, much less kill her."

Despite everything, Miltiades was glad. He didn't want this dumb kid to turn out like himself. "Glad to hear it."

"Of course," Rocky continued, "I'm not sure what to do with my life now. I've spent the last three years training myself to stop Xena. Now that I'm not doing it . . ." His voice trailed off.

Miltiades looked at the remains of his tavern. "You any good at construction, kid?"

Miltiades' tavern was harmed during the production of this motion picture.

HORSING AROUND

Lyn McConchie

Xena woke. It was mid-morning by the angle of the sun.
Her mouth felt like the inside of a hen roost and her skin
itched with drying salt. She scratched absently, her eyes going to the slender figure that sprawled beside her. They'd
made it to shore. But where that shore was Xena was uncertain. The storm had blown too many days. At her side
Gabrielle rolled over and groaned.

"My mouth feels like a sandpit."

"Best we find some water."

Thankfully they'd left Argo with a friend before they took
ship. The poor beast would never have survived. Xena flared
her nostrils, searching into the light breeze for water scent.
Behind them tall dark trees grew thick, spreading down almost to the sand's edge. They wouldn't grow so well without water. The breeze changed direction slightly. Xena
nodded.

"I think there's water within those trees. To the south-
east." She staggered to her feet, the carry sack fastened to
her waist swinging with her movements. "Up!"

She gripped Gabrielle's shoulder. The younger girl

dragged herself to her feet and, leaning on Xena, made her way to where the scent of water became stronger. Behind them Gabrielle's sack was left almost buried and unnoticed in the sand. Several hundred yards farther on and past the headland, within the edge of the trees, a tiny spring glimmered. The water ran only a few yards before it sank into the sand's edge and vanished again. Gabrielle flung herself full-length and drank. Xena knelt, drinking from one cupped hand. The other lay curved over her sword hilt.

"We'll need something to carry water." Gabrielle looked back toward the beach. "I had a water skin in my bag. I'll get it." The water had given her renewed energy. She dashed off.

Xena sighed and followed. There was a water skin in her own bag, but she let Gabrielle retrieve hers. It would make the girl feel better to do something useful. A gentle smile curved Xena's mouth. The sort of smile few but animals, babies, and Gabrielle ever saw. It vanished as a sudden cut-off shriek floated back to her. She should have known better. Any time her friend went out of sight there was trouble.

The sound of wood meeting metal smote her ears as Xena raced forward. On the beach Gabrielle was fighting, her staff in constant motion. Xena slowed a second to evaluate. Two enemies. One a smaller, lighter man who pranced, dagger in hand, around the edge of the fight. He limped. Gabby must have got in one blow and the small man had no intention of receiving another. Probably he felt there was no need to anyway.

The other man was huge. He wielded an axe with some skill, but Gabrielle, lighter and faster, was having no trouble staying out of reach. Her staff deflected the blows despite their power. But if just one of those massive blows landed squarely, she'd die. Xena moved in. The big man turned his attention to her, she opened her mouth to speak soothingly. Suggest that there was no need to fight. Her eyes met his and she shut her mouth. Berserker. No chance of his listening to reason. They couldn't outrun him. And he'd fight so long as she or Gabrielle lived.

She hadn't sought this fight. She knew Gabrielle wouldn't have started anything either. That meant the attack had been unprovoked. If two people had to die Xena had no intention of allowing it to be themselves. She closed in warily. A few minutes later the opening she awaited came and her sword blade licked out. The big man went down swinging his axe savagely in a backward blow at her as he twisted. Xena struck again. He snarled at her as he died.

Behind her there came a high shriek again as the small man attacked Gabrielle. The girl's staff spun first one way then into reverse. It cracked him hard across his knee then came up to strike one side of his head as he half-fell. He groaned and slipped to the ground. A fading glare transfixed them.

"I curse you. May—" his voice slurred before clearing again. "I hope she tears your hearts out, you . . ." His voice trailed off as he shuddered and went still. Gabrielle would have knelt to check the body but Xena snatched her back.

"Wait. He could be faking. Let me." She checked the man swiftly. "No, he's dead." She glanced up. "I suggest we collect your bag and get out of here. If this pair had friends they may not be pleased at what's happened." She knelt, however, and checked belt pouches quickly. Her eyebrows raised at some of the items.

Gabrielle turned to gather up the water-sodden leather bag. She swung it onto her shoulder and followed her friend back to the spring. There, they filled their water skins and evaluated the contents of the travel bags. They both had water skins, eating knives, and flint; Gabrielle's stock of herbs was ruined but her salves were intact, and Xena had her whetstone, spare dagger, and items to repair her armor.

"I've got food, too." Gabrielle held up half a smoked sausage and a chunk of hard cheese triumphantly. She looked down the seemingly endless line of trees and sand. Her smile faded. "Where do we go, Xena? I couldn't understand what that man said to us. Where are we?"

"I'm not sure." She'd understood the dying words but didn't want to say so just now. "Somewhere in the northern lands."

Gabrielle blinked. "That far. The storm took us that far!"

"I think so. Settlements here are often on the coast. If we keep walking along the shore we should find one sooner or later. Or a path that will lead us to one." She began to walk along the edge of the shore where the sand firmed into earth under the tree fringe.

"It's going to be cold tonight without blankets."

"I know. We'll light a fire."

They walked steadily. There was no reason to hurry and exhaust themselves, Xena thought. If more trouble appeared it was better they still had enough energy to fight. Toward late afternoon her eyes noticed a thread of a path striking off into the trees.

"Gabrielle," she pointed.

"Do we follow it?"

"We do. Stay behind me." She could smell smoke. It would have seemed a homely scent. Suggesting a fire, hot food, and perhaps a bed, but for the undertone Xena was getting whenever the wind blew harder. Burned wood, yes. But there was more to it. She slipped through the trees, Gabrielle a blond shadow at her heels. Another gust brought the smell more strongly and both women halted, then ghosted on. They'd smelled that scent before. Somewhere ahead there was death. A wave of Xena's hand and Gabrielle drifted away to the left of the path. Xena went right. They closed in on a scene of devastation.

There'd been a sturdy log cabin here once. Perhaps as recently as two or three days ago. Now it was partly burned. The body of the builder lay in front of the entrance. He'd died from one massive blow, which had crushed in his head and one shoulder. Xena moved to where the well-tanned hide curtain, which would have cloaked the doorway, had been flung aside.

"We have a blanket."

"We have to bury him. If we do that I think it would be fair to take anything we can use."

Xena nodded and for the next half hour they sifted through the cabin's contents. They found a robe of rabbit furs only slightly singed. Smoked fish and meat hung on one half-burned rafter, candles, a coil of braided rawhide rope, another of string, a good axe and an ancient, rust-eaten sword. Once they were done, it was becoming dark.

"We'll spend the night down the path aways," Xena said

quietly. She'd seen the look on her friend's face. Gabrielle hadn't wanted to say anything, but the idea of sleeping by the body was bothering her. "Gather firewood, I'll start a fire. Tomorrow we'll lay the man inside and burn his cabin. The ground's too rocky to dig a grave the wolves won't find."

"Is that the way the people here do it?"

"Some do. It's the best we can manage anyhow. His gods will understand." Her tone closed the conversation and Gabrielle went to find dry wood. Xena took up a handful of the dry pine needles from beneath a tree. She heaped them into a tiny cone, added a sheath of dry twigs and struck a spark onto the tinder. Gabrielle returned with firewood just as the spark flared. Something caught her eye and she gave a small crooning sound as she dumped the firewood.

"Oh, you poor little thing." She approached the tiny animal making soft sounds of reassurance. It trotted to meet her. "Oh, poor baby. Did you belong to that man?"

Xena had looked up quickly at the first words. Seeing what their visiter was, she had returned to the fire. With it burning well, she was free to look at the creature. Gabrielle was cradling a kitten. It couldn't have been more than six or seven weeks old. It was a ball of black fluff with huge, innocent, blue eyes. It cuddled into Gabrielle's arms as she brought it to the fire, purring at the warmth and looking up hopefully.

"It's hungry."

"Try it with some of that smoked fish you found."

The kitten didn't have to be invited twice. It fell on the fish, ate hugely, then fell asleep in Gabrielle's lap while the two women made their own meal.

"We can't leave it here to die."

"How did I know you were going to say that."

"Well, we can't."

"Just so long as it doesn't cause us any trouble. Speaking of which. What happened down on the beach with those men?"

Gabrielle looked disgusted. "I have no idea. I went to pick up my bag. They came out of the trees and attacked. The little one was in front, so I tripped him. I hit him on one knee and he screamed. The big one went crazy and started swinging that axe." In her lao, the kitten had opened blue eyes and seemed to be listening as intently as Xena. "I'd have tried to run but I thought if I turned my back I'd get a knife in it."

"Almost certainly. No, you did the right thing. I didn't want to kill them but the big one was a berserker. Once they start fighting they don't stop until they're killed. The other man was probably his shield brother. With his friend down he had to avenge him or die trying."

Gabrielle looked to where the ruined cabin was hidden by the dark. "Do you think they killed that man?"

"He was killed by an axe blow. It's likely." Remembering the man-sized cheap copper ring she'd found in the berserker's belt pouch and the white mark on the dead man's finger, Xena thought it very likely. The pair had probably made a career of robbing lone dwellers and chance-met travelers. It explained their instant attack on Gabrielle.

"And they left the kitten to die. That's awful."

Xena smiled. "I daresay they never saw it. Kittens aren't always stupid. This one probably ran away and hid. It came out when it saw you." It would, she reflected. Animals knew a sucker when they saw one. "I'll take first watch."

She sat, back to the low fire, sword across her lap and ears alert for unusual sounds. Warm under the fur robe Gabrielle slept, the kitten curled up under the robe with her. It looked as if they had a traveling companion. Well, so long as it wasn't a nuisance. They were on foot. Carrying a kitten wouldn't slow them. It wasn't as if they had to be anywhere. She woke her friend at midnight and found the kitten joining her when she lay down.

In the morning they ate, then went to do what had to be done at the cabin. Xena carried the body inside and laid it onto the bed. In the limp hands she placed the old sword they found. The injury that had slain the man had been struck from the front. Let his god know he'd died fighting. Unobtrusively she slipped the ring back onto the bruised finger. It fitted as if made for it—which, she reflected, it possibly had been.

They heaped the bed and filled the cabin with pine branches. The resin would burn like a torch. It was as well the cabin was in a clearing. Xena had no desire to set half the forest afire behind them. She took one of the candles, setting it in a mat of tinder. Then she lit it.

"Let's go. By the time that burns down far enough to start the fire we'll be long gone. If anyone comes to the smoke I don't want them finding us still around."

Gabrielle stood looking at the body. Her voice came softly as she stared up at the sky, the kitten sitting solemnly at her feet.

"We don't know your name, but we did the best we could. I hope your god understands it isn't your fault if we were wrong. We'll take care of your kitten. Don't worry about her." She stood in silence a moment, then turned away. They shouldered their bags, Gabrielle scooped up the kitten, and they were off. Treking along the edge of the shore toward the east. They walked steadily all that day. Toward sunset they halted, moved into the trees, and made camp.

"No settlement."

Xena shrugged. "There'll be one sooner or later. We just have to keep walking."

The kitten had scampered off into the trees. From the depths there came sudden kitten cries for help. Gabrielle was on her feet and running before the first one had died.

"Gabrielle, no. You don't . . ." Shutting her mouth on the rest of the warning, Xena followed. She arrived in time to find her friend waist-deep in a water-filled dip retrieving a frantic and soaked kitten.

Gabrielle looked up. "I think the bank gave way."

"On you or the kitten?" Xena's tone was dry as she hauled on an outstretched hand. "Go back to camp and get yourself and that creature dried off before you both get pneumonia." She glanced around at the banks before she left after them. No sign of any slip. And the banks sloped into the water. Why hadn't the animal climbed out again if it *had* fallen in. The night passed peacefully after that.

The next day was more walking. Supplies would be gone very soon at this rate. They needed to stop and find food. Xena slept after her watch and woke to find Gabrielle looking guilty as she cradled a very round-stomached kitten.

"What happened?"

"She didn't know. It was my fault. I should have watched her. She was just hungry."

Xena tipped out the bag. The last of the smoked fish and meat had vanished. Remaining still were the brine-soaked sausage and cheese. Clearly the kitten hadn't fancied the taste although small tooth-marks decorated the edges of both items, suggesting she'd sampled them in case.

"I'll go without. I made you bring her."

"I found rope and string at that cabin. I can set snares tonight." She eyed the defiant kitten. "If we get too hungry we can always eat that."

Gabrielle opened her mouth to protest, realized her friend was joking, and subsided.

The sausage and cheese are edible, but only just. They finished the last crumb around the fire that evening, after Xena had set her snares. Morning found empty snares and emptier stomachs. They walked most of the day, Gabrielle carrying the kitten, which made their day miserable with repeated wails for food they didn't have.

"We'll camp here."

"It's only afternoon."

"I need time to hunt. There may be something I can find, and I'll set snares again."

They both searched once they had settled on a campsite. There seemed to be nothing. No berries or nuts, no sign of anything edible. Here and there were traces of animals. But none looked recent. Once something moved. Xena pounced and stared down at her quarry. Fat lot of use that'd be to the three of them. At last, grimly, she set the snares and returned to the fire Gabrielle was tending. The kitten howled at her hopefully.

"Did you find anything?"

"Not really. But one of us can eat." She tossed the knife-impaled mouse corpse to the kitten and watched the baby fall on the meal with growling enthusiasm. "There's good water. Drink as much of that as you can. It'll help." Replete on mouse, the kitten came to curl into her lap. "I may as well take first watch. Nuisance here won't like being disturbed."

She settled herself, back against a tree, and watched as Gabrielle slept. At some stage the kitten rose and wandered off into the trees. Xena looked after it. "I'd suggest you stay there," she said very quietly. "Except Gabrielle would keep us here for days searching." Besides, they'd have been out of food by now even if the kitten hadn't stolen what they had. They needed to find food. Too many days walking without food on this deserted coast and they'd weaken. Gabrielle woke when her watch turn came.

"Where's the kitten?"

"Gone for a walk. She'll be back. Don't worry. If she gets into trouble, I'm sure she'll yell."

She rolled herself within the door curtain and slept. Gabrielle sat alertly, her ears listening for sounds of a kitten returning. When that happened there was no need to listen. It sounded like a cross between a cattle stampede and the infernal sound Picts made with something they called a musical instrument. Everyone else had other names for it. The women had heard one once and agreed with everyone else. Xena came out of her curtain in one leap. Gabrielle was on her feet already trying to decide where the sound was coming from.

That it was approaching was not in doubt. But the trees tended to deflect sounds, so direction was hard to determine. The women moved back to back just as a shrieking kitten shot into the clearing and up a tree. Hard on its furry heels came a large, irritable-looking boar. It paused beneath the tree to utter a few heartfelt threats. Then it observed it had company. It had no time for them either. It accelerated straight for Gabrielle, who dodged hastily behind the kitten's tree.

The boar ploughed through the fire, spun, and returned around it to where Xena waited. She leaped to one side and drove her sword into the joint between neck and shoulder. The beast faltered. The kitten chose that moment to fall out of the tree. It landed under the boar's nose. The boar slashed, the kitten skittered sideways. Gabrielle popped out from behind her tree, brought her staff down hard on the boar's skull, and vanished again. The animal's eyes rolled.

Xena stepped up from behind and to one side of the beast, raising her sword again. The kitten shot forward under her feet and Xena barely escaped tripping over it. The boar emitted a grunting roar, Gabrielle emerged again, seized the kitten, and Xena's sword came down. The boar fell over. Everyone sat down to recover, apart from the kitten, who was playing king of the castle on the enemy's body.

"Well, we have food." Gabrielle's tone was tentative.

"By a miracle." Her friend agreed. "It is also a miracle neither of us is dead along with that pig. If I didn't think it unlikely I'd say your kitten led him right to us." Xena eyed the bouncing kitten dubiously.

"Maybe she did. To say sorry that she ate our food. At least we eat now."

"It'll be tough, but beggars can't be choosers. I do have some salt left. Help me drag the carcass away a bit. I don't want blood all over the camp."

They skinned, gutted, and carved. Strips of roast boar proved surprisingly tasty. The kitten got her share raw, chopped for her into tiny scraps by Gabrielle. When they moved on a day later they carried enough meat to last several days. Xena planned to try fishing once the meat began to run out.

Once it did, they found the fishing wasn't bad. So long as they kept a very close eye on the kitten, who liked fish even more then they did. Gabrielle hooked the first one using a scrap of the boar, the string they'd found in the cabin, and a fishhook bent from a broach pin. She placed it behind her, returning to fish again. She hooked a second, went to put it with the first. Only to find the first fish was gone. Not that she had to look far.

She left the kitten with its prey and tucked the second, larger fish in her carry sack. It was quickly joined by a third and fourth. Xena emerged from the forest holding leaves pinned into a basket.

"Berries. How's the fishing?"

"Wonderful. I've got a couple of good-sized ones." She pointed at the carry sack. Xena looked inside.

"There's nothing here."

Gabrielle stood up. "That . . ." she followed the marks in the sand. Both fish had been too big for the kitten to carry, fortunately. At the end of the marks she found the kitten energetically hauling a fish along the beach. "Give me that. What did you do with the other one, you couldn't have eaten it."

From behind her Xena had begun to chuckle. "She didn't. Look here. She buried it. I think she planned to come back and collect it later." The kitten flung itself at the uncovered fish. Gabrielle stooped to pick it up and Xena seized the kitten by the scruff of its neck. "Listen. Friends share. You won't starve." Gabrielle giggled as the kitten was lectured. The baby appeared unrepentant. It still liked fish.

Days slid past as they traveled along the deserted coastline. Both women were beginning to wonder if the whole land was empty of people. There were plenty of fish, but the salt had run out and saltless fish is tasteless, even if filling. At the high-tide mark on the third day they found a hollow in some rocks. It had once been filled with sea water that had since evaporated. The hollow now held rather sandy salt. They scooped up every grain with care. But signs of life or not they kept up the night watch. Which was just as well. On the eleventh night after their arrival in this land, Gabrielle heard a sound. Her hand slipped out to touch Xena's shoulder. It was pressed in return.

From the dark three men came running. The fight was brief but ferocious. With two men down the third gave back. Xena pursued. She didn't want him following them for however long it took to find a settlement. He wove through the trees, running like a deer until she lost sight of him. Xena halted. It occured to her it was strange Gabrielle hadn't followed. In sudden fear she turned and raced back along the trail. Gabrielle was sitting white-faced by the fire, staff in hand.

"What's wrong?"

"I think I sprained my ankle. I fell over a tree root." She exhibited an already swollen ankle. Xena bit back a groan. Gabrielle was still talking. "I'm sure if I bind it tightly I'll be able to walk." Xena wasn't so sure but she kept silent. The kitten crept out of the dark and cuddled up. Gabrielle hugged it gently. "You can't say she brought that lot into camp this time."

"No, this time it was all their own idea."

They'd stay in camp a couple of days. After that she'd see if Gabby was all right.

Gabrielle wasn't. When it came time to walk the pain was so great she fainted. She recovered to find Xena cradling her, thinking.

"We'll have to stay here awhile longer. But we need food. Will you be all right here alone while I go down to the beach and catch fish?"

"Of course. We'll be fine." The kitten looked up and mewed as if in agreement. Xena found an unwilling grin stretching her mouth.

"You look after her, small one. I'll bring you a fish."

She trotted down the path, worrying as she went. They needed a horse, a pony, even a donkey would do. Something to carry Gabrielle until her ankle healed. She scanned the beach, then chose a rock jutting into deeper water. If she did well, there would be no need to leave her friend tomorrow.

At the camp, Gabrielle was drowsing when twigs snapped. She jerked upright—too late. A nicely judged blow smacked against the side of her head and everything blurred. Her hand dropped away from the staff. She saw a figure approaching, already unlacing hide breeches. She struggled to rise, to fight. The kitten jumped from her lap, dimly Gabrielle was aware of a yell of rage, footsteps crashing away into the trees. They did not return.

She came fully conscious again sometime later. Her head hurt but that was all the injury she had. The kitten was sitting beside her purring. How much of those events had she dreamed? She heard footsteps returning and reached for her staff before Xena came into view.

"I got five, all good fish. I won't have to . . ." her voice broke off as soon as she got a look at the camp. "What happened, are you hurt? Your head is bleeding." Even as she questioned she was kneeling to examine the cut. "Not serious. I'll clean that and salve it. It'll be fine. You didn't try walking and fall, did you?"

Gabrielle shook her head, gasping as the headache stabbed. "No, that man came back. The third one who got away last time. He hit me. I can't remember properly after that. He yelled as if he was angry, then he ran off, it sounded as if he was chasing something. He didn't come back."

"He didn't . . . ?"

"No, he was going to but whatever happened happened before he did."

Xena shut her eyes briefly. Thanks be to whatever had saved her friend. She busied herself in silence cutting up fish to bake in embers. Gabrielle leaned back, concentrating on persuading the headache to go away. The kitten concentrated on the fish, purring when she was given a whole small one to herself. With that eaten she scurried into the trees. She had something urgent to do.

She was gone almost the entire night but wandered back at dawn. With her came a horse. A short-backed, stocky animal without saddle or bridle. It was unshod, a sort of medium bay in color.

"Who do you think it belongs to?" asked Gabrielle.

"No idea," Xena said cheerfully. "But it'll carry you to a settlement. Once we get there we can let it go. The owner may find it."

She broke camp, boosted Gabrielle and the kitten onto the broad back, and with a length of rope about the horse's neck led it off down the shore. A godsend finding a horse out here, just when they needed one. She didn't like the way Gabrielle breathed. That blow on the head and lying on the cold ground until she came to had given the girl a fever. Xena pushed the horse, finally getting up behind her friend and riding as well so they could make better time. The animal was becoming lame when, two days later, they walked into signs that a farmstead was near.

A long time ago one of Xena's men had been a man of the north. She could speak enough of the language to have the horse shod. Clearly the beast had never worn shoes before, but the smith was used to that and the horse was given no option despite vigorous resistance. There was no other mount to be had but they could buy supplies now and a small amount of fever drink. Xena paid with a silver penny from the belt pouch she had looted. Then they rode on. Three days more and they reached the outskirts of a large settlement.

At the edge of a rise Xena slowed the horse. She slid from its back, tethered it, and made camp back inside a screen of brush. Then she spoke.

"Stay here with your friend. I'll get more medicine for that fever. Once you're well again we can ride in and take passage out of here."

The fever drink was easily obtained, enough of it for several doses. Xena rode back on the weary horse, left him enough rope to graze, and turned to Gabrielle with the herbs. They worked quickly enough. By the end of the next day the fever was gone and the girl's strength was returning. Xena left her long enough to ride back into the settlement. The ship she'd heard talk of was in. Readying for the passage back across the seas to Albion. She made arrangements.

At the camp Gabrielle was up packing and chatting to the kitten. "You'll like it where we're going." She scooped up the small furry body and mounted the horse. Slowly, with Xena walking beside, they made their way down to the beach. "When will the ship be here?"

"In the morning." The kitten dropped over the horse's shoulder. It appeared to vanish as small paws touched the sand. Under Gabrielle the horse twisted. The shape shortened in body and legs and a startled Gabrielle abruptly found herself sitting astride the back of a naked man. She vaulted hastily away. He attempted to rise and howled. From where the women stood they could see the horseshoes securely nailed to his palms and feet. Both women recognized the missing attacker. Xena's sword lifted.

From one side someone cleared their throat. "I thought it only fitting. He wished to ride you. Instead it was he who was ridden." She chuckled softly. "Go well, I will find a smith for this one. I think he would be rid of his shoes." Both women spun to stare.

Nearby stood a tall powerful woman. Blond hair flowed past her shoulders in thick, glistening plaits that reached to the ground. She wore silvered armor and at her side was sheathed a gem-hilted sword.

Xena nodded politely. "You were the kitten, Why?"

"One cursed you in my name. I came to see if the curse should bind. I saw. You are of my kind, battle daughters. Ferocious in war, large in heart toward the weak. Your ship will come with the dawn." She extended her hand toward Gabrielle, who took it. The long fingers traced a rune on the back of the small calloused hand. "Let the captain see that." She whistled softly. From the sky, a chariot came slanting down, drawn by large cats. One winked at them. A wave of her hand and the man was flung aboard. "Go with my favor, battle daughters. A following sea and a fair wind." The chariot faded upward.

Gabrielle stared after her. "Who was that?"

"Freya, I think. At least we're rid of that kitten. In the morning we can get out of here, our own gods are bad enough." She grinned. "Although I don't think I've ever seen anything sillier than you sitting on that man—unless it was the look on your face when he changed." They were still giggling weakly when the ship arrived.

THE HUNGRY LAND

Mary Morgan

Gabrielle tried to wake up. She knew that she slept, but this dream had gone far enough. In it, she dreamt that the earth had softened beneath her and she was starting to sink. The soil covered her face grain by grain. In panic, she opened her mouth to call for her friend, and drew in a breath. Earth flooded in. She gagged on the dirt, and the noise that she made must have awakened her partner. Still trapped in the dream, she saw Xena rouse and walk over to watch while the earth covered her eyes, while it drowned her. But this was only a dream: she knew that. Very few of her dreams were prophetic. So why was she frightened?

Gabrielle woke. Something hissed in her ears, and her neck ached. Carmine blotches floated in front of her eyes. She rubbed at their lids with her fingers. These felt cold; their skin was like ice and was rough with fine grit from the ground they had rested against. Wary, she opened her eyes. The sun shone full in her face, though it had failed to warm the rock she was leaning against. Hours must have passed. "Trust me. I've dozed off again," she thought with embarrassment. "Just sit down to rest while I wait for Xena, close my eyes for a minute and I'm away," she taunted herself.

Though it was hardly surprising. She had been sleeping badly, here on the plateau, waking exhausted and plagued by a nagging anxiety. Three nights in all, each troubled by dreams. And she'd been dreaming just now. As she realized this, Gabrielle felt her heart falter, then quicken. "I'm terrified," she thought with amazement. "But of what?"

She reached for a water skin, to sluice the foul taste of her doze from her mouth, and looked around her. So there was nothing to see but rocks scoured by the wind, hollows scabbed by gray patches of snow. She'd seen worse. So most of the provisions had gone. They'd survive, even Argo. So Xena had been strangely determined to take this route, although it was plainly out of their way. And so now she had gone on ahead, scouting, she said, though she'd sounded impatient when she'd told her to wait and to rest. So her partner was late. She'd be back, perhaps with a rabbit or two. So there'd been dreams. Gabrielle stopped: she couldn't remember the dreams. Just the fear. It struck her again, so hard that she sucked in her breath. Cold air scorched her lungs and made her eyes water.

Then she heard hoofbeats. Argo returning: she knew the mare's gait, and there was no one else foolish enough to be up here. She stood up and saw Xena, riding with negligent ease, her face dour. But her partner was pleased. Even this far away, Gabrielle knew what that scowl covered. Relief. Even elation. "Now what?" she asked herself, and then waved. Deep inside, her fear snickered knowingly. She ignored it, focused on Xena, who now towered above her. When the warrior, wordless, reached down a hand, Gabrielle took it, let herself be hauled into the saddle. "Let's see what she's found," Gabrielle thought. A new feeling flowered inside her, and she knew it by name. A sense of foreboding.

Xena rode for two hours, angling north, away from their trail. Noon came and went. The sun, chill and white in the sky, slipped over her shoulder, threw their shadows under their feet. Xena pushed Argo hard, Gabrielle saw with surprise. The mare's coat had darkened with sweat, her sides worked like bellows. "Hey," she said softly, then tried again, pressing harder round the warrior's waist to get her attention.

"Patience, you'll see soon enough," Xena said.

"No hurry. There's plenty of time. Give Argo a break." She felt Xena take a quick breath and then shift. Her friend's knuckles briefly showed white as she pulled on the reins. Argo slowed and then stopped. Xena waited while Gabrielle slid to the ground, then swung down herself with consummate grace.

"Sorry, Argo." Xena reached down a skin, poured water into her hand, then rubbed it over the mare's muzzle. "What was I thinking?" she said to herself. She filled a cupped palm with more water and let Argo drink.

Gabrielle, watching, felt the fear flare once again, and silently echoed the question.

They reached it soon after. Gabrielle gasped when she saw. "It's so lovely," she said, when she'd recovered her breath. Words rose in a swarm in her brain. Numbly, she sorted them out. The land fell away into a crater that stretched past the horizon. The air rising from it was hazy, as though it were heated. It swelled into a dome that quivered and shook. Where it moved, rainbows crawled over its skin. When she looked down, she saw green. Cushioned and vibrant, a pelt of lush green.

"Come on." Xena's face shocked her, it was so flushed. "Race you there." The warrior turned, ready to plunge down the slope into the forest below through a gap in the rocks rimming the crater.

"Wait." Gabrielle swallowed, tasting fear once again. What was going on here? A forest? Here on this plateau with its fuzz of thin moss and its pools capped with crazed layers of ice? "Something's wrong."

"What's wrong?" Xena turned. "Just once in a while, can't you leave out the pros and the cons? This is a gift, and you know what they say about gifts."

Gabrielle did, though the horse she thought of was Trojan. "It's well off our route," was the best she could do by way of objection. Everything else just sounded plain daft.

"It's north of our route, but we can still bear due west. And take a break. Hunt, make good our supplies. There'll be plenty of prey down there." Xena flung out her hand, palm slightly cupped, forefinger pointing. "A conqueror's gesture," Gabrielle thought. The sort they gave statues. She tried to muster her doubts, but her partner abruptly got tired of talking, pivoted round on her heel, and bounded away down the path.

"Yes, there'll be plenty of prey down there. Now." Gabrielle flinched at the thought, wondering where it had come from. Her head was starting to swim. The rocks looked like teeth, which meant that the path was a throat, waiting to swallow. She shuddered. This place repelled her, but Xena was down there, in the trees' shadow. Gabrielle straightened her shoulders and wrapped Argo's reins round one of her hands. Defeated but dogged, she followed her partner, leading the mare, sinking into the crater.

The sun shone strongly in her dream. If she looked directly over her head she could see a blue sky. All around, though, the forest grew. She turned slowly, taking it in. Bark glowed like copper, leaves hung like slices of emerald. Huge flowers seemed to float without weight, carved from ruby and amethyst, from topaz and pearl. Lovely but armored, Gabrielle thought; each surface here would gash or bruise or pierce. A feeling blossomed inside her and rose in her throat. As it did so, the world started to spin. At first she thought she must have grown dizzy, but she soon saw the truth. The forest was moving around her. The shapes of the trees had all changed. Limbs crooked at their joints, straightened again, twitched and scuttled. Leaves became wings that unfurled, jewelled on the surface, dusty beneath. Compound eyes flickered shut and then opened, focused on her, judging the distance. As the forest swept down, she choked on the fear in her throat.

Why was she so tired? Gabrielle hoisted herself to her feet and reached for her share of the gear, meaning to pack it.

When she swayed, Xena looked over her shoulder from where she stood saddling Argo. "Sit down, Gabrielle."

Gabrielle looked at her closely, then sat down. Cold

coiled inside her: Xena's face had been blank. Perhaps there was nothing behind it, but Gabrielle trusted her instincts with Xena. She knuckled her eyes. "What would be worse? To make a mess of her chores, or to uselessly keep out of the way? Whichever she did, Xena would secretly fume." She stayed put and considered the previous day.

It had been hot. Perhaps that was why she had felt so wretched. And the air here was so thick. It clogged her lungs, shimmered with insects, was heavy with pollen. Trying to see through it strained her eyes. Anything farther than a few paces away seemed to lie behind water, or glass. Then, this path was so tricky to follow. It wound through the forest and was easy to miss. Roots writhed across it, making for treacherous footing. Branches and briars snaked into her path, snagging her hair and her skin.

Xena strode through all this. Where Gabrielle stumbled and doubted the path, Xena trod it down as if on a conqueror's road strewn with petals. She'd left the mare with the bard and pushed on ahead. From the bounce in the warrior's stride, Gabrielle knew that Xena would have chosen to walk whatever the state of the trail. She plainly loved it; the motion, the pace, the play of her muscles as they took on and vanquished the trail. She even defeated its shadows. Up ahead, where these lay thickest, they seemed to surrender to Xena's black hair and dark armor so that she grew ever taller and stronger.

Gabrielle had tired long before dusk. She had stopped for a moment, meaning to call out to Xena, but her partner had gone round a bend in the track. Sighing, thrusting a hand through her hair which was matted with sweat, the bard had moved on, trying to blank out the ache that burned in her muscles, her sides. She thought back with regret to the plateau, its clear, icy air, and lifted an arm to sweep sweat from her brow. Trickles dripped into her eyes, making them sting. Vision blurred, she had rounded the corner and seen with relief that Xena was squatting a handful of strides up ahead. Green light shone in a circle around her, water lapped at her feet. A glade with a stream, somewhere to camp for the night, Xena said.

There were fish in the stream, but though she'd felt hun-

gry before, Gabrielle ate little. The fish had tasted like mush
on her tongue, and she was exhausted. She'd kept dozing
off, only to have Xena nudge her awake. The third time,
Xena gave up. "You can eat what's left in the morning,
when you feel better," she had said, taking the platter out
of her hands. "Now let's see to these."

Gabrielle had looked down when she said that, at her
arms, at her legs folded beneath her. They were covered
with scratches, most shallow and beaded with droplets of
blood, but some deep. She'd been vaguely surprised because
she'd not felt them. Now she watched Xena moisten a rag
and dab at the wounds. She was taking her time, but Gabrielle sensed that she felt ill at ease. The bard flinched when
she realized this, and Xena winced in response. All the
same, she did not move any closer, but still kneeled only
just within reach.

And this morning? Things had been worse. Food choked
her, while Xena kept even more distance between them. Gabrielle read rage in her partner, and impatience, both barely
tamped down. "She will leave me," she thought in despair,
but good sense denied it. "She loves me. She'll find a way."
Thinking this, although she'd been up for scarcely an hour,
she felt sleep steal upon her, and the first, smothering touch
of a dream.

*The ground that she lay on was hot, getting hotter. A desert?
She opened her eyes, saw sand stretch in every direction.
But there were rocks here and there, and in their shade,
drifts of snow. She stood, and an icy wind slashed at her
skin. She wrapped her arms round her waist, pulled them
tight. Only the soles of her feet still felt warm. She looked
down. The ground was dimpling, was sifting, seemed pim-
pled and cracked. Out of the cracks and the pits, tiny black
shapes heaved themselves up, many legged, scrabbling for
purchase. They tottered and staggered, spread limp, dragging rags, which soon dried. Stretching these, the ants
swarmed and swirled, filled the sky. It turned the color of
milk, shot through with rainbows. Though Gabrielle covered
her face, she felt the insects invade her, clogging nostril and*

mouth. When she screamed, they filled her chest and consumed her.

Xena kicked out the fire and smoothed soil over its remains. Through the mist, she could make out the sun's disk as it rose over the trees. "It will be a hot day," she thought. Another hot day. She shivered, feeling hairs rise all over her skin, and a jolt of excitement ran down her spine from her neck to her tailbone. But these conditions were taking it out of her partner, slowing Gabrielle's steps, draining her strength and her normal high spirits. Xena looked over to where Gabrielle was still sitting. The bard had fallen asleep again, her head lolling forward, her hands lying limp, palm up in her lap.

Xena walked over to squat down beside her, and gave her shoulder a vigorous shake. "Wake up now," she was saying as Gabrielle's eyes flickered and finally opened. "It's time to start out."

"Oh." Gabrielle blinked. Embarrassment colored her skin, masked her unusual pallor. "Sorry. Must have dozed off." She got to her feet, reaching out to steady herself. Then she snatched her hands back. "Xena?"

The warrior fought to relax. What was this? Had she stiffened when Gabrielle touched her? "What is it with me?" she enquired of herself. "Just now, had she wanted to kick Gabrielle awake? And last night?" She closed her eyes briefly, remembering how moisture had flooded her mouth, how her skin had grown hot as she swabbed away blood, how she had wanted to lick it. She shuddered, disgusted. Aloud she said, "I wish I could give you a rest day, but we have to keep going." She reached out herself, was relieved when her fingers made contact with Gabrielle's skin easily, willingly, with no pricklings of distaste. "That's more like it," she told herself. "Must be this place. It's getting to me."

"The sooner we're out of here the better," she said aloud to Gabrielle, as the bard stretched, then joined her in walking toward the mare.

"Yeah. What is it with this place? Why haven't we seen a single living thing except insects and trees?" Gabrielle scuffed her toe in the dirt and looked around her, scowling.

Xena looked, too. The land opened up for a while and the path smoothed. She could ride Argo. She swung herself up, surveying what lay around her. She still couldn't see far. Trees all around, and where there were none, brush and grasses sprang up, some as high as her head. And all this was up here, on this high, freezing plateau. Yes, something was wrong, but she couldn't say what. So she shrugged, and offered no other answer.

The bard went on talking anyway, softly, as though she was thinking things out for herself. "It's so overwhelming. Like it's in a fever. And it seems to be, well, so defensive." She kept pace with the warrior, planting her staff firmly into the ground, swinging her feet in a steady rhythm.

"Almost the old Gabrielle." Xena let herself smile, just a quirk of her lips, and just for an instant.

"No," the bard said, even more softly, "not defensive. It's aggressive. Ferocious." She took a few more strides.

Xena glanced down at her partner. Now and then, the reddish gold hair flipped back a little. She saw an arc of pale cheek, streaked with dust. When Gabrielle was quiet her mouth was shut tight. Little lines pinched its corner, a deeper one tracked up to her nose. Her skin shone with sweat. She kept her eyes down, on her feet. "I should stop," Xena thought. "Should make her ride Argo, at least." Worry ruffled the surface of what she felt for her bard, and she nearly leaned down, wanting to smooth back Gabrielle's hair, soothe her skin.

Then a sudden gust of impatience overtook her. "Weakling," she heard her own voice whisper inside her head. "That's all she is. Why tie yourself down?" Shocked, seared with shame, she rammed her heels inward. Argo leapt straight into a gallop. "I'll scout ahead," she made herself shout back over her shoulder. But even while she raced away from the bard, something inside her expanded, spread its wings with delight.

Soon she kneed Argo north, leaving the track. When the mare balked, blinded by grasses, she hammered her sides with her heels, driving her on. Foam spattered her legs before long, but she kept up the pace. The world was a tawny tunnel of heat that turned here and turned there, shooting her through it. She laughed out aloud, wanting never to stop.

Then she came to a river, and had to, though she ached to go on. For a moment, she thought that she could, and leant forward. But Argo tossed up her head, danced to one side, whinnied and snorted. Xena leapt from the saddle and ran up to the bank, thrusting her hand in the water, scooping it up, splashing it over her face. At her side, Argo stepped up. Remembering barely in time, she grabbed a rein, made sure that the mare took her drink slowly.

At length Xena calmed, looked around. She could see the forest started again on the farther bank, and that, since the river curved to the north, they need not cross it. She felt disappointed, and watched the river sweep by. It was in full spate, tossing tree trunks, swirling them round in its currents. Xena knew how it felt, and feeling the same she plunged in. Once over, she nearly did not return, nearly pressed on at a run into the forest. She knew she could keep going forever, make endless demands on her body, stay drunk on its heady response.

At this moment something jumped in the river, falling back with a splash. Alert, she turned back to its waters, saw the tiny commotion again. Trout. Her partner loved trout. Xena grinned, stepped into the waters, snagged herself supper for two. She swam back briskly, vaulted on Argo, then turned to go. "Tamed and house trained," her voice sneered at herself. "Don't you want to be free?" She shut her ears and rode back.

Gabrielle was still walking. From a distance Xena watched the small figure toil through its own dust. Something smote her, and she heard herself grunt in reaction. She rode down to the bard, who stopped and looked up at her, white-faced and panting. Xena sighed, then swung her up.

"I'm okay. Argo can't manage two in this heat," Gabrielle said after her breathing had steadied. It had taken some time. Her voice was burred with exhaustion.

"Rest." Xena was curt. She tried to soften her voice. "We'll all manage." She felt the small woman relax, felt her own tenseness start to grow slack. Impatience gripped her, a desire to be up and be running. Then Gabrielle's head settled into her shoulder as she slipped into sleep and the warrior could wrench back control of her feelings. "What's going on?" Xena asked herself. "Why do I never get tired, while she just gets weaker?" But the only voice that replied mocked her for betraying her strength by caring for weakness. Fighting it left her tired, after all.

In this dream, she woke to the sensation of being smothered again. I must be under the ground, the bard thought groggily, and tried to move her arms, to fight against whatever confined her. Touch told her, as well as the green light filtering in when she opened her eyes, that instead she was wrapped in thick, sappy vines. Heavy odors wafted from flowers whose vermilion petals drooped and lapped at her face. They had some darker fluid running through their veins. She had been left there: perhaps she had even been bound. She felt sick with fear, and with desolation. Choking, she bit at a stem that seemed to be trying to force its way into her mouth. Something that tasted like copper flowed over her tongue. A red spray spurted out, blotching her skin and everything in sight. "Blood," she thought. "My blood."

Xena watched Gabrielle. Light from their fire's dying embers flushed the face of her partner, making the sweat glimmer. What had she muttered just now? Something about blood? Xena shivered. It was the second night now. While Gabrielle had barely woken since yesterday, the warrior had not slept at all. Hours ago she had made a fire, prepared tea and some food, forced a little into the bard, all the time fidgeting, longing to be somewhere else, anywhere else. Once Gabrielle had stopped chewing, had fallen asleep again as she sat there, Xena had barely taken the time to settle her down on her blanket before striding off.

For a time, her desire to be moving had contented itself with circling their camp, but this didn't last long. She had felt like a horse on a lunging line, goaded into a gallop, but forced to stay always in the same place. She had made another circuit, then another, then suddenly, helplessly, had given way, had raced off, back along the way they had come. Scorning the track and its bends, she had plunged straight through the forest. Not so long after she reached the rim of stones that bordered this unsettling land, having raised barely a sweat.

Now she was back, and still not at all tired. She was stronger if anything. But she was very afraid. What had she been thinking of? Not Gabrielle, not for a second during that run. Nor of herself, but only of running; of being free. She looked down at the bard. It would be so easy to leave her. To just turn around and disappear into the forest. "But she'll die here," she whispered, to no one.

"Then spare her that misery," someone replied, and her hand curled and strayed, hovered over her sword hilt. "That way you'll be free." Yes, she'd be part of the forest, and free. She clenched her hand, stared at the fist she had made. Then Gabrielle shifted, twisted uneasily, and moaned. Old habit made Xena start forward and reach out a hand.

The moment it touched the younger woman's hair, swept a strand off her forehead, her hand knew. It could no more cut off itself than harm Gabrielle. This steadied Xena. She rested her knuckles lightly on her partner's cheek, and hissed at the heat she could feel. The bard was burning up. Fetching her water skin, wetting a rag, she wiped Gabrielle's face gently, concentrating on the task, on the fact of Gabrielle's presence, and her need.

Gabrielle moaned again, muttered indistinct words, though Xena thought she heard her name. Then the bard groaned, twisted round, lashed out with her hands. Xena caught them, held them down. "Wake up, Gabrielle. Wake up. It's only a dream." She said this again and again, and though it calmed the bard she did not awake. Xena grew afraid she never would. In the first light of dawn, she realized the bard's eyes had opened, and met Gabrielle's feverish gaze. "Help me, Xena." Her voice was dry and frail, like a dead leaf. "I can't wake up."

In her dream, she was watching Xena run. The warrior ran endlessly, tirelessly, racing through dense stands of trees as though tracing wide avenues, not threading narrow paths. She saw her, it seemed, from every direction at once. As though she were a leaf on one of the trees Xena ran past, as though she were moss on a stone Xena's foot touched.

Repletion swelled all around. Something had been excited, something was being sated. The land gathered itself, ripened, grew more. Gabrielle realized she knew this because she was the land. Because she had been eaten alive by the land.

Xena readied Argo, strapping on their packs swiftly. She fondled the mare's ears. "Follow us," she whispered into the nearest, hoping the mare could. Then she turned back to Gabrielle, lifted her into her arms. The bard's eyes were closed once more. She lay quietly. Xena, dipping her head, could hardly make out a heartbeat. Panic rose inside her, but she squashed it. With Gabrielle in her arms, she started to run.

The forest thickened before her. Trees stood against her, lashing out limbs, flailing roots. She ran on, dodging and turning, surefooted in spite of its tricks. Then it changed its tactics, cajoled her, bled more of its strength into her, trying to drug her, whispering, "Be one with me, share my strength." She tapped into that strength, fed it into her muscles, gripped the bard tighter, ran still faster. It tried to deceive her, turned the trail back on itself, meaning to swallow them both. "West is there," she said to herself, and forged her way to it.

When the land started to rise, she knew she was near to the border. "Almost out," she breathed to her partner. "Hang in there." The slope became steep, and then steeper. Xena's feet slipped in soft soil and she slowed, looked around for bare rock and then made her way to it. She'd feel safer with that under her feet. She checked Gabrielle, feeling her pulse fast and faint under her fingers. Anger flared, and she lifted the bard, settling her over her shoulder. After that, using one hand and her feet, she climbed to the lip of the crater.

There were stones on this side as well, tall and white. She started toward them, expecting to pass them in seconds, for the slope leveled off here, becoming a rim of black soil. But she couldn't get near them. One step, a second, then her feet rooted themselves in the earth. Light dimmed and time slowed. Her heart beat at her temples, shook her bones, which yearned to be free of her flesh. Gabrielle's weight bore her down and she sank to her knees, settling the bard on the ground just before herself. Then she looked up at the sky and she screamed.

"You can't leave," the voice whispered to her when she was done and could hear it. "You're already part of the forest. You soaked in its strength. It's part of you now." She stiffened as something behind her opened its mouth, prepared to engulf them. Xena sobbed. She looked at her partner's white face. "Turn round and come back," she heard in her head. "Be rid of your burden. Savor your conquest." Its laughter mocked her.

Xena stopped fighting the forest, allowed its raw strength to race through her. Her thoughts gathered power, ignited in starbursts of flame. Through the dazzling eruption, she spotted a possible way. "I'll give it conquest." She drew out her sword. "It's revolted by weakness. Let it have what it wants." She tightened her grip on the hilt. "Feed it. Distract it." She brought the sword down, watched it part flesh, watched the blood spurt and soak into the ground.

Summer began on the slopes of the plateau. Grass grew in patches down here, fine bladed and sweet, dotted with gentians and rock rose. Argo sniffed it and pranced like a filly, then rolled on the sward. In sheltered corries juniper dozed, blue green in the sunlight. Rowan trees rooted in clefts in the rock, colonised gullies above tumbling streams. Lower down silver birch clustered, striping the ground with their shadows.

Gabrielle observed this intently. It helped to dispel the chill wisps of dream that still clung around her. These accused her, showing her winter come to the land high above, mists settling as frosts overnight and fuming as fog in the mornings, ice slicking the ponds. At night it was harder to fight them. Then she saw fungi dry to a crust and collapse into powder, grasses bleach and wither, rattle and snap in the wind, leaves brown and shiver, die and fall. "She did it for you," the land claimed in her dreams. "It's your fault." Gabrielle would shudder and wake, afraid that it was.

In a grove by a pool near the base of the plateau, Xena sat, perfectly still and staring at nothing. A breeze scented

with wood smoke startled the face of the pool, making it
flinch, and stirring her hair as it passed. Gabrielle saw her
push the strands back. Then the bard turned her attention
back to their fire. Now that the water was hot, she could
make tea. Steam drifted up from the cup and she sniffed at
it, frowning. She picked up a small package and peeled back
the wrapping. The comb that emerged was still brimming
with honey, and she drizzled some into the tea. That was
better, she thought, scratching her arm. Two angry, red
mounds showed what she had paid to the bees.

She let the tea cool, just a little, then walked over and
settled herself down by her partner, glancing up at Xena's
face. "Here." She held out the cup. When Xena didn't react,
she said, mildly, "It'll get cold."

The warrior roused herself. She reached out for the cup,
and sniffed at it, then raised it to her lips. She took a small
sip, then another. Holding her peace, Gabrielle waited till
she had finished the tea, then leaned over and took the cup
back.

Xena glanced at her. "Did you get stung?" she asked.

Gabrielle displayed her arm. "Cheap at the price." She
awarded her partner a cheerful grin.

Xena studied the stings, then her face. "Thanks." Her face
relaxed a little. After a moment, stiffly, she returned Gabrielle's grin.

The bard leaned back into her briefly, then turned matter
of fact. "So let's change that dressing. Okay?"

Xena rose and went back to the fire, where she watched
Gabrielle assemble a bowl of hot water and some cloths.
When that was done, she presented her arm. Taking her
time, Gabrielle undid the knot, then unwrapped the bandage,
damping the innermost layers. She took a deep breath just
before she pulled them away. The wound had been deep.
She remembered its puffy, wet lips, glistening red just below
the rag that Xena had used as a tourniquet.

But once the cloth was clear, she sighed with relief.
Xena's familiar magic had asserted itself once again. The
wound looked cool, the flesh around it healthy. A mere two
days, and the thing was nearly healed. Gabrielle examined
her neat little stitches carefully as she bathed them, sorting

her thoughts. Xena's arm was okay: now, what about Xena? How could she get her to talk?

In the end, she just said what had burned on her tongue from the moment she woke safely outside the forest. "Would you rather have stayed?" When Xena said nothing, she felt her eyes prick and then water. "Some help you're going to be," she railed at herself, appalled by her doubt and her fears. She kept her head down and felt tears slide down her cheeks, wanting to wipe them away, but hoping the warrior would not notice.

She was aware first of Xena's fingers, gently catching her tears. Then her voice. "The only thing I was sure I wanted, was to stay with you," Xena was saying.

Gabrielle felt herself smile and looked up, to share it. But there was still more to be said. "Do you feel you've left something behind?" she probed gently.

Xena's eyes went inward. "No." Then she dropped her hand, locked it tight in her other. "That's why I'm afraid, Gabrielle."

Gabrielle leaned in as close as she could, wrapping her hands around Xena's. "Tell me," she coaxed.

"I'm afraid that I brought out what I went in with, and that it poisoned that place. That what happened was me." Now she was weeping.

Gabrielle tightened her grasp. "Say something," she screamed at herself, "say something to mend this." She felt Xena shake, and draw a deep breath, muscles tensing, ready to move. "She'll run away, just to save you. You've got to stop this."

The words rose to her tongue without thought. "You brought us all out. Argo, and me, and yourself. It's you who saved us."

"I put you at risk." Xena kept her eyes on their hands, but stayed still. "The darkness inside me felt at home in that place. And I didn't leave it behind me. I wanted to cut it out. When I gave the forest back what it had given me, I was trying to do that as well. But I couldn't."

Gabrielle remembered the depth of the cut, and shuddered. "No. That place was the risk. Not you. I felt it before we even got there. So did you." She loosed one hand, used it to grasp Xena's jaw, raise her head. Once Xena was look-ing back at her, was paying attention, she said, "If you had left anything there, I'd go back to get it. Understand?" She surprised herself with her fierceness.

Xena's eyes widened. "Gabrielle," she said softly. "How can you say that?"

"I mean it." Gabrielle made herself pause. This was too important to rush. "You're not a good side and a dark side, Xena. You're not two people, a good one and a bad one. What you are is someone who has conquered your darkness, like you conquered that land. You wouldn't be you without it."

She watched Xena take each word, consider it carefully. When she was sure her partner was ready, she added, "And I love you. All of you." And then held her breath.

Xena said nothing for a moment. Instead she smiled, widely. Then she asked, "How about a new dressing?" She lifted the arm with the wound, raised an eyebrow, managed to look rather like Argo demanding a treat.

Gabrielle remembered to breathe. When she knew that she could, she replied, "Okay. Hold still."

Under Xena's incredulous eyes, she reached for the comb, dripping honey on a scrap of clean cloth.

"You planning a bear hunt?" Xena asked. "With me as bait?"

"You remember the healer in that last village? She told me about this. Said it stopped infections and made the dress-ing easier to take off later. I've been wanting to try it." Gabrielle looked up, realized that Xena had snatched back her arm. "Humor me." She grinned. "It's not as though you couldn't handle a bear or two, after all."

"I prefer it in tea," Xena grumbled. But she lowered her arm, held it out.

"There," Gabrielle said, when she had finished. "All done. Who knows, perhaps we've made medical history here."

Xena examined her arm, then her friend. "Xena: warrior guinea pig?" Her voice sounded injured.

Gabrielle chuckled, then, suddenly unsure of herself, dropped her eyes. "I should have asked you first." She tried for a lighter tone. "I needn't put it in the story."

Xena placed a hand on each of Gabrielle's shoulders, dipping her head till her brow touched the bard's. "Nah," she said. "We're in this together."

HOMECOMING

Gary A. Braunbeck

AND

Lucy A. Snyder

It was a perfect evening; the twilight was achingly gorgeous, clouds of delicate purples and reds and oranges framed the dying sun, and on the opposite side of the sky the moon was rising in a silvery crescent; the cool Achaean breeze was filled with the scent of wild jasmine, and the only sounds were the pine needles crackling beneath Argo's hooves and the quiet creak of the saddle and Xena's leather armor. Gabrielle wished she could freeze time and hold the evening in her mind forever.

Indeed, evenings did not come any more lovely or peaceful than this.

So this feeling probably won't last much longer, thought Gabrielle. *It never does.*

As if the gods didn't want to disappoint her, that was the moment Something Happened.

A low rumbling thunder rippled through the clearing sky. The air was suddenly electric, and the hairs on the back of Gabrielle's arms rose as her body was washed in chill. The rumble rose and rose until the ground practically shook, and

Gabrielle finally saw it: a shooting star. The meteor flamed bright as it tore across the sky, coming closer and closer.

Xena whispered an oath, her eyes widening at the sight.

Argo whinnied and reared in fright.

"Steady, steady, girl!" Xena slid out of the saddle and reigned in her scared steed.

"Xena, it's coming right for us—" Gabrielle said, looking frantically around for something to hide behind.

The meteor screamed as it fell earthward in a steep angle. The green tops of the tall pines nearby ignited as the star's fiery corona grazed them, and both Xena and Gabrielle were knocked flat by the sudden blast of sound and heat and an incredible boom as the earth jolted and the meteor smashed into the ground a hundred yards away and drove forward with a might to rival the wrath of the gods.

Then it was over. Gabrielle climbed to her feet with the aid of her staff and stared at the charred, ten-foot-wide track the meteor had gouged through the forest. Her knees felt rubbery as she realized precisely how close they'd just come to dying.

"Is it a good omen or a bad omen that that thing almost killed us?" Gabrielle tried to make it sound like a joke, but her voice was shaking far too badly.

Xena was petting Argo and whispering reassurances in the horse's ear. The poor beast was shivering, but slowly calming down.

"I always take survival as a good omen," Xena said. She paused, staring at the charred track. "We should go see if anyone was less fortunate than us."

Gabrielle followed as Xena began to lead her horse toward the track. "I don't see how anyone could have survived if they were caught in the path of that thing."

"If they didn't survive, they'll need a decent burial. And I want to find that meteor. M'Lila once told me that the iron from a fallen star makes a far finer sword than any earthly metal." Xena drew her sword and examined the edge with a critical eye. "This blade has served me well, but it's got some deep nicks. I know a good swordsmith in Amphipolis who owes me some work."

"Everyone you know owes you something," muttered Gabrielle.

"And what's wrong with that?"

"Nothing—if you're a tax collector. No wonder people are always trying to kill you."

"What's life without friends?" replied Xena as they made their way toward the impact site.

The charred ground crunched beneath their boots. Fortunately, none of the fires started by the fallen star had spread; the forest was green and the ground well-soaked from recent spring rains. The track continued for another mile, and in the dying light they finally saw it: a flattened, silver egg that was a little smaller than one of the great elephants Gabrielle had seen in the traveling animal shows from Egypt. The egg, which was mostly buried in the earth it had plowed into, was covered in strange hieroglyphs. It was cracked down the middle, and a blue light glowed through the finger-wide fracture.

"That doesn't look like any fallen star I've ever heard of," Xena said.

Gabrielle heard a baby's frightened wail. The tiny voice was faint and strangely distorted; it didn't sound entirely human.

"Did you hear that?" Gabrielle asked, feeling oddly dizzy.

"Hear what?"

Gabrielle heard the cry again, though she couldn't quite make out where the voice was coming from. It was almost as if she heard it inside her own head. She stepped up to the egg and put her hands against the silvery shell. The metal was still hot, but not too hot to touch.

"Gabriel, don't touch that—"

"I think there's . . . there's a baby inside! We need to get him out."

She stuck the butt of her staff into the crack and began to lever the crack open wider. "Can you help with this?"

Xena joined her and together the two women pulled and pried at the crack in the egg. The metal shell gave way with a groan. The two halves rocked apart, shimmered, then collapsing into twinkling motes of stardust.

There on the ground lay an extraordinarily homely infant

swaddled in a fine, gray cloth. The baby's skin was a deep, mottled blue, and his head was topped with a fuzz of shocking red hair. His eyes were black as ripe olives.

Gabrielle knelt and picked up the baby. The moment she touched him, her mind was filled with a kaleidoscope of images:

The terror of birth. Angry voices, accusations, fear. A quiet place, Mother's whisper: *Don't worry little one, I'll send you down to a pretty mountain while I talk some sense into your Papa. I'll get you tomorrow night when things have calmed down.* Gentle hands placing him in the silver egg. The egg floating earthward . . . then the cold, black shadow of Brother's jealous, paranoid rage. *You should never have been born, bastard brat!* A powerful blow, and the dizzying, sickening sensation of the egg falling from the sky. The bone-jarring impact, the roar of flames and bitter smoke.

The baby's fear and confusion were a palpable vibration that coursed through Gabrielle's body. He blinked up at her as if to say, "What's happened? Where's my mama?"

"I don't know where your mama is," Gabrielle whispered. "But it's okay, you're safe now."

The image of the mountain flashed through her mind again. Gabrielle recognized it: Mount Ampeli, a day's travel away.

Xena stepped up to her and pulled back the cloth covering the infant's face. His little blue head was as round as a honeydew, and his huge black eyes were wide with fright. "That's one *ugly* baby."

"He's not ugly!"

Xena sighed, leaned in for a closer look, then pulled away. "Gabrielle, I have seen many babies in my life—cute ones, beautiful ones, chubby ones—and I'm telling you that the sight of this thing—"

"—baby . . ."

". . . whatever—the sight of this *baby* would make Medusa shriek and run for cover."

"I think he's kind of cute."

Cute for a monster, maybe.

"*Xena!* He isn't a monster!"

"I didn't say he was!" Xena's blue eyes flashed with indignation.

"Yes, you did, I heard you . . . *think* it. . . ." Gabrielle trailed off, her eyes widening with realization.

"You heard my thoughts?" Xena asked incredulously.

Girl's getting high from all this smoke. . . .

"It's not the smoke, Xena. I can hear what you're thinking."

"No, you can't, that's impossible!"

"Can."

"Can't!"

"Can!"

"Fine! Then what am I thinking now?"

"You're thinking I've lost my mind, and you wish we'd never gone looking for the fallen star, and your left toe hurts from kicking that hard-headed pirate last week, and you're wishing you could scratch that itch in your—"

"Okay! Enough! So you *can* read my mind."

"Told you."

"Why can you suddenly do this?"

Gabrielle looked down at the baby. "I think he's done it so he can communicate with me."

"And *what,* exactly, are *we* supposed to do with it?" Xena asked. "I don't know about you, but I'm not known for my tender maternal instincts."

Gabrielle touched the baby's cheek. Once again, she got a clear image of the mountain. "We need to take him to the top of Mount Ampeli. The baby's mother told him she would be there to get him tomorrow night. I know where it is, Xena, it's just a day away to the west. There's some really great wild grapes growing on the south face—"

"Damnation! We're supposed to be in Amphipolis four days from now . . . this side trip is going to make me miss my mother's birthday party!"

Gabrielle shrugged. "It's not like you remembered to get her anything."

Xena looked at her feet, embarrassed. "There's a merchant in Amphipolis who—"

"—specializes in helping thoughtless daughters who forget to buy their mother a birthday present?"

". . . well, *of course* it sounds bad when you say it like *that*. . . ."

Gabrielle got an image in her head of Xena kissing Saul, Amphipolis's very buff young blacksmith and laughed loudly. "It's not your mother's party you're worried about missing, is it? Well, I've heard Saul's forge is pretty hot—"

"Stay out of my mind!" Xena snapped.

"Then stop thinking so loud." Gabrielle looked at the baby and became serious. "Xena, we *have* to take this side trip. It's not like we can just give this baby to the nearest kindly farmer to raise . . . he doesn't *belong* here. We've got to get him back to his mother."

Xena sighed. "All right, all right, you win. You're right. Besides, it's nice around here this time of year . . . it'll be a fun trip. And what's the worst that can possibly happen to us way out here in the countryside?"

A few bars of twanging lyre music jangled through the evening air. *Danggg a dang dang dang dang dangggg. . . .*

"You had to ask," said Gabrielle.

Xena leaped to her feet, drawing her chakram with her left hand. Gabriel stood with her, the baby cradled in the crook of her left arm and her staff at the ready in her right hand.

"Who's there?" called Xena.

A dozen people in gold-trimmed white robes emerged from the trees. A few of them carried lyres and tambourines, and others carried tall staves.

A tall, thin man with a shock of graying black hair stepped forward. "Greetings, strangers. I welcome you to our forest. My name is Cephtis."

Xena inclined her head in greeting but she did not put down her chakram. "You're Asterians, aren't you? Star worshippers."

Cephtis smiled indulgently. "That's an oversimplication, but yes . . . we are Asterians. Our oracle told us that one of the Star Mother's chariots would fall from the sky tonight, and that a child would survive." He nodded at the swaddled baby. "Is that the child?"

Xena nodded.

Cephtis clapped his hands. "Ah, what *wonderful* news that

such kind strangers were here to save the babe from certain death! Please, give us the Star Child. We will ensure that he is returned to his people."

Gabriel took a step back, shaking her head. In her mind, she could see the baby lying naked on a cold stone altar. Cephtis stood above the child muttering incantations as he raised high a silver-bladed knife.

"No. You're going to kill him," she said.

Cephtis laughed. "Nonsense! He won't die; he will be *reborn* as a new star. And the blood he renders unto us will ensure a bountiful harvest next year."

Crazy freaks, Gabrielle heard Xena think.

Xena stepped grimly forward, drawing her sword with her free right hand. "You can't have him."

"But you must understand," said Cephtis in an annoying singsong voice, "that the blood of a Star Child, besides ensuring a bountiful harvest, also possesses remarkable curative powers, and the warlord upon whose land we have erected our holy temple suffers from a terrible degenerative skin disease. The blood of this child will cure him, and thus ensure that the Asterian Temple will remain standing, a beacon to the True Believers who shall travel—"

"Do you ever stop to take a breath or are you *that* in love with the sound of your own voice?" spat Xena.

Cephtis's face darkened. *"Give us the child."*

The musicians had put down their instruments and opened their robes to retrieve studded clubs. The others brought their staves to the ready.

"Over my dead body," Xena hissed.

"As you wish—and it was *such* a lovely evening, too." Cephtis looked toward the others and said: "Take her!"

The cultists rushed forward, ready to brain the two women. Ululating wildly, Xena catapulted herself toward the mob, swinging sword and flinging chakram.

And that's when Something Else Happened.

Gabrielle instinctively pulled the baby closer to her chest and looked down to make sure that he was all right, and as she did so the baby closed his eyes tightly and began to make the softest of mewling sounds, and the more he made the sound, the louder it became, and the louder the sound became, the more the baby's face turned from its usual blue to an increasingly deeper purple.

You pick now *to make your first poopy?* thought Gabrielle.

But a moment later she knew that wasn't the case at all, because as the cultists rushed Xena, swinging down with their clubs and staves, the weapons suddenly met with resistance and were bounced backward, out of their hands.

Xena's weapons met the same fate. Her chakram, which she'd flung at the noggin of a particularly burly Asterian, whanged off the invisible wall and knifed harmlessly into the ground. As she swung her sword to parry another cultist's club, her sword bounced back with such force she had to use both hands to hold on to the weapon.

The cultists retrieved their weapons, tried again, but could not strike Xena.

"Well, this is interesting," said Xena, retrieving her chakram.

It was then that Gabrielle caught a glint of multi-colored light reflecting off something smooth and curved above Xena's head; the more she stared at it, the more Gabrielle came to realize that what she was seeing was the light of the setting sun glittering off the surface of something like a large bubble that surrounded her, Xena, and Argo.

She looked at the baby and smiled. "*He's* doing it, Xena! The baby is protecting us!"

Xena sheathed her sword and looked first at the baby— its face was still purple and intense with the effort of generating the invisible wall—then at the bewildered and powerless cultists.

"Suddenly I find this child much more attractive."

"You'd better," said Gabrielle. "But look at him—it's hurting him. He can't keep this up much longer." She looked at Xena. "Do you have some sort of plan?"

Xena quickly mounted Argo and extended her hand for Gabrielle to join her. "Fleeing springs to mind. Come on."

Gabrielle took Xena's hand and climbed up onto Argos' back, slipping one hand around Xena's waist.

"Let's ride! Yah!" Xena dug in her heels and snapped hard on Argo's reigns and the horse took off at a strong gallop, the protective field remaining around them even as they moved at such speed.

The cultists chased them for a little while, but Argo's speed soon proved too much for them. Many of them turned and ran back to mount horses of their own.

The baby let out a sigh of relief soon after, and Gabrielle knew the invisible armor was no longer surrounding them.

"He protected us for as long as he could," said Gabrielle, pulling the baby close and listening to him breathe. He *seemed* to be all right, but how could she be certain with such an unworldly child?

He opened his dark eyes and looked at her. And smiled.

She leaned down and kissed his forehead. "Good boy," she whispered. "Thank you."

The road they now found themselves traveling was little more than a rutted tract of hard-packed dirt meandering through a skeletal tunnel of near-barren tree branches. The night became an usually cold one, and the trees, sensing this, seemed to slumber against the chill. Tendrils of mist snaked from between the trees and lay across the road like a blanket of living snow; shifting, curling, reaching upward to ensnarl Argo's legs for just a moment before dissolving into nothingness. Overhead, the moonlight straggled through the branches, creating diffuse columns of foggy light that to Gabrielle's frayed nerves became fingers from a giant, ghostly hand that at any moment would fist together and crush all of them. She was aware, as if in deep nightmare, of shadows following along from either side of the road—silent, misshapen things, spiriting along with the mist for a while until she snapped her head toward them, then they would disappear in slow degrees, mocking her anxiety, melting back into the darker, unexplored areas of the night-silent forest. These shadows called to mind far too many campfire tales and old wives' stories of the strange woodland creatures—neither fully human nor fully beast—that were said to inhabit this section of the land.

"Not the most inviting of paths, is it?" said Xena.

"I was just thinking the same thing."

"Have you seen them?"

"Seen what?"

Xena looked over her shoulder. "Those figures trying to hide themselves in the trees behind us."

"Yes. Do you think they might be the creatures that the legends speak of?"

"I think they're Asterian scouts."

"But how could they have picked up our trail?"

"They're fanatics, Gabrielle, not idiots." She hastened Argo's step.

"Listen," whispered Xena. "If those are Asterian scouts, then it might be best if you stay close to my thoughts. Any unnecessary conversation might alert these things that we are aware of them."

"We need to find a place to rest. The baby can't be out in this cold."

"There's a farmhouse ahead—can you see it?"

Gabrielle squinted her eyes against the night and could make out the shape of an old structure of some kind. "I see something."

"Shelter is shelter." Xena gave Argo's reigns a sharp snap and the horse broke into a trot.

"Gabrielle?"

"Yes?"

"About that 'staying close to my thoughts' thing?"

"Uh-huh?"

"Well . . . if you happen to see Saul around, I'd appreciate some privacy."

"I never get to have any fun. . . ."

The farmhouse was dark, and so they crept by it and decided instead to stay in the massive barn that lay several hundred yards away from the house. Once inside, Gabrielle was delighted to find that it was rather warm, and there was plenty of hay for them to use against the night chill, and—best of all—there was a nanny goat to provide milk for the baby.

She hoped the baby would accept the milk, and he did, rather hungrily.

"He worked up quite an appetite for himself," said Gabrielle.

"He saved us from a nasty little mess, that's for sure,"

replied Xena. "If he wants to *eat* the damn goat, I'll kill it and put it on a spit over a fire." She paused, then added, "Could you let him know I said I'd do that for him? I think he should know I'm on his side."

"But do you think he's cute?" said Gabrielle, holding the baby up for Xena to take.

Xena winced, swallowed once, then took hold of the baby and held him out in front of her as if he were something smelly she'd found by the side of the road. "I think he's . . . adorable."

Gabrielle smiled. "Only adorable?"

"You're really going to make me pay for calling him ugly, aren't you?"

"That is my plan, yes."

Xena sighed in frustration, then pulled the baby a little closer to her. "I think he's lovely. I think he's gorgeous. Why, in the history of history itself, never has there been a more remarkable, beautiful, angelic, breathtaking, dazzling, wondrous child than this one."

"He knows you're making fun of me and he doesn't appreciate it."

"How do you know what he's thinking? Can you read his mind, as well?"

"No."

"Then how can you be sure that he feels that way?"

"Because he just peed on your boots."

Xena looked down. "Oh." Then, looking at the baby: "Sorry. I didn't mean to make fun of Gabrielle. I *do* think you're pretty adorable, though."

"Only adorable?" said Gabrielle.

"Don't start with me."

"Okay."

A few minutes later—Xena's boots satisfactorily wiped clean and Argo happy with a bag of oats they'd found by the door—Xena and Gabrielle climbed up into the hayloft, covered themselves and the baby against the chill of the night, and soon fell asleep.

In the morning, they would continue their journey to Mount Ampeli.

Providing, of course, that Nothing Else Happened.

•   •   •

Gabrielle awoke to the sound of voices. She peered down through the gaps in the loft boards and saw Ares, the handsome God of War, facing Xena in the barn.

"What do you want, Ares?" Xena asked.

"You're in over your head, Xena. This baby is bad news, for all of us." Ares stroked his black goatee thoughtfully. "We'd all be better off if you'd kill the brat and be on your way to Amphipolis."

Xena stepped close to him. "Kill him? Why is one little baby such a threat to big bad Ares, huh?"

"It . . . it shouldn't have been *born*, Xena. It will upset the balance of things. Zeus doesn't like it, and neither do I."

Ares took a breath as if he were going to elaborate, then seemed to think better of it. "Just kill it, Xena. Kill it and be on your way. If you don't, I can almost guarantee you'll be dead before midnight."

Xena laughed contemptuously. "Oooh, like I've never heard *that* one before. I have no intention of hurting this child, Ares, and I have even less intention of getting myself killed. Get out of here. You're wasting your breath and my time."

Ares glared at her. "Someday, Xena, you're going to say the wrong thing to me at the wrong time and it's not going to be pretty."

Before Xena could respond, Ares was gone and the baby was awake and mewling for more goat's milk.

"Thank you," said Gabrielle.

"Why are you thanking me?"

"You could have said yes to Ares."

"Tell me something I don't know."

Gabrielle looked down at the baby. "He needs us."

"I know."

Gabrielle took Xena's hand. "Have I told you recently how wonderful I think you are?"

"I'm touched, I'm moved, I tingle." Xena pulled her hand away. "Let's get ourselves together and get the hell out of here before Ares decides to pull something."

"What are you doing in my barn?" demanded a voice behind them.

They turned, and saw a burly middle-aged man in a simple, green farmer's tunic standing in the doorway brandishing a wooden pitchfork.

Gabrielle quickly covered the baby's face with his swaddling cloth before the farmer could get a good look. "Uh, we were just—" she began.

"We're just travelers, and we came upon your barn late last night. We were dead on our feet, and we didn't want to wake you," Xena said. "We can pay for the oats and milk we've taken—"

"Say, you look familiar." The farmer frowned in brief concentration, but then his face brightened into excitement. "You're Xena! The Warrior Princess! Oh, what an honor it is to have you in my barn! You saved my sister and her kids from Draco at Poteidaia!"

"Your sister lives in Poteidaia?" asked Gabrielle, surprised to meet someone this far south who knew of her hometown.

"Yes, she's a weaver named Chloe . . . long auburn hair, three kids and a husband named Aristus?"

"Oh, I know *her*—" Gabrielle began.

"Look, we've really got to get back on the road," Xena said, nudging Gabrielle with her elbow. "It's a long way to Actium,"

We can trust no one, Xena thought pointedly.

"Oh, please don't go so soon!" said the farmer. "Join us for breakfast! My wife is cooking eggs and porridge . . . and she's got the most amazing story about a child who fell from the stars last night! She's been dying to tell the tale to someone besides me. Apparently, her church is looking all over for the baby. There's even supposed to be a reward for anyone who has news of the child's location."

He stared at the swaddled infant in Gabrielle's arms. "You two haven't heard anything about a Star Child, have you?"

"Not a thing." Gabrielle smiled at him sweetly.

"We thank you for your offer, but we really must be on our way," Xena said.

"In that case, I wish you a safe and speedy journey." The farmer saluted Xena and headed back to the house.

Gabrielle carried the baby to the goat to give him some

more milk and to change him while Xena gathered their equipment and saddled Argo.

"We've got to get out of here before his wife comes out to chat," Xena said.

"I don't remember any women in the group that attacked us yesterday; maybe she won't recognize us," Gabrielle.

"It's not worth the risk. Bad enough her husband saw us; hopefully my story about us going to Actium will throw them off our trail."

They rode all day, stopping only to change the baby and for a brief lunch of grapes from an abandoned vineyard and dried meat and hard cheese from Argo's saddlebags. The sun was just dropping below the horizon when they came to the foot of Mount Ampeli.

"Are you sure this is the place?" Xena asked.

"Yes; I've been getting very clear images from the baby. Now all we have to do is get to the top . . . and wait."

Wild grapes and olive trees grew along the mountain's slopes, and the top of the mountain was weathered, bare rock. They left Argo in a cusp of trees near the base and began their climb. The climb was much steeper than either one of them had anticipated, and for a few minutes they had to stop so Xena could fashion a basket to hold the baby—one which Gabrielle could carry upon her back like a quiver. It took them longer to gather the wood and vines to do this, and by the time they began their climb again, the moon was rising high in the night sky

Gabrielle, at Xena's insistence, took the lead. She came to the bulge, went over, placed her foot firmly on the edge, and found a solid hold on what felt like a root with her left hand. Pulling upward, kneeing and toeing into the blessedly cooperative stone, kicking steps into the shalelike rock wherever she could, Gabrielle positioned both hands and one foot before moving into a new, higher position.

The mountain was starting to shudder in her face and against her chest. Her own breath was whistling and humming crazily against the stone. The rocks were steep, and she labored backbreakingly for every inch. Her shoulders were tiring and her calves ached and the muscles in her arms felt like iron. Panic was courting her, reminding her that her fear of heights was perhaps the greatest terror in her life, and now she had gone and put herself halfway up one of the steepest mountains in all the land, and it was only the thought of the baby she carried upon her back and what she would see somewhere above that kept her going. Taking hold of a firm root in the mountainside, Gabrielle pulled in a deep breath, counted three, then released it as she pulled herself up another nine inches, over a small outcropping, and reached a wide ledge that was only a few dozen yards from the summit.

She did not see the shadows moving behind the large stones that surrounded her.

Nor did Xena, until a bolt shot forth and went straight through her chest, emerging in a straight, deadly, bloody line from her back.

Xena's eyes met Gabrielle's the moment before Cephtis and a small group of Asterians began to emerge from their hiding places.

Gabrielle's heart shattered at the sight of Xena—powerful, indestructible Xena—dropping to her knees and falling backward, blood trickling from her mouth.

Gabrielle moved toward her.

No! Came Xena's silent command. *The child, Gabrielle, you have to think of the child! Get him to the top of the mountain. You can't . . . waste time on me. . . .*

"Xena!" screamed Gabrielle.

"I am sorry," said Cephtis, kneeling down and pressing the palm of his hand against the bolt, pressing it in deeper.

Gabrielle began backing up the mountain toward the summit.

She felt Xena weakening. This was by far the deadliest wound the great warrior princess had ever suffered, and if something wasn't done to help her soon. . . .

Cephtis rose to his feet, surrounded by his followers—all of whom now pointed their crossbows at Gabrielle and the baby.

"If you willingly give him to us," the Asterian leader said, "then we will let you live. If you refuse, then we will kill you where you stand."

"Go to hell."

Cephtis's eyes grew dark and cold. "Don't think I won't tell them to fire. If a bolt should happen to hit the child, well . . . that would be a problem if it died before the sacred ceremony, but we have ways of staunching the loss of any blood."

Gabrielle looked at Xena, remembered her friend's command, then turned and ran with all she had in her.

Cephtis gave the command and the Asterians fired their crossbows.

Though each Asterian had aimed carefully, no bolt struck its target.

For the baby had once again closed his eyes and, purple-faced, raised the invisible wall of armor around Gabrielle. She knew that he would have done it sooner had he sensed any danger, but the Asterians had surprised him as much as they had Xena and Gabrielle.

But this time the field did much more than protect Gabrielle.

It lifted her from the surface of the mountain and held her in its invisible grasp.

Shrieking, then taking a deep breath in order to keep her wits about her, Gabrielle opened her eyes and saw that the baby—perhaps growing stronger each time he used his powers—had commanded this field to lift not only her, but Xena and the profoundly confused Argo, as well.

Tears streaming down her cheeks, Gabrielle looked upward toward the night sky, saw a brief flash of what she at first thought was lightning, and then gasped as that bolt of lightning expanded and curved, becoming solid and wide and so very, very large.

She was looking at a giant floating pyramid made from the same silvery metal as the baby's meteor egg, only it was easily twice the size of the mountain, and shone bright as the full moon.

A door opened at the base of the pyramid, and a sunset-colored light bled down, pulling her, the baby, Xena's unconscious form, and Argo upward, and as Gabrielle stared into the light, mesmerized, she asked the baby a question—

—*What's going on?*—

—and was suddenly overwhelmed by the tidal wave of sensations; she heard thoughts and sensed dreams and absorbed myriad impressions as they were passed from psyche to psyche with compulsive speed and more sensory layers than her brain, anyone's brain, *anything's* brain could possibly absorb. The atmosphere was packed with millions upon millions of swirling, drifting, reeling bits of consciousness. At that moment she was attuned to the majestic cacophony to such a degree that she heard, as plaintive and delicately strained as any rhapsody, the murmur of every cell; the percussive sounds of termites banging their heads against the floors of their dark, resonating nests; the drumming feet of mice; the synchronic rustling made by flowing blood as it brushed against arterial walls; the clicking of synapses; the introverted cries of a million lonely people shrieking their anguish into the cold, empty, uncaring night; and Gabrielle realized that somewhere, underlying all life, there was a continual music of living that had been playing since life began, and that its sounds, its rhythms and pulsings and tones, were the refrain of something more, the distant memory of the chorus from an earlier song, a sub-organic score for transposing the inanimate, random matter of chaos into the enigmatic, lavish, magnificent, improbable, ordered dance of living forms, rearranging matter and consciousness into miraculous symmetry, away from probability, against entropy, lifting everything toward a sublime awareness so acute, so incandescent and encompassing she thought everything within her would burst into flames for the blinding *want* underneath it all—

—and in this communion she was given the answer to several secrets about the universe, about the worlds within worlds that she passed through every day without even realizing it, and though much of this knowledge was hidden away in her mind, echoes of knowledge and magic and the power of the gods, even though she experienced all of these sensations without actually comprehending them, the baby's response—its gift of celestial communion—nonetheless gave her the courage to go on.

A blink, a burst of light, a pressure in her chest that she

was certain would cause her heart to burst, and she felt something hard and cold beneath her back.

She opened her eyes to find herself in a pale gray room that seemed to be made from clouds. The vaporous edges of the cloud walls shifted constantly, curling and uncurling to form an endless procession of arcane hieroglyphs.

Standing before Gabrielle was a tall, beautiful Egyptian woman with skin the blue of a clear summer sky. Her night-black robe shimmered with a thousand stars. She held the Star Child in her arms.

"I am Nuit, goddess of the sky. I thank you for saving my little one." She smiled down at the baby, who gurgled happily in response. "He is the son of your father god Zeus. We should not have made love . . . but Zeus certainly has his share of masculine wiles. My husband, Geb, the earth god, was angry for a while, but I have calmed him. Unfortunately, the little one's older brother, Set, fears any competition. When I tried to send the baby safely down to the mountaintop while I spoke to Geb, Set interfered, and made sure the Asterians would find him. He also convinced your god of war that the child is a danger to both our pantheons. The child is no danger to anyone, god or man, and I have plans to keep him out of the affairs of both worlds from now on.

"Again, you have my deepest thanks for helping my child."

"You're welcome . . . I guess." Gabrielle looked around and saw that Xena had been laid out on a cloud altar. "Can you . . . can you help her?" She gestured at Xena.

"Of course, a simple request."

Nuit raised her hand, and the bolt protruding from Xena's chest shimmered, dissolved into a million particles of gray-tinted light, and vanished. The wound in Xena's chest began to close, pulling back in her spilled blood, and in a few moments Gabrielle heard her friend groan and mutter, "Oh, *damnation* . . . how many horses fell on me, anyway?"

Gabrielle started over toward the table, but was stopped when Nuit placed a hand on her shoulder.

"For your own protection, for the sake of your sanity, and

for our protection, as well, I am afraid that I cannot allow you to remember what has happened here."

"But the baby, he—"

"He shared with you some of the Knowledge that is awakening in his mind, and much of it is Knowledge that Mankind is not yet ready for. I also promised Zeus and Geb that no mortals should learn about our affair and the baby's true parentage. I am very sorry."

Gabrielle looked around the cloud room, then, finally, at the baby. "Can I say good-bye?"

Nuit smiled. "Of course."

The goddess held the baby out. Gabrielle took the child and held him close. "You've been quite the little visitor, haven't you?"

The baby replied by wrapping one of its tiny hands around Gabrielle's finger.

"I'm going to miss you," she whispered to it. Then: "Even if I can't remember what you gave to me, I want to give you something to remember me by. It's a lullaby I remember from when I was a child. I never knew who used to sing it to me, or where it came from, but I want to give it to you now."

And then she sang: "May the night be your friend, and may dreams rock you gently; may you never know hunger, and may you love with a full heart; and may the bright, smiling stars light your way, until the wind sets you free. . . ."

Then she could sing no more.

She kissed the baby on its forehead, then gave him back to his mother.

From behind her she could hear Xena say, "Gabrielle?"

"Yes?" She turned to face her friend.

"I want you to know that, from this day forward, I shall never, *never* doubt your judgment or abilities again. You showed me that the heart can be stronger than any weapon. You proved yourself the equal of any warrior—of any *ten* warriors. I just wanted you to know that."

Gabrielle stared at her for a moment, blinked, then said: "Nearly dying has made you all squishy. I don't think I like it."

Argo chuffed her agreement.

A moment later the cloud room filled with a light purple vapor, which Gabrielle breathed in deeply . . .

Xena and Gabrielle came awake to find themselves sitting at a table in the Staggering Satyr Tavern. The tables were littered with wineskins and tankards, and people were passed out all over the floor. Argo was just standing there, snorting and pawing the straw-covered floor and staring down at them quizzically.

"What the—" croaked Xena.

The remains of a cake of some sort lay on a platter in the center of the table.

"Where are we?" asked Gabrielle.

Xena looked around and shrugged. "I . . . I'm not sure. I remember that we were on the road to Amphipolis and we. . . ." Her eyes suddenly grew wide. "Oh, no."

"What is it?"

Xena pointed toward the tavern doorway. "I think we're already here—I mean, *there*—I mean—"

"One hell of a party, wasn't it?" said Xena's mother from the tavern doorway. "Never in my life did I dream that my daughter would give me a birthday party that lasted nearly two days!"

She approached the table and stood over Xena, smiling. "Looks like the two of you don't remember much."

"That's one way of putting it," said Gabrielle.

"Well, no matter, as long as you enjoyed yourselves."

"Oh, yes," said Xena, not very convincingly. "It was . . . one hell of a party."

"Good," said her mother, then leaned down. "Now, dear daughter . . . where's my present?"

As Fate Would Have It

Jody Lynn Nye

"Sounds like you had quite an adventure, sir," the tavern-maid said, refilling the chief mercenary's mug.

"Indeed we did," the man said, gulping down a draught of beer and dashing his hand against his scruffy beard to clear away the foam. "I mean, what chance did we have with *her* jumping here, there, and everywhere, screaming like a fury, and throwing that . . . that flat round thing . . ."

The tall woman in bronze and leather at the end of the bar clapped a circlet of metal down on the rough plank counter.

"Chakram," said Xena, "but I've never been to Parcae-lion."

"Xena!" The mercenaries leaped up, scattering benches and chairs. In their haste to get away, they forgot to open the tavern door. Three man-shaped holes in the wall dropped dust down to the dirt floor.

"Funny," her small blonde companion said, watching them go. "You usually have to *throw* them through the wall."

Xena sat down on the bench as the tavern owner and his

staff hurried to clean up the mess. "That's the third band of thugs who've said they met me in Parcaelion."

"They have to be mistaken," Gabrielle said, frowning at a lamb bone before returning it to her empty trencher.

"You're right, of course," Xena said, drily. "There are so many warriors matching my description in Greece . . ."

"So we're going?" Gabrielle asked, brightly.

"Of course." Xena pursed her lips in a small smile. "I want to know how my reputation has managed to precede me so effectively."

"It can't be far now," Gabrielle said, pulling on her mount's reins. They had been riding into the mountains for three days, and her rear was getting a little sore. The mare danced to a halt, no doubt glad of the break, too. Gabrielle swiveled her head around to study the olive orchards on the hillsides the road wound through. "The man back in the last village said we'd be there when we found trees already in fruit. Here they are. It's amazing. Only a dozen miles back the trees are still just flowering."

"Strange, isn't it?" Xena said, studying the heavy gray-green clusters and the profusion of dully gleaming leaves clinging to the branches of the trees. She pinched an olive and felt the flesh already thick on the seed. "Almost as if spring comes earlier for them here than other places."

"The road is in good shape," Gabrielle pointed out. "They must be well-off to be able to maintain the track so well. No potholes, even though the rains have been heavy this season. And look at those fences! How'd they get lath fences to stay together so well? The wood hasn't even grayed."

"I don't know," Xena said. "The gods favor them for some reason."

Her horse raised his head and whickered.

"He smells blood," Xena said, raising her head, too. Her keen ears picked up the distant but unmistakable sounds of metal on metal. "There's a fight up ahead." She dug her heels into the stallion's side. "Hee-*yah!*"

The golden horse shot away. Gabrielle sighed and kicked her mount into a gallop to follow. "I suppose it's no use suggesting the subtle approach?"

• • •

To Gabrielle's experienced eye, the village did indeed seem to be blessed by the gods. The surrounding fields were burgeoning with crops. Grainfields under the wide blue skies were full of swaying golden stalks. Fat melons in plenty sprawled along healthy, large-leafed vines. Grapes glowed like green jewels among the leaves in the vineyards. The sheepfolds were loud with the high-pitched bleating of spring lambs. All the buildings beyond the entry gate had been well-built of wood and stone, and painted in brilliant colors. The only jarring note was the battle going on in the center of the town market.

"Romans!" Gabrielle shouted to her companion. At least twenty of the red-cloaked foe were scattered through the village square, either breaking down doors or fighting hand to hand. The townsfolk defended their homes, but they had only makeshift weapons, and little skill in the art of war.

Xena had evidently already noted the enemy's presence and decided on a course of action.

"Ayaiaiaiaiaiai!" she shrilled, spurring her horse into the midst of the town square. She drew her sword, stood up in the saddle, and somersaulted into the thickest part of the action, landing feet first on the back of a surprised Roman. By the time Gabrielle pulled up, unsheathing her twin battle knives, the tall woman had already engaged four legionaries armed with gladii and long, square-topped shields. By the look of surprise and dismay on their faces, Gabrielle guessed they never dreamed that a raid on a small Greek town would bring down a legendary one-woman protection force upon them. Two-woman, she corrected herself hastily. Though she admired Xena and thought of her first when it came to puissance in battle, she was half of this fellowship. They stood together, now and forever. She vaulted out of her saddle and ran to help.

If the citizens of Parcaelion were taken aback to see a six-foot, black-haired warrior maiden or a five-foot-something, blonde, knife-wielding Amazon leap into their midst, they covered it well. The Romans, on the other hand, were surprised. Xena gave them no time to react. She dodged from side to side behind a cart full of vegetables as one soldier stabbed at her with the short sword, spearing gourds, onions, and lettuce instead of his intended prey. He lost sight of her for a moment, and cast around, letting his sword drop. Xena burst out from amid a display of baskets and kicked the surprised man in the chin with one sweep of her booted foot. The soldier went over backward.

His companions rushed in to attack, but their huge shields got in the way within the tight quarters, preventing them from maneuvering. Xena let out a wild yell and spun, coming up under the guard of the third man. She grasped his sword arm, twisted the weapon out of his wrist, and swung him hard against his friends. Their banded breastplates clanged. She swung her partner again. His head knocked into his companions', one after the other. All three men fell to the ground, unconscious.

"These are pretty soft," Xena said, dusting her hands together. "Caesar ought to be ashamed of the way his empire has declined." She looked around for her next opponent.

"No!" a woman's voice screamed from across the small agora. Xena shoved her way through the milling crowd to a small cloth shop. The owners, a pleasant-faced woman with brown hair and a nervous, pudgy, black-haired man, barricaded the door with their own bodies, trying to prevent a trio of legionaries and their decurion from entering. The unarmed weavers had no chance of keeping the soldiers out for long. Xena strode over and tapped the officer on the shoulder.

"Pardon me," she said. The officer turned his head. She elbowed him in the jaw, then swept the chakram out of her belt with her free hand and flicked it into the air. The two soldiers attacked with swords. She only had to parry with them each briefly before the shining ring ricocheted off three walls and bounced off their foreheads. The chakram made its last strike and rebounded into Xena's hand. She observed, satisfied, as the men staggered backward against the nearby wall, eyes crossed. When they recovered their wits, they started running out of the village, pursued by the rest of their troop. The officer crawled, then stumbled to his feet.

"Halt!" he cried. "What about the Child of Fortune?" He

looked back at Xena and the others massing behind him, then ran after his men.

Gabrielle came to stand beside Xena, sheathing her knives. "What does *that* mean?"

Xena raised an eyebrow, watching the Romans flee down the road. "I don't know, but we're going to find out."

Once the enemy was out of sight, the citizens began to clean up the town. Wounded men and women were loaded onto stretchers and carried into the tavern.

"Let's see if we can be of any help," Xena suggested to Gabrielle. The two of them followed into the hall.

Gabrielle looked around, her heart going out to the injured, who lay moaning while others flitted around them with medical impedimenta. The weaver who had been defending his shop was bent over the litter of a boy whose arm had been slashed. He straightened up with a start as Xena approached him.

"Xena! I mean . . ." the weaver gulped, "how pleased we are to see you, Warrior Princess. You've saved us all. And Gabrielle. We are grateful for your help in our time of need."

"And you are . . . ?" Xena asked, pointedly.

"Clodias, headman of this village," the man said, sketching a deep bow to each of them. He tugged at the collar of his tunic, clearly nervous. "Forgive my manners! I should have introduced myself at once. Your fame precedes you, fair ladies. I presumed . . . I mean, I feel as though we already know you."

"That's interesting," Xena said, looking around. "Nice place you have here. But I've never seen it before, have I?"

"No! I assure you, Warrior Princess, that this is the first time you've visited our town. Er. Welcome! Welcome! We will have a feast in your honor, you and Lady Gabrielle, for defeating the Romans who would have pillaged our homes. Just as soon as we have cared for the injured."

"That's not necessary . . ." Xena began.

"Please!" Clodias threw his arms wide. He seemed fond of grand gestures. "Let us show our gratitude. We have wine, fruit, meat, good bread . . ."

As he spoke, the tavern owner and his family hurried to

the cooking area and began to bustle around with cooking pots. Other townsfolk hurried out and returned with more tables and benches and two large chairs that they set at one end of the grandest table almost, Xena thought, as if they had rehearsed the exercise. They carefully kept from making eye contact with her or her companion.

Gabrielle said in a low voice, "Romans don't just raid houses for nothing. What were they looking for?"

"I don't know. I think Clodias and the others are trying to get up the courage to tell us."

". . . and so, I wish to offer a toast to those brave warriors, brought to us by fate just when our needs were greatest. I give you Xena. And Gabrielle." Clodias, standing at the foot of the table, raised his goblet to the visitors. The others echoed him.

Xena offered them all a smile that went no farther back than her lips.

The simple room had been transformed from a tavern and a makeshift hospital to a beautiful dining hall. An expensive embroidered cloth covered the boards of the table, with individual cloths to match at each place. Goblets and trenchers of colored glass picked up the winking firelight from the torches and lamps overhead. Platters of food and pitchers of wine, water, and ale were replenished by the healthy young servers as soon as they were emptied. Two youths with lyre and sistrum sang throughout dinner. They had unusually good voices. Xena knew most of the tunes and would have enjoyed joining in, but she held back. Until she found out precisely what was going on, she didn't want to allow her guard to drop. No one would meet their eyes for long.

"I have to admit, the food was as good as they promised," Gabrielle said, pushing back a little from the green plate before her.

"Almost as though we're being fattened up for the kill," Xena commented drily.

Gabrielle almost told her she was being too suspicious, but the furtive atmosphere was beginning to irk her, too. She began to regret the fennel salad and that second helping of raspberry puree mixed with snow.

"Do you think there's poison in the food?"

"No. I think it's something in the air. Time to clear it." She cleared her throat and stood up. "Citizens of Parcaelion, you honor us with your generosity. We've enjoyed your feast and the entertainment, but I think it's about time you tell us the truth."

The lyre and sistrum rattled into silence. The men and women around the table blanched, glancing furtively at one another. Xena went on relentlessly, turning to catch each person's eyes before they hid their gaze from hers.

"I've run into a *number* of strangers recently who say they met me here in Parcaelion. You all know I've never set foot here before, so they have to have seen someone else." Xena let her voice go cold. "I don't like it when someone impersonates me. I don't have to meet her, but you'd better tell her that the charade is over."

Clodias sprang up. "I swear to you, good lady, that no one in our village has ever pretended to be you."

Xena glared at him. "Are you telling me that *all* those people were mistaken?"

"No, Warrior Princess," Clodias said, hanging his head.

"Well, if you haven't got one or more people pretending to be me, who beat up those men?"

Clodias twitched with discomfort. "You did."

"I did?" Xena said, taken aback. She exchanged incredulous glances with Gabrielle. She'd been ready for a confrontation with a country girl in homemade leather armor or a retired swordsmistress. "How—no, never mind. *Why?*"

"We needed your help, Xena." The weaver's wife, Thisbe, rose from her seat.

Clodias gestured to her to sit down. "You will surely have noticed the beauty of our town. We have been well favored by the gods. Our children are never ill. They grow strong and beautiful, as you have seen. Our crops are more plentiful than any of our neighbors'. The sheep always bear twin lambs, and the cows and goats give more milk than we can ever use—but you must not think that we are greedy. We share always with those who are less fortunate."

"And what is the source of all your good luck?" Xena asked.

After exchanging glances with her husband, Thisbe brought forward a ruddy-haired girl of about six years of age. She was dressed in the same fabrics as the others, but on her the fine linen seemed to shine. Her large, appealing eyes were a heavenly blue, and she had a sweet smile.

"My foster daughter," Thisbe said.

"She's beautiful." Xena knelt down beside her and clasping her small hands in her large ones. "Hello. I'm Xena. What's your name?"

"Ianthe," the girl said.

"This child? She is why everyone has been invading your village?"

"Yes," Clodias said.

"What's so special about her?"

"Nothing."

But Xena could tell the weaver was lying. She lost patience with him.

"Why do they call her the Child of Fortune?" Gabrielle asked. "I heard the Romans say that as they were . . . leaving."

"Er, she's our luck," Clodias said, nervously. His calloused hands twisted in the fabric of his tunic. "She means a great deal to us here. And it's why you've helped us so often. Or rather, why you will."

"Not me," Xena said coldly, rising to her feet. "Our work here is done. We'll be going now. Thank you for the feast."

"Oh, but, Warrior Princess, you must stay," Thisbe said, wringing her hands.

"There's no *must* about it," Xena said, looking at her curiously. "Why would I need to protect one little girl when she has a whole village to raise her? You have enough wealth to build a castle to hide her away from anything."

"We don't want to do that," Clodias said.

"Why not? It would keep her from harm."

Clodias put out a hand in appeal. "We want her to grow up happy. If we shut her away she won't be able to run, to play in the sun with other children. We want her to enjoy being a child."

Xena was touched by the simplicity of the answer. "Then, what?"

"She's nearly old enough to go back to . . . her mother and her aunts. We only need to care for her a little longer."

"I wish you good luck in doing it," Xena said, patting the girl's hand before letting go. "Come on, Gabrielle." She strode toward the door of the tavern. The others sprang up from their places to follow, as she knew they would.

"Oh, please," Thisbe begged, "you can't go! We need your help!"

Xena spun on her heel, so that Clodias nearly ran into her. He stepped back a pace, intimidated. "Then, tell me the truth. All of it."

The expression on their faces shifted from terror to worry to resignation.

"Very well," Clodias said, torn between needing her to know and not wanting to admit to a very angry warrior that she'd been lured into a situation without her knowledge. "Ianthe is the daughter of Lachesis."

"Lachesis?" Xena asked, raising her eyebrows. "The Fate?"

"Yes," Thisbe said. "She was brought here to us at her birth. Parcaelion was founded in service to the Fates, the Parcae. Lachesis brought her to us. It is impossible for her to take her eyes off the work of keeping every life in the world running smoothly. They care for even the gods' strands of life. You know how it is for a working woman. She knew—who better?—that Clodias and I could not have children of our own. We offered to raise her as our own until she was of an age to go back to Olympus."

"In return," Clodias said hoarsely, "our crops are plentiful. No one falls sick or even has a run of bad luck. In six years we've never seen a locust or a weevil. But six months ago word leaked out that we had a Child of Fortune in the village—a misunderstanding of what she really is: the child of Fate. They thought we had treasure."

"In a way we did," Thisbe said, looking ashamed. "Our good fortunes would cease if she was stolen from us. That's when we started to let it be known that you were protecting her."

"And you did," the girl said. She made her way between

the adults and came over to Xena. She held out a mirror made of crystal in her small hands. "See."

Xena stooped to look into it. At first, the warrior saw only her own face. Before she could protest that nothing was happening, the image swirled into gray nothingness. Then, a shadowy figure wrapped in a cloak, flanked by two other figures, approached a visibly younger Clodias and Thisbe, and handed them a small bundle. Scenes flitted by of the baby Xanthe growing into a child playing with her friends. More scenes unfurled before Xena, of the people of Parcaelion giving alms to the needy, making offerings in their temple, opening celebrations to visitors. Xena felt awe. The child was a seer.

"These are good people," Ianthe's light, high voice said. "They meant well, truly. This is what would have happened had you not come."

The visions became darker. One after another, Xena watched as groups of intruders invaded the village. Each time, people were wounded or killed, and the village burned and destroyed. The carnage was horrific. Men and women alike died by the sword, or by fire, or by torture. The child herself was taken prisoner or slain by greedy barbarians. Or Romans. Or thieves. Gabrielle, beside Xena, made a choking noise and headed outside. Xena herself continued to watch, grim-faced, until the visions ended and the crystal went blank. She took a deep breath, wrenching herself with relief back to the present.

"But these disasters didn't occur," she said. "She's alive."

"That is because you saved us," Clodias admitted. "Otherwise, she is dead many times over. Her enemies would have succeeded without you."

"How? How is it that I helped you but can't remember doing it?"

Clodias's mouth opened and closed several times before he could produce words. "We . . . er, we stole from your future to defend our present."

"That sounds like it would take divine power," Xena said, frowning. "Does Ianthe also possess the power of the gods to play with the order of humans' lives?"

"No," said a voice behind Xena. "But we do."

Xena turned, immediately on guard. Three women stood in the hall, silhouetted against the golden light of the torches. The golden-haired one at the left, holding a distaff, was young and pretty. The wrinkled crone at the right held a pair of shears that gleamed with the same silver as her hair. The auburn-haired woman in the middle with the measuring tape in her hand resembled Ianthe so closely Xena knew at once the villagers had been telling the truth. Clotho, Atropos, and Lachesis, mother of Ianthe. The Fates. The townsfolk dropped to their knees.

"Greetings, Xena," Clotho said. "You don't seem surprised to see us."

"No more than you are," she said, standing at ease with her hand braced on her belt. Gabrielle reappeared at her side. Her friend was a little pale, but she stood tall.

"The people of Parcaelion appealed to us for a champion to defend my daughter," Lachesis said. "You were the chosen one. You have served well. Or you will."

"No," Xena said flatly. "I don't like being forced into fights that are not my business."

"Not even for the sake of mercy?" Thisbe asked. She came up to wrap an arm around her foster daughter's shoulders.

Xena glared down at her.

"You never *asked* me to help. You assumed that I would."

Thisbe cringed, holding the little girl close. Ianthe buried her head against Thisbe's bosom. "Great warrior, I don't know what else we could offer you in exchange, but you'd be saving this child's life! You saw the visions. That is what will happen—what will have happened—if you leave now. Please, help us protect her. I love her. She is my heart."

Xena snorted. Gabrielle knew her friend was thinking hard. She had a soft spot for children, and the little girl was pretty and charming. Ianthe came over to take Xena's hand and looked up into her eyes. That seemed to make up Xena's mind for her.

"All right," she said, turning back to the Fates. "Tell me. Tell me how, and what."

"All things are fated to happen," Atropos said, in her creaky voice. "You would have met all of these ruffians and brigands—later on. But for the sake of my niece, we tied the strand of your life into loops so those encounters would occur earlier in their lives." She nodded to her sister Clotho, who gently picked through the hank of threads in her hand to pull forth a robust strand of darkened bronze twisted into complicated knots.

Xena eyed it. "And how many people will die in the future because I wouldn't be present at those other encounters?"

"If you aid us," Atropos smiled, her thin mouth another wrinkle in her lined face, "none. You will fight the battles that have come before and are to come. If you agree, there will be no more beyond those. We know."

Gabrielle looked at the Fates suspiciously. "How many?"

Clodias fidgeted. "Four bands of thieves in the last two months."

"Four?" Xena exclaimed.

"Six in all," the headman admitted.

"Six?"

"Plus one that you dispatched today," Atropos said. "But there are three yet to come. You must defeat them all to protect Ianthe."

"Nine battles?" Xena asked. "You are asking too much."

The people of Parcaelion burst out in protest.

"But, Warrior Princess," Thisbe said, "you already *have* fought them. Please, Xena. You're a mother, too. Save my child."

Atropos swept her hand across, cutting off all argument.

"I offer you an inducement, Xena," the crone said. "If you will be my niece's champion I promise you this: in days to come, when death is certain, if you call upon me I will hold back my shears. I make this offer to no one lightly. You will make the decision when to use it. I give you free will. What do you say?"

Xena smiled grimly at the demigoddesses. "You already know I'm going to do it, don't you? And not just for a 'Get-out-of-Hades-free' card. I'll do it for her."

"Of course," said Lachesis, placidly. "It's foreordained."

"I don't believe in fate, you know."

"We know," Clotho said, with a smile. "But we believe in you."

"All right." Xena let her voice drop to a cold whisper. She looked the Fates in the eyes one by one. "Let's get it over with."

"Wait," Gabrielle blurted out. "I can help. I have to be with her."

"You are," Lachesis assured her. Clotho displayed the twisted cord of Xena's life. Another, lighter strand of blue and silver was wound tightly against it and tied through three of the loops. "The thread of your life is twined with hers."

Gabrielle stood back, pleased, embarrassed and honored all at the same time. "Well, all right then."

Xena drew her sword and chakram, and braced her feet on the ground.

"Let's do it," she said.

Clotho spun out the bronze thread and passed it to Lachesis. The second Fate drew out the knotted section, swung it into a loop, and crossed the strands.

Xena was plunged into a moonless night. It took a moment for her vision to clear. When it did, she realized she was standing in the middle of the market square. Only the tiniest flickers of fire peeked out through curtains and shutters. The village slept.

She became aware of figures moving stealthily toward the village gate. In the faint starlight, she could see that the wings of the gate stood ajar. The shadows moved erratically. They were coping with a heavy and irregular bundle that wiggled. A stray starbeam glanced off bronze hair as the child Ianthe wrenched her face away from whatever the villains had covering it. She let out a shrill cry for help.

Dogs woke up and began to bark. The sounds of stirring arose in the houses as people stumbled out to see what was wrong.

"Ianthe!" Thisbe's voice cried in the darkness. Clodias appeared behind her bearing a torch just crackling to life. The kidnappers broke into a run. Xena was right behind them.

Burdened as they were, they couldn't move very fast. Xena circled around and met them at the gate, which she shut behind her with a *clang!*

She counted six figures. Men, by the sound of their breathing. Poachers, or worse, by their stench. Her eyes were getting used to the dark now. Ianthe's face was a pale dot.

"Put her down, and you won't get hurt," Xena advised them.

"Get her," a hoarse voice whispered. She heard the unmistakable whisper of metal leaving leather sheaths.

"Eeedeedeedeedeee!" Xena warbled. She brought up a foot and kicked the first man in the face. The villagers ran up with torches while she dispatched one of the ruffians after another.

As soon as the last man was on the ground and Ianthe was restored to her weeping foster-mother's arms, the scene changed. Xena found herself blinking in strong sunshine on the hillside on the road a little way out from Parcaelion. A party of four steppe raiders, clad in black leather and armed to the teeth, were riding toward the village.

She addressed them from her perch beside a cluster of olive trees.

"You're far from home," she said. Surprised, they looked up. "You wouldn't be looking for an easy target, would you? Because I have to disappoint you."

Swords hissed out of scabbards as the men spurred their sweating horses up the hill toward her.

Xena grabbed hold of an overhanging branch, and swung herself at the lead rider.

He was too canny to fall for a trick like that. He reined his horse around and sharply to the right. That gave Xena the opportunity to leap into the saddle behind him and grab him around the throat. She turned her sword pommel down, knocked off the man's helmet, and hit him sharply over the skull. He sagged, and she threw him off the horse. The body rolled down under the hooves of the other horses, making them dance. Xena brought her unwitting mount the rest of the way around in a circle and charged the three warriors.

It didn't take her long to deal with the remaining raiders. She took out on them the frustration she was feeling against the Fates. How dare they claim that her every action was foreordained? She knew she had free will, that she and she alone made the decisions as to what she would do. Xena braced herself against an onslaught by one of the grinning warriors, who rode toward her with sword held high. Without thinking, she whipped the chakram out of her belt. No, she thought. That's probably what they are ordering me to do.

Instead, she dragged her sword around and felt the satisfying strike of metal on metal. She screamed her war cry, spurring her horse in the face of her enemy. They didn't stand a chance against her. None of them did.

By the time she was finished, the townsfolk had heard the noise and come running out to see what was going on. In the crowd, Xena spotted Thisbe cradling Ianthe, who watched her with those old, old eyes.

The third raid was conducted by Phoenicians, who had no doubt been the first ones to misinterpret "fate" as "fortune." They didn't want bloodshed, and were happy to flee intact, promising never to return to that part of Greece.

Fourth and fifth were gangs of thugs and common thieves who had sworn they'd met Xena in Parcaelion before. She was glad to understand at last that not only were they not mistaken, but time was beginning to fall into its normal order. She was relieved. Six battles at full fever pitch were beginning to tell on her, coming on top of a full day's riding, fighting with Roman legionaries, and a rich meal. She sensed that her reactions were slowing slightly.

"This is surreal," Gabrielle said, watching Xena deal with the mercenaries they had encountered in the tavern three days before. "She's here beside us, but she can't see us." Her friend seemed to exist within the boundaries of an arena that began within arm's reach of the feast tables on an evening. Inside the circle Xena was outside, in daylight.

"She stands with one foot in the future and one in the past," Atropos said, without looking at Gabrielle. One of the unshaven men leaped on Xena's back and tried to strangle her with a cord. She struggled, her face growing red. Two men, the worse for having taken some telling punches and strikes from Xena, staggered toward her, swords drawn. Xena lifted her feet, letting all her weight hang from her neck, and kicked out, sending the mercenaries reeling. She let her legs drop, bent over, and threw the third man over her head. He fell on the fourth man. Lachesis watched avidly. From Clotho's skein she chose a thread and held it out to Atropos, who snicked it short. The third man got up and shook his companion's shoulder, but the fourth man didn't move.

Gabrielle watched the goddesses in horror. Until that moment she hadn't really believed in their power. Now she had proof before her. They had the power of life and death, which they exercised without the least trace of emotion.

Taken aback by the death of their fellow adventurer, the remaining three backed away from Xena, who pursued them, ululating all the while. Only Gabrielle, who knew her so well, realized that Xena was beginning to flag.

"Let me help her," she pleaded with the Fates.

"Of course," said Clotho, spinning out the bronze thread. Between her fingers there appeared to be a knot, but it wasn't a flaw. Gabrielle's blue-and-silver strand joined it at that point.

She had only time to say, "Thanks," before she was swept up into the action.

Xena was whisked away from her sight of the mercenaries running away. She saw a brief flash of the Romans arriving in Parcaelion, and herself arriving at the gates. Suddenly, she felt a comforting presence at her back. Familiar. Gabrielle.

"Hi," the blonde woman said, peering over her shoulder. "Can I play, too?"

Xena smiled. "I thought you'd never ask."

They found themselves in a field of withered leaves and torn vines. Gabrielle guessed the season to be winter, with the crops long gathered in, but the new planting not yet done. Around them were at least twenty rough-dressed men armed with rusty swords and farm implements. This was the future, she reminded herself. These were things that hadn't happened yet. Time was yet unformed. They were now affecting what was to come. It felt . . . godlike.

She didn't have time to explore the sensation before the enemy moved in on them. She drew her knives and stood at the ready.

Together she and Xena saw off the first gang, who had sensed easy pickings and were readily scared off by the presence of experienced warriors. The next incursion consisted of two strong, fierce women, rogue soldiers from Lesbos, who had to be nearly killed before they would withdraw.

Gabrielle took a few deep breaths as the chakram whizzed back into Xena's hand. The scene changed. They were back in the agora. Romans seemed to pour in from everywhere, shoving the market carts aside, knocking people to the ground as they broke into every house, searching for the child Ianthe.

"They've called in an entire century," Xena said, grimly. She was breathing very heavily now. Gabrielle was worried. They had to defeat the foe to return to their normal place in their lifelines. How could they battle so many soldiers?

Gabrielle spotted Thisbe and Ianthe running into an alleyway behind their home. A dozen legionaries funneled in after them. Xena reached out to snag Clodias away from two Roman soldiers who were beating him. She brought his face close to hers.

"Where does that go?" she demanded, pointing. "Is there a way to head them off?"

Clodias saw his wife and foster child disappear with the Romans in pursuit. He paled. "Follow me."

He led them into another small street. Xena could hear men shouting to one another, and hoped they hadn't yet caught up with Ianthe.

To her relief, the woman and girl emerged from the narrow passage. Thisbe gasped when she saw Xena, and ran toward her. Ianthe cried out and stumbled, falling to her hands and knees.

"Ianthe!" Thisbe started back toward her. Xena grabbed

the woman and swung her into Gabrielle's arms.

"Hold on to her!" Xena started running as the Romans came pouring out. She screamed a war cry that startled some of the legionaries into halting. It was enough of a distraction for her to pull her chakram and send it ricocheting off the stone walls of the alley. The steel circlet knocked into the temples and jaws of several men, taking them out of the equation. The quarters were tight enough that the rest of the men had to climb over their fellows to get at her.

But the first soldier was still standing. It was the same man Xena had defeated before—could it only have been that afternoon? He clenched his teeth in a bitter smile as the two of them circled. The child cowered between them at their feet. Xena watched the Roman's eyes, waiting to see where he would strike. He swept up his gladius. Xena countered, raising her sword to catch his blade. He parried and stabbed upward, trying to get under her guard. Their swords rasped together to the hilts. Xena could smell sweat, fear, and garlic on him. He disengaged, shifted a few feet to the side and lunged again. Xena admired his skill even as she diverted his stroke, knocking his blade out of line.

The Roman didn't like being bested. His eyes ablaze, he leaped at her. Xena sidestepped and smacked him on the back, sending him staggering. She had to twist suddenly to avoid landing on the weeping Ianthe. Off-balance, Xena's heel skidded on the smooth-flagged street. She went down, dropping her sword. The Roman wheeled around and leaped across her prone body. She grabbed for his booted foot, but missed. He stood over her, his sword raised on high. Xena braced herself.

But he didn't chop at her. Instead, with a vicious smile, the Roman brought his weapon down toward Ianthe's head. The girl screamed. Xena stuck out a desperate hand. Ianthe was just out of her reach.

Xena cried out, "Atropos, no!"

The man froze in place, the sword's edge just a hair's breadth away from its target. All of the combatants had stopped moving.

The Fates shimmered into existence beside Xena. She got to her feet.

"So you used my gift for her," Atropos said, with her wintry smile. A narrow pink thread rested within the open maw of her scissors. She drew the shears away, leaving the strand intact. "Generous of you."

"You know I couldn't have it any other way," Xena said.

"Of course not," Lachesis said. Thisbe clutched the girl to her bosom and brushed her off, making motherly clucking noises all the while.

"They will withdraw now," Atropos said. "He was angry at you for losing his commission. It was not a good enough reason to return here. He will retire in disgrace. Your task is at an end. There will be no more attacks."

Xena straightened up and sheathed her sword. "Good." She waited for a moment. The Fates stood, smiling at her as the scene around them blurred. They found themselves back in the dimly lit feast hall.

"You have our thanks," Clotho said.

"And ours," Clodias added, swinging his arms wide as if to embrace the warriors. "You are welcome here any time. We will throw another feast for you! We will sing your praises!"

"I think we've seen enough of Parcaelion," Xena said, backing away from his exuberance. "Now and forever." She walked to the door and glanced back at Gabrielle. "Are you coming?"

"And we're leaving again, without getting a chance to rest, *and* without any kind of reward," Gabrielle said, shifting in her saddle. Not only did her rear end still hurt, but her muscles ached from fighting. She had a number of bruises and grazes from bumping into stone walls.

"Except having saved that child from her enemies," Xena said, staring straight ahead. She, too, sat her horse gingerly. After ten battles she must have been sore all over.

"Which you would have anyway," Gabrielle pointed out. "It's a shame that Atropos didn't give you another second chance to keep for yourself. That could come in useful in the future."

Xena smiled ruefully, meeting her eyes at last. "She knew

I was going to use it to save Ianthe. I was never meant to be able to keep it for later."

"That's really unfair, after all you did for them!"

Xena shook her head. "They'd never give anything away. Fate isn't generous. You should know that by now."

"That," Gabrielle said, "is why I like people more than gods."

"Maybe we have done some good," Xena said, thoughtfully. "We've ensured that that child has time to learn more about human ways before she returns to Olympus. Perhaps she'll come to change things."

"Now *that*," Gabrielle said, with a grin, "is a future I'd like to see."

XENA AT THE BATTLE OF SALAMIS

Jaye Cameron

"Gabrielle, please, please, tell me a story," begged Anyte, a twelve-year-old beauty. (As Gabrielle looked into her young blue eyes, she could almost see her own sister Lila.) More than anyone else, Anyte hungered for Gabrielle's tales of Xena and the Way of the Warrior, and the girl pestered Gabrielle for stories as soon as the bard sat by the fire.

"What shall I tell you about this time," laughed Gabrielle.

"Tell me again how Xena saved me from both my cruel father and the arms of Poseidon and brought me here to live with you."

Gabrielle began to speak using the singsong, low-pitched voice of the storyteller. As she spoke, the fog that crept in toward their campfire seemed to disappear and the hoarfrost that was already settling on the twigs seemed to melt. Anyte could almost feel the soft, salt air of the Aegean Sea and see the hills of the Greek mainland as they captured the sunlight that was so brilliant in that part of the Mediterranean.

"Ten years ago, Xena still considered herself an apprentice in the Way of the Warrior. She had mastered the weapons of the land and was skilled at the strategies that brought victories in the forests, hills, and plains. Now, the Way led her to the sea where the sleek fighting ships sped with the dolphins through the deep waters. Xena had heard tales of a mighty queen in the Persian Empire named Artemisia, who was said to be one of the most brilliant admirals in the fleet of the great King Xerxes. Xena wanted to join her and learn her secrets, but she never imagined that on Artemisia's ship, she would fight one of the greatest naval battles the world had ever known, or that she would fight against her old friends the Greeks.

"Xena traveled to the northern shore of the Aegean Sea and reached the Hellespont—that narrow strip of water that separated the Aegean from a great inland sea with water so dark people called it the Black Sea. The warrior princess at first looked for a small boat to charter to cross the Hellespont, but then she thought again. If she were going to learn the secrets of naval warfare, she should be prepared to survive the sea's challenges. This forbidding spot where the tides swept the water through narrow, rocky straits would be a perfect test for her. She offered a prayer to the sea god, Poseidon, and dove into churning waves. The waters from the Aegean Sea—warmed by the Mediterranean sun—were not as cold as those of the northern lakes where Xena had first learned the strong strokes that pulled her through the current, but the bite of the salt surprised her for it is even saltier than the great oceans that surround her land.

"As she rhythmically swam through the current, she tried not to think of the stories she had heard of monsters who lived in the deep, salty water. Storytellers told of sailors who had been pulled under the wine-dark sea by beasts with tentacles like snakes that held the power of six men. Others told of great fish whose teeth could break through the strongest bone. Xena had learned not to recoil from such fearful thoughts, but instead to embrace them—her warrior nature almost made her wish for a monster to challenge her so she could prove her great strength. 'Well, actually,' she thought honestly, 'I'd probably have to depend on my quick wits to defeat the great sea beasts if they are truly as formidable as the poets say.'

"Engaged by these thoughts and almost hypnotized by the strong swimming strokes, Xena crossed the two miles of the straits and climbed onto the rocks of the shore. The salty water dried quickly on her skin as she stood in the sun, leaving white crystals on her tanned body. 'I'm going to dive into the nearest river, even if it is as cold as the North Sea, to wash this salt off,' Xena thought. 'Poseidon can keep his salty, monster-filled home.' She then started walking south along the eastern edge of the Aegean toward Artemisia's kingdom.

"Xena soon came to the kingdom of the Lydians, who had become fabulously wealthy with their invention of a wondrous thing: instead of trading for goods, the Lydians had taken precious metals—silver and gold—and formed them into regular round pieces with the imprint of their kings and gods. These they called *coins* and used them to trade for whatever they needed. This system was so convenient for merchants that Lydia had become a crossroads for travelers seeking to sell their goods. These coins were so wondrous, that the Persians had adopted them to use throughout their empire and even the Greeks were starting to make some of their own. Xena shook her head in some disapproval as she passed a Lydian merchant guarded by many armed men. 'People now kill to steal these coins,' she said to no one in particular. There would always be work for those who followed the Way of the Warrior.

"Six days after she had crossed the Hellespont, Xena had covered the two hundred miles that brought her to the kingdom of Caria on the southwestern edge of Asia Minor. She slowly traveled south to the city of Halicarnassus to present herself to Queen Artemisia. Like Lydia and many other small kingdoms, Caria was part of the great Persian Empire, and the Persian kings had wisely allowed their subject peoples to keep their own customs and rulers. In this way they ensured the loyalty of most, and this was how Artemisia continued to be queen while belonging to the empire. For this trip, Xena was not exploring the far-flung lands of the empire, which encompassed exotic peoples and animals. Her single-minded goal was the huge naval yard where Xerxes had spent a vast fortune building the greatest navy the world

had ever known, and where Artemisia served as admiral in
the great king's navy.

"As Xena slowly traveled south, she became aware that
all was not peaceful in Caria. Centuries before, Greek colonists had established city-states on the coast of the kingdoms that bordered the eastern Aegean. Like Greeks
everywhere, the enterprising colonists had focused on trade
(and accumulating these new coins that the Lydians had
made famous). However, also like Greeks everywhere, these
on the edge of the Persian Empire were fiercely independent.
The Persians had been willing to leave the Greeks pretty
much to themselves, but they installed pro-Persian leaders
in the city-states. The Greeks resented even this level of
interference, and a few years before Xena's arrival, some of
the cities had revolted against Persian rule. The rebellion
had begun in Miletus, a rich coastal city in Artemisia's kingdom. The Persians had crushed the revolt and virtually destroyed Miletus, but that did not bring peace.

"Xena heard excited stories from Greeks in the shoreline
villages—Athens and Sparta on the mainland would avenge
their defeat. Greeks would never live subject to the shame
of 'barbarian' rule and would rise up to smite the Persians.
Xena also heard complaints in Persian villages, where people resented the arrogant Greeks who would not learn their
lesson. The warrior princess shook her head as she once
again saw people eager to fight."

"Why didn't Xena leave that region since war was brew-
ing?" Anyte asked, briefly breaking the storytelling spell that
Gabrielle was weaving.

"Did you ever see Xena be moved from her purpose simply because of a fight?" the bard answered. "I was more
worried than Xena, and I wasn't even there. I had vivid
dreams in which I saw Poseidon rear out of the sea and
smash ships to kindling, and I saw Aphrodite weep because
people were too busy killing each other to make love. I tried
to call to Xena in my dreams and my thoughts, and though
she told me later that she had dreamed of me, she did not
return. Now let me get back to my story and tell you of the
court of Queen Artemisia.

"Xena entered the courtyard of the great palace at Halicarnassus and admired the gardens and fountains that graced the huge entryway. The doorway to the palace itself was a great archway covered in thinly pounded gold, so when the setting sun shone on it the brilliance almost blinded any late-afternoon visitor. Xena had known that there were many wealthy, independent women in the Persian Empire, and she now could see that Artemisia, queen of Caria, was one of the wealthiest. Caria lay next to wealthy Lydia, and had fine ports on the Mediterranean to serve the growing trade from the Greek city-states. The shrewd queen knew how to make the most of her kingdom's location, but her prosperity depended on good relations with the Greeks. The rumors Xena had heard seemed to threaten these ties, but the great queen seemed unperturbed when she greeted Xena in the magnificent hall of her palace.

" 'Xena, my warrior sister, welcome to Caria. Tales of your adventures have reached our lands from the songs of traveling poets, and I'm delighted to meet you in person.' Artemisia was dressed in the flowing robes of Persian women, made of light blue silk so finely spun that they seemed almost transparent. Her hair was as dark as Xena's own, but was piled on her head in a mound of curls crowned with a finely wrought gold band. As delicate as Artemisia appeared, Xena was not deluded into underestimating her—when the queen gave Xena a welcoming hug, the warrior princess could feel Artemisia's strong arms and shoulders. Artemisia was as formidable a warrior as Xena herself, but more experienced in naval warfare. Xena was hungry to go beyond the necessary pleasantries and see Artemisia's famed warships.

"Artemisia sent servants to show Xena to her quarters, where she could bathe and borrow royal robes to dine. Once she was refreshed, Xena joined the queen at a sumptuous feast where servants brought delicacies that had clearly come from all over in the eastern Mediterranean. As they ate, they shared stories of battles they had fought and enemies they had defeated—Xena was thrilled to be in the company of another warrior woman. Suddenly their pleasant dinner was interrupted by loud voices coming from the courtyard. As the door slammed open, both Xena and Artemisia were on their feet with swords drawn. They moved so quickly that even the royal guards were taken by surprise. A man dressed as royalty burst in surrounded by his own guard. Upon recognizing the intruder, Artemisia relaxed and laughed: 'Cyaxares, what are you doing bursting into my home uninvited? Just because you are king in your own land of Calyndia does not mean you are welcome here.' Xena saw the hate in the man's eyes and kept a firm grip on her own sword.

" 'I've come to demand that you marry me,' said Cyaxares. 'I'm tired of waiting for you to choose from among your suitors. I am the strongest, and when we combine our kingdoms, we will rival even great King Xerxes himself in wealth and power.'

" 'Never,' said Artemisia. 'When I decide to marry it is because *I* choose my husband, and I can assure you I will never choose you. Don't ever presume to enter my presence uninvited again, or I won't be so patient.' Her eyes had grown as hard as Cyaxares's and the queen had made a secret signal, which caused a heavily armed force to enter silently and surround the king and his men. Cyaxares reconsidered his position, and he, too, let out a cold laugh. 'I was only kidding, Artemisia. Of course, I know you are queen in your own land. I am really here with a message from Xerxes. Let me join you and your warrior friend with a cup of wine and I'll tell you the exciting news.'

"Artemisia allowed Cyaxares to sit down with them, but Xena kept her sword close at hand and her wits steady. She took no more wine and drank only fragrant rose-scented lemonade. 'What is your news, Cyaxares?' asked the queen. He replied, 'Xerxes has lost patience with the Greeks. His mother, Atossa, has finally persuaded him to invade the Greek mainland and conquer the city-states that had so arrogantly interfered in the revolt of your own city Miletus.' Cyaxares spoke with the excitement of a man who sees the chance for plunder. 'The best news is that the fleet will sail in the Aegean to support Xerxes' land forces as they cross the Hellespont and invade Athens. Xerxes wants you to bring five of your ships, and I will join the Persian forces with three of mine. Now is our chance to prove once and for all that we are masters of the sea and that Athens' fledgling navy cannot withstand us.'

"Artemisia's eyes shone as the imagined the impending battle, and the queen poured a large cup of wine for Cyaxares as they toasted the upcoming fight. 'I will even share secret news with you as a mark of my goodwill,' said the king. 'I have been contacted by a Greek traitor who wishes to defect and seek his fortune within the Persian Empire. He tells me he brings a gift of great value to Xerxes, and if I will gain him an audience, he will help me in the battle. He commands a warship, and will send me a message if we engage and throw his support to me. This should gain us additional advantage when the battle comes.' Artemisia laughed scornfully, 'You can depend on traitors, but I count on my own wits and strength in a battle. We'll see who ends up better off,' and she ordered more wine and cakes.

"Xena had some conflicting emotions. She could feel the excitement rise within her—what she always felt before a battle. She loved the anticipation that caused her muscles to tense and her brain to clear. However, she was not certain about this fight—she had many good relations with the Greeks and was not eager to offend their gods and goddesses, who had always shown her favor. She could imagine armed Athena rising to join the Greeks against her.

"Later, when she and Artemisia were again alone, she expressed another reservation: 'If I were going into battle on land, I would not want that snake, Cyaxares, guarding my flank. Is it also important to trust your companions in naval engagements?' 'Yes,' said Artemisia. 'I know that Cyaxares would be very happy if I died in the battle, because then he could try to take my kingdom. With me alive, he knows he cannot. I will not marry him, and I can easily defend my lands from him. But, I can watch my own flank, and with you at my side, we will be victorious. Tomorrow, we'll get the ships ready and see the messages from Xerxes that will give us our assignment. You will learn naval warfare in the best possible way—by joining in battle.'

"The next morning, the women once more donned their battle armor, and Xena accompanied Artemisia to the harbor. The warrior princess was amazed by what she saw—

these were huge warships, the likes of which she had never seen. 'What kind of ships are these?' asked Xena in surprise. 'They are triremes,' answered Artemisia, 'the latest ships of war. Each has three banks of oars on each side, with the oarsmen rowing on three different levels. It takes twenty-seven oarsmen on each side at each level to move the giant ships.' 'I can see the ports through which the oars will fit on two levels,' said Xena, 'but how can yet more oarsmen fit at the top?'

" 'Do you see that extension out from the deck? The top oarsmen fit their oars onto that outrigger, and they can thus row skillfully without tangling the oars with the men sitting below. The 170 oarsmen can move the trireme with great speed through the water. In addition, the trireme will take thirty more on board: ten soldiers to fight off any who would try to board, four archers to attack the opposing soldiers, and fifteen deckhands to help where needed. Finally, the ships carry the two most important people: a flautist, who pipes time for the rowers and a *trierarch*, the ship's commander who steers at the helm.' 'Only ten soldiers and four archers?' exclaimed Xena incredulously. 'How can any commander hope to win a battle with so few soldiers?' Artemisia laughed. 'Ships are no longer used simply to move soldiers from one place to another. They are weapons in themselves. Look at the bow of this magnificent trireme.'

"Xena walked to the front of the sleek vessel and saw that the bow extended far out just below the waterline, and it was covered with bronze plates so that it was a huge spear that could be driven home by the force of the oarsmen rowing. Xena gazed into the painted eyes of the ship that were just above the ram; eyes to guide the warship in its fearful purpose.

" 'With the ships themselves as weapons,' explained Artemisia, 'practiced oarsmen and, most important, a skilled helmsman can ram and sink any other ship on the water. Our triremes allow us to control both the seas and the all-important ports. Our spies tell us that the Athenians have just built a fleet of triremes, but our Phoenician-trained oarsmen will outmaneuver the Greeks, and there is not a better admiral on the sea than I!'

"Xena looked again at the eyes painted on the warship and thought of the two hundred men who would be spilled into the sea as the pointed ram penetrated the wooden walls of the opposing trireme. It seemed as if the eyes were those of the sea monsters that lived in the Mediterranean to prey on humans—they seemed to glint in anticipation of the upcoming battle that would send corpses into the sea. While Xena explored the ships and the harbor, Artemisia went to receive her orders. That evening they sat together again and planned the upcoming campaign.

" 'Xerxes is bringing over eight hundred ships to support his land campaign.' Artemisia said. 'We are to guard the merchant ships that will supply his army and make sure that the Athenian fleet stays out of the war. Xerxes will surely defeat the Greeks in this campaign, then there will be no more threat of Greek revolts in our lands. We leave in three days; you will ride on my ship, and this battle will complete your education in naval warfare!'

"That night Xena's dreams troubled her and showed how torn she was about the upcoming battle. She did not want to help Xerxes' forces defeat the Greeks, who had always been her friends. She did not want to offend the Greek gods, who had shown favor on her, but she did not want to miss what would be the most exciting naval battle the world had ever known. Finally, just before dawn, she had a dream that was the most vivid of all. In it I appeared with the goddess Athena as vividly as if we were real. 'Gabrielle, what are you doing here?' asked Xena in her dream. 'What do you want me to do?' 'I come with Athena to tell you to sail with Artemisia. The goddess has a task for you that you can only fulfill from Artemisia's trireme.' 'What is it?' asked Xena, but the dream spirits did not answer; they faded away into the soft predawn light. But Xena awoke from the dream refreshed and strong of purpose. She didn't know what awaited her, but she knew it was her destiny to sail with Artemisia in Xerxes' forces.

"Xerxes' land army had great success at the beginning of the engagement. His engineers had built a great pontoon bridge across the Hellespont (where Xena had swum) and the whole army crossed without even getting their sandals wet. They defeated the Spartans at the Battle of Thermopylae, although not easily, I must confess. They found a Greek shepherd to betray the Spartans who so nobly stood against even the Immortals, the elite Persian guard. With the pass taken, Xerxes' army swept down the Greek peninsula; Athens was in its path.

"The frightened Athenians sent to the Delphic oracle to ask what they should do, and as usual the oracle gave a reply in the form of an ambiguous riddle: 'Take refuge behind a wooden wall that shall help thee and thy children.' Some Athenians took this quite literally and built a wooden palisade on top of the Acropolis, where they awaited the Persians. However, the Athenian leader Themistocles gave a different interpretation to the oracle's advice: He said the 'wooden walls' were Athens' new wooden ships, and most of the Athenians evacuated the city to an island—Salamis—just off the coast of Attica. Salamis lay just at the head of the Bay of Eleusis with narrow channels on the eastern and western ends of the island that led into the bay. The straits were no more than a couple of miles wide—not suitable for a pitched battle with hundreds of triremes.

"The Persians swept into Athens and, after a fierce battle, burnt the temples and the palisade on top of the Acropolis. Citizens on Salamis could see the smoke rise from their beloved city as the Persians looted anything that was left there. The Greek fleet was beached on the east side of the island of Salamis and now it was left to the Persian navy to finish off the victory.

"Xerxes called his generals and admirals together to decide the best course of action. The Athenian leader Themistocles wanted to lure the Persians into a trap in the narrow straits, so he sent a slave pretending to be a spy to tell Xerxes that the Greek fleet was going to escape out of the straits to flee their trap at Salamis. Xerxes wanted to strike right away to defeat the fleet and seal his victory before the weather turned difficult. It was already September, and the fleet could not sail in the winter. Artemisia stood up in the council: 'Do not sail into the straits, great king. It is surely a trap, for the speed, maneuverability and greater strength of our navy will be lost in the Straits of Salamis.

Just as a few Spartans could hold off the Immortals in the pass of Thermopylae, do not give the Athenians the same chance to trap the navy.'

"Cyaxares shouted down Artemisia. 'Do not listen to this weak woman. Leave it to the men in your navy to win this battle for you. If Artemisia does not have the heart for Greek blood, leave her here on shore to wait on your majesty while I lead my ships into the straits and destroy the Athenian navy.'

"Faced with the pressure of the upcoming winter weather, Xerxes decided to risk all on the attack on the Greek fleet at Salamis. Against her better judgment, Artemisia joined the fleet; she could not resist taking her ships in against the best that the Greeks could throw at her. Just before dusk, the Persians moved two hundred ships to block the western channel near Salamis; the Greek fleet would not be able to escape that way. Then at midnight, the rest of the fleet— over three hundred triremes, including Artemisia's and Cyaxares's—lined up at the head of the eastern straits. Xerxes himself had set up a golden throne on a hill overlooking the water, from where he could watch the battle. Just before dawn, the Greeks dragged their galleys down to the water, boarded, ran out their oars, and waited for the signal. At dawn the dramatic movements began.

"The Greek trumpeters sounded and the flutes on all the triremes—Greek and Persian—struck up their tunes. To the rhythm of the flutes, men pulled at their oars and the galleys began to move out into the channel. As the two fleets closed, the Greeks in the center of the line backed water with their oars so the center collapsed. Seeing the Greeks backing up, some Persian admirals were convinced they were fleeing and, shouting their war cries, they charged into the breach. But the Persians did not know the local seas as did the Greeks, and they were lured into a trap. A great swell of water that periodically flowed from the channel caught some of the Persian ships from behind. Some were knocked out of line and others were turned broadside to be exposed to the killing thrust of the Greek rams. The famed mobility of the Persian sailors was of no use in the narrow straits; the ships collided with each other, and as Persian ships sank the confusion only increased."

"But Gabrielle, where were Artemisia and Xena?" Anyte broke in eagerly. "Were they in the straits? Were they in danger?"

"Of course they were," Gabrielle answered. "Artemisia placed her ships on the right flank of the line as far away as possible from Cyaxares, whose ships were on the left, where he had been told he could meet the Greek traitor. Thus, neither were drawn into the trap in the center and escaped the immediate danger. However, both were left with the new danger of how to escape from the straits as the victorious Greeks began to chase and surround remaining Persian vessels.

"Now hush child while I tell you how Xena's and Artemisia's skill in war helped them fulfill Athena's purpose.

"As Artemisia led her ships in the right flank of the line, there was not enough room to turn to have the mighty bow strike the Greek ships that were rapidly approaching. Then Xena saw the skill of the admiral. As Artemisia came close to a Greek ship she let out a shout and the oarsmen on the right side quickly pulled in their oars as the trireme sped so close to the Greek ship that the side of Artemisia's trireme sheared off the oars on one side of the opposing vessel. The Greek ship was crippled and Xena and the archers could pick off opposing Greeks. Now Artemisia had room to turn, for it was past time to get out of the straits while they still could. As they rowed out, two fleet Greek ships chased them and were gaining on them. Artemisia urged her men to row more quickly, but then she saw a ship blocking their way. It was Cyaxares!

"He had turned his ship slightly so that he blocked their way while he was waiting for the Greek ships to catch them and destroy them. Xena and Artemisia saw him standing at the helm, slowing his ship, and they saw the evil smirk on his face as he believed he had succeeded in trapping Artemisia. The queen of Caria slowed her ship, looking around for an escape. Xena felt the rage of the warrior rise in her; this was the rage that drove the Viking berserkers to fight blindly, and the rage that led Hercules to his heroics. She saw Cyaxares's ship through a bloodred haze but her mind was icy clear. 'Artemisia,' she shouted, 'speed up and ram him.' 'I can't, Xena' said the queen. 'Xerxes is watching and will kill me for treason if I make it out of here.' 'Don't argue,' Xena roared, with her teeth bared in the look of the wolf, 'ram him now.'

"The two warrior women stood at the helm as the flautist sped up the cadence. Artemisia's ship sped through the water directly at Cyaxares. Too late he saw their purpose and tried to turn his trireme to speed away. They had the momentum and the bronze tip smashed into the trireme, accompanied by the sounds of splintered wood and screams of oarsmen who felt the bite of the bronze in their flesh. The ship sank rapidly and Artemisia's ship swept over the drowning men as it continued its way out of the straits.

"This bold act brought some immediate benefits to Artemisia and her warrior companion. First, the captain of the Greek ship that was chasing them assumed Artemisia was helping the Greeks, so he veered off to turn his attention to other Persian vessels. Remarkably, Xerxes' counselors who were watching the battle (that was rapidly turning into a rout) misunderstood the action. One advisor remarked to Xerxes as the king sat on his golden throne placed on the high cliff overlooking the straits, 'Master, do you see Artemisia, how well she fights? Lo, she has sunk a vessel of the enemy.' Xerxes replied, 'Are you sure the valiant ship is really that of Artemisia?' 'Yes,' replied the counselor, 'I recognize her standard on the prow.' The king of the Calyndians had lost his standard early in the engagement, so Xerxes could not recognize his ship and simply assumed it was Greek.

"It seemed that Artemisia would break free of the trap unscathed, but there remained one more Greek ship blocking their way—the ship of a Greek traitor, Criton, who had conspired with Cyaxares to betray the Greeks and defect to the Persians. He had kept his ship back with the Calyndian vessels, away from the heart of the fighting. With the victory clearly going to the Greeks, Criton had not yet decided what to do. He stood on deck and watched as Artemisia's ship approached. Should he attack her ship and restore his reputation with the Greeks, or should he turn and continue to seek his fortune with the great King Xerxes? He had his gift for Xerxes with him—his beautiful two-year-old daughter, with hair like the sun and eyes the color of the sea. She was as lovely as Aphrodite herself, and Criton planned to give the child to Xerxes. She would be raised in the harem and trained in the arts of love. Then when she was twelve, she would be given to the king as a concubine to please him in his old age."

"That's me!" interrupted Anyte. "Why would my father have planned such a cruel fate for me?" The girl looked crestfallen as her eyes lost the excited fire they had when Gabrielle told of the battle. She once again resembled the hurt, haunted child whom Xena had brought to Gabrielle so many years before.

"I'm sorry, child," the bard said gently. "Know that there are evil people in the world who care more for power and wealth than they do for the helpless ones in their charge. There is no crime greater than to betray that trust. But remember, you were beloved of Athena. It was she who sent Xena to save you. Now let me continue the tale. Try to forget the evil as you hear how the Way of the Warrior brought your salvation."

"Xena saw you, a frightened child on the deck, and the rage rose up in her again. In the sun that shone brightly on the carnage of the battle, Xena saw a vision of Athena smiling, and the warrior princess knew this was why she was here. 'I will save the child, Artemisia. Pull your ship close and shear the Greek ship's oars off. When it is disabled, I will board, and as soon as I am clear with the girl, ram the ship of that traitor and escape back to Xerxes. The skilled admiral didn't hesitate, and she drew her ship close to attack. Before Criton knew what was happening, Artemisia had drawn close, ordered her oars pulled in, and disabled his vessel. As Criton shrieked with rage, Xena leaped on board.

"With sword and boots, Xena quickly dispatched the foot-soldiers and archers who guarded the deck and she kicked many overboard while slashing the others. Then she approached the helm, where Criton had grabbed you and held a knife to your neck. 'If you want this child to live, you will immediately leave my ship and tell Artemisia to pull away. Otherwise, I will kill her now and swim away from this place!' Criton shouted. He cut your neck, drawing blood to prove his resolve." (Anyte fingered the scar she still bore as she listened to Gabrielle's account.)

"Xena neither answered nor hesitated, but faster than the eye could see, flung her chakram at the hand that held the knife. The razor-sharp circle spun through the air and cut Criton's hand, forcing him to drop the killing blade. As the lethal circlet ricocheted off the mast and returned to Xena, Criton screamed in pain and rage: 'You still will not have her! Poseidon or the sea monsters can claim this child.' With these brutal words, Criton used his good arm to fling Anyte into the sea on the far side of the ship.

"You had hardly begun to sink below the waves in the powerful current of the straits when Xena dove into the water and swept you into her strong arms. She surfaced and swung you around to her back and told you to hold tightly to her neck. You didn't need to be told twice, and you held on with strength remarkable in so small a child. Xena began to swim, stroking strongly to the Greek mainland where Xerxes' forces guarded the great king on his golden throne. As Xena swam, she heard the sickening crash of a bronze bow striking Criton's wooden ship. Artemisia had struck true, and Xerxes witnessed her prowess again. Herodotus, the Greek historian who preserved the details of this battle, recorded Xerxes' words as he watched most of his ships sink and Artemisia victoriously escape the trap: 'My men have become weak as women, and my women strong as men.' Both Artemisia and Xena would have laughed at his pointless comparison, but they didn't hear it as they were too busy finishing this day's work.

"Xena brought you on shore safely and was letting you rest a moment before moving on. She did not intend to return to Xerxes' court, but instead take you straight north up the Greek peninsula to bring you home to me. But she took a moment to look back at the carnage of the Battle of Salamis. The fight, which had begun at dawn, had lasted for eight hours. The Persians lost more than two hundred ships, while the Greeks lost only forty. The surviving Persian ships fled, and never again engaged the Greeks at sea. Athens had proved itself to be the master of the eastern Mediterranean.

"As Xena looked at the bodies of men and the wrecks of mighty triremes, her mind was lost in reflections on the battle. Suddenly a hand grabbed her ankle and pulled her down; it was Cyaxares! He, too, had swum from the wreckage of his ship to the shore near Xerxes. He had been resting behind a rock when Xena brought you ashore, and now he pulled Xena down and reached his hands around her neck. 'I'll get even with you right now,' he growled, 'and I'll take this little blond gift to Xerxes myself. Once I tell him how Artemisia rammed my ship she will die horribly and I'll have her lands. She should not have challenged me!'

"His hands closed tightly around Xena's throat, cutting off her air. Even as her eyes began to dim, the rage of battle rose in her once more. With superhuman determination, she reached for her breastplate and drew the dagger she kept hidden there. With her last ounce of strength she drove it deeply under Cyaxeres's ribs to his heart. She grinned as she heard his death rattle and felt his hands loosen on her throat. 'Here's my last gift to you, Artemisia,' Xena thought as she shoved the body off to the side.

"The Greek historian Herodotus would write that no one from the Calyndian ship survived to tell of Artemisia's act, so she continued as Xerxes' favorite admiral. Indeed, when Xerxes needed someone to take his children back to his own lands in Asia Minor, the great king entrusted them to the queen of Caria, who had proven herself that day to be the greatest captain of the Persian fleet. Xena's trip home with you was uneventful, and you have been with us ever since, growing stronger and wiser every day."

Anyte sighed with satisfaction as the spell of the story faded and the fog once more shrouded the woods around the campfire. "I'm going to follow the Way of the Warrior just like Xena," she said energetically.

Gabrielle laughed and said: "But remember, without the Way of the Bard to preserve the stories, the Ways of the Warriors would be no more than forgotten fights."

A WEAPON OF FLESH AND BONE

Tim Waggoner
AND
Russell Davis

Xena paused in her long walk and took a sip from her dwindling water supply. The sun beat down on the dead landscape, searing the already tiled and broken ground. She saw no living vegetation, and the only evidence that there ever had been any was the occasional leafless tree desperately clinging to the dry soil. She had not seen any sign of water in this place since Athena, Goddess of Wisdom and Battle, had banished her here.

Xena removed the wide leather thong that was holding her long, dark hair in place. It was damp with her sweat, and she quickly pulled her hair back into place and retied it. She had traveled across the length and breadth of the known world (as well as the not-so-known world), and she was no stranger to deserts. This one seemed almost familiar, as if she'd been here before. But then all deserts were alike: hot, mind-numbingly boring and—unless you were well prepared (and thanks to Athena, she was not)—deadly.

At the farthest edge of the horizon, she could make out a variation in the landscape—a hill, maybe a tall building. Distance was deceptive in this heat, and there was no telling what it was. Still, it was a destination of sorts, and it wasn't as if she had anywhere else to go. She started walking toward the whatever-it-was, mindful of the fact that she had no armor and no weapons, and that if she met anyone hostile she'd be in deep trouble.

"Damn you anyway, Athena," she muttered and adjusted the straps of her pack. Three days ago—or was it four?—Athena had come to her in a dream.

"Xena," the goddess said, *"you are a warrior princess, of that there is no doubt. But what my brother Ares has failed to impress upon you is that being a warrior is not about the sword, or your precious chakram, but about using your mind. You've been clever, but only at the last moment, when there was no other choice. And there's a difference between cleverness and wisdom. I intend to teach you the latter."*

"Why?" Xena asked.

"Simple," replied Athena. *"Because your arrogance displeases me, and your suffering at my hands will certainly annoy my brother Ares."* The goddess chuckled. *"With wisdom comes humility. Or death. Which do you think you will find, Xena?"*

"I don't fear you, Athena!" Xena shouted. "I have faced the challenges of the gods before and lived to tell the tale!"

"That was then, Warrior Princess," Athena said. *"This is now. When you awaken, this dream will be over, but your nightmare will have only begun."*

Xena had woken to a nightmare, all right. Gabrielle was gone, as were all of her weapons and belongings. Instead of armor, she found herself garbed in a simple, gray tunic, the sort of outfit a servant might wear. On the sun-blasted ground next to her was a pack containing three skins of water, and enough dried meat for only a few spare meals. She had eaten the last of the food yesterday, and she had only half a skin of water left. Whatever was in the distance, Xena hoped to find food and water—especially water—there. It would be awfully hard to learn wisdom *after* dying of thirst.

As the sun continued pounding down on her, Xena contemplated calling upon Ares. But she knew that would be hopeless—the War God despised weakness of any kind, and most likely, He would be unable to help her here, in whatever hellish place Athena had sent her. *Besides,* she thought to herself, *I think Athena's wrong. I don't always reach for my sword when there's trouble.* Still, she knew she had no choice but to continue to play the goddess' game, so she trudged onward, one aching step after another, trying desperately (and without much success) not to think about cool, clear, life-sustaining water.

The punishing sun had finally edged toward the horizon when Xena realized she wasn't alone on the desert landscape. Off to the west, she could just make out the form of a rider on horseback. Was the rider male? Female? It was impossible to tell from this distance. Though she was incredibly thirsty, Xena was still a warrior, and long-practiced caution won out over thirst.

How's that for using my head, Athena? she thought. The goddess didn't respond, not that Xena had expected her to. Xena scanned the desert all around her, checking to make certain the rider didn't have any friends with less-than-noble intentions who might be approaching from a different direction. Seeing no one else, she began heading toward the stranger. The rider wisely kept the horse to a walk. Ride a mount any faster in this heat, and you'd soon be serving up a meal of horseflesh for the vultures.

Xena judged she had crossed half the distance to the rider, who was moving at an angle northeastward to her, when the stranger reined the horse to a stop. She'd been noticed. Xena halted to give the rider a chance to look her over, decide if she was a threat. It would be the rider's choice whether to make contact or not. If the rider elected to move off, Xena could hardly run the stranger down on foot, certainly not as weak as she was.

The rider sat motionless for several long moments, a blurry figure obscured by a curtain of shimmering heat, watching. Finally, the rider tapped heels to horse flanks and began moving toward Xena at a slow trot. She could have merely waited for the stranger to arrive, let the horse do the work for both of them, but she resumed walking. As the rider drew near, Xena stopped and stared.

The stranger was a young woman in her early twenties, if that. She had straight black hair and, while not unattractive, had a hard face, as if she were formed of marble instead of flesh. Her eyes were clear and as coldly penetrating as those of a hawk. It was . . . herself. Xena, as she had been not long after being ostracized from her home village of Amphipolis. The girl was somewhat slimmer of face and limb, of course, and her flesh bore fewer scars than that of her older self, but it was her—garbed as a desert tribeswoman, in a white robe and cloth headpiece for protection against the heat. However, Xena knew that beneath the robe the girl wore cheap leather armor, and at her side a sword that was only slightly more expensive. The rider brought her mount close to Xena (but not within arm's reach) and stopped.

"Are you a pilgrim or a fool?" the girl asked in a voice hard as flint.

Xena blinked. "Pardon me?"

"You must be one or the other. No one else would risk crossing the desert on foot. My guess is you're a fool."

Xena had to keep from smiling; it was just the sort of thing she would have said at that age. "Oh? And why is that?"

"Your pack isn't very large. I doubt it contains more than three water skins. Hardly enough for this heat."

The horse's saddlebags bulged, and Xena knew they were crammed full of water skins, a supply for both rider and mount. She imagined she could smell the water within the bags, and she had to fight the urge to take a step forward.

Xena knew there was any number of explanations for her younger self's presence. Perhaps she was simply a hallucination brought about by the heat, or if she was real, perhaps her true appearance was masked by sorcery. Or maybe Xena faced some manner of shape-changing demon; she'd seen (and killed) far stranger things in her time. But none of those explanations *felt* right. Her instincts told her that this woman was exactly what she appeared to be: Xena's younger self. But how . . . ?

Time as you know it is meaningless to the gods, Athena's voice whispered in her mind. *Time is a river, and mortals are like fish; I merely plucked you out of the river at one point—your present—then walked along the bank upstream and dropped you back in at a different point—your past. Nothing to it, really. With a bit of help from my cousin Chronos, that is.*

So it was true. This young woman was Xena, during a time in her life when she was still learning the way of the warrior, but before she had begun to travel down the dark path of blood and conquest. If she could only tell her younger self of the evil that lay ahead of her, perhaps she would be able to avoid—

You walked the path the gods ordained for you, Xena, Athena mind-whispered. *You are not here to change it.*

No, Xena thought back. *I'm here to learn "the difference between cleverness and wisdom." And I suppose you've brought me face to face with my younger self because she's even less prone to thinking before acting than I am. An awfully elaborate lesson, wouldn't you say, Athena?*

Athena didn't reply, but Xena had the impression that the goddess, wherever she was, was smiling.

"Has the sun addled your brains, old woman?" Young Xena sneered.

"Addled? *Old?*"

"You just stand there looking at me like you've lost what few wits you had to begin with."

Xena bristled. She'd never been one for social niceties, but she didn't recall ever being this obnoxious. She opened her mouth, prepared to give her younger self a rather large piece of her mind, but then she thought better of it. After all, she was the more mature (not *old!*) of the two, and therefore she should act like it.

"I beg your pardon," Xena said. "I'm afraid the trials of the last few days have indeed taken their toll on me. I was a member of a merchant caravan that was beset by desert raiders. The bandits killed everyone, looted our wagons, and then set them aflame before riding off. I alone survived, by the grace of the gods. The thieves took all our weapons and most of our supplies. Luckily, they missed a bit of water and food. It wasn't much, but it was enough to keep me alive for the last several days." *Not bad for improvising*, Xena thought.

Young Xena frowned. "You survived an attack by bandits without a mark on you?"

Xena thought fast. "I was struck on the head during the initial attack. The raiders assumed I was dead and left me while they fell on my companions."

Young Xena's frown deepened into a scowl, and Xena thought her younger self wasn't going to buy her story. But finally she snorted and said, "Fools. They should have cut everyone's throat before leaving to make sure there were no survivors."

Despite the oppressive heat, Xena felt a chill slide along her spine at the casual cold-bloodedness of her counterpart's words. Young Xena reached into one of her saddlebags and brought forth a skin of water. "Here." She tossed the skin to Xena, who caught it easily. Xena pried loose the stopper and drank, forcing herself to go slowly. Although she desperately wanted to drain the entire skin, she knew better. Conservation of water was key to survival in the desert. Plus, it would be rude to take it all.

She finished, replaced the stopper, and held the skin out to her younger self. "My thanks."

"Keep it. I have more."

Xena nodded. "My thanks again." She put the skin in her pack.

"My name is Xena," her counterpart said. "I'm a . . . traveler."

Xena smiled. "This seems a strange place for sightseeing."

"I'm curious as to what lands lie on the other side of the desert."

Xena knew this was a lie. She understood now why this desert had seemed familiar to her before. It was because she had traveled it during her youth, seeking a legendary tribe of desert folk who were reputed to possess the power to make themselves invisible during battle. She had eventually found the tribe, only to discover their abilities had been greatly exaggerated. While they could not render themselves unseen, they could move like striking serpents when they fought, nearly faster than the human eye could follow. She had stayed and studied with them for a time and had learned much.

"And who are you?" her counterpart asked.

Xena couldn't very well give her true name. It wasn't that her younger self would suspect the truth; this Xena, while not completely inexperienced, would have had only a few encounters with magic so far, and was largely unaware of how truly strange and wondrous existence could be. No, it would be merely awkward to name herself Xena, and it might raise questions that she'd prefer not to answer. So she gave the first name that came to her.

"Gabrielle."

Young Xena's lips twitched into a sneer. "A silly name," she muttered.

Gabrielle shrugged. "It's served me well enough over the years."

A silence fell between them, one that young Xena finally broke by gesturing toward the object on distant horizon. "I take it you were heading there."

"Yes, though I'm not sure exactly what 'there' is."

"A place to be avoided, or so I've been told in the villages where I've stopped to refill my water skins. People say it's a temple of some sort, dedicated to some manner of evil god." She sniffed. "Not that I put much stock in ghost stories."

Xena remembered now. She had originally avoided the temple, not out of fear (though despite her younger counterpart's words, Xena knew that was part of the reason), but because she had been so intent on finding the warrior tribe and learning from them all that she could. She had a tendency to be somewhat . . . obsessive in her younger days. Thankfully, she had matured since then.

Don't say anything, Athena!

The goddess' chuckle drifted through her mind.

"You can come with me, if you wish," young Xena said. "I can drop you off at the next village we come to." Her lips drew back from her teeth in a gesture too cold to be called a smile. "Or we could seek out the raiders who attacked your caravan and take vengeance for your fallen comrades. Whichever you choose, you're going to need to be armed."

Young Xena reached into her robe and drew forth a dagger. With a catlike flick of her wrist, she hurled the blade hilt-first toward her older self. Xena started to reach up to catch the dagger, but her hand froze, and the hilt thunked painfully into her shoulder. The knife fell to the sand.

Young Xena smirked. "Sorry," she said, sounding anything but.

Xena scowled, but didn't reply. The last three days had taken their toll, that was all; she was still just as fast as she ever was. She wasn't getting slow, getting . . . old. *She wasn't.* She bent down to retrieve the dagger, but as she reached for it, her hand froze once more.

No weapons, Warrior Princess, Athena mind spoke. *I sent you with none, and you will be unable to wield any as long as you remain in the past.*

Xena concentrated, bending all of her will to overcoming the enchantment, but it was no use. She couldn't move her hand so much as another inch toward the blade.

She straightened and faced her younger self. "I thank you for your offer, but I practice a philosophy of"—she gritted her teeth—"nonviolence. I cannot accept the dagger."

Young Xena looked at her as if she were mad, but all she said was, "Can you at least return it to me then?" She held out her hand.

Xena wasn't certain whether she could or not. She bent down, reached for the blade, and this time she was able to close her fingers around the hilt. She stood, stepped closer to her younger self, and returned the dagger. Xena didn't even try to hold on to the knife, for she knew she wouldn't be able to.

Young Xena tucked the blade back into her robe. "So, are you going to ride with me or not?"

Xena considered. She couldn't very well continue walking through the desert on her own. Before long, she was sure to perish, and she harbored no illusions that Athena would step in and save her at the last moment. The gods played for keeps. On the other hand, she wasn't sure that continuing to have contact with her younger self was a good idea either. She didn't know whether she was capable of changing her own past—after all, she had no memories of meeting a Gabrielle when she originally crossed this desert—but there was always the possibility. Why else would Athena have forbidden her from attempting to warn her younger self of the dark path that lay before her unless the past could be changed? By continuing to have contact with her counterpart, Xena might well alter the course of her life in some unknowable, disastrous fashion. She might end up getting her younger self killed.

No, best to leave things as they were. The course of Xena's life had been far from perfect—*very* far—but it was her life, and for better or worse, she would play out the hand she had been dealt.

"Again, my thanks, but I believe I will continue on toward the temple." She smiled. "Like you, I place little stock in ghost stories. Perhaps there I will be able to rest and regain my strength before I attempt to return home." And if it really was a place of evil, then it was most likely the challenge Athena had sent her here to deal with.

Young Xena shrugged. "Suit yourself." She held out a hand.

Xena frowned. "I don't understand. I told you, I wish to go to the temple."

"And I heard you. I'll drop you off before continuing on my way."

Xena definitely remembered bypassing the temple when she had sat in her counterpart's saddle. She had to make sure that her other self continued onward without stopping at the temple if she wished to avoid changing her past too dramatically.

"There is no need. It is not far."

Young Xena scowled. "All the more reason for you to let me give you a ride."

Thinking quickly, Xena replied, "My philosophy of nonviolence does not permit me to allow any sort of harm to come to another. As I said, I do not believe the temple is haunted, but if it is, I cannot risk any ill befalling you because you chose to aid me."

Young Xena smirked. "I can take care of myself, old woman."

Xena ground her teeth. This little snip was damn lucky Athena had taken away her weapons along with her ability to use them! She'd have liked to take the flat of a sword-blade to her younger self's posterior right then. "Of that I have no doubt, but I would rather continue on to the temple alone. My thanks for the water, and good luck on your journey." She turned in the direction of the temple and began walking, hoping that her younger self would become exasperated and ride off.

"You know what I think?" Young Xena called out after her. "I think there's another reason you don't want me to go to the temple, a reason that has nothing to do with your supposed 'philosophy.' "

Xena kept walking.

"I think you know more about the temple than you're letting on. The rumors of evil are just lies designed to scare people off, to keep them from finding out what the temple truly contains."

Uh-oh, Xena thought.

"What is it? Gold? Diamonds? Rubies?" Young Xena's voice was thick with avarice.

Xena had forgotten that twin missions drove her younger self: in order to protect her homeland, she intended to become a great warrior—the greatest the world had ever seen—and raise an army to follow her. Becoming a great warrior meant learning all that she could about the martial arts, hence her reason for seeking out the desert tribe. But building an army took riches, and Xena had constantly been on the lookout for ways to obtain the money she would need to build a proper fighting force.

Xena stopped walking and turned to face her young counterpart. "No, that's not it at all, I—"

"Hi-yah!" The other Xena dug her heels into her horse's sides and snapped the reins. The mount surged forward in response, its hooves sending up showers of sand.

"Wait! Don't!" Xena shouted as her younger self flew past, grinning, but the young warrior continued to pick up speed as she drove her horse on toward the temple.

"Damn it!" Xena swore, and began walking as fast as she dared. As she continued on her way, she couldn't help thinking that both of them were doing exactly what Athena wanted them to.

The sun had set, and an almost full moon had risen before Xena reached the temple. A chest-high wall of gray stone surrounded the building, and the main entrance was nothing more than two wind-scoured marble pillars, broken hinges the only remains of gates long since gone.

Xena stopped before the entrance and listened for sounds of life, but heard only sand blowing against the walls. Stepping quietly into the courtyard, she felt unseen eyes trained upon her, but the moonlight revealed only the muted stones of the temple, sand drifts, and the abandoned horse of her younger self. *No doubt she's gone inside to look for hidden treasure*, Xena thought.

In the center of the courtyard, a well and drop bucket beckoned, and Xena crossed to it as quickly as her aching, weakened legs would allow. If she had any hope of facing whatever challenge Athena had placed before her (not to mention extricating her younger self from whatever trouble she had surely found), Xena needed water, and she needed it *now!* With trembling hands, she lowered the bucket into the well, and after a considerable descent, she heard it splash down. *Thank Ares*, she thought as she slowly began to pull the full bucket upward. *I've got a fighting chance now.*

But before she could slake her thirst, the sands exploded as the swirling forms of the temple's scimitar-wielding guards appeared all around her. They had been lying in wait, buried beneath the surface sand. An obvious trick, one she would have anticipated if she hadn't been mind-weak with thirst. Xena released her grip on the bucket's rope and whirled to defend herself, even though she knew it was useless, for she was both weaponless and incapable of violence. *Still, I've got to try.*

Letting forth an ululating war cry, Xena leapt forward, grasping at the helm of the closest guard with the intent of swinging his body into the others. But her movements were slowed by the depredations she'd suffered during the course of the last several days, and he caught her as easily as he would a child. Grinning, the man violently twisted her arm around and shoved her to the ground. Spitting sand, Xena sat up and came face-to-face with several scimitars glinting cold and deadly in the moonlight.

A voice from the temple patio called out. "Do not harm her! We can use her for the sacrifice." The words were not Greek, but rather spoken in a desert dialect that Xena had a small degree of familiarity with, though she was far from fluent.

Xena was hoisted roughly to her feet, and she got her first good look at the speaker. Garbed in the robes of a priest, her captor was a tall man with a black, bedraggled beard and the blazing eyes of a fanatic.

"Is this how you treat all your guests?" Xena asked haltingly, for it had been some years since she had spoken this language.

"Silence, water stealer!" he said. "Or I will have my men cut out your tongue."

Xena nodded, not particularly impressed by the threat. There had been a time when she might have said the same thing. Besides, she was too busy planning her escape to pay full attention to the priest's words.

"Escape," the man said, as if reading her mind, "is impossible." He grinned as his men pushed her forward. "Besides, where would you go? You have no water."

He's got a point, Xena thought wryly. Besides, she was certain this was where Athena wanted her to be. "What is this place?" she asked, ignoring the priest's threat.

"The Temple of Naal," he responded in the reverent tone of a true believer. "A mighty water demon who came to this land centuries ago as the servant of a powerful but foolish wizard. One day, the mage made the mistake of lowering his guard, and Naal destroyed him. The demon-god then raised up this temple as a place of worship and sucked the waters from the soil. This land was once fertile, but it is now a desert for miles in all directions thanks to the all-powerful Naal."

"Let me guess," Xena said. "You're the demon's high priest."

"That is correct. While I once had another name, I am known now only as the Aquifer: the Bringer of Water. I perform the sacred rites of Naal, Naal provides water—" he gestured at the well.

"And the tribes for miles around do whatever you tell them to, or they go thirsty," Xena finished.

The priest smiled wryly. "I see you have an excellent grasp of the finer points of theology. But Naal's blessing does not come without a price. Ordinarily, one of my guards would have offered his life to ensure the well remains filled for another month. But there's no need for that, not now that you are here—a stranger and a water stealer to boot. Tonight, your blood will quench Naal's thirst, and in return, He shall quench ours."

"Big surprise," Xena muttered. *If I had a gold coin for every two-bit priest who tried to sacrifice me to his "almighty" god* . . .

Aquifer glanced up at the moon. "Enough talk; the time is nigh for the ceremony to begin. Come, your companion awaits you on the altar."

"Companion?" Xena asked.

"Yes." Aquifer peered closely at Xena. "She resembles you a great deal. Is she a sister, perhaps?"

In a matter of speaking, Xena thought. She shook her head.

"Perhaps she is from the same tribe, then." The priest shrugged. "It doesn't matter. She arrived earlier, lusting for more than just water. She quickly discovered that my guards are more than capable of defending against looters as well as water thieves. Still, she fought well, killing several of my warriors before she was subdued. A pity to see so much blood spilled so wastefully."

Xena couldn't help feeling a rush of vicarious satisfaction at her younger self's limited victory. At least one of them could still fight.

"It's time to enter the temple," Aquifer said. "Out of respect for Naal, you must be silent from this point on."

"Or what?" Xena asked. "You'll kill me?"

The priest chuckled. "Of *course* we're going to kill you, but if you're silent, we won't cut out your tongue first."

Xena nodded. "Right. The tongue thing. I almost forgot."

The guards escorted the warrior princess into the Temple of Naal.

Xena was laid on a stone altar next to her younger self. Both women were bound, strips of leather wrapped tightly around their wrists and ankles, biting painfully into the skin. Periodically, young Xena struggled against her bonds, but Xena the elder didn't bother. She knew escape didn't lie down that road.

The chamber, which she took to be Naal's sanctum sanctorum, wasn't particularly impressive. Dirt floor, stone walls, domed ceiling, guttering torches for light . . . but the central feature of the chamber more than made up for the room's simplicity. In the middle of the floor was a pool with a radius of fifteen feet. The water was the purest blue, the color so bright and rich that it almost seemed to glow with an inner light. The pool wasn't still, though; the water swirled round and round in a miniature maelstrom, which Aquifer called the Gyre. Silently the water spun, and not a single drop was flung forth from the pool. The overall effect was quite eerie which, Xena supposed, was the point.

On the other side of the Gyre the bodies of five guards—those slain by her younger counterpart—were laid out upon the floor, heads nearest the maelstrom's edge, feet pointing away from the water. Two of the remaining guards stood at the chamber's entrance, hands resting on the hilts of their scimitars, while two more took positions near Aquifer. Whether these guards were supposed to protect the priest from his captives or from his god, Xena didn't know.

Aquifer knelt before the Gyre (but not too closely, Xena noted), chanting a prayer in his desert language. The guards joined in, filling the chamber with reverent tones that held more than a hint of madness.

"This is a fine mess you've gotten me into, old woman!" young Xena whispered.

"I don't recall telling you to sneak into the temple and try to steal a demon's treasure." Despite her words, though, Xena felt guilty. Her younger self would not have ended up bound on Naal's altar if it hadn't been for her interference.

Was it possible for the same person to die twice, in two different times, at two different ages? If Xena couldn't think of a way out of this situation, and fast, she was going to find out!

Young Xena struggled against her bonds. "If I could just get loose, find my sword . . ."

"It wouldn't make a difference. This isn't a problem that a sword can solve." She was about to say more, but then the prayer ended and Aquifer stood. He reached into his robe and brought forth a wicked-looking dagger with a gold hilt encrusted with blue diamonds—diamonds the same color as the water that swirled in the Gyre.

"The time has come." He stepped toward the altar and raised the blade. Ceremonial the dagger might be, but its edge looked sharp enough to cut through bone.

Think, damn you, Xena! Think!

Aquifer turned his head to shout toward the water. "Naal! Water-Giver, Life-Bringer! Lord of the Depths, and King of the Waves! Come forth to accept the gift of blood that I offer in your name!"

The priest's words echoed in Xena's mind. *Gift of blood . . .*

From within the swirling waters of the Gyre, a long sinuous shape stretched forth. At first Xena thought it was a serpent of some kind, but there was no head, no eyes, no mouth. It was a tentacle, but one unlike any she had seen before. During the course of her wanderings, Xena had done her share of sailing, and she had seen octopi and squid, but this tentacle belonged to a far different creature. The skin was leathery, more like lizard hide than the flesh of a sea beast. Its color was a sickly whitish-green, like something that had lain too long at the bottom of a foul, dark sea. The appendage was covered with tiny puckered dimples, and it emitted a fetid odor of rotting flesh and vegetable matter.

As the tentacle extended farther into the chamber, what Xena had at first taken as dimples opened to reveal tiny rows of sharp, yellowed teeth. The tentacle was covered with mouths; hundreds of them, and they all thirsted for the same thing—blood.

. . . that I offer in your name.

And then it came to her, but she realized that the weapon wasn't one she could wield.

"Xena," she whispered harshly, "offer the blood of the guards you killed to Naal!"

Young Xena's head snapped around to peer at her, then she nodded in understanding. "Naal!" she shouted. "In your name, I offer the blood of the five slain guards!"

Aquifer let out a shriek of surprise and anger. His eyes blazed with fury, and for an instant Xena thought he would plunge the diamond-encrusted dagger into her chest. But instead the priest turned away from the altar and began rapidly chanting to his god in an attempt to regain control.

But it was too late. Four other tentacles streaked forth from the Gyre to join the first, and all five wrapped around the bodies of the dead guards. The mouths went to work and within seconds, the corpses had been drained completely of all fluid and had become dried, flattened husks.

The priest screamed in fury. He turned and ran toward the altar, dagger raised high.

"Naal, kill Aquifer and the remaining guards," young Xena shouted.

A writhing tentacle shot out of the pool and wrapped itself around Aquifer's waist. He was pulled, shrieking, into the swirling maelstrom. When they saw what happened to their priest, the guards tried to run, but they weren't fast enough. Moments later, the two Xenas were the only ones left in the chamber.

"Not a bad idea," young Xena said, "for someone who doesn't believe in violence."

Her older counterpart smiled, and let the comment pass. "Thanks." She didn't know if her next idea would work or not.

One tentacle remained just above the surface of the swirling waters, swaying back and forth slowly, like a trained snake awaiting its master's next order. Xena looked at the smugly smiling version of herself, and said, "You probably ought to have him cut us loose."

Young Xena nodded. "Naal, cut our bonds," she said.

The tentacle withdrew into the Gyre momentarily, but then reappeared, clutching the ceremonial dagger. With surprising gentleness, Naal cut the leather thongs, freeing the two women. The tentacle then withdrew back to the pool, dropped the blade into the water, and resumed its waiting position above the surface.

"You were right," Young Xena said.

"About what?"

"When you said this wasn't a problem a sword could solve. I guess steel isn't the answer to everything, eh?"

"No," Xena said thoughtfully, "I don't suppose it is."

They got down from the altar and stood looking at the pool, and at Naal's sole remaining tentacle.

"What's it waiting for?" Young Xena asked.

Xena shrugged. "Another command, I suppose."

A dangerous glint came into her younger counterpart's eyes. "If I could command a beast like that—"

"Don't even think about it. You saw how easily it turned against Aquifer and his men. How long would it be before the demon turned on you, one way or another?"

Young Xena nodded, though she didn't look too happy about it. "So how do we keep anyone else from coming along and taking Aquifer's place?"

"Simple. Tell him to destroy it, and then start running."

"Naal!" Young Xena commanded, "destroy this temple!"

A terrible, inhuman shriek bubbled up from deep within the Gyre and hundreds of tentacles burst forth from the pool, questing for the very foundations of the ancient temple.

Both Xenas ran like hell.

It took Naal several hours to reduce the temple to rubble. The two Xenas stood some distance from the temple wall and watched as most of the building disappeared into the swirling sands. When the tentacles finally reached the wall, they could see how each stone was literally shattered with water from within, as though each tentacle had the power to dissolve rock. It was an eerie sight, and both Xenas were silent. By the time the moon set, it was over.

"Well," the younger Xena said quietly, "you don't see that everyday."

Xena smiled to herself, thinking how many times she'd said that over the years when some strange thing or another had happened to her during her travels. "No," she replied, "I guess you don't."

"Now what will you do?" the younger Xena asked.

"Go home," Xena said. "At least I hope so."

Her younger self looked at the horizon, where the sun was just beginning to lighten the sky. "It's almost daybreak," she said. "Are you going to rest first?"

"Well, the gods know I'm tired enough," Xena admitted. "You could probably use a little rest yourself."

Young Xena shrugged. "Plenty of time for sleep when you're dead," she replied.

I wonder when I changed my mind about that? Xena thought to herself. "So you'll be moving on?"

"Yes," she said, and then added, "You're no fighter, Gabrielle, but you're welcome to come with me—at least to the next village. If nothing else, you think clearly, which is more than I can say for most people I meet."

"Thanks," Xena said. "For the compliment and the offer. But my path lies in a different direction than yours. Who knows? Maybe we'll meet again someday."

"Maybe," said young Xena. She reached into her saddlebags and removed two water skins. "Take these," she said. "I wish it were more, but it's all I can spare. I don't know how long I'm going to be out here."

Xena nodded, slipping the skins into her pack. "Thank you again."

Young Xena mounted her horse, and looked down. "It's the least I can do, since it appears I owe you my life. That's not a debt I'll be forgetting, and one day, maybe I'll have the chance to repay it."

Xena smiled. "I'm almost sure of it," she said. "Good journey to you, Xena."

"And to you, Gabrielle," she replied. She touched her horse's flanks lightly, and started into the desert.

For a few moments, Xena watched her younger self ride away. Then she had a notion.

"Xena!" she called.

The horse stopped, and her younger self looked back. "What is it?"

"You're going the wrong way," Xena said. "The tribe you're looking for lives to the northeast."

Young Xena turned the horse around and trotted back. "What do you mean?"

Xena smiled up at the younger version of herself. "The warrior tribe you seek—their village lies in the northeast. You were headed west."

"How do you know what I seek?" Xena asked.

"Only pilgrims and fools cross this desert, and I already know you're no fool. And the only pilgrimage worth making out here is to the Langdia tribe—the invisible warriors."

Young Xena scowled suspiciously. "Who are you?" she demanded.

"Definitely not a fool," Xena replied with a chuckle. "Go on, now. You should be there in a few days, and time is precious."

Young Xena sat motionless for a moment, then turned her horse northeast. "I've had enough strangeness in one day to last me a lifetime. I don't know who you are, 'Gabrielle'—if that truly is your name. But thanks for the tip."

"You're welcome. Good journey."

Young Xena raised a hand in farewell, and Xena watched her ride off into the desert. When she was certain that her younger self wasn't going to return, she picked up her pack and carried it to a nearby rock—a leftover piece of the temple wall sticking up out of the sand.

She lay down with her head on the pack, and as the sun crested the horizon, she slept—falling deep into a dream of Athena.

The goddess was garbed in a white robe, and olive leaves adorned her brow in a wreath. But her left arm held a sturdy, white shield, and in her right hand she gripped a wicked-looking spear. "So, Xena," the goddess said. "Have you learned anything?"

Xena thought for a moment before answering. "Acceptance," she replied.

Athena smiled. "Of what?"

"Of who I am, of the path I've chosen. Or the path that was chosen for me."

"A good start," Athena replied. "What else?"

"That the only real weapon I've ever had is me—my mind, my knowledge—used when the time was right."

"Truly the beginning of wisdom," Athena said approvingly.

"You still haven't told me why you felt a need to teach me this lesson," Xena said.

"You have gifts, Xena. And gifts such as yours don't just come from one god, such as my arrogant brother Ares. Your abilities come from all the gods—and how you use such powerful gifts must be carefully monitored."

Xena nodded. "I understand," she said, then added, "but I don't have to like it."

Athena laughed. "No," she said, "you don't. While Acceptance and Understanding are cousins, they're usually far distant relatives from Enjoyment."

Xena laughed, too. "Now that's wisdom," she said.

Athena sheathed her spear across her back, and grasped Xena's arm. "We are sisters, of a sort, Xena. Once, long ago, I lived and fought, and even loved, as you do. There are many different types of wisdom. I wanted to make certain that you had the most important kind—wisdom of the self. You are who you are, Xena. And acceptance of that is truly wisdom of the highest order."

Xena put her hand over Athena's. "Thank you," she said. "It's good to be reminded of that."

Athena nodded. "And now, it's time for you to go home. When you awaken, no time will have passed, and you will know this dream for what is was—a dream. You have done well, sister. I am pleased."

Xena smiled, and kept her silence. She began to feel herself floating, and looking up—or was it down?—she could see Athena fading into the distance. The light grew slowly brighter, and she was eventually forced to close her eyes. It became so intense that Xena feared opening them, but then suddenly, the light dimmed, and she could hear a familiar voice . . .

"Xena!" Gabrielle called. "Xena, wake up!"

Xena stirred, and opened her eyes. "Gabrielle, what is it?"

"I couldn't wake you," she said. "And from the way you

were tossing and turning, it looked like you were having a nightmare." She peered closely at Xena. "Are you all right?"

Xena looked around. They were in the same peaceful forest clearing where they had made camp the night before. "I'm fine. What time is it?"

"First light," Gabrielle said. "Time to move on."

"Move on?"

"Yes," Gabrielle said. "We always move out at first light."

"Not today," Xena said, closing her eyes.

"What?" Gabrielle asked.

"Let's sleep in," Xena replied. "I'm really in no big hurry to get to the next battle—wherever it is. I imagine we'll get there in time either way."

Gabrielle frowned. "Have you been drinking?"

Xena laughed softly. "No, Gabrielle, I've been sleeping. And I'd like to do that for a while longer, if you don't mind. Trouble or adventure will no doubt find us in the near future. Let's enjoy the quiet while it lasts."

Gabrielle shrugged, and lay down beside her companion. "If you say so. Though this isn't really like you," she added.

Xena thought of the her younger self's words: *Plenty of time for sleep when you're dead.* "This morning, it's exactly like me," she murmured.

THE TENTH WONDER OF THE WORLD

David Bischoff

It was tough sometimes being a Warrior Princess. Especially when you started off able to do just about anything you cared to and then found a conscience.

Xena, Warrior Princess, was musing on this the very day she got a chance to be a villain again (thanks to Salmoneus). She woke up in a foul mood and felt like kicking something—or preferably somebody.

Sleeping on the other side of the dead campfire was Joxer, Something-Less-than-Warrior-Prince. Joxer was snoring. In fact, Joxer was snoring very loudly, which was what had woken Xena up at this early hour. The doofy bad-excuse-for-a-soldier sounded like a titan gargling rocks through a megaphone. Xena's first impulse was to get up and cut off the megaphone, and if the offensive head came off too, well, so be it.

"Gods!" said Gabrielle, Xena's friend and chronicler, sitting up, her blond hair tousled and matted. "Who's attacking us now?"

Xena drew her sword. Her buckles rattled as she stalked

across the campsite. "Joxer's demons. I'm going to exorcise them."

"HarrrrrKKKKKGHHHHH!" commented Joxer. "HarrrrrrKKKKKKKKKKKKGH!"

"Xena!" said Gabrielle, admonishingly.

It seemed as though she were back years and years ago. Back when she could do whatever she wished, whenever she pleased, and the wind was in her hair and anger was in her blood. "Gabrielle, I'm doing the world a favor!"

"Xena! We all have annoying habits," said Gabrielle.

"Yes, but Joxer's habits are all annoying!"

"By Zeus, your war cries for instance. Boy, they sure get my goat!"

Abruptly, Xena's crabby feeling wrenched away from Joxer. She squinted below her brunette bangs, her teeth clenched. "What's wrong with my war cries, little Miss Perfect?"

"I mean, come on, Xena," Gabrielle said. She lifted up her childlike nose and opened her mouth. A frightful yodeling ululation rose up toward the treetops. A rank of birds screeched away, and a group of squirrels ducked for cover. "It sounds like Aphrodite looking in the mirror and finding a zit. Fingernails on a cave wall, Xena."

"I'll give you fingernails!" said Xena. She showed Gabrielle her hand, clawed up like a harpy's. Only once she had it out, she realized that how ludicrous it looked and choked back a laugh.

"Hmmmm. Yes. You and Callisto and a catfight?" said Gabrielle. "I'm afraid she'd win the scratch-your-eyes out in a flip of a dinar!"

They both started chuckling. Xena felt better. Gods, what would she do without this sweet and intelligent person by her side? Gabrielle not only kept her sane in a world of crazy gods, cranky monsters, and far too much adventure, she helped make life rich, wonderful—and sometimes funny as Hercules with a charley horse. "Just don't tell that to the bet makers," she said, pinching her friend's chubby cheek.

A clueless whine rose up from the prostate lump below them. "Would you two shut up? I need my beauty sleep!" Joxer rose just long enough to give his female companions a nasty look, then rolled over and went back to sleep.

Gabrielle raised an eyebrow. "Sorry. Go ahead. Kill him."

"Hades would never forgive me," said Xena.

"You're right."

"Are we up?"

"Up and ready for the road to Athens!" said Gabrielle.

"Good." She sheathed her sword. "You deal with the horses? I get to kick Joxer's skinny butt."

"I was sort of hoping I could."

"Tell you what. Let's just tickle him. He's so much more amusing that way."

The warrior and the storyteller surrounded their friend, gazing down with smirks.

"Oh, it's fun to be mean sometimes!" said Xena.

Joxer squirmed and yelped to both their extreme satisfactions.

The road to Athens!

Xena knew it well. It was a good road, one with just enough thieves and brigands to keep her skills honed. Olive trees, blue skies, the invigorating sun of Greece! Ah, it was good to be alive sometime, and moments like this, with a cool spring breeze whipping her night-black hair, and the taste of a jerky breakfast still in her mouth and the prospect of a decent bath ahead of her: yes, these were the moments that gave Xena's life exactly what it needed. She'd taken and given her share of pain. Now that she was passed that conquering and destroying nonsense, she could poke her handsome nose up and take a good clean sniff of—

Euuuuh!

"Joxer? Is that you?"

"What?" The soldier grunted moodily. He hadn't said much at all since the tickling episode, which was not like Joxer, who made chatterboxes sound positively reticent, at all.

"Something smells like a bull ox in heat! You're upwind from me, and all I see ahead is bright red and blue flowers, green grass, and a bubbling brook." Xena was a woman of action. She kicked her heels into her beloved steed and moved downwind. Her olfactory environment improved immediately.

"Oh, dear. Joxer! Are you using that stuff the Seer of Sarcek gave you."

"Stuff?" said Xena.

"Perfume. Aphrodisiac perfume, to attract women," said Gabrielle, her voice tart. "From ancient Egypt."

"Joxer! I was wondering why I had been gripped with uncontrollable desire," said Xena in a singsong voice. "Please, O stud of studs. Drag me off my horse and ravish me! Take me, brave soldier. I want to feel your manly need!"

"Okay, okay. I've dipped into a little something to get the ball rolling. I mean, women usually flock all over me," said Joxer. "I mean, the ones that I want, anyway." He curled a lip at the sight of Xena and Gabrielle. "But after a long trek, I like to smell good even before I have my bi-monthly bath. All right? Is that a good enough explanation for you."

"This aphrodisiac. What's it called?" said Xena.

"Pharaoh Gnomes," said Joxer, suspiciously. "And it's not an aphrodisiac. My personality attracts all the sweet women I can handle."

Xena's eyes lit up. "Pharaoh Gnomes? From Egypt? Joker, those are ground up mummies!"

"Nonsense!"

"Look. I know Egypt. Do you know Egypt? I know Egypt, Joxer! Cleopatra herself has given me fashion tips. I hope that stuff didn't cost you much?"

"It cost him ten dinars!" said Gabrielle. "Boy, it does stink, doesn't it?" She yanked Argo up to ride abreast of her friend. "Have you got someone you're trying to impress in Borgos, Joxer?"

"He's already impressed me!" said Xena. "And don't look now, but there's a group of sows hot on our heels with roses in their mouths!"

"Borgos! That's right, we're hitting Borgos today!" said Gabrielle. She swung around to look at the soldier with the floppy earflap helmet. "Joxer. Doesn't that old girlfriend of yours live in Borgos? The one who dumped you for the

Spartan general? What's her name? It's on the tip of my tongue."

"I don't know what you're talking about," said Joxer. "It is true that I have loved many a woman and many a woman has loved me. I, after all, am a hot-blooded man, and a lover supreme as well as a soldier of skill and accomplishment. However, I have never, Gabrielle, been dumped!"

"You know, Joxer," said Gabrielle. "With a mouth like yours you have to remember that you just talk about everything. And as a writer, I tend to write things down. In fact," Gabrielle reached down in her saddlebags and rooted around in her scrolls. "I remember something very specifically you wrote and it was about a woman you cared for and it concerned Borgos and—"

"Nonsense!" said Joxer. "Poppycock!"

Xena shook her head and smiled. Oh, the pride of men! She knew pride well enough, as a Warrior Princess, but generally all that was well-deserved and tempered with enough humor and modesty to make it palatable. However, it was generally not women who were struck down by the gods because their egos got too uppity.

"Joxer. Beware hubris."

"Hugh who?"

"Pride, Joxer," said Gabriel. "When a man's head gets too big, the gods become upset and strike him down. Don't you know your Euripides?"

"Well, Aristophanes and I go out drinking together whenever we're together. He says that I inspired a whole new kind of play." The soldier looked bright and happy. "He's called it 'comedy.' "

"Well, hubris leads to tragedy," said Xena.

Tragedy. She thought about tragedy a bit, and she thought, sadly, about the men she had loved. Suddenly, she felt much more compassionate toward Joxer. She felt bad that she was giving him such a hard time simply because he wanted attention from women who didn't ride around slaying monsters and saving the world for a living.

"Joxer, you know—Borgos. I understand the women are particularly beautiful and soft and loving in this part of

Greece. I have heard of many a man who has been loved here. That's not such a bad thing."

"Joxer!" said Gabrielle. "I want to see this!"

And so did Joxer. "Yes, that's true. I suppose it's the olive oil they use here. Very good for a woman's skin. You know, my dear mother swore by olive oil. And you know there's all kinds of olive oil that can be used, too, for all kinds of food, ailments, and general lubrication!"

"Gee, Joxer. You must use extra-virgin olive oil!" said Gabriel.

Joxed grinned. "I do! Extra extra virgin! Why do you think I tan so nicely!"

Gabrielle shot Xena a look.

Xena shook her head and lifted her eyes to Olympus.

And sometimes she thought the gods were fools.

"Well, Borgos is all well and good," said Gabrielle. "Personally, though, I'm eager to be in Athens again."

"Well you should," said Xena. "That's why we're going, isn't it? You're going to talk amongst some other storytellers? Tell some stories. Get some tips on hyperbole and metaphor?"

"I know those girls!" said Joxer. "Ooh la la! All the same, you're right. Borgos women will be just fine." He suddenly looked sheepish and sweet. "And I have to admit, there is someone special there. I mean, there's someone who might be there—but it has nothing to do with this ointment I have on! Absolutely nothing."

It was a ways to Athens, and they had decided to stay a day or two in Borgos. Relax, take baths, get supplies. Eat and drink. Borgos had a reputation for being a safe crossroads for travelers and Xena intended to make the most of it. Adventures were all very well, but time to pause, reflect, and maybe even a stop at a temple for a little meditation might be a good idea.

It took them another two hours to reach the small town, and the whole way, Joxer's spirits rose. He regaled them with a story about his youth so unencumbered by climax or even significant event that Xena quickly realized that it was the kind of tale that Gabrielle labeled a 'shaggy unicorn' tale.

However, after they passed a few huts and cottages on the outsirts of the town, it didn't take long to figure out that something was up.

Something quite out of the ordinary.

"Xena! Look!" said Garbrielle. "What's going on. A circus? A carnival?" She was pointing up to a huge sign at the edge of town with an arrow pointing toward the city gathering spot. "Olympic games?"

"In a small town like this?" said Xena. "I don't think so."

They were walking toward the town, leading their horses. It was hard going because of all the people heading toward the event.

"It says 'wrestling,' Xena. It has to be part of the Games. Or something leading up to them."

Xena examined the letters.

Yes, those were the letters that spelled out *wrestling* in Greek. But what was wrestling doing in Borgos?

Xena was well aware of wrestling. It was a sport practiced by men. An organized sport, it was a marvelous person-to-person conflict of holds and takedowns and final pins that channelled men's aggressive natures into a fighting art. Wrestling was the stuff of champions, of Olympic games, and it elevated humankind toward something noble.

In fact, she'd had a boyfriend once who had taught her all about wrestling. His name was Ironicus, and he was a handsome younger soldier who eventually had to leave her life. Yes, when she wrestled with Ironicus, whether she got the pin or she got pinned, they both liked it, and no matter who won on their private mat, they both ended up satiated winners a little later on.

Ah yes.

Wrestling!

Xena approved!

"Good!" she said. "This will be fun. We can watch some genuine athletic competition. Drink some wine, eat some food. I can't think of a better way to relax, after our baths."

"I don't know," said Gabrielle. "I think I've had enough of sweaty men throwing each other around!"

Joxer cocked his head and threw out his chest. "I happen to have won awards for my wrestling abilities!"

"Because you used olive oil?" said Gabrielle.

"No. Of course not. Because I'm good at it. In fact—"

However, before Joxer could regale them with accounts of his wrestling prowess, Xena heard an uproar.

She looked off the road. A group of men were attacking a short, bearded fellow, kicking and roughing him up. The short man was outnumbered to the extreme. One to six. In short, he was taking a nasty beating. Xena was no Hercules, so she had to work herself up to care—but a sentence from Gabrielle was enough to push her on:

"Xena! They're beating up a little guy, the bullies. He needs help!"

Xena shrugged. Why not? She'd hoped to have a few days of rest, but frankly, she hadn't done her push-ups today and this was a pretty good opportunity for exercise.

She pulled one of the attackers around, a swarthy man with a mangy beard. "Hey, big guy! Why don't you pick on someone half your size!" The man tried to strike her, opening himself up for just what he got: a fist in the solar plexus. He doubled up and fell right into her knee.

Gabrielle was whacking about with her staff, disposing of two of the attackers. Joxer was trying to get up after a bad stumble.

Ignoring the fate of his mob companions, a fat man was punching the short, bearded guy. "I want my money back!" The man was yelling. "I want my money back."

"Immediately. No problem. With interest! Shall I polish your sandals?" cried the man on the bottom.

Xena recognized that voice. However, she was so into her warrior punch-'em-up mode that she didn't even pause to try and put the voice and a name together. She just pulled the fat man up. "Can't you deal with life with anything else but violence? Well, neither can I!"

Eyes blazing, she kicked him, then chopped him in the neck. The man went down in a moaning heap.

Xena turned to the victim of this mass attack, lying on his back, scuffed and dirty and looking generally the worse for wear. He was short, with short, gray hair, no muscle tone, a big nose, a paunchy stomach, flashy clothes, and a neatly grown beard. He smiled under a bloody nose.

"Xena! Am I glad to see you!"

"Salmoneus!" Xena put her hands to her hips, feeling duped—a feeling she felt often around this man, whom she'd encountered far too many times. "I should have known."

"Well, are you just going to stand there and be regal and superior or are you going to help your old, dear friend up!"

Grudgingly, Xena reached down and pulled Salmoneus up.

Salmoneus. Schemer supreme. Con artist. Player. The Get-Rich-Quick King. "Do you owe these people money?" said Xena.

"I wouldn't say that!"

Gabrielle held back on a staff swipe and gawked over. "Salmoneus! You owe everyone money!"

"A dinar here, a dinar there!" said the man shrugging. "Soon everyone will thank me. I shall have dinars galore for all!"

"Hey!" said Joxer. "You! Could I talk to you about that bridge you sold me!"

"Please, please—can't you see I'm broken in half! I have to live to fulfill my earthly debts!" said the despondent fellow.

The guy that Xena had laid out struggled to his feet. "Wow! I'd pay to see this Amazon in a cage match!"

A crooked smile cracked across Salmenous's supple features. "Xena! Am I glad to see you!"

"Cage match?" said Xena. "Happy to see me?"

Salmoneus dusted himself off. "Gentlemen!" he said, raising his hands. "I am so glad you caught me. There's been a dreadful misunderstanding! I was just headed out here to greet the replacement for today's title match. Please. Go back and tell all that we have a special fight today. Alas, Crag the Boulder was unable to make it today—however, in his place, against Skullface—we have, straight from the Peloponnesian Rumbles—Xena the Magnificent!"

The men rising up looked at Xena, rubbing their sore spots. "Looks good, looks good," said one.

"What about this one!" said the bearded fat guy.

"Yeah! Geez, she's tough!"

"Oh yes. And her deadly tag-team friend—No Holds Bard!" said Salmoneus. "No scoot, scoot! You'll have a sight you'll never forget. You've just seen the Tenth Wonder of the World warming up on you! Wait till you see what she has in store for Skullface!"

Rumblings of approval arose from the men. They got up and hurried away.

Xena turned to Salmoneus. "You want to tell me what this is all about?" She shook her head. "Wait a minute. Two and two are coming together. You're a sports promoter. You're putting on some sort of exhibition."

"Oh, Xena!" Salmneus clapped his hands together with glee. "Smart and beautiful. Yes, yes. Wrestling, Xena. Wrestling!"

"That sign," said Gabrielle. "Yes!"

"You know, I'm not bad with the old arm!" said Joxer, flexing and showing a pretty miserable bicep.

"Not arm wrestling," said Salmoneus, smiling.

"Wrestling wrestling?" said Xena. "You've talked people into watching men hug each other, grunting for hours and hours!"

"Oh, not that boring amateur stuff," said Salmoneus, flapping his arm dismissively. "That's for wanna-bes. I'm talking about something that I, Salmoneus of Acme, Incorporated, have devised." He clapped his hands together. "And Xena, it's working better than my PouchGorgons!"

"I bought one of those!" said Joxer. "Cute little thing! I think Callisto stole it though. Got any more?"

"Oh, that was so last year!" said Salmoneus. "And you know, the gods are definitely smiling on me."

"Looks as though they were kicking your butt a moment ago," said Gabrielle.

"Oh, just a little bump on the nose of life," said Salmoneus. "But wrestling, Xena! Not amateur wrestling." His eyes became big orbs of joy and greed. "Professional wrestling!"

"Professional wrestling?" said Xena. "Isn't that an oxymoron?"

"Somebody called Hercules that once," said Joxer. "Isn't that an insult?"

"Professional wrestling, Xena. Pageantry. Sport. Carnival!" said Salmoneus. "All wrapped with popcorn and wine at concession stands. Wonderful fun, and a nice box office."

"I sure don't get it," said Gabrielle. "You're telling me you've figured out a way to get people to pay you to watch half-naked men roll around over each other?"

"Yes!" said Salmoneus.

Xena shrugged. "Do we get to watch for free?"

"You do! And Xena—I'll pay you to fight one of my guys. And Gabrielle—I'll pay you to announce a match and maybe even to tell a story. And Joxer"—Salmoneus looked over toward the eager warrior wannebe—"Joxer, I'll pay you to keep your mouth shut."

Joxer shook his head. "I'm not very good at that. I'm very good at fighting, though!"

"Then I'll pay you for both, though you'll have to be lower on the card."

"We could use some money for Athens," said Gabrielle. "And I not only get to tell a story . . . Sounds like I'm going to get a pretty good one out of this, too!"

"Oh yes, oh yes! I'm so happy." Salmoneus spread his arms out. "Come, come my dear friends. You've not only saved my hide, you've made me a very happy man! And something tells me that all of you will be a hit in Borgos this very day!"

Xena sighed as she looked at her eager companions.

Something smelled bad here.

But then, so did she, and it looked like they might just earn enough money for a few days of bathing here.

On the outskirts of Borgos, in a glade, a goddess and a fairy princess sat under hair dryers.

"Oh, Puck!" said Titania, looking at her nails as they were being polished by an attendent fairy. "I don't think this color quite goes with my eyes. What do you think, sweetie?"

The goddess took a drink of wine, then examined the proffered nails. "Absolutely fabulous, darling. They will glow in the dark awesomely."

"Do you think Oberon will like them?"

Aphrodite, Goddess of Love, nodded. "Oh yes, yes, dar-

ling. Although I must say, chartreuse is rather bold for se-
duction. I myself go for the warmer colors." She sighed
extravagantly, adjusted the fairy blowing on her hair after
that delicious oleander shampoo. Oh dear, though, poor Ti
could be so boring sometimes. She was absolutely obsessive
about Oberon, which was odd, since she'd done absolutely
nothing to put them together. And after that business with
the guy with the jackass head that Obie had laid down on
his babe—sheesh, Aphrodite had told him that she could set
her up with some other guy, easy, but no . . . Titania had to
be sweet and forgiving. The way she was going, she was
going to give world-class hypernatural bitches a good name!

"You know, Aphie, sweetie," said Titania. "I just can't
understand you. You can have any god in Olympus, any
man on Earth. And you choose a solo chariot to drag your
beautiful behind around in—" Titania winked. "So to
speak."

Aphrodite shrugged. "Don't go there, Ti. Please. A girl
has got to have a sense of individuality. You know, things
weren't always so good for us. Like Hera was saying just
the other day, in the days of the titans, women were kept
barefoot, pregnant, and making ambrosia sandwiches for the
men's poker games." She smiled. "Liberation is absolutely
fabulous, darling. I'd advise you to try it, sometime."

"What? And lose Obie? No way! He may have a thing
for changelings and he may Puck up once in a while—but
there's no guy who knows what a woman wants deep down
better than Oberon."

"But I thought, sweetheart, that he was the Fairy King,"
Aphrodite smirked.

"Sweetie. There's a very good reason I glow in the dark
sometimes!" said Titania. "You just keep your warm-colored
nails off of him, that's all I can say. He's mine. Besides,
you know, I think you and Ares are really meant for each
other."

"That bastard!" said Aphrodite. "As if! One of my little
boy Cupid's arrows went kafluey one day. That's all." She
examined herself in the mirror. Perfect. She kissed her image. What a delight it was to be perfect. She took another
deep gulp of wine and held her goblet out for a refill.

"Well, I guess that Ares does get a little rough sometimes, him being the God of War and all, but he is absolutely gorgeous and I've heard that he knows how to get a woman up to Olympian heights. Just heard, mind you, Aph. No personal experience."

So next the little housefrau was probably going to suggest cards. She was fun to gossip with, but when she got to talking about settling down, it was purely dullsville.

"I'm bored," said the Goddess of Love. "Heard any good limericks lately?"

"No, sweetie," said Titania. "But I have to tell you, there's this utterly wonderful new thing going on."

"Do tell!" said Aphrodite.

"Show is much better than tell." The Fairy Queen snapped her fingers. "The birdbath, Pixel!"

An attendant fairy scampered off.

In a trice, he was back, holding a large birdbath, slopping a bit of water. With a grin, he turned it sideways. Aphrodite flinched, expecting to get drenched. Instead, the water stayed in the birdbath, and started to glow.

"Cool," she said. "What is it?"

"Oh, just a fancy vision mirror. Great way to follow mortal stuff, you know. What fools these mortals be! But you probably know that."

"I've had a giggle or two with Hercules."

"Demi-god. Anyway, he's a hunk, and there's one that not even you could hold down. No, Ares is the one for you, sweetie."

"I'm getting bored again!" said Aphrodite.

"Look. It's happening in Borgos tonight. And oh, it is so awesome!"

Aprhodite arched an eyebrow in a show-me kind of way. "Okay. "Let's have a look."

The birdbath water flickered.

An image fluttered into view.

Aphrodite watched with faint curiosity. Titania could get excited about fairly mundane things. Anyway, the very idea of a fairy finding out what was hot before the Goddess of Love was just too, too . . . Too!

"Here it is. Look at this!" said Titania.

It was a large arena. In the middle of it was a square ridged by ropes. Two men were grappling with each other. At first, it looked like one of those silly old Olympian matches. However, the men didn't just stay in one place and grunt and groan a lot.

They started throwing each other all over the ring.

"What is this?" said Aphrodite.

"It's this new invention," said Titania. "Puck likes it. He says he's thinking about doing something with the fairies like it. It's called 'professional wrestling.' "

Hmmm. That was all well and good. Watching half-naked men wiggle around was quite amusing.

However, almost immediately, something else attracted Aphrodite's attention.

"There. By the ring!" she said, standing up. "What are they doing there!"

"Who?"

"Her! Butch Cassidiphonos and the Sundance Bard!"

"Xena and Gabrielle!"

"I told you it was all the rage! And aren't they the hippest, sweetie!"

Aphrodite scowled. "I'm the hippest! Me! Me, Aphrodite! Why, I'm unstoppable without arms! With them—I'm more than anyone can handle. Not you, not Ares . . . not the Warrior Princess and her Girl Friday."

"Chill, girlfriend!" said Titania. "You are, you are! But someone has to clue you in sometimes. And sometimes it's me, okay?"

Aphrodite nodded. She had felt a tantrum coming on, but she'd stopped it. She'd just had her hair done, after all.

She watched the proceedings and a smile started to creep onto her blemishless, classically beautiful face.

"The newest rage, huh? And Xena is there—" she said. "I'm beginning to get an idea, Titania. And it's not only a perfect cure for boredom . . . I can fix that Warrior Princess once and for all."

"What's Xena done to you?"

"I'm a goddess. And a damned good one, too. And do you think Ms. Warrior Princess goes to my temples and worships me, as she should?"

"But Xena doesn't worship any god or goddess."

"Exactly. Which is why she has to be taught a lesson."
Aprhodite smiled slyly. "Say, Titania. Why don't you and I
go there, darling—and Puck with their heads a bit!"

Titania grinned. "I'm there, sweetie. Faster than you can
shake a spear!"

The crowd in the arena was huge.

Xena was impressed. Whatever she could say about Salmoneus, he was an entrepreneur and showman supreme.
Where most people just settled for bread and circuses, when
he was on, Salmoneus could conjure up cake and carnivals!

Gaily colored banners fluttered all about. The smell of
roasted chestnuts hung in the air alongside sweet wine and
mirth and barbecuing fish and goat. There were exotic dancers dancing hither and thither and jugglers balancing balls
and the whole event had an attitude of anything can happen.

"Well, I guess I'd rather have a bath first," she said. "But
if I'm going to work up a sweat in competition, why
bother?"

Gabrielle and Joxer were sitting beside her under the awn-
ing. "Exactly. Plenty of time for that later." Gabrielle was
busy scribbling something on a parchment. She seemed in
some other universe. Xena understood. She was composing
something. At first, Gabrielle's artistic side was annoying.
It meant that when Xena wanted attention from her friend,
she couldn't get it. Gradually, though, when she came to
understand her little bard better, she knew that she had to
have these times drifting in the cosmos like some kind of
dreamy kite. She'd come back soon enough, and when she
did she generally brought back something charming.

"Where's Salmoneus?" asked Joxer. "He said he'd have
something exciting for me to do!"

"Well, he has to come back eventually if he wants me to
wrestle. I'm not sure exactly what the rules are!" said Xena.

There was what Salmoneus had called a 'warm-up match'
going on, and Xena had to admit, this professional wrestling
stuff that the fellow had concocted was quite a bit more
active than the pure stuff.

At the base of the arena, surrounded by the crowd now,

was a ring rimmed by rope and in this ring, two burly guys looked as though they were going to tear it down before the "real matches" got started.

One of the men, in a red cape and purple shorts, had been announced as "Mister Godlike." He'd pumped his muscles a lot and had kissed the air, and generally looked a bit like what Iolaus Aeolus thought he was sometimes.

The other guy was called "Alexander the Greater." He had started immediately pounding on his chest and creating quite a noise. Now he was winding up his opponent in the ropes and kicking him unmercifully.

"Where the dignity?" said Xena. "Where's the grandeur? Where the majesty of sport?"

"Gee, Xena," said Joxer. "No wonder Salmoneus wanted you! Looks like you when you get in a fight!"

"Joxer. Your mouth. My fist. Let's not get them too close, okay?"

"Okay. Sorry. Hey . . . you know, it's kind of fun! I mean, look at them. They're flying all over the ring. And gosh . . . now one's out of the ring. They're all over the audience. Wow! This is kind of exciting!" Joxer stood. "Alexander! Get him, Al. Get him Al!"

"Joxer!" said Xena. "If the real Alexander heard you say that, he'd stop conquering the world and start conquering your skinny butt!"

Joxer, moping, sat back down.

The match ended soon, but not until a few trash receptacles and audience members were thrown around. Sure enough, Alexander the Greater got his opponent down on the mat and held him there for three counts . . . *bam bam bam*. The victor of the match was roundly booed by the growing audience. But they seemed to enjoy the booing and they seemed to be glad.

"He didn't play fair!" said Xena. "It's a contest, and he didn't play at all fair. Why did they let him get away with that—Why did they let him win! He shouldn't win? What's wrong here?"

"I guess Salmoneus is going to tell us all about that, Xena," said Joxer. "Look. Here come the announcers."

A Greek chorus of twenty men and women in the masks

of comedy and tragedy filed out into rows in front of the ring.

> *"Heed! Oh audience of stature and grace.*
> *Listen to the next chapter of this tale of glee and*
>   *woe.*
> *Here comes another heel and babyface*
> *The Great Big Gorilla and the Cathartic Shmoe!"*

The chorus filed back out again.

"What was that?" said Xena.

"A fascinating narrative device!" said Gabrielle. "Dramatic devices. Incorporated with sport! My goodness."

"Aristotle must be rolling in his grave!" said Xena.

"Gee. I saw Ari at the last Bard-A-Thon. He seemed pretty darned healthy to me."

"He won't be when he gets a load of this!" said Xena.

"Zounds!" said Joxer. "Get a look at those bruisers! And Xena—they've got more leather on than you!"

"What? Where?"

Xena swivelled her head and immediately saw what Joxer was yapping about. From opposite sides of the arena, two men were making their way down toward the ring. One man was so bald his head shone in the sun. He wore a leather collar studded with spikes. He was dressed in black leather that bulged with much more fat than muscle. He looked as though a permanent scowl had been tattooed onto his jowly face and sported a handlebar mustache with points as sharp as Xena's sword.

The other guy looked like a beefier version of Hercules, with long, beautiful hair and gleaming teeth. He too wore leather, as Joxer had pointed out—only it was clearly well-designed leather, much more to Xena's taste. As he descended the stairs he would pause from time to time to flex his muscles for the audience. When they cheered, he would lean over, cupping his ear, as though to drink in every last bit of their praise.

"Shmoe! Shmoe! Shmoe! Shmoe!" cried the crowd.

"Grandstander!" said Xena.

Once in the ring, the pretty man held up his hands, held back his head, and yelped a war cry

"Yip . . . Yip . . . Yip . . . !"

Joxer laughed. "Xena! That sounds just like you!"

Xena was not amused. "Too high," she said.

Apparently, the big bruiser in black leather and metal studs was not amused either. Even as the Cathartic Shmoe was giving his vocal chords their exercise, the Gorilla pounced. He started pounding on his opponent with all his might, beating him to the mat.

"Hey! That match hasn't started yet!" said Joxer.

"That's a villain! I'm going down and dealing with him!" said Xena. She stood, but Gabrielle grabbed her arm.

"Hang on, Xena. Let's see what's going to happen!" She grinned. "Besides, a moment ago, you wanted to do that to Goldilocks."

Xena nodded. Yes, that was right.

Clearly, as a member of the audience, she was allowed to revert to her previous nature. Hmmm. As she watched the Great Big Gorilla throwing the Cathartic Shmoe around the ring she found a smile beginning to creep up around her lips.

Hey. This was kinda fun.

The match took another turn. Finally, the Schmoe reversed a hold. He laid the Gorilla low.

"Pin him!" cried Joxer. "Pin him, Shmoe!"

Shmoe did nothing of the sort. Instead, he went to the corner, and climbed up on the ropes to the top of the turnbuckle. "Get up, Gorilla! Get up!" cried Xena.

The Shmoe stood for a moment and raised his arms, as though getting strength from Zeus himself. Then, as the crowd roared, Shmoe launched himself out and out some more—

—and landed right on top of the Gorilla with a huge slam.

"He killed him!" said Joxer. "That big guy's dead! He's going to bleed all over the place. I just know it." Joxer looked ill.

Then, finally, Shmoe covered the Gorilla, pinning him to the mat. The referee, who had thus far been standing well clear of all this, moved in and started slapping the mat.

At the very last moment, the Gorilla pushed up with such strength that Shmoe was launched a good two yards into the air.

"Yes!" said Xena. "Go, Gorilla."

"But Xena. You were about to go down and pound that guy yourself. He's bad!"

"He didn't steal anything from me," said Xena, eyes flashing.

About five minutes later, after more leaps and bounds and crashes, the match ended with the Cathartic Shmoe finally drop-kicking Gorilla to the mat, and then holding him down long enough for a count of three.

"What a fight!" said Joxer. "My goodness! It's even better than your fights, Xena—and without a chakram."

The crowd cheered wildly. The Gorilla snarled and showed them all his underarms as he got up, while Carthartic Shmoe blew kisses.

Xena folded her arms together and mulled the situation over while Gabrielle and Joxer bought food and drinks from a vendor. They both seemed happy and gay and thrilled to be here. Xena was a little more cautious, however. It looked like Salmoneus had a winner here—but then, the guy's plans usually blew holes. If she hadn't happened along today, he'd be tied up on a tree branch by his thumbs now.

Still, even though these "wrestlers" looked pretty ferocious, there was no question that she could take on any of them. That was what Salmoneus counted on surely: the sight of a woman throwing a man around, that vision of speed and might and cunning and skill and, yes, art and beauty that was Xena, the Warrior Princess, putting ugly brutes in their place. Even as she thought about the prospect of listening to the cheers of the rabble as she laid blow upon blow to her opponent, as she flipped him and whipped him—a tiny smile crept over her face.

The Old Xena. Yes. Maybe the Xena of Old had her place. Maybe the Xena the Conqueror could be let out today for a little air. Yes, and according to Salmoneus, she would even be paid for her trouble.

A hand fell on her shoulder.

Xena turned around, ready to fight.

"Whoa! Xena! Friend and true believer! It's just me," said Salmoneus. He grabbed a nearby chair. "Anything these three want, all day—on the house. And give them back any money they've given you." Salmoneus rubbed his hands together, his eyes glowing. "So what do you think, my friends? What say you about my new entertainment scheme?"

"I'm entertained," said Joxer, mouth full of gyro. "When do you want me to beat the stuffing out of someone, Sal?"

"Soon enough, soon enough, Joxer," said Salmoneus. "Have some more wine. Eat, drink, be merry!"

Xena shook her head. "Don't tell that to Joxer! He'll eat so much he'll throw up all over his opponent."

Salmoneus's eyes glowed even brighter. "What a roar that would get! Quite all right, quite all right! We'll fix you up in a special warrior's outfit, Joxer. Just relax and enjoy yourself."

Gabrielle stepped forward. "I'm preparing a tale that will have all the audience laughing and crying—at the same time!"

"Don't tell me—The Epic of Xena's New Brass Bra . . . just kidding, just kidding! Terrific. Just head over for wardrobe, Gabe—They'll want to fit you out in something appropriate for your performance."

Xena fixed the slippery man with a frown. "What about me, Salmoneus. I'm having second thoughts about all this—"

Salmoneus's face fell. "But Xena! You're the main attraction! You saw what was going on a couple of hours ago! With this crowd all worked up, if there's no main event— why, they'll tear me apart! You don't want that, do you?"

"A little tar and feathering might help your complexion, Salmoneus," said Xena. "But no. I've made a promise. And as we keep on running into each other, I'm sure someday you'll be able to pull my fleece out of the fire. No, I'm just wondering who it is I'm supposed to be battling? After those last two, I have to wonder if I'm in a competition or a carnival."

"Yes, Xena. Exactly."

"I don't want to lose my dignity, Salmoneus."

"Your dignity will remain intact, I promise!"

"Who is my opponent, then? Some smelly pile of hair beating his breast? Some cranked-up egomaniac?"

"No, Xena. You're going to be wrestling with a handsome, well-mannered fellow, I promise. A local favorite. He fights fair, he doesn't brag—and he even smells good."

"Thank Zeus for small favors," said Xena.

"Good. That match won't be for a little while yet. Another hour or so . . . come on down to the backstage area. We'll spruce you up a little for the stage. They're going to love you, Xena. The crowd will just eat you up!"

"Hmm," said Xena. "Well, I guess there are worse ways to spend an afternoon."

"Excellent! Wonderful!" said Salmoneus. "And look. Here are the announcers to tell you what you can expect in the next match! You all enjoy yourselves, and we'll see you down in the backstage area soon!"

"What a nice guy," said Joxer, already with a silly grin on his face from the wine. "I like him. A lot!"

Xena shook her head, still troubled. "Something's fishy about all this. Very fishy indeed."

Oberon, the King of the Fairies, squirted some lemon on a piece of squid sauteed in olive oil, then popped it into his mouth. He chewed for a moment, then washed it back with a swallow of drink from a goblet.

"How's the calamari, Ares?"

"A little chewy for me, Obie."

The King of the Fairies shrugged. "So have a brewski and don't chew much."

Ares, God of War, sat at the table in front of the feast that his host had laid out for him. There were fruits and cheeses galore. There were dishes of exotic fishes and stuffed grape leaves. There were pitchers of wine and vats of strong ale. A servant fairy was rubbing his neck. Ares didn't go in much for the seafood he got inland. After hanging around in Poseidon's kitchens, you got spoiled. You had to face it. Fish was best fresh, and you couldn't get any fresher than eating it under the Mediterranean itself.

But he hadn't come here to eat seafood.

Ares snapped his fingers and held up his goblet. "Brewski. Whatever that is!"

Three fairies, back wings fluttering like anxious hummingbirds, lowered themselves and poured Ares a healthy portion of drink.

"My own personal homemade beer, Ares," said Oberon. "Yeasty for the feasty!" The strapping, half-naked guy belched and laughed. He wiggled off the last of his sandals and laid back his Grecian locks against the Lounge-A-Recliner and laughed. "I break it out for special occasions. Now I've got two reasons! Your visit, my good friend! And sport on the Vision-Pool!"

In front of the pair of supernatural entities, two fairies patiently held up a birdbath. Its water, defying gravity, gave off a perfect image of sporting activities—elsewhere. Ares only half paid attention. Something about odd-looking men grappling in an area in front of cheering fans. The only sport that Ares got much of kick out of was, of course, bloodsport. Give him a couple of armies having at it over discus-throwing any day!

Some of the suds got on his perfectly groomed beard as he drank. Foul stuff! Tasted like old boots were somewhere in the grainy mix! But if he didn't finish it, he would certainly offend his host. He picked up a silk napkin and dabbed it off.

"What is this, anyway?"

"Wrestling! And quite exciting, too!" said Oberon, eagerly. "Why, the stuff in Athens pales. I don't know how they do it, but these mortals are quite inventive."

Ares grunted. "No swords, no arrows, nothing deadly! Scant blood. And no death at all. What's the use, I say."

Oberon shrugged. "Each to his own, pal. So, to what do I owe the honor of your visit? I thought you were off on the other side of the world, getting the aborigines to bash each other to death with their didgeridoos!"

Ares shrugged. "They're too busy dreaming to have wars. Better pickings in civilized countries, Obie. As a matter of fact, since I was in the neighborhood, I thought I'd drop by. It just so happens that my lieutenant in the Mischief and Mayhem Department tripped and fell on his sword and is now washing Hades' dishes, if you know what I mean. So I'm scouting for a new guy and I can't think of a better candidate than that world-class scamp, Puck. I—"

"No," said Oberon, flatly.

"I'd pay him well, and I'd pay you as well. I'm a wealthy god, Oberon. Not only that, I can promise you good luck in any wars in the future!"

"Oh. Right. The Fairy Wars. Come off it, Ares. Fairies don't have wars. We're too busy having fun, when we're not hiding from trouble in the forest. Let soldiers and wrestlers fight, I say. Just call me a voyeuristic soul."

Ares gritted his teeth. Damn! This was going to be harder than he'd thought. Of course fairies could have wars, but he didn't want to use that strongarm card unless he had to. But there were more ways to skin a sphinx than one!

"Where is the likely lad, by the way?"

"Puck? Oh, he's not even around. I sent him off, scouting for changelings. They grow up fast, those changelings. Gotta keep fresh ones in stock."

"Suppose I keep you in changelings for eternity, Oberon! You and Titania both! Just think! No more fights! No more Midsummer Night Screams!"

"Come on! Those are fun!" Oberon winked. "And you know, after a fight with Titania . . . The sex? Ooo la la!"

Ares grunted. What he wanted to do was to take one of those fruits and—

Calm down, calm down . . . boyo—he told himself. Oberon was clearly a sporting soul, and sporting souls had Achilles' heels.

While Oberon wasn't looking, he dumped the brewski in a flowerpot and switched to wine for a while. He watched the proceedings of the sporting event that the Fairy King was observing.

Life was good.

Too good.

There had to be more war! More excitement! Mankind needed war to develop. Once they got what they needed, they could become like gods. And once that happened, he could be their number one god.

Ares smiled to himself.

Yes, and then he could take War a notch higher, and put him on the Throne Where He Truly Belonged . . .

Zeus had ousted the titans.

Sometime, surely it would be Zeus' turn to move over for Destiny!

"Yes!" cried Oberon, standing. "Go, Shmoe! Go!"

Ares fixed an eye on the events in the ring in the pool. Yes, a wrestling match . . . And a particularly wild one.

"Oh, he won't win," said Ares.

"He surely will! The Gorilla hasn't a chance!"

"I'll bet you a thousand dinars the Gorilla will win!"

"Bet taken!"

They watched the match. The Cathartic Shmoe won. Ares pretended the loss of a thousand dinars was a tough one. He paid up promptly and Oberon pocketed.

"You're right. This is most fascinating," Ares lied. He watched for a while longer, then said, "Wait a moment. Isn't that Xena the Warrior Princess in the crowd?"

"Yes! What a babe, eh? Too rough for me, but I can look, huh?"

"Believe me, you can't handle Xena," said Ares, shaking his head with genuine rue.

"I sure would like to!" said Oberon. "Looks as though she's going to be wrestling today, though, so I can watch. I'd say, frankly, that the wench will win. And win decisively."

"You do, do you?" said Ares, thoughtfully. "So, who's she up against?"

"Someone by the name of the Alexandrian Athlete!"

"Hmmm. Well, that sounds good to me. I'll tell you what, Oberon. I need a chance to win my money back. I'll bet you another thousand dinars—and, oh, this wonderful changeling prince in Africa I know of. Gorgeous child and will do you proud. I'll bet you that the Alexandrian Athlete will best Xena the Warrior Princess this day in their wrestling match."

"Not for Puck, you villain!" Oberon was grinning, eyes filmed with drink.

"No. But a wager's loss must have some sting for the

loser and reward for the winner. Shall we say—Puck's services for a month?"

"A month? Well . . . that's not so bad," said Oberon. "Besides, Xena lose? I've been watching her! That wench is a winner. All the way, Ares. And I've heard she's gotten the best of you, more than once."

"Well then, Oberon. You'll want to bet with me, and watch her do it again, eh?"

Oberon nodded with finality and extended his hand. "Bet!"

They shook and that was that.

Ares loaded his plate with food, got himself another pitcher of wine and settled down with the King of the Fairies.

"Oh. I've got to get back to Olympus for a bit and tell the servants to hold off on the nectar and ambrosia for the evening. I mean, it's okay if I have dinner with you, isn't it!"

"Of course!" said Oberon. "Just be back in time for the last match! I want to watch your face when you lose!"

Ares slapped his fairy friend on the back, then left the bower with a crooked smile on his handsome face.

"Xena! Xena!" cried Salmoneus. "You're here!"

Xena looked around. The backstage area was total pandemonium. Along with her was Joxer and Gabrielle, both well wined and dined and looking more than ready for their parts in the show. They seemed to take the noisy place in stride, and totally trust Salmoneus to tell them what to do.

Xena, of course, was less trustful. Not only had she had her own experience with the man. She'd had a few talks to Hercules, and had heard some of Herc's encounters. The big-hearted lug was more amused by Salmoneus than she. His inventions were particularly funny to Hercules—but worst of all sometimes Herc thought they made sense.

"Fast food!" Xena could hear the demi-god's good-natured voice now. "Now that idea has a future."

Future shmuture. Now was always the important thing to Xena. She had a black past, and a doubtful future. So she took exactly what was her plate, wolfed it down with zest, and spat the seeds out at the gods. Generally, anyway. She couldn't help the do-gooder part that had taken over. And look at where it got her. In the middle of bread and circuses—with Salmoneus grinning at her through a mouth smeared with jam and butter.

"Yes, I'm here, Salmoneus. Where's my opponent?" said Xena.

"That's a very good question. That's okay, the Athelete wasn't the guy that people wanted to see. Now you're the person the crowd wants to see fight. But you know, we'll find you someone quite fit to fight. If absolutely necessary, we'll just glue a wig onto the Gorilla."

Xena made a face. "What kind of contest is this?"

"A brand new sort, Xena! And you can see that the people love it. And what is Greece? Why absolutely nothing, if not a democracy!"

"Democracy?" said Xena. "What's that?"

"Uhm . . . never mind. Look, why don't you just go over there and they'll set you up with makeup and a costume."

"Costume . . . what's wrong with what I have on now?"

"Hmmm." Salmoneus stood back and examined her. "Brass bra. Lots of leather and studs. A bounty of bare flesh. Come to think of it, you're quite right. But I think you might need just a touch more mascara plus a whack of the old pancake."

"I'm not wearing breakfast for anyone."

"Look. Trust me. You're going to look fabulous. And speaking of fabulous . . . Here's Joxer." He put an arm around Joxer. "Joxer, you're up next."

"I am!" said the wobbling warrior with a silly smile on his face. "Good. Who do I wrestle! I'm ready!"

"Excellent. And Gabrielle. You can do your little reading or whatever before Joxer goes to it with his opponent. Then all you have to do is to announce the match!"

Gabrielle smiled. "Piece of cake!"

Salmoneus hustled them over to wardrobe and makeup.

"Psst!" came a voice from behind Xena. "Hey, Hot Stuff! Like, que pasa, dudette leatherette! Can I borrow your lipstick?"

Xena looked over to the stands. "Oh my gods. Trouble comes in pairs!"

Sitting in the stands were two women. It was the one in the shawl and robe that bothered Xena. Despite the extra clothing for the usually overexposed vixen, she recognized Aphrodite. The other woman—just as beautiful, if not more so—she didn't know at all. She was also dressed in a robe that hid all but her face. Her blue eyes stared out with curiosity and mischief and a Bacchus-may-care sparkle that only an immortal could own.

"Xena, this is my good friend Titania, Queen of the Fairies," said Aphrodite.

"I'm not going to touch that line with a ten foot minotaur!" said Xena. "But anyway, hello. I'm Xena."

"I know, I know! Warrior Princess! Your reputation preceeds you," said Titania. "I understand you're going to stand up for womankind in battle today against a nasty old male."

"We're here to give you some sisterly support!" said Aphrodite.

"We're here to cheer for you, Xena—and roundly jeer the opposition."

Xena sighed. Boy, this was the pits. When sporting events attracted the attention of goddesses, there was more trouble than she cared to handle. Why, oh why had she picked up ethics? She'd promised Salmoneus that she'd fight—and now, she knew for certain that she should be making like a fig tree and leaving!

She took a deep breath. Best to keep this as dignified as possible.

Xena bowed. "I thank you, Aphrodite. I thank you as well, Titania. I am honored by your interest. I beg for your approval in this effort in the name of our sex."

The two supernaturals giggled. "You're right," said Titania. "So earnest!"

"She's a heroine, don't you know?" said Aphrodite. The goddess started fluttering her eyelashes. "We can't all be helpless waifs, waiting in high white towers for men to rescue us. We can't all be Helens of Troy with men fighting for us! We women need powerful symbols of steel and fire to put us right up there with those arrogant guys!"

"I do like those sandals, Xena. Where do you get them?" asked Titania.

"I took them off a warrior I'd just beheaded," said Xena. She was becoming annoyed with these prattling pretties.

"A big-footed warrior," said Aphrodite. "But then, he was probably sleeping at the time."

"I'd say we have a winner here," said Titania. "I like her! Xena, be assured that I am betting on you in your upcoming wrestling match."

Xena bowed. "I am grateful for the vote of confidence." She turned to Aphrodite. "Is that why you've come here, Aphrodite—to win money by betting on me as well?"

"Actually, I was hoping to get hair-styling tips from your friend Gabrielle." The goddess shrugged. "Just leave them at my nearest temple."

"We tend to avoid your temples."

The goddess's eyes flashed. "And just why is that, Xena? Is there no feminine solidarity in this universe?"

"Frankly, I think we should get this love thing straightened out so there's not so much suffering involved here in this world," said Xena. "The day you get real, Aphrodite, I'll be worshiping you night and day."

"Real? Real? I don't know what you're talking about!" said Aphrodite. "I am what I am! You mortals have no control. No control whatsoever."

"Ooooh. Claws in, sister!" said Titania. "This one has spunk! I like her!"

"She's a troublemaker!" said Aphrodite. "That's all right. She'll age. And then she'll be kissing my marble toesies with all the rest of the groveling female mortals, just for a whiff of that sweet, sweet stuff . . . love."

"You know, Aphrodite," said Xena. "You peddle the stuff like opium. You gods are what you are—that's for sure. We mortals get to choose. That's life, Aph. I'm here now doing a friend a favor. I saved his life, and I just want to do what's right. Used to be I was angry. So angry I don't think I was really human. But being human means something. Love? I guess that's a part of it. But only a part of it, Aphrodite— and with all due respect, I'm just trying to do what's best and what's right for the few mortal years I have to me to make this world a better place."

Aphrodite sniffed. "By besting some male wrestler?"

"For too long mankind has suffered under the yoke of life. But women have suffered under the yoke of life and of mankind, Aphrodite. I just want to show women that the odds can be evened a bit."

"I like her!" said Titania. "I like her a lot!"

"Hot air!" said Aphrodite. "We'll see how she fares in the match. In any case, I told you it would be amusing, didn't I, Titania?"

"Oh, and it truly is. My blessings on you, Xena!"

Xena bowed to Titania. Then she made a mock curtsey to Aphrodite and spun on her heels and headed off to watch the proceedings in the ring.

Supernaturals were here.

Things were getting weird.

Oh, the noise! The terrible noise!

Banging and clanging! Such a dreadful din, thought Ares as he stood outside the hulking manse. Carefully, he stuffed wax into his ears, just as he always did when he visited his cousin, and then went into the heat and flashes of the factory.

Hephaestus was working, as usual. He was by his forge, with his hammer and anvil, banging away to beat the band.

"Phest!" said Ares, waving at him to attract his attention. "Yo. Cousin Hephaestus. Hey there! What's up!"

The huge, swarthy god grunted. "Apollo's chariot wheel. Damned speed demon! I keep on telling him, slow down! Slow down! You think he listens to me. No. So while he sports with the women, I get to fix his flats!"

Hephaestus was not only big, he was squat and very ugly. He had muscles, upon muscles too, and if there was a god of big apes, it was cousin Phest. Sweat rivuleted down his chest.

"Ooooh. Sounds frustrating. Sounds like you could use a bit of fun," said Ares.

"I don't go in for battles, Ares. You know that. What do you want?"

"Let's just say, I just want to let you know that I respect you, Phest. I do. And I'm watching out after your interests."

"So, you need a new sword. New armor?"

"You're so thoughtful. No, Phest. There's this mortal down on Earth. She's been saying things about you. Terrible things. I just thought you should know."

The god stopped his work. "Saying things? What things? Who?"

"Xena. Warrior Princess!"

The god's big brow furrowed. He looked hurt. "I know of her. Bad girl gone good. What's wrong with me, though?"

"Good? Well, if you can call it good. She's absolutely gone puffed up with pride if you ask me. She's going around saying that she's such an amazing fighter that she can wrestle any man."

A smile cracked Hephaestus's ugly mug. "That woman? She probably could."

"Phest, she's saying that she's so good she can probably beat a demi-god."

The stumpy guy grunted. "Hasn't she given Hercules a heave-ho or two?"

"So good, she says that she can even wrestle a god!" Ares' eyes glittered.

"Hurrumph! Well, that's overweening pride, isn't it? Hubris? Hmm. Getting a bit uppity. Doesn't sound like Zeus should get her with a thunderbolt, though, does it?" The gruff guy chuckled. "Waste of good womanflesh, I say. Ares, maybe you should take her down a peg or two."

"Actually, Xena says that she couldn't best me. 'Only the lower, insignificant gods,' " she said. "Gods like, say—Hephaestus!"

The god stopped banging. He turned, squinting at Ares. "She said that?"

"Want to see an instant replay? I can conjure it, you know."

"Spare yourself."

"Wouldn't it be fun, Phest—if you gave Xena her come-uppance . . . personally? Zeus wouldn't mind. Hera would appreciate it. Xena's down there now, taking on all comers.

All you'd have to do is to pin her to a mat. One. Two. Three. That's all."

Hephaestus grunted.

"I know you're busy, but you deserve a rest. It would be a good lesson for Xena. And a break for you."

"What would Apollo say?"

"Look, you've got plenty of wheels around here. Give him one of those." The God of War got close to the burly being and whispered in his ear. "Besides. Imagine! Getting all that leather and bouncy flesh. Pounding it onto a mat. Covering it with your vast and powerful frame. Feeling her squirm beneath you! Making her cry out, "Hephaestus! You are the most vulcanizing man in the universe!"

The god's big nostrils snorted. His eyes were red. "She does deserve to have her big behind kicked, doesn't she?"

"Are you god enough to do it, Phest?"

"Yes! I am!" With a growl, the god slammed his job down with a clangor that echoed through hall. "Lead on, Ares!"

"Citizens of Greece!" proclaimed Gabrielle. "I come to you today with a timeless tale of heroism and courage!"

"What a cutie!" someone yelled.

"How did you squeeze into that outfit, babe! Looks like you're trying to squeeze out already!"

Xena winced. She could barely watch the proceedings. But she had to. It was like watching a chariot wreck.

Gabrielle stood in front of the town of Borgos in a two piece purple and red something that was really closer to a purple and red nothing. Her hair had been teased into a garish cloud and so much makeup had been trowled onto her face that she looked like an Athens prostitute. The only thing that could have possible kept her going up there was that she'd drunk a considerable amount of wine.

"I tell you a tale of the brave and noble Joxer—Warrior Supreme," she said.

Someone threw a piece of rotten fruit. "Cut to the fight!"

"We want the Main Event!"

"Joxer! The mighty and brave soldier. The warrior with

moxie! Listen to the tale of his encounter with the evil Callisto!"

Salmoneus shook his head. "I thought the outfit would work. Crowd's too worked up. Excuse me, Xena." He went up to the edge of the ring. "Gabrielle. Looks like they want some action. Just announce the fight."

"But I have . . . an epic . . . story . . . to tell . . ." Poor Gabrielle was weaving.

"Just say—Jocular Joxer versus—King Slammer!" stage-whispered Salmoneus.

"Right! Friends! Greeks! Countrymen! I give you . . . Jocular Joxer versus King Slammer!"

"I'll clobber him! I'll nail him! I'll beat him bad!" said Joxer, psyching himself up.

Out of his usual ridiculous outfit, the fellow looked even more ridiculous. Salmoneus had robed him in some kind of furry yellow tights with red ribbons on the shoulder. He still wore his floppy eared helmet, which he had insisted on, making him look even more ludicrous.

Coming down the aisle on the other side of the arena was the man whom Gabrielle had announced as King Slammer. He was seven feet tall, with hands the size of hams. He wore a black eye patch and a bull-size ring through his nose. He hardly seemed to have to even lower the ropes to get into the ring.

"I have to fight—him?" said Joxer.

"Go get him, brave warrior," said Salmoneus, pushing Joxer toward his fate.

Again, Xena had to wince. She felt helpless. No way she could help her friend and companion here. This wasn't a matter of life and death. Joxer would be all right—she hoped.

Fortunately, the ordeal was over for everyone—including Joxer—with startling swiftness. Joxer, finally game, put up his fists in a comic attempt to fight the mammoth. However, King Slammer easily avoided one blow, caught another in his big hand. He grabbed Joxer by the side, lifted him up—and then up some more!

"Ahhhhhh!" said the crowd.

"Ohhhhhhh!" said Gabrielle.

King Slammer brought Joxer down on the mat so hard, Xena's teeth hurt. The impact exploded out to the crowd. Then the behemoth fell upon the fallen hero.

The referee fell to his knees, slapped the mat three times, and that was all for Joxer.

The crowd went wild. King Slammer bounced to his feet and jounced, absorbing the applause.

"What a pop!" cried Salmoneus. "What a pop!"

"Joxer's head went 'pop'?" said Xena.

"No! Joxer's fine! That's just an expression. It means an audible sweep of excitement through the crowd."

"Let me look at Joxer's head first," said Xena.

The referee was helping the fallen warrior out. Surprisingly, Joxer was quite conscious.

"Joxer! Are you okay?"

"What happened?" said Joxer. "Yes, I'm okay, and I'm ready to fight. Let me at him! Let me at him!"

"It's over, Jox," said Xena. "You go off and have another drink. I'm just glad you're alive."

Joxer shook his head. "I'm still ready to fight!" However, he allowed Gabrielle to lead him away.

"He's not only still alive, he still wants to fight! That kind of fall should have put him out for a day."

Salmoneous grinned. "I wouldn't let that happen to a friend," he said. "This is pro wrestling, Xena. Which—ah—brings us to a little matter I need to deal with. You're up right after this next match, and I need to speak to you about something . . ."

Xena shrugged, baffled. "All right, Salmoneus."

Salmoneus waggled his finger. "Why don't we come over here and have a little chat, shall we?" He gently led Xena to an enclosed area, out of earshot of anyone else. "Now, Xena. You've been very good to help me out here. Everyone is very excited about the match."

"And they will be more excited," said Xena. "When I win."

Salmoneus kept his grin, but it lost some of its luster. "That's what I need to speak to you about, Xena. You see, there's something about pro wrestling that obviously you don't understand."

"What's not to understand."

"Ah . . . Well, Xena. Let's just put it this way. I need you to put your opponent over."

"You bet I will. Right over my shoulder, onto the mat!" Xena mimed her decisive, victorious move.

"Ah. No, Xena. You need to lose," said Salmoneus. He was still smiling.

"Lose? You mean—lose the match . . . on purpose!" Xena could not help but betray astonishment. "Throw the match?"

"That's right. It's called a 'work.' "

Xena grabbed the little man by the front of his shirt and yanked him forward. "You mean—you bet against me, you wretched—"

"Of course not!" He chuckled, then flinched a bit. "Oh well, maybe a dinar here and there with total suckers or losers. But can't you tell, Xena—does this look real to you?"

Xena felt that somehow reality had cracked below her feet and she was about to tumble into total chaos. Fighting had been her life for so long, the whole idea of fights that were not actual fights, but so called 'works' was . . . was . . .

Blasphemy!

"You charlatan!" she said. "I'm going to rip your tongue out and feed it to the dogs! I'm going to tear your heart out with my teeth and then spit it into the sewers! I'm going to—"

"Oh, Xena! Wonderful. Save it for the fight! Tell that to your opponent. Xena, you're absolutely perfect. You'll make the other wrestlers look like flower pickers!"

Xena let him go with disgust. Damn him! Salmoneus knew her well enough to know she wouldn't hurt him, not really. "What about Joxer though! That looked real. You didn't tell him to put his opponent over, did you?"

"Joxer? Why bother? What a loser!"

"You're cruel," said Xena. "You're heartless and cruel."

"Xena, I've never killed anyone," said Salmoneus calmly. "I give value for money. Sometimes I play a little fast and loose with reality and illusion." He shrugged. "But maybe I learned that from the gods, eh?"

"The gods! There are no moral lessons there!' "

"You tell me about morality, Xena, when all the blood is

off your sword. What I'm doing now is a show. It's fun. The people like it. It's a hell of a lot more fun that pokey old Olympic wrestling. Everyone wins, because everyone gets value. And the losers most of all, because what other losers get paid the same amount as the winners?"

"But the art of sport! The value of competition! Is nothing sacred to you, Salmoneus?"

The glib man chuckled. "Yes! My word. And your word, Xena. And you said you'd help me. Now I'm not saying that you have to not do your very best. I'm not saying that you have to look at all weak. We'll throw in some interference. That will cause you to lose. Everyone will win that way. The people threatened by powerful women will feel better. And the audience who will see a gallant and brave and courageous female in action will be inspired. Because you are an inspiration! You're the tenth wonder of the world!"

"And who's the ninth wonder, Salmoneus?"

"Why—me, of course."

He'd done it. Salmoneus had drained away every bit of her righteous indignation. All that was left was her word. And that was sacred to her as well. He'd just asked her to fight. He hadn't asked her to win.

"All right," she said. "All right. A half-hour of my life. Then I get to take a bath, right?"

"Absolutely. With my own special bubble-bath solution, Xena. All part of the package. Now—the Alexandrian Athlete should be here any—"

Suddenly, the ground shook.

Xena started. She looked around. Earthquake? No it was just a pounding—not a continuing tremor.

"Xena!" bellowed a voice. "I am here to wrestle!"

Xena looked at Salmoneus. "That's the Alexandrian Athlete?"

"No! I don't know what—"

Xena strode over to the side of the ring.

Standing at the top of the arena, all eyes turned his way, was a big, squat man holding a hammer. He wore a leather apron and heavy boots. The smell of ozone and hot coal hung in the air.

"That," said Salmoneus. "Is the ugliest man I've ever seen in my life!"

"No. That," said Xena, feeling her heart drop to her knees, "is the ugliest god you've ever seen in your life!"

"I am Hephaestus!" cried the god. "And I have heard the challenge of the Warrior Princess. I accept!"

The voice roared through the arena, and all of Borgos and a goodly portion of Greece.

Ares could almost hear it and feel it without the aid of Oberon's magical fairy contraption.

"This wrestling!" said Ares. "Full of surprises! Who would have known they had a god on the card!"

"That . . . that's Hephaestus!" said Oberon, spilling his beer as he sat up from his chair. "Isn't he the strongest god—"

"No. I am!" said Ares, proudly.

Oberon waved the remark away. "A god! Against a mortal? And a mortal woman!"

"But it's the fabulous Xena, Obie! In fact, I'm starting to realize that I'm going to lose the bet. She can beat Hephaestus in a heartbeat!"

Oberon was deathly still for a moment.

Then he turned to Ares.

"You were gone an awfully long time, Ares," he said.

"What? Are you accusing me of cheating?" Ares raised an eyebrow. "Careful there, my friend. There haven't been fairy wars for a long time, like you say, but I think you'd look rather gallant in a general's uniform!"

Oberon shook his head.

"It's just—a god wants to fight Xena? I don't understand, Ares!"

"One word, Obie. Hubris. The woman's pride has brought down the wrath of the gods." Ares grinned. "And it looks like the wrath of the gods is just like life—nasty, brutish and short!"

The god stumped down the steps of the Arena. With every step that Hephaestus took, the place shook and rattled. There was a hush all over the stadium. People seemed petrified. This, clearly, was no ordinary wrestler.

"Here I am!" cried a man running down from an entrance. "I'm ready for battle. I am the Alexandrian Athlete. Show me this woman Xena!"

"She's mine!" said Hephaestus. He grabbed the Alexandrian Athlete, held him up in the air for a moment, squirming and kicking, and then heaved him into the crowd.

Xena nodded. "Yep. That's Hephaesteus all right. A god of few words, and fewer brains."

"I don't understand," said Salmoneus. He turned to her, looking honestly terrified and apologetic. "Xena. You have to believe me. I had nothing to do with this!"

"I know it. And I'll forgive you, if you'll grant me one wish, my friend."

"If I can, Xena. You want to know the back way out."

"No. I want out of my agreement to get my opponent over." Her eyes blazed. "A god wants to wrestle me? Sure. Why not. But if a god wants to wrestle me—and I win. I want to win . . . clean!"

"Oh Xena . . . yes. Yes, of course. Just don't get hurt!"

"I think it's a little too late for that, pal."

Quickly, Xena divested herself of her sharp objects. Then she stepped to the ring, pulled herself up, and stood defiantly before the new arrival.

"Hey, Hephaestus. Wrong guy! I'm Xena. Down here! It's called a mat, sport! It's what you use when you wrestle! Don't trip on your shoelaces."

The god looked down at his boots. They were tied well enough, but the alarm in his face caused the crowd to laugh.

"Arrrrrrghhhhh!"

Hephaestus stamped down the stairs.

When he was at the edge of the ring, Xena pointed at him. "Hey, fella. No foreign objects!' "

"They're all Greek!" rumbled the god.

"No, no. The hammer!"

"Oh." Hephaestus dropped the hammer, and then lumbered up into the ring. "All right, Xena. Come and get what you've been looking for—"

"Looking for. I'm not looking for—"

Hephaestus lunged.

It didn't take a genius to feel the god's power vibrating through the air. However, he'd gone totally physical, so he could be fought. Xena could tell that much. That didn't mean he could be defeated. It just meant this would be a match.

At the last moment before he could grab her, Xena ducked and hurled her weight at Hephaestus' ankles. The god went down, whacking into a turnbuckle so hard that it went down with him. The god followed it over the edge of the ring, pulling the ropes and the other turnbuckles to the ground.

The crowd went wild with approval.

Xena ran over to the edge to jump on the guy, to try and pin him, but he was already getting up.

She backpedaled as he roared to the edge. With surprising swiftness for his size, he got up into the ring again and regarded Xena.

"You are good, Xena! I respect that. However, now you must have a little of that pride mashed out of you."

He advanced.

Xena let loose her war cry.

She launched herself at the god. Her feet hit him square on the chest. He gave hardly at all, and rapidly Xena found herself on the floor.

Before she could scrabble out of the way, the god's hands were down on her. She gasped as he wrenched her up from the floor. Then he tossed her into the crowd.

She landed in a jumble of "oofs" and "ows."

People were hurrying away. She was just getting back up, still conscious and ready to have at it, checking in with her Inner Self and ready to rip with some "Yip Yip Yips" sufficiently powerful to shred paint off walls, when two hands were laid upon her. Xena felt their puissance immediately. She turned and beheld the source of all this power.

Two feminine smiles.

"Hi, Babes!" said a familiar voice.

The other, of course, was none other than Aphrodite, Immodest Goddess, and hackles automatically rose just at the sight of all that makeup. "Xena, sweetie. You're fighting the good fight. To be honest, we came to cause mischief."

"But something bad is going on," said Titania, "and it looks like its boys versus girls, and we're rooting for you."

Xena was about to refuse their help. But then she caught sight of a muscle-bound, maddened god snorting her way. She could smell him already, and he smelled of sweat and blood and ages of inequality.

"What? I get to go godlike like Callisto?" she said.

"Well, I'm godlike," said Aphrodite. "And still I don't want to face combat with the likes of Hephaestus. No, Xena. Just do what you do so well. And know that we're here!"

"Self-confidence, hon," said Titania. "It will work miracles."

The hand of the god fell down upon her. "Nuts to that!" cried Xena. "I want some magic!"

The god dragged her halfway down the aisle, and then tossed her into the ring. He hopped up and said, "Lie down for me, and this will go easier, woman!"

Xena snarled. She picked herself up. "I'm not even into metal, guy!"

Hephaestus roared and charged her. The Warrior Princess charged as well, only instead of meeting him halfway, she jumped, somersaulted, and sailed over him. She dropped a few "Yips" along the way for good measure. She landed, turned, pounced. She caught the guy around the ankles and tugged. The result was profound. She had just enough strength to stop his feet. The rest of his bulk kept on going and Mother Earth did the rest with her blessed gift of gravity.

WHAM!

Hephaestus went down so hard he cracked a hole in the floor. The canvas sagged beneath him.

"Go Xena!" she heard Gabrielle yell, and it was enough to give her another lift. She got up and she jumped right onto the god's head. Again, Mother E's gift pushed her down hard enough to mash Hephaestus's head, just raising up, back into the mat.

The crowd went crazy, yelling and screaming and roaring its approval.

Xena danced a bit for them, then, just before the hamlike hands reached for her she skipped back.

She assayed the damage.

Hephaestus got to his feet. He turned. Before he just looked annoyed. Now, he looked mad.

"What's wrong with you, woman?" he said. "Are you crazy! You don't fight the gods! And you don't insult them, either."

"I never insulted you! And I'm here to fight because I promised to fight. I didn't know it would be a god! Are you dim?"

The remark registered as an insult. Hephaestus stepped out of his hole. Xena danced back away from a blow, and circled the ring, staying out of reach. How long she could keep this song and dance going she had no idea, but probably not for long. In fact, as she turned, the god caught her by her hand and swung her around. He lifted her up and this time there was no quick release. He turned Xena round and round and round and pretty soon she felt as though her brains were going to get expelled from her ears.

Then Hephaestus brought her down onto the mat so hard, it broke again. Only this time there was a lot less godlike muscle to keep things together. Xena could feel her consciousness threatening to run away from this madness. Sheer ornery willpower kept her going.

The big figure of the god was falling down upon her for the pin. No, he wasn't fooling around. Once that bulk got on top of her, there was no hope short of Zeus' intervention.

Xena scrambled. With all the speed she could muster she pulled herself away. Hephaestus slammed down where she'd been with a gratifying "Oooof!"

Xena backed up against a leaning turnbuckle. She climbed up the ropes and was about to make a suicide run at the god, when suddenly she was aware that, ringside were Aphrodite and Titania.

"Hey, Heph!" cried Titania.

"Buckle up!" yelled Aphrodite.

They were standing right there and they did the most astonishing thing that anyone had ever seen supernatural creatures do.

Titania lifted her top and gave the God of Metalworking a look at an astonishingly naked pair of breasts.

Aphrodite turned, leaned over, and mooned him with her bare buttocks.

The god of fire stood, jaw dropping, frozen with astonishment.

And then Xena noticed.

"Buckle up!" The Goddess of Love had yelled, and sure enough, there was a buckle on Hephaestus's belt. Such was the god's build that the only thing that kept his pants up was that belt. Xena's mind was not slow. Knowledge was better than magic any day.

Xena attacked.

With quick movements, her hands undid the buckle. Raging, Hephaestus grabbed for her, but missed. She moved around, gave his pants one good, sharp tug and again Mother Earth's good gravity helped out.

The pants fell down.

The God of the Forge, it turned out, was wearing bright, white and red polka-dotted bikini underwear.

With a howl he reached for Xena, but Xena jumped out of his reach. He cracked upon the floor.

The whole arena fell into whoops of laughter.

Hephaestus went bright crimson, all the more so to see Aphrodite pointing and laughing at him along with the rest of them.

"Hephaestus!" said Xena. "Who put you up to this? Who told me I could beat you! I can't beat you!"

"Ares! Ares said you needed taking down," said the god, getting up and, with what dignity he could manage, pulling up his trousers and rebuckling them.

"I'm so sorry. Ares has tricked me before as well." She shook her head. "You're a good god, guy. I like you. Let's not fight, okay? It's not really fair for either of us, huh? Let's do what we do and be ourselves. If you want to fight, why don't you fight Ares? Now, I'd pay to see that."

"She's right, Hephaestus," called Aphrodite. "I can get him if you like. How about a no DQ match, huh? I'd put my money down on you for that!"

"You would?" said the god.

"You're the best, Heph," said Xena. "I'm glad you're here. I've never been able to tell you before how much I appreciate what you do. You work hard. You're beautiful, Heph. Absolutely beautiful, and you make beautiful things. I look up at Apollo everyday and I think, now, the dawn and sunset and the sun itself would not be half so wonderful without a hardworking Hephaestus."

The God of Metal slammed a fist into a hand. "Get him, Aph. Let's do this!"

Two days later, the party strode down the road from Borgos to Athens, relaxed, well fed, happy and smiling.

"I still can't get over that fight!" said Joxer. "Hephaestus just mopped the mat with Ares."

"I already have my story poem composed," said Gabrielle.

> *"And then the mighty god of iron gave him a suplex*
> *And Ares, champion of war, became a champion-ex"*

The group chuckled, Xena most of all. She liked it when her friend and companion rhymed her verses, particularly when they were funny verses.

"We'll never see the likes of that match again!" said Xena. "And from the look on Ares' face, I think we'd better avoid him for a while. I heard he's paying Oberon a huge amount for a PR campaign just to spin control the shame!"

"Men!" said Gabrielle. "Song and poetry are so much more fun and creative than battle. Even if it's fake battle."

"I guess there's not much of a future for 'professional wrestling,' is there, Salmoneus?"

"I'm giving it up, that's for sure," said the small man. He picked a few troublesome feathers from his arm. "I'm going to be taking baths all week in Athens. I itch! Tar is hell on my skin! Xena! Why did you let them do that?"

"Better than the hanging that you probably deserved, Salmoneus."

"The people of Borgos may have been entertained for a while," said Gabrielle. "But I don't really blame them for being upset. That arena is going to cost a bundle to rebuild after Hepheastus and Ares tore it apart."

"The look on Ares' face when he got slammed through

the latrines!" said Xena. "Aphrodite says she heard the gods themselves chortling. Even Hera was giggling."

Xena, Warrior Princess, took in a big breath of Grecian air and looked up at the sky with wonder.

Life seemed a little sweeter to know that there were gods who listened to reason, even if you had to pull their pants down first.

But it was even sweeter, knowing that some gods wore polka-dotted underwear.

LEAVING THE PAST BEHIND

Melissa Good

The market square was full of life, vendors competing for customers with ribald shouts, and colorful banners draped over every available square inch of space. Small children ran in and out of the booths, playing and laughing as they dodged older travelers, who browsed and bickered with the sellers for goods ranging from cloth to baubles.

Along one length of the market, three women strolled, taking in the chaos and sidestepping the more excitable revelers. The tallest of the three, a striking, dark haired woman in brown leather armor lead the way, fending off the odd drunk or thief with a well-practiced shove.

"Some things never change," she commented to her companions. "Even after all this time."

"Does it feel strange, Mother?" the woman on her left asked. She had a shorter, slighter build and mouse brown hair. "Being back in Greece?"

The taller woman shrugged. "Hadn't thought about it." She glanced to her right, at the slim blond woman who was idly fingering a bit of cloth. "Where'd they get that color from?"

"Reminds me of India," the blond woman replied. "You know what does feel strange, Xena?" she said suddenly, pausing to look around. "Knowing how few people there are left who might know us."

Xena considered that. "That may not be all bad, Gabrielle." She put a hand on her shoulder. "At least for me." Her eyes searched the market intently. "I left a lot of enemies frozen in our past."

"At least yours are in the past. Wish I could say that," the brown haired woman muttered. She pulled the thin, fragile cloth over her shoulders closer about her.

Gabrielle wandered a few paces farther down the lane, and paused at the bench of a parchment maker, who looked up at her and smiled as she gently touched a creamy white sheet.

"Wrap some up for you?" the parchment maker asked.

"No thanks," Gabrielle said, turning away and almost colliding with Xena. "Hey!"

"Sorry," Xena said. "Didn't see you."

Gabrielle gave her a wry look before she gazed around the market. "It is kind of nice to be home, though," she admitted. "Come on, Eve—there's a stand over there selling baklava. My treat." She paused as she heard a gentle throat clearing behind her. "Didn't you want to get a new bracer, or something, Xena?" she asked the warrior pointedly. "Don't let us keep you."

"Did I?" the taller woman replied with a touch of annoyance. "I guess I did. See you two later." With that, she turned and left, disappearing into the crowd without another word.

Eve and Gabrielle exchanged glances. "Did we do something?" Eve inquired warily. "I didn't think she liked shopping."

Gabrielle turned and led the way across the market. "She doesn't," the blond woman said. "But she knows I do." Gabrielle hesitated briefly. "Or anyway, I did and she knows her birthday's coming up."

"So?" Eve followed Gabrielle's tanned shoulders through the crowd. "What does that mean?"

Gabrielle stopped in front of a stall with carved wooden

toys. She picked one up, a hobbyhorse, and smiled as it wagged its head at her. Then she put it down and smoothed its yarn mane down with one finger. "That'll make some little kid happy," she concluded, in a quiet voice, before she turned toward Eve. "That means? Well, I usually get her something."

Eve digested that. "Okay," she replied. "That's good, right?"

"Not really." Gabrielle sighed, moving on to a stall that had strips of leather and hide draped over it. "She hates being reminded of her birthday."

"Oh." The brown haired woman fingered a piece of tanned skin appreciatively. "Nice," she murmured. "So, why do you do it then, if she hates it?" She gave Gabrielle a curious look.

Gabrielle held up a piece of dark leather, measuring it with her eyes. "Why?" She seemed to consider the question seriously. "I guess because she's my family."

"Oh," Eve said, again, obviously still at sea. "But . . . if she doesn't like it . . ."

Gabrielle put the leather down, and faced her. "It's not that," she explained. "She doesn't really hate it, I think she really likes it, but she has to pretend she hates it because everyone expects her to hate having a fuss made, which I actually know she really likes." She paused. "Got it?"

Eve nibbled on her lower lip. "Tell you what," the former Roman champion said, "I'll take your word for it."

"Good choice." Gabrielle agreed. "So, what are you going to get her?"

"Me?"

Gabrielle looked around, her pale green eyes a little amused. "The horses are back at the inn, so yes, you," she replied. "She's your mother. I know getting something from you would be very special for her."

"You just said she hated getting presents," Eve protested. "We went over that, remember?"

Eve sighed. "I . . . Gabrielle, I don't know. I have no idea what to get her . . . I . . ." She paused awkwardly. "I hardly know her. It's just so strange."

"No." Gabrielle put a friendly hand on her shoulder.

"That's not strange. The fact that I used to change your diapers, and you're now older than I am is strange," she said. "Picking a gift for your mother is easy. Keep it basic and functional, and you've got it licked."

Eve rubbed the side of her face. "You've got a point," she admitted. "Okay, where do we go first, the wine maker or the weapons shop?"

"You catch on fast." Gabrielle grinned at her. "Though, she does like a little bit of luxury once in a while."

"She does?" Eve asked. "Like what? I know where we can get Roman bath oil," she offered.

Gabrielle thought about that. "Not exactly what I had in mind." She muttered . . . "C'mon." She led the way deeper into the market, with Eve trailing after her.

It was late afternoon before they made their way back to the inn. Xena was there first, seated inside the busy common room at a decently sized table with a jug of wine and a half-finished plate. Gabrielle and Eve took seats at the table next to her, setting down their several packages each.

"Hi." Gabrielle broke the silence, noting her friend's grumpy expression. "Something wrong?"

"Just a mix up with a few jerks looking for trouble without the sense to quit when they were ahead," Xena replied, rubbing one hand with the fingers of the other.

"They picked a fight with you?" Gabrielle asked, dumbfounded.

Xena shrugged. "They had no idea who I was, Gabrielle," she told her. "No reason they should, remember?" She reminded her friend.

"Maybe you should have told them, and saved yourself the time," Eve commented. "Scared them off."

Gabrielle frowned thoughtfully.

"Yeah," Xena said, after a slight hesitation. "Maybe I shoulda tried that." Then she shrugged. "Nah, they wouldn't know my name from Hades.' " She flexed her hand. "Looks like it's getting crowded in here." Eve moved her chair a little as a heavyset man pressed by her. "I thought I heard them say something about a festival tomorrow."

Xena rolled her eyes. "Great. Maybe we should get out of here while we can."

Gabrielle gave her a tolerant look, and snitched a bit of meat from her plate. "C'mon, Xena. It's just a little harvest festival. Maybe it'll be fun," she said, as she nibbled the beef. "It's been a long time since we've been to a party."

The tall warrior picked up her mug and took a sip, eyeing the room with a slight scowl. Then a thoughtful look crossed her face. "You could be right, Gabrielle," she said. "It has been a long time. Maybe you should dust off some of those old stories you used to tell, and try out a new audience."

Caught very off guard, Gabrielle stared at her friend for a long moment before she shifted uncomfortably in her seat and let her eyes drop. "No, I don't think so." She answered slowly. "I think I left that part of who I was in the past." With that, she got up and took her packages. "I'm going to put these away. I'll catch up with you later." Then she turned, and, without turning or looking back, pushed her way through the crowd toward the rooms they'd paid for.

Xena watched her go with a look of mild consternation.

Eve picked up an empty goblet and fiddled with it. "That wasn't what you were going for, was it?" she asked her mother.

Xena sighed. "No," she admitted briefly. "It wasn't."

"Maybe she just isn't into that anymore," Eve suggested.

"No, she's just trying to convince herself she isn't," Xena disagreed, then glanced up. "Have a good time shopping?"

Eve grimaced, but accepted the change of subject. "Not really, but the baklava was great."

Her mother nodded slowly as her eyes searched the crowd, thoughts racing behind the surface of her pale blue eyes. "Maybe sticking around for the festival isn't a bad idea after all."

Eve's brows contracted. "I thought you didn't like festivals."

"I don't. But they can have their uses," Xena replied with a mysterious smile. She took a sip of her wine, and stared at the crowd thoughtfully.

●   ●   ●

The next day dawned bright and cool, the scent of flowers and baking already on the wind before dawn. Gabrielle walked slowly through the waking town, absorbing the simple sights of people living their ordinary lives around her.

It was hard for her to feel like she had anything in common with them. Her life had been so fractured lately, so many changes coming at her from so many directions that she found herself searching for connections to these people who looked so much like she did, and it was hard to see any at all.

It was very much like being in limbo, she thought. Even going home to Poteideia held its own fears and complications, not the least of which was whether or not her family was still alive. What would she say to them if they were? Her parents would be aged and her sister . . . Gabrielle sighed, and hugged herself. Her younger sister would now be twice her age and they'd have even less in common than they ever had before.

A feeling of being watched came over her. Gabrielle concentrated, listening intently as she detected very soft footfalls trailing behind her. Then a small smile crossed her face as she recognized the pattern of them as one of the few familiar things left in her life. She turned to see Xena behind her and stopped, crossing her arms and waiting for her friend to catch up. "You're slipping, Xena. I heard you."

"I wasn't trying to sneak up on you," the tall, dark haired woman stated as she came alongside her companion. "Can't I just be enjoying the weather?" She gave Gabrielle a look.

"Yes, you can." Gabrielle felt a little abashed. "Sorry."

Xena's expression gentled. "You seem a little on edge," she commented. "Anything you want to talk about?"

"That used to be my line," Gabrielle murmured, half to herself, then sighed. "Sorry, Xena. I'm just out of it a little, I guess. Maybe everything's just hitting me at once." She looked around. "Coming back home made me realize just how long we were gone, frozen in the ice," she said. "I feel so out of place."

Xena put a hand on her shoulder. "Try not to think about it," she advised. "We can't change what happened, Gabrielle. We just have to move on."

"I know." The blond woman straightened up a little, taking on a more serious expression. "Things have changed, we've changed, and I do have to deal with that." She reached up and covered Xena's hand with her own. "But thanks for asking."

Xena studied her quietly. "Maybe you'll find you haven't changed as much as you thought, Gabrielle."

"Wishful thinking?" Gabrielle smiled wryly.

"Personal experience," the warrior answered. "Anyway, c'mon. Let's go see if we can find some trouble to get into." She playfully tweaked a bead hanging from Gabrielle's halter. "You owe me a baklava."

"Oh I do, do I?" Gabrielle decided to forget about her problems for now, and concentrate on enjoying the day. "And like we ever have to look hard for trouble," she added, as she followed Xena's tall form through the slowly increasing crowd.

The festival was brash, and boisterous. Wine and ale flowed freely, and the celebration spilled out of the market and through the town. Music clashed from two different areas, one a dancing square filled with sweating, laughing people, and the other the outside of the inn. Trestle tables had been set up there, and a large group was downing mugs and singing bawdy songs.

Gabrielle leaned against one of the now-closed market stalls, trying to catch her breath after joining in the wild line dance they'd just finished. She hadn't recognized the steps, but the tune had been familiar, and watching the other dancers had provided enough of the moves to get her going. It had been fun, and she'd enjoyed it, even though she'd totally failed in her attempt to get Xena to join the line as well.

Speaking of Xena. Gabrielle pushed off from the post and looked around, trying to spot her companion in the crowd. Usually, this wasn't much of a problem, since Xena's height tended to make her stand out, and also because crowds tended to give her space even when the warrior didn't ask for it. But Xena was nowhere to be found, so Gabrielle decided to walk through to the other side of the village and look for her. She edged past a group of giggling girls and headed through the square, evading the friendly hands of passing revelers intrigued by her unusual clothing. As she passed an open pit with a huge pig roasting over it, something in the air made her pause and turn.

Quickly, her eyes searched the crowd, looking for the disturbance that had caught her attention. It hadn't been a scream, really, more of a—

"Run!" A man bolted between two of the stalls, stumbling right past her. "Run!"

Gabrielle grabbed his arm and dug her boots in, dragging him to a halt with difficulty. "What's going on?" she yelled over the music. "Hey!"

The man twisted wildly in her grasp. "Lemme go! We got to get ouuta here! There's a . . ." He pointed behind him. "Big old . . . a bunch a . . . there's bad guys comin'!"

Gabrielle winced as a gust of wine-laden breath hit her in the face. "What? Are you sure?" She could now hear more people coming, and the yells were starting to disrupt the festival. "Who are they?"

"Lady, I dunno!" The man yanked his arm free and stumbled away. "Gotta get away from 'em . . . Hey! Run! Run!"

The square started to dissolve into chaos. The music abruptly stopped, and people started turning around, cries of anger and surprise going up. Several arms pointed toward the main gates to the village, and somewhere near there, several horses neighed. Gabrielle heard the sudden, distinct clash of steel, and she followed the noise, pulling her sais from her boots as she ran full tilt toward danger.

Not because she'd lost her mind, either, but because if there was trouble somewhere, chances were that's where Xena was, and if Xena was there, and trouble was there— Gabrielle wanted to be there, too. That's just how it was with them. "Xena!" Just on an off chance, she let out a bellow as she ran, dodging the villagers running in the other direction. "Xena!"

Gabrielle bolted between two rows of huts as the noise grew louder. Just as she passed a wall, an arm reached out and grabbed her, pulling her around the corner of the wall and jerking her into a rough embrace. "Hey!" She struggled, then recognized the body pressed against her. "Xena!"

"Shh!" the warrior hissed into her ear, and released her.

"There you are." Gabrielle took a breath. "What's going on? I heard all the yelling, and I heard fighting this way. Where did you go? Where's Eve? What's happ—" Her words got cut off as Xena clamped a hand over her mouth.

"I don't know. Eve's getting the children to safety." Xena pointed to where a group of frightened youngsters were being guided into a nearby hut with sturdy-looking walls. "I heard from some guy they've been getting hit by slavers looking for kids. Go with Eve, and make sure they're safe, okay?"

"Okay." Gabrielle pulled Xena's hand off her face. "But what are you going to do?"

"Gabrielle, don't argue. Just go take care of those kids. I'll be fine." Xena turned her around and started walking toward the building, her hand on Gabrielle's back. "Slavers aren't going to be looking for the likes of me."

Gabrielle glanced at her, before she gave in and joined Eve. "I don't know . . . you're nice and strong looking. They might take a chance." She saw the glowering expression. "Okay, maybe not. But be careful!" she yelled after her friend as Xena pushed them all inside and closed the door. Gabrielle heard a scraping as something heavy slid against the wood from the outside, and she realized they were locked in. "Great."

The children were running around in confusion, ranging in age from toddlers to adolescents. Eve was struggling to carry two of the smaller ones, so Gabrielle put herself to the task of organizing the rest. "Okay . . . listen to me, everyone," she spoke above the crying trying to put confidence in her voice like Xena had taught her. "Hey!"

Her yell got their attention, and the children turned her way. "Okay, everything's going to be fine," she told them. "But you have to be quiet, and not scream, so people can't hear you." The childish voices, she reasoned, would easily penetrate the walls. "Everyone sit down, and I'll make sure no one can get us in here, all right?"

The crying subsided, but didn't evaporate. The children mostly milled around, but they stopped yelling as she circled the hut, and made sure the window covers were locked down tight. The room was for storage and had boxes and bales stacked in neat rows, but nothing really else in the way of things to sit on or diversions for children who were scared and panicking.

Gabrielle finished her inspection and went over to Eve's side. "You okay?" she asked Eve, who was hanging grimly on to one toddler, his feet kicking against her legs.

"Oh yeah," Eve replied with a grimace, "never been better."

Gabrielle smiled. "You sound just like your mother." She put a hand on Eve's shoulder. "Turn him over, and he'll stop doing that."

Doubtfully, Eve complied, cradling the child in her arms, and sure enough, he stopped struggling and blinked up at her, sticking a thumb into his mouth. Eve looked up at Gabrielle. "Thanks for the tip."

Gabrielle was about to answer when several of the children started screaming again. She sighed, and went over to them quickly. "Hey! We have to be quiet, remember?"

The crying only got louder. "He kicked me!" the loudest girl squealed. "And he pulled my hair!"

"Did not!" the boy yelled back. "You're just a crybaby!"

"Shh!" Gabrielle hissed at them.

"Mama!"

"Baby-baby!"

Gabrielle took a page from Xena's book and clamped a hand over each tiny mouth. Now the other kids pointed and laughed, squealing in delight. Frantic, Gabrielle glanced at the door, then took a deep breath and let out a yell that momentarily silenced even the noisiest of the children.

"All right. Now look" she told them, "this isn't a game. You all could get hurt if you don't be quiet."

Several of them hiccuped, but they stayed quiet. "Now, how can we keep it that way?" Cautiously, she released her two little captives, who giggled.

One of the older girls came forward. She was of medium height, and had two unevenly braided pigtails hanging over her shoulders. "I know," she stated confidently. "The scary lady tole me how." A tiny chorus of little voices agreed.

Gabrielle put her hands on her hips and gazed down at the little girl. "Oh yeah? How?"

The girl tipped her head back and looked confidently at Gabrielle. "We will be quiet if you tell us stories." She almost chanted it. "That's what she said."

"Yes!" Several of the children started hopping up and down.

Gabrielle stared at her blankly as she tried to absorb the words. "What?" She knelt down so she was at eye level with the tyke. "Who said that, sweetie. Who told you to say that?"

"The scary lady," the girl replied stolidly. "She said you know lots of good stories."

" 'Bout tigers!" one boy yelled.

"Sea monsters!" another one added excitedly.

"The scary lady," Gabrielle repeated softly, a suspicion growing. "Was she really, really tall?" She held her hand far over her own head. "And had long, dark hair, and really blue colored eyes?"

The child nodded. "Yes," she agreed solemnly. "The scary lady."

Gabrielle looked up over the girl's head, and caught Eve in mid-smile, which she immediately wiped off her face. "Wait a minute." She stood up. "Waaaaiiit just a minute."

The little girl tugged on her leather belt. "Won't you tell us?" she asked wistfully.

"Yeah!" The children all gathered around Gabrielle, pulling on bits of her clothing, and urging her with piping voices.

Gabrielle looked at Eve, who held her stolid expression for a beat, then shrugged and smiled, lifting both hands up in sheepish guilt.

"Please?" The little girl took Gabrielle's hand. "She said you would, if we asked nice."

Gabrielle eyed the small faces watching her intently. "She said that, huh?"

The girl nodded.

Could she? Gabrielle had consciously tried to forget about her stories, concentrating on developing and honing her warrior skills instead. It seemed much more practical, given that their lives seemed to consist mostly of fighting and danger lately.

"Please?" The child moved closer and grasped Gabrielle's hand.

Gabrielle surrendered both to the children's wishes and her partner's tricky scheming. "Okay," she said. "Come on. Everyone come over here and sit down, and I'll see what I can come up with." She sat down on a low box, and the kids settled in a ring around her, the straw ground cover rustling as they squirmed into place.

Then they all just looked up at her, with wide-eyed, innocent faces. Somehow, looking back at them, Gabrielle found it much easier to forget everything she'd been through in the last few nightmare months and reach back into an older part of her. The part that still dreamed, sometimes.

The part that could still be awed, and charmed, and amazed by something so simple as an unlikely friendship, which had never stopped showing new facets. "How would you all like to hear a story about the scary lady?" she asked them.

The kids all looked at each other. "Is it scary?" a young boy asked, timidly.

"Not this one," Gabrielle reassured him. "It's about how the scary lady saved Solstice."

"Okay!" The kids clapped and one crawled over to sit right at Gabrielle's boots, playing with one of the laces.

Gabrielle took a deep breath, and then just did it. "Once upon a time, there was a really sad Solstice. . . ."

Eve waited for Gabrielle to relax and settle into her story, and then she got up and walked silently over, sitting down at the edge of the circle of children to listen. She was sure she'd never heard the story before, but somehow parts of it felt so familiar it was almost as though she had.

When Xena had pressed her into service for her little plan, Eve had been doubtful. It hadn't made much sense to her, since she felt forcing her mother's friend into doing something she obviously didn't want to do wasn't a very good idea.

But now, as she watched Gabrielle's face grow more animated, she had to admit that maybe her mother was right.

It was almost like seeing a completely different person.

"... And Xena knew that if she didn't change the governor's mind, the children wouldn't get to have Solstice," Gabrielle said. "So she came up with a plan."

"Was it a good plan?" one of the boys asked.

"Xena's plans are always good plans," Gabrielle answered wryly, a sudden smile transforming her face. "Though you don't always think so at the time. This one had a donkey in it."

"A donkey!" the children chorused. "What was his name?"

"Tobias," Gabrielle said. "And he had to help me to fly."

"Oooo."

When Gabrielle came to the end of the tale, she realized the sounds outside had petered out, and peace had once again descended over the village. As she looked up toward the door, it opened, and Xena slipped inside the room, giving her a wave, and a confident grin. "Well well," Gabrielle greeted her. "If it isn't the scary lady."

The children all turned to look.

"Looks like it was all just a misunderstanding," Xena spoke up. "Couple of guys got into a fight at the gates, things got out of hand, that's all."

"Oh, really," Gabrielle said, with a very droll grin.

"Yeah, sorry." Xena shrugged. "Looks like you've got things under control in here, though, huh?"

Gabrielle gave the little boy on her lap a hug. "Yeah, I sure do," she agreed. "We've been having a great time, haven't we, guys?"

"Yes!" the children cheered.

Now the bard pointed at the warrior in the doorway. "Okay, kids—now, go on over there, and Xena will be glad to show you all that stuff I told you about. Her sword, and her chakram. Go on."

The kids scrambled to their feet and made a rush at the door.

"Hey ... hold on." Xena looked alarmed at the miniature raiding party. "Whoa ..."

"Hang on those little leather straps." Gabrielle called out. "She loves that!"

"Hey!"

The children swarmed over the startled warrior, reaching up to grab at her leathers, small voices piping questions. "Can you give us a ride?"

"Did you really climb up a chimney?"

"Does your horse talk?"

Xena backed away with a dozen of them clinging to her armor skirt. "Wait . . . let go of that . . . Gabrielle!"

Gabrielle only smiled as she watched the children chase the warrior out the door. She chuckled softly as Eve crouched down at her side.

"Was . . . that really a true story?" Eve asked skeptically.

"Sure was," Gabrielle told her. "Why?"

Eve shrugged. "Doesn't jibe with the Xena I know," she replied bluntly.

"You're wrong," Gabrielle said. "It's just a side of her you don't remember seeing." She added, thoughtfully, "But I do."

Eve decided to drop the subject. "You're not really mad at her, are you?"

"No," the bard replied, with a gentle smile. "Sometimes her methods are like having a rock dropped onto your head, but once you get over the headache, it's usually worth the pain." She got up and brushed the straw off her legs as she headed toward the door.

Eve regarded the retreating woman, and shook her head. "If you say so." She got up and followed, catching up to Gabrielle within a few strides.

They emerged into the village square, once again restored to its party atmosphere. A group of village men were standing near the entrance to the inn, talking. They gave Gabrielle and Eve curious looks as they walked past.

"Hey, that's the one!" one man muttered. "That's the one the kids were talking about."

Eve hastily pulled her scarf closer, and turned her head, but Gabrielle glanced thoughtfully at the group before abruptly changing direction, and heading right for them.

•   •   •

Late that night, Xena approached the inn at last, well satisfied with her day's work. The festival was winding down, only a few stragglers were left roaming in the streets with arms around one another, desperately trying to find a way home through the fog of ale.

She stopped by the stable first, greeting their horses with a pat on their noses, and adding the last supplies she'd gotten to their saddlebags. The twenty-five years they'd spent frozen in time had led to certain changes, Xena had found, and she'd taken advantage of the marketplace to add some new things to their baggage.

Metal, for instance. Xena sat down on a hay bale and examined her finds. A new type of bit, for one thing, with joints that would make it more comfortable for the horses to wear. She held it out to show Argo II. "See?" The horse snuffled it, then went back to munching on hay. "Everyone's a critic." Xena put the bit inside her bag, along with strips of well-cured leather to rewrap her sword hilt and cakes of fragrant soap. She also laid under the bags two new thick wool blankets for the coming cool weather and a half-hide of leather to make repairs to her armor.

The last thing she took out and lay on her knee. It was a package wrapped neatly inside a woven bag that contained sheets of parchment and a collection of quills. Xena studied it for a moment, then shrugged, and leaned over to open the top of Gabrielle's pouch, slipping the package inside, then retying the flap over it. "She can only kill me once," Xena told the horses, who nickered at her in seeming amusement. "Don't worry, there are a lot of things I can use that stuff for if she doesn't wanna write on it. It won't get wasted."

"That's true."

For a split second, Xena thought the horse had answered her, and her eyes widened, before she recognized the voice and turned around. Gabrielle was in the doorway to the stable, leaning against the wood and watching her. "Thought you were busy inside."

Gabrielle walked over and seated herself on the bale next to Xena. "I was," she admitted. "Somehow . . ." She paused, and gave Xena a meaningful look. "Those people in there got the idea that I had some entertaining stories to tell."

Xena didn't react. "Maybe the kids told them," she suggested blandly.

Gabrielle just smiled. "Maybe," she agreed. "But I'd rather think it was because I have a friend who loves to meddle in my life when she thinks she's right about something."

Xena smirked a little, then turned to face Gabrielle. "I didn't think I was right, I knew it," she proclaimed confidently. "Didn't I?"

Gabrielle took her time in answering as she considered how she'd felt. "It felt strange," she admitted. "We've been through so much lately, I really didn't think there was much of that ability left in me." She pulled out one of her sais and examined it. "It's like anything else, though, I guess. I never thought I'd feel natural using these." She paused. "Or killing in battle. It's all what you get used to."

Xena remained silent, unsure of what to say.

"But you were right," Gabrielle continued, quietly. "Thanks."

Xena put a hand on Gabrielle's back. "I know it's been rough," she said. "But we'll make it."

Gabrielle nodded slowly. "As long as we have each other to count on, I think we will." She looked over at Xena, who smiled. "I've got one more story to tell over at the inn. You want to come listen? Eve's up there holding a spot for us."

Xena looked surprised. "Eve? Didn't think she'd be interested in all that old history." She started toward the door, laying an arm over Gabrielle's shoulders as they walked together.

"Oh, she isn't," Gabrielle replied, with a smile. "But she's been fascinated by learning new things about her mother."

Xena paused, giving her friend a startled look. "She has?" She thought a moment. "What kind of things?"

"Good things," Gabrielle reassured her seriously. "All about the people we've helped, and the places we've been . . . the things we've done . . . you know—everything."

They walked on a few more steps. "Everything?" Xena raised an eyebrow, and smirked just a bit.

Gabrielle pulled on her earlobe. "Well . . . almost everything," she admitted, clearing her throat slightly.

"Uh-huh." Xena chuckled. "That's what I thought."

They walked together from the stable to the inn. The sky was dark, and full of stars, and an air of peace seemed to be evident around the village. Xena drew in a breath of the cool night air, and decided that all was well that ended this nicely. "So what story do you have left to tell?" she asked her friend.

"Oh . . . it's part of a long one," Gabrielle told her. "I've been telling it all night . . . all about battles, and adventures, and this wonderful, epic friendship." She put her hand on the door. "Problem is, I don't have an ending for it yet."

Xena gazed at her, puzzled. "You don't?"

"No." Gabrielle opened the door, and gestured for Xena to enter ahead of her. "It's still a work in progress." She followed Xena inside, greeted by the crowd calling their names, strangers no longer.

ABOUT THE CONTRIBUTORS

Jennifer Roberson has published twenty-one novels, including fantasy series such as the "Sword-Dancer" saga and the "Chronicles of the Cheysuli," and has contributed more than twenty short stories to anthologies, collections, and magazines. She has also edited two fantasy anthologies, *Highwaymen: Robbers and Rogues*, and *Return to Avalon*, a tribute to the late Marion Zimmer Bradley.

Robin Wayne Bailey is the author of a dozen novels, including the Brothers of the Dragon series, *Shadowdance*, and the new Fafhrd and the Grey Mouser novel *Swords Against the Shadowland*. His short fiction has appeared in numerous science fiction and fantasy anthologies and magazines, including *Guardsmen of Tomorrow, Far Frontiers*, and *Spell Fantastic*. An avid book collector and old-time radio enthusiast, he lives in Kansas City, Missouri.

Diane Duane has now been writing professionally for twenty years. Besides creating her own universes, such as the "Young Wizards" and "Middle Kingdoms" worlds, she has also worked extensively in other creators' territories—counting among these her forays into animation (everything from *Scooby-Doo* to *Gargoyles*), comics (including *Batman* in animation, and *Spider-Man* in prose), and of course Star Trek, in comics, novels, and on the screen. She lives with her husband, Peter Morwood, in a quiet corner of County Wicklow in Ireland, pursuing galactic domination in a leisurely way, with the assistance of three cats, four computers, and six hundred or so cookbooks.

Esther M. Friesner is no stranger to the world of armed-and-dangerous women warriors having (a) created, edited, and written for the *Chicks in Chainmail* series, (b) graduated from Vassar College and (c) raised a teenaged daughter. Her son, husband, two cats, and warrior-princess hamster treat her with accordingly appropriate awe, which has nothing to do with the 30 novels she has had published, the two Nebulas she has won, or the over 100 short works she has written besides this one.

Josepha Sherman is a fantasy novelist and folklorist whose latest titles include *Son of Darkness* (Roc Books), *The Captive Soul* (Warner Aspect), *Xena: All I Need to Know I Learned from the Warrior Princess*, by Gabrielle, as Translated by Josepha Sherman (Pocket Books), the folklore title, Merlin's Kin (August House) and, together with Susan Shwartz, two Star Trek novels, *Vulcan's Forge* and *Vulcan's Heart*. She is also a fan of the New York Mets, horses, aviation, and space science. Visit her at www.sff.net/people/Josepha.Sherman.

Greg Cox is a diehard "Xena" fan who has also written numerous Star Trek novels, including *The Q Continuum, Assignment: Eternity*, and *The Black Shore*. In addition, he is the author of several novels based on Marvel Comics characters, including The Gamma Quest trilogy, starring the X-Men and the Avengers, and two Iron Man novels. Greg lives in New York City, where he has occasionally been known to drop in on "Xena Night" at Meow Mix.

Keith R. A. DeCandido was once referred to as a "pop-culture demigod" by an Albany newspaper, which led to his parents arguing over which one was the deity. Among the media universes he has played in: Young Hercules (*Cheiron's Warriors* and *The Ares Alliance*), Star Trek: The Next Generation (the novel *Diplomatic Implausibility*, the comic book *Perchance to Dream*), Buffy the Vampire Slayer (the best-selling books *The Watcher's Guide* and *The Xander Years Volume 1*), Marvel Comics (*Spider-Man: Venom's Wrath*, half a dozen short stories), Magic: the Gathering (*Distant*

Planes), and Doctor Who (*Decalog 3: Consequences, Missing Pieces*). Visit his website at DeCandido.com.

Lyn McConchie lives in New Zealand, and has had nine books and around 125 short stories published. Two of her novels, *The Key of the Keplian* and *Ciara's Song*, are fantasy collaborations with Andre Norton. Future books include *Beastmaster's Ark* and *Beastmaster's Circus*, both set in another Andre Norton universe. Crippled in a 1977 accident, Lyn owns, lives, and works on Farside Farm, on New Zealand's lower North Island. There she lives in her 19th-century farmhouse with two Ocicats, 6,000 books, and says it's the perfect ambiance for a genre writer.

Mary Morgan is English and lives in Hertfordshire. She teaches and writes, not necessarily in that order. Among her enthusiasms are the theatre, photography, classical literature, and anyplace that (unlike Hertfordshire) has mountains and is close to the sea.

Gary A. Braunbeck is the author of the acclaimed collection *Things Left Behind*, as well as the forthcoming collections *Escaping Purgatory* (in collaboration with Alan M. Clark) and the CD-Rom *Sorties, Cathexes, and Human Remains*. His first solo novel, *The Indifference of Heaven*, was recently released by Obsidian Books, as was his Dark Matter novel, *In Hollow Houses*. He lives in Columbus, Ohio, and has, to date, sold nearly 200 short stories. His fiction, to quote *Publishers Weekly*, ". . . stirs the mind as it chills the marrow."

Lucy A. Snyder lives in Columbus, OH, the test-marketing capital of the known universe. She comes in three flavors (RedHat, SuSE, and MacOS9), and may theoretically exist in an alternate dimension as a bottle of Merlot. She should be kept in a cool, dry environment free of excessive exposure to sunlight and politics. She may be found on the Web at http://www.sfsite.com/darkplanet/ or in anthologies such as *Civil War Fantastic*, *Guardian Angels*, and *Bedtime Stories to Darken Your Dreams*.

Jody Lynn Nye lists her main career activity as "spoiling cats." She lives northwest of Chicago with two of the above and her husband, author and packager Bill Fawcett. She has written twenty-two books, including four contemporary fantasies, three SF novels, four novels in collaboration with Anne McCaffrey, including *The Ship Who Won*, a humorous anthology about mothers, *Don't Forget Your Spacesuit, Dear!*, and over sixty short stories. Her latest books are *License Invoked*, co-authored with Robert Asprin, and *Advanced Mythology*, the fourth of the Mythology 101 series.

Jaye Cameron is a world traveler and an avid student of history. She imagines the past coming vividly to life while she treks to out-of-the-way places. Perhaps inevitably, fictional characters (like Xena) creep into her recreations of historical events, and maybe these figures improve the already-riveting reality of the past. She invites you to the eastern Mediterranean, where an epic battle is about to take place, with the notable addition of a certain warrior princess . . .

Tim Waggoner is the author of two novels: *The Harmony Society* and *Dying for It*. In addition, he's published close to sixty short stories and several hundred articles. He teaches creative writing at Sinclair Community College in Dayton, Ohio, and his Web site is located at *www.sff.net/people/Tim, Waggoner*. Recent anthology appearances include *Single White Vampire Seeks Same, Villains Victorious*, and *Guardian Angels*.

Russell Davis is the Managing Editor of Foggy Windows Books, a new publishing house launching in 2001. His writing has appeared in numerous anthologies including *Merlin, Civil War Fantastic*, and *Warrior Princesses*. He was co-editor of the anthology *Mardi Gras Madness*. He lives with his wife, their two children, and a psychotic cat in southern Maine.

David Bischoff was born in Washington, D.C., in 1951, very close to where Michael Rennie and Gort landed in *The*

Day the Earth Stood Still. One of his favorite books as a child was Edith Hamilton's *Mythology.* He attended the University of Maryland and graduated in '73. Thereafter he worked for NBC in Washington, where he started writing stories and novels. He know writes full-time, including nonfiction books and articles in his repertoire. His latest books are *Philip K. Dick High* and *Tripping the Dark Fantastic* from Wildside Press.

Melissa Good is a senior support analyst and network engineer for Electronic Data Systems, currently living in Pembroke Pines, Florida. She has written two scripts for *Xena: Warrior Princess,* and is working on a third, has published two full-length novels, *Tropical Storm* and *Hurricane Watch,* with a third in progress. She has also written a television pilot based on those novels that is currently in preproduction. Future projects include development of the series, further novels, and the attainment of a CCNP certification.